HELL BOUND BOOK 1

LUST

SARAH HEGGER

Cover: Deranged Doctor Design

ISBN: 978-1-990731-24-2
ISBN: 978-1-990731-25-9

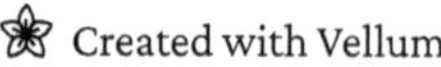 Created with Vellum

To Chris, who is always my anchor when all hell breaks loose, and also my partner in hell raising.

Board meetings—bored meetings—might be the death of Edme. Three hours and counting, and by Edme's estimation, they weren't even approaching the halfway mark. She weighed up the benefits of lobotomy by mechanical pencil.

"Right." Peter smoothed his salt-and-pepper Clark Kent do into a place it had never left. Looking around the table, being sure to meet every eye, he flashed his sparkly white veneers. "Our favorite part. Play selection."

Christ! Eddie barely kept the eye roll internal. She'd forgotten that particular nugget of soul evisceration on the agenda.

"Smashing." Lillian clapped her slender, elegant hands and beamed at her husband. "This is my favorite part."

Peter winked. "I know it is, poppet."

Giggling, Lillian flipped her gleaming raven hair over the heroin-chic protruding bones of her shoulder and batted her big greens at Peter. "I know you know it is."

Peter smoldered. "Poppet."

"Babe," Lillian purred.

Jesus kill her now. Eddie threw up a little in her mouth. Across the table, she caught Bianca's quickly masked shudder of ick. Bianca was new to the scintillating world of the Paradise Players of Claymont, Ontario. Eddie's grandmother, Dee, had brought her into the fold a couple of months earlier. That would be about a month before Dee had up and disappeared on her first cruise with Jean-Claude, and left Eddie to suffer death by bored meeting. And Peter.

Unfortunately, that cruise had set in motion a domino of subsequent cruises, and Jean-Claude and Dee were currently shuffle-boarding their way to Alaska, leaving Eddie to die by increments every first Wednesday of the month.

Perched beside Bianca, hanging on to the edge of his seat by his bony ass bones, Rodney shot his transparently white hand into the air. "Um...Mr. Chairman." He tapped on the mouse pad of his laptop. "I believe a review of the budget would be in order before we commence with play selection."

As treasurer of their community theatre group, a review of the budget was always in order in Rodney's world.

One quick thrust with the BIC up Eddie's nose had to hurt less than this.

"Oh, Rodders." Lillian wrinkled her adorably upturned nose. "Must we?"

"Yes, Lillian." Rodders tightened his thin lips beneath his precisely clipped mustache. "The budget"—he pointed to his screen—"will form the basis from which we select our season. How many plays we intend to stage, the cost of rights, production costs." His dark eyes gleamed with the feverish delight of a man in numbers nirvana. He slid a glance to Eddie. "The ongoing costs of maintenance to the building and projected repairs."

Dee owed Eddie so big for this, and Eddie was keeping the

sort of detailed inventory that would make Rodders cream his pressed chinos.

They were all looking at her, even Patty had paused crocheting another baby blanket for her next grandchild to peer over the top of her half-moon glasses at Eddie.

Words! They were expecting words from her.

"The...er...maintenance costs are the same as last year." Eddie did her best impersonation of a woman with her shit together. "And no new projects planned for this year." None that Dee had told her about anyway.

Dee had been a little short on detail as she'd ridden—or sailed—into the sunset with Jean-Claude.

"See." Lillian pouted. "We don't need to discuss the budget at all." She shimmied her shoulders. "We can just get to the good part."

"Poppet." Peter threw her the indulgent look of a man besotted with his much younger wife. How much younger was open to constant speculation as Lillian was as tight with her age as she was with her carbs. "Rodney keeps us all on the straight and narrow. He's the GPS on our magic bus. He keeps us all traveling in the right direction."

"Fucking budgets." Patty sniffed and jabbed her hook into the wisteria wool. "Suck the godsdamned life out of all of us."

Eddie was with Patty.

A snort came from Bianca's general direction before she dropped her gaze to the scarred tabletop. "Sorry."

"May I proceed, Mr. Chairman?" Rodney's mustache twitched.

"Proceed," Peter intoned, voice thick with the weighty import of a doomsday prophet.

Eddie dropped her gaze to her well-worn, paint-splattered leggings. She picked at a smear of vermillion as Rodders launched into his big moment. Her top eyelids started their dangerous drift towards her lower lids as her busy night threatened a takeover that would drive her system into shutdown. She'd dreamed of *him* again last night. Slate blue eyes, tawny brown hair, bone structure to crack a walnut on, and that outrageously pillowy mouth. The way he looked at her as if she was working a stainless-steel pole at The Brass Rail and he wanted to make it rain hundred-dollar bills.

The murmur of voices around her blurred into a meaningless monotone, lost in the savage throb of the only word her dream man had spoken to her. "*You.*"

You. One syllable, three letters, loaded with incinerating, sweat-filled possibilities and spat out of that any-way-she-wanted-it mouth and directed right at her.

"Didn't we do *The Importance of Being Earnest* last year?" Bianca's three pack a day, chew you up and spit you out, bad girl rasp penetrated Eddie's lust fog.

"And the year before." Patty snorted. "And every fucking year before that."

"*The Importance of Being Earnest* is a classic." Peter leveled a glacial glare at Bianca. "In the the-ay-ter, one can never underestimate the impact of a classic. You are new to our little thespian community, and perhaps you don't fully comprehend the traditions, the reputation of our theatrical endeavors."

"The audience loves it," Lillian twittered. "Our audience comes back every year to see it."

"Yes." Bianca twined her black-polished hands in front of her on the table and leaned forward. "And I love it. Great play." She smiled and took the tension in the room down three levels as she did. Bianca had one of those smiles that invited everyone to trust her. "And we should definitely do it later in the season, but how about something new to start off with?"

"New?" Rodney looked alarmed.

"Right." Bianca turned her everything-is-lovely-here strobe

smile at him. "Something that would showcase Lillian's talents even more."

Lillian straightened. "We should avoid falling into a rut."

"Peter falls into your rut every night," Patty murmured.

"I mean," Bianca said, "Lillian does a fantastic Gwendolen, the best I've ever seen."

Blushing, Lillian simpered, "I do my best."

"Poppet." Peter eye-humped her. "We count our blessings every day to have you with us."

"But wouldn't it be even better if we gave her greater scope for her talents?" Bianca had their number and pressed the advantage home. It was masterful stuff, and Eddie suppressed the desire to applaud. Man, she had to ask Bianca how she did that. "A play where she could soar to the heights of her gift," Bianca said.

"I did work professionally." Lillian lowered her sooty lashes. "Three seasons at the NAC before the joys of marriage and motherhood called me to a higher purpose."

"Our audience doesn't want modern." Rodney sent a wave of icy water over Bianca's performance. Even seasoned veteran Lillian had nothing on their newest board member. "They come back every summer and expect to see what they saw the summer before. They have remained faithful to the Paradise Players for years."

"Our patrons have been loyally supporting us since our inception," Peter said.

"Older than fucking dirt, the lot of them." Patty coughed. "Older than me."

The unwelcome reality check of last summer and seat H24, who had literally died laughing at the age of ninety-three and hadn't made it to the exit on her own steam, crept into the boardroom. Nobody had noticed poor H24 until Eddie had let the cleaning crew in between the matinee and the evening show. RIP, H24.

"You're right, Rodney." Bianca winced. "Tried and true is for the best."

"Good." Peter did the nod equivalent of a man shuffling his papers into order. "So, we'll follow tradition. Start with *The Importance of Being—*"

"Babe." Lillian laid a hand on Peter's arm. "Let's not be too hasty."

Rodney snapped his laptop shut. "We just discussed this and agreed that we would not deviate from our norm."

"No." Lillian raised her forefinger and cocked her head like a magpie eyeing a button. "We agreed that perhaps a modern play might not be the best way to go."

Mustache twitching, Rodney reddened. "But—"

"A moment please, Rodders." Lillian batted her lashes at him. "And while I absolutely agree that our first priority is to our loyal fans, I do think they would enjoy a little spice." She trilled her cut glass laugh. "*Un soupçon de variété.*"

"Our audience doesn't want variety." Rodney's mustache was in serious danger of frog marching off his top lip. "They want what we always give them." He jabbed his forefinger into the table. "They come here every summer, every tourist season, and expect to get what they want. We rely on them coming back."

"Lillian would make a fabulous Masha or Blanche DuBois," Bianca cooed.

"I had marvelous notices for my Blanche," Lillian lisped. "Transcendent, one critic called it."

"Bums on seats, people." Rodney threw his hands up—the only sane man in a world gone mad. "It's all about bums on seats."

"But maybe we could go for even more...er...bums on

seats," Bianca said. "Shakespeare is always popular. Wonderful name recognition."

Eddie gave her points for not flinching on the words bums on seats, but the mention of Shakespeare had her paying closer attention. They didn't do Shakespeare at the Paradise Players because Dee steered their ship away from the bard and with damn—pun intended—good reason.

"Shakespeare." Peter stared into the middle distance where visions of directorial brilliance sparkled. "Everybody loves Shakespeare."

"Our audience doesn't come for Shakespeare," Rodney sputtered.

"No, they don't." Eddie added her two cents before they got too far down the Shakespeare road.

"But, Rodders." Lillian dimpled at him. "Don't you think it's time to challenge ourselves?" She pressed a hand to her chest. "I, for one, would relish the challenge." Tossing a smile at Peter, she added, "Not that I don't love playing Gwendolyn, babe, because you know I do."

"The reason *The Importance of Being Earnest* works, Lillian, is because it's a comedy and people like comedy," Rodney snarled. "We sell out every year. A comedy. Light, frothy, not too demanding of our community actors and lots of bright costumes. We keep to what we can do without screwing it up."

Rodney had been so close and blown it on the finish. Much like Eddie's last boyfriend. How long ago had that been exactly? A year, two. Jesus, it could not be three years since she'd gotten any action. Three years? Except her desiccated lady garden begged to differ. Three. Fucking. Years. No wonder she was creating dream sex gods.

Had she really just called her vagina the lady garden?

"Excuse me, Rodders." Lillian drew back, leaking afront and wounded sensibilities. "I believe that some of us at the

Paradise Players could, indeed, rise to a greater demand without screwing it up." The last three words were spewed out of her puckered, bright red mouth with venom and accompanied by a side of death stare.

Patty grunted. "Too old for Ophelia."

"I am not too old for Ophelia." Lillian glowered at Patty.

Patty shrugged and started another row.

"Maybe we can come to a compromise." Bianca smiled.

Even Lillian settled down from rapid boil to vigorous simmer.

"Maybe." Bianca leaned her elbows on the table and kept that smile radiating. "We could compromise by starting with Shakespeare this year and do Earnest later in the season?" She shrugged. "After all, the company knows it so well, it wouldn't need much rehearsal time at all. And we already have all the sets and costumes."

Rodney opened his mouth to argue and then shut it again. "That doesn't sound too revolutionary."

"And." Bianca's indigo eyes gleamed. "This year is a kind of Shakespearian anniversary. Wonderful promo opportunities. It's the four hundredth anniversary of the publication of the folio with all his plays. And it wouldn't have to be one of the longer plays."

The alert button in Eddie's gut started to chatter. No reason to overreact yet. Shakespeare had penned a lot of plays before and after the Scottish one. All was not lost yet, or to keep it topical, all could still end well. "I agree with Rodney, people like comedies. So why not combine the two ideas and have a Shakespearean comedy? I've always liked *A Midsummer Night's Dream*. That's a comedy."

"Hmmm." Peter tapped his top lip. "Midsummer is a marvelous romp."

"It is." Bianca nodded enthusiastically. "Except." Her face

fell and she looked at Lillian apologetically. "Are the female roles as strong as we would like?"

"Fucking fairies," Patty muttered.

"*The Taming of the Shrew* has a great female role." Eddie couldn't believe she'd suggested that, but sue her, she didn't think fast on her feet.

Peter gave her the look of astonishment she'd deserved. "Eddie!" He shuddered. "*Shrew* is so not appropriate in today's world."

"Kate is abused." Lillian sniffed.

"*Twelfth Night?*" Eddie had to keep them away from the tragedies and far, far away from that one specific tragedy.

"The tragedies are where the real acting chops lie." Bianca led them all down the path Eddie didn't want them on. "And we can all agree that our Lillian would thrive on a challenge."

Dee had brought this shit stirrer into their midst. Dee who should have known better. Dee who had left her with very few instructions but had reiterated the one Eddie had known since childhood. They could never, ever, do the Scottish play.

Eddie's alert button wailed into a full-blown siren.

Patty huffed. "Theatre to slit your wrists by."

"There is such scope in the tragedies," Lillian whispered, eyes alight with dangerous possibilities.

"*King Lear*," Eddie yelled.

"Well, yes." Bianca smiled at her.

Eddie steeled herself against that smile. Bianca needed to shut her mouth.

"But the lead female role is Cordelia, and she doesn't have many lines." Bianca went right on digging them into a deeper hole.

"Can't have a geriatric Cordelia," Patty said with a smirk at Lillian.

Peter threw up his hands. "I've got it."

No, no, no, no, no. Eddie prayed to every saint she didn't know and the two she did. *Please say* Hamlet, *any of the kings, bloody* Romeo & Juliet.

"*Macbeth!*" Peter beamed.

"No," she bellowed, way past the point of subtle. "We can't do *Macbeth.*" Not under any circumstances. The one rule even wild child Dee followed without question: Never do *Macbeth* at The Paradise Theatre.

"Oh, babe." Tears swam in the jade depths of Lillian's eyes. "Lady Macbeth is a wonderful role."

"And you'd kill it." Bianca led them straight into hell.

They'd all be dead if they did *Macbeth.* Eddie had to put a stop to this. Any play but *Macbeth.* "We can't do *Macbeth,*" she yelled.

All gazes snapped her way, a range of expressions from bewildered to offended hit her all at once.

Lillian recovered first. "Why ever not?"

"Yes, Eddie." Bianca cocked her head. Something flickered in her purple eyes and disappeared too fast for Eddie to identify.

"Not too long either," Rodney said. "Less chance of people falling asleep in the middle."

With all eyes still on her, Eddie panicked. "It's bad luck. Everybody knows that."

"Oh Edsie." Lillian giggled. "Surely you don't believe that old superstition."

"A witch's curse." Bianca chuckled. "Especially when there's no such thing as witches."

Yes, Eddie did believe that superstition. Furthermore, combining the oh-so-real witch's curse in *Macbeth* and the oh-so-vital fact that the Paradise Theatre was built right over a portal to hell, seemed like the worst idea she could imagine.

Lillian beamed at the table. "Shall we vote?"

TWO

Four days after losing the battle of *Macbeth*, Eddie still couldn't reach Dee. And four long, sexy nights with wonder hot man glaring and simmering at her in her dreams had kept her tossing and turning.

Peter hadn't hung about once the play selection was done, and already auditions for fucking, fuckity, fuck-fuck *Macbeth* were taking place in the theatre.

Not for Lady Macbeth—oh, no. Even worse. Today they were auditioning witches, and damnit why didn't Dee answer her phone?

Edme hit her grandmother's contact and waited for the call to connect.

Thank you, Jesus! It was ringing.

"*Oui*," Jean-Claude answered.

"Hi, Jean-Claude?"

"Deandra's telephone—" Jean-Claude enunciated carefully in his heavily accented English.

"Could I speak to—"

"—who is speaking?"

Goddamn delay on the line.

"Eddie, darling?" Peter called from the auditorium. "Are we ready for our auditions?"

No, they damn well were not. Not in this lifetime. Eddie wasn't clear on what the effect the Scottish play would be on the hell gate exactly, but Dee had definitely mentioned catastrophic and irreversible in the same warning.

"Gimme a minute, Peter," she yelled back. Eddie dashed through the sound lock on stage right and into the institutional looking passage behind the stage door. The front of the Paradise Theatre was all bygone era glamor, the back—pure utilitarian of the hospital variety.

"It's Eddie," she whisper-yelled into the phone. "Can I speak to Dee?"

"Eddie?" Jean-Claude's tone brightened in delight. "It is so good to talk with you. Dee, she is not here."

"Look it's rather urgent. Do you—"

"—she is getting the cocktail—"

"—know—"

"*Pardon?*"

"Could you maybe, find—"

"Eddie?" He yelled down the line. Clearly a raised voice would overcome any time lag or spotty connection.

"Yes, it's Eddie." She forced a constipated smile for the small group of hopefuls clucking together in the greenroom and held up her hand to indicate five minutes. "And I need to—"

"Dee is not 'ere."

Eddie's Converses squeaked on the beige vinyl-tiled floor as she paced to the rehearsal room. Barrie looked up from his script sides and raised a questioning brow.

She shook her head and waved for him to carry on.

Barrie took a deep breath and intoned. "*Ma, ma, ma, ma, ma, ma, maaaaaah!*"

Mouthing sorry to Barrie, she ducked into the coat annex, blocking out the smell of sweaty feet wafting up from the motley collection of shoes and boots. "Yes, I heard you but—"

"Dee is having the cocktail," Jean-Claude bellowed. "Cock. Tail."

"Excuse me...um...Edme?"

Eddie whirled at the tap on her shoulder, her autocorrect on her name faster than Google. "Eddie."

"*Oui*, Eddie." Jean-Claude shouted happily. "Dee, she is not here."

"Eddie." Whitney's pretty face folded in consternation. "Sorry, I didn't know you were on the phone." Regret swam in her treacle eyes. "But is the audition going to start soon?"

"Dee is having the cocktail with friends." Jean-Claude declared in the tone of a man unveiling the newest and brightest creation. "She is making so many friends, and they invited her to have the cocktail. I did not want the cocktail. So, I am here in the cabin."

"A couple of minutes." Eddie managed a smile for Whitney.

"That's great." Whitney beamed. "Only—"

"*Ah, non.*" Jean-Claude made a truly Gaelic *pfft* of regret. "She will be longer than a few minutes."

"—have another audition for *Newsies* at four." Whitney grimaced and shrugged. "And I—"

"Ah!" Peter loomed in the opening to the coat annex. "There you are, Eddie darling. I really think we must be getting on." He gave her a gently chiding look and tapped his empty left wrist. "Time is running on, and the talent is waiting."

"One minute," Eddie tossed in the general direction of Peter and Whitney.

"*Non*, Eddie." Jean-Claude raised his voice to ear splitting decibels. "I have told you. Dee she will—"

"Is that Jean-Claude?" Eyes shining, Whitney leaned closer. "Could you tell him I said hi?"

Along with every other under forty in the Paradise Players, Whitney had fallen prey to Jean-Claude's tall, dark, and cut beauty. Unfortunately for them, Jean-Claude had an eye for older women. And unfortunately for Eddie, Dee was always on the lookout for the Jean-Claudes of this world.

At the mention of Jean-Claude, Peter stiffened like a pissed off pound mongrel. "Dee had no business leaving at this time. As the the-ay-ter's resident operations manager, she knows this is our busy time."

"Tell him they're doing *Newsies* at the Rockridge Theatre," Whitney whispered. "Jean-Claude's tenor would be perfect." She pursed her lips. "Do you think he'll be back in time? I can tell them if he will be and maybe they can keep a part for him."

"Jean-Claude is way too old for *Newsies*," Peter snapped. "He's at least forty."

"No." Whitney shook her cloud of walnut hair. "He's only thirty-five and he looks so much younger."

"Hello, Whitney!" Jean-Claude yelled down the line. "Hello, Peter. We are on the cruise, Dee and I. The cruise to Halaska."

"Right." Eddie did what she did best and took the reins. "Jean-Claude, please tell Dee to call me back. It's urgent." She hung up before Jean-Claude could tell her where Dee was again. "Whitney." She turned to the young actress. "Have you filled out your audition form?"

Whitney's face fell. "No, but I act here so often. I just thought—"

"We're still going to need you to fill in that form." Eddie produced a tight smile and the line nobody would argue with.

"Insurance purposes." Then she turned to Peter. "I'll get the first group out to you."

"*Pah, pah, pah, pah, pah, pah, paaaaaaah.*" Barrie's mellow drone drifted over from the rehearsal room. He'd arrived to audition for the title role. A firm believer in professionalism, Barrie liked to set an example for the younger volunteers by always "preparing". Even though he already had the part, and warming up was as much a waste of time as attending the auditions.

Peter popped his head into the rehearsal room. "Sounding good, Barrie."

"She stood at the balcony door, inexplicably mimicking him hiccupping and amicably welcoming him in," Barrie responded.

"Good job." Peter tossed him the thumbs up. "Warm up the old instrument."

Barrie responded with, "Red leather, yellow leather. Red leather, yellow leather."

"Solid professional." Peter nodded and tugged his cuffs into place. "Always a pleasure to work with." He yanked open the sound lock door and disappeared into the blue-lit darkness.

"I didn't see any auditions forms." Whitney pouted. "They weren't in the greenroom."

Eddie pointed to the stack in the inbox marked Audition Forms on a shelf near the greenroom door.

Flushing, Whitney folded her arms. "I haven't got a—"

"Pens, right there." Eddie got out in front of Whitney's hovering objection before she lost her shit completely. She consulted her clipboard and stuck her head into the greenroom. "Trina, Sue, Kathryn, we need you on stage please."

She strode to the rehearsal room.

Barrie was chewing each syllable, his mouth working like it

was filled with toffee as he chattered, "Unique New York. Unique New York. Unique—"

"Barrie." Eddie motioned the stage door. "We need you on stage please."

Straightening his shoulders, Barrie raised his chin like a conquering hero. "Which—"

"Act four, scene one." Eddie turned and strode for the workshop. At least there she would be guaranteed a few minutes to get it together. Maybe auditions didn't really count. Maybe it had to be a performance. Even as she considered it, her heart sank. It wasn't the play itself; it was the stupid damn witches. Truly damned witches in this case.

Chatter of actors making their way on stage drifted toward her as Eddie welcomed the cool, cut-lumber-scented interior of the workshop. Fitful afternoon light struggled through the dusty windows positioned beneath the twelve-meter-high ceiling.

Paradise Players had never done *Macbeth*. Never! Because Dee had been there to stop it, and before her, Dee's mother. Eddie's mother had been next in line, but Rosabella had terrible taste in men and had taken her traveling shit show of a love life on the road. If Dee were here, she could call the guardians and warn them what was about to happen.

Detail fuzziness aside, Eddie was clear this would end badly—very, very badly. Like end of the world, apocalyptic event bad. And Dee was having cocktails on a cruise ship heading to Alaska.

The key was not to panic. *Think, Eddie, think.* Perhaps some preemptive smudging might help.

Through the double doors leading to the stage, Trina's piping, shrill voice said something indecipherable. Another woman responded.

Eddie didn't need to hear the words. Those three witches

would be double troubling and cauldron bubbling soon enough.

Habit had Eddie looking around to make sure she was alone before she called up the app on her phone. Technology had reached its sticky fingers into the paranormal world as well. The app opened, and Eddie keyed in the password Dee had given her, on pain of death to keep secret. Eddie's death that was. An effective incentive never to share the password as it turns out.

Three dials appeared on her screen, each surrounded by a moving circle of light. The dials kept track of the stability of the hell gate. Right now, each dial was resting in the green zone and not moving, indicating the hell gate was stable.

"Double, double toil and trouble. Fire burn and cauldron bubble." Onstage, the witches had reached the spell, and Eddie held her breath.

Two things were worse in Dee's book than *Macbeth* hitting the Paradise stage. The first would be letting the good people of Claymont, Ontario—and the rest of the world—know that they lived on a bona fide gate to hell. And the second was Eddie contacting the guardians. The whole pain of death—hers—reason was trotted out for that one too.

The meter on the left dial twitched and edged clockwise around the circle.

Eddie's heart thumped uncomfortably.

The dials receded back to green, and she let out her breath.

From stage, the witches went at it a second time. "Double, double toil and trouble. Fire burn and cauldron bubble."

All three dials flickered and bounced.

Argh! This was so not good. Those stupid dials never moved, but now they were edging toward the yellow zone.

The floor beneath Eddie's feet vibrated. A screwdriver bounced on the workbench and clattered to the floor.

Eddie's heart nearly went into orbit, but the dials went back down to their starting position.

Sometimes the workshop floor did hum and vibrate. It was only a few bits of concrete and some piping that separated it from the portal that shall not be named in the basement. Perfectly normal. To be expected even.

The girls on stage gave it gusto as they went into the third and final chorus of the curse. Each word came through loud and clear, pounding into Eddie like the march of doom.

All three dials surged into the yellow, paused, and then inched into the red zone.

Red for danger. Red for unstable hell gate. Red for colossally bad shit happening.

The workshop lurched under her feet and sent Eddie sprawling on her ass. She dropped her phone, and it skittered over the workshop floor and shot under the circular saw table. Even from here, Eddie couldn't miss those glowing red circles of oh-shitandfuck.

Muffled squeaks and cries of alarm came from the stage.

Light flared beneath the door leading from the workshop to the basement. Bright enough to sear Eddie's retinas and make black circles dance through her vision.

And then the stench hit her. Rotten eggs and four days in the sun roadkill. Scrambling for her phone, she retched and coughed, praying her quick sandwich lunch wouldn't make an appearance.

The onstage squeals turned into cries and grunts of disgust.

"Ewww! What is that smell?"

"Oh my god, it stinks."

"Kathryn! Was that you?"

And then Peter called for his salvation. "Eddie?"

Peter would have to wait his turn behind the stench and

the glowing light from the basement. And the possible minions of hell on their way to take over the world.

Shadows flickered under the basement door.

You know what hell had? Demons, Satan, dead souls of really shitty people like murderers and child molesters.

The basement door groaned and shuddered and then sprung open.

Screaming, Eddie threw up her hand, which was so fucking useless she had no idea why she did it other than she was out of any better option.

"Eddie!!!" Peter's bellow grew closer. "Are the toilets clogged again?"

The light from the basement door blinked out, and the smell started subsiding.

A form hopped into the workshop. A small form. Actually, tiny, like insect tiny.

Eddie stared at the thing like she was losing her mind, because that was a distinct possibility. There'd been earth quaking, bright light, and that disgusting smell. And now... "A grasshopper?"

The dials on her phone flickered and drifted back to green.

"*Chirrup!*" Feelers working the air, the grasshopper sprang toward her.

Now Eddie wasn't an insect sort of girl, but looking after a theatre meant a certain amount of wildlife of the vermin category. Snatching up her phone, she checked that it was working.

It was working. And the dials were definitely indicating the hell gate was stable again.

She felt strangely let down. All that fuss over a grasshopper.

As it hopped closer, the details of the grasshopper got clearer. It was a weird blue gray with an armor plated carapace. Slightly bigger than your average garden grasshopper, with a bulbous head, but all in all, not enough to cause all the fuss and the dire warnings. Thank you, Jesus, she hadn't given in and called the guardians anyway. Dying over a grasshopper looking thing was not the way she wanted to go out.

"Everything's fine, Peter," she called and grabbed a dustpan and the broom. "The…er…septic tank might need checking."

Threatening or not, that nasty bug was heading back where it had come from. All bugs might very well come from hell anyway.

Scooping the bug into her pan with the broom, she flipped on the light to the basement.

Feelers twitching, the bug squatted in the pan and eyed her through bulbous, red-rimmed eyes. Yup, she didn't want that ugly bastard taking up residence in her theatre.

She edged past the silent furnace and squeezed between the oversize propane tanks and the wall. She tapped the icon on her phone that would open the door.

A latch clicked, like it had the couple of times Dee had allowed her to come down here with her, and the wall opened.

Granted, this was the only hell gate Eddie had ever seen, but it was a disappointing swirl of gray and black smoke on the floor just over a meter in diameter and tucked into the far side of the three meter by three meter room that housed it.

Particles of ash lay around the swirling smoke, the only indication that anything had happened. Other than the fuck ugly squatter in her pan.

The bug shifted. It made a high-pitched squeak and then leapt onto Eddie's hand.

"Shit!" The pain shot up Eddie's arm in a searing blast of heat as the little fucker sunk his teeth in and bit her.

She shook her hand, but the bug stuck, hanging on by its teeth.

Agony pounded through her arm like she'd thrust it straight into a mound of burning coals.

"Ow, ow, ow." Dancing like she hoped nobody was watching, Eddie hopped around and flapped her arm to dislodge the thing.

Either it wasn't a fan of her moves, or her flailing had shaken it free, but the bug flew off and sailed straight into the hell gate.

The mist moved faster and emitted a loud burp before returning to its languid swirling.

Eddie's arm throbbed in time to her heartbeat as she checked the dials on her app again. All dials safely in the green and homicidal grasshopper back with his psycho friends.

With a quick sweep of the ash, Eddie trudged back up the stairs to the theatre. She had auditions to finish.

THREE

Dream lover—she wished—paid Eddie another visit that night. Caramel-and corn-streaked hair blew over the sweat-sheened angular planes of his face. His icy gaze narrowed in concentration on something she couldn't see.

And was that blood?

Dried, rusty stains crusted one nostril and stroked over the chiseled planes of his chest. Grunting, he swung a massive axe.

Eddie felt the reverberation through her own muscles as the axe struck an invisible target. Her arm jarred with the initial impact, juddered as the axe met resistance, followed by the release as the axe completed its arc.

Vermillion sprayed from the edges of the double headed blade and spattered warm and sticky against his face.

That was definitely blood.

Gross! And she recoiled, her sensations separating from him.

Now she stood to the side, and she could see the mass of

tangled, roiling bodies. Blades flashing, guttural cries of pain, harsh grunts, the stench of blood and fire. Dream lover—she wished—stood in the center of a war zone. Only like a historical war zone with weapons that looked familiar but also different.

A hulking beast leapt in front of dream lover—she wished —and opened its mouth and roared. Five-inch canines dripped globs of saliva down its oxlike face. Its eyes glowed black and red, and light gleamed off the silver-tipped edges of its horns. Swollen, exaggerated muscles bunched beneath its russet skin as it raised a huge war hammer.

Eddie wanted to shout a warning to dream lover—still wishing.

"Shade!" Oxman roared.

Shade. His name was Shade. It clicked into place perfectly with his sensual beauty.

In her dream, she whispered his name. "Shade."

He turned, that glacial stare locked on her. "You."

"Watch out," Eddie screamed, but her voice didn't meet the movements of her mouth, and nothing came out.

Whirling, Shade swung his axe. His biceps swelled as he cleaved Oxman's ugly head from his grotesque body. Unlike before, this dream made blood lust pound in her pulses. She wanted to fight something. Kill.

The battle receded into a blurry mist around Shade. Shadows danced through the mist, but the sounds muted as Shade turned and looked at her again. His beautifully sculpted mouth, almost feminine in its lush hedonism, parted, and he whispered that word again, "You."

His voice was deep and resonant, and it rolled like a coming thunderstorm over her senses and tugged at some-thing visceral in her core. "What have you done?"

Eddie jerked awake. Her heart pounded and sweat slicked

her skin as she blinked the familiar details of her bedroom into focus.

Chest of drawers opposite her bed, large window beside it showing a pearly predawn sky, shadowed doorway to her attached bathroom.

Like the other dreams about him, this one had been disturbingly real and intense. Only given a choice, she'd go back to the less martial dreams she'd had before. In those, she'd found herself popping in on him like a phantom peeping Tom.

Shade.

She kicked the tangled sheets away from her legs. The springs of her cast-iron bed frame creaked in protest as she wrestled her limbs free.

He'd spoken to her, his gaze accusing, his voice as clear as if he'd whispered those words in her ear. *"What have you done?"*

What had she done?

Her arm throbbed in a visceral reminder. She clicked on her bedside lamp. Four distinct puncture wounds had raised, swollen edges and looked much larger than yesterday. They throbbed like a son of a bitch, and bruising circled the holes. It looked like the bite from a much larger beastie, like a dog.

She padded into her bathroom and unearthed the Polysporin from beneath the sink. Her bathroom was one of her favorite parts of living in the old playhouse. Tiny black and white octagonal tiles made floral patterns on the floor and harkened back to the theatre's turn of the twentieth century origins. A cast-iron claw-foot tub and shower combo lent itself to quick cleanups and long, bubble scented soaks equally. She'd liberated the large, ornate oval mirror above her sink from props storage, and was not giving it back. Her vanity she'd converted herself from an antique washstand.

She gave her bite a thorough wash with her antibacterial

chain store face wash and slathered it with the poly. It took an opera of hisses, whimpers, and squeaks to get through the process, but she was satisfied she'd done the business.

Dressing for the day in her standard black leggings and long-sleeve T-shirt, she grabbed a quick toast and coffee breakfast in the kitchen she and Dee shared and took the dingy, dank back stairway down to the theatre.

Theatres could be creepy places when they were empty, like the echoes of countless people and plays still clung to the air. In these spaces, kings had lost their heads, people had lost their hearts, dreams had died or been fulfilled, and the magic of creation lingered in the walls and floors.

Eddie loved the laden solitude of the Paradise Theatre, and she found her way by memory through the windowless backstage spaces. *Macbeth* callbacks were scheduled for evening, and until then, she had the place to herself. As a child, she'd clambered after Dee into all the magical spaces the theatre offered. The wardrobe room bursting with the colors and textures of costumes. The props room housing a treasure chest of bottles, hatboxes, weapons, music boxes, pictures, and anything else that had been used on stage. The furniture storage resembling a dusty bric a brac store.

In the fall, she and Dee would haul everything out and clean it all before organizing and putting it all back in time for the winter play season to begin and the community volunteers to scamper through it like destructive toddlers in their special playground.

After yesterdays' excitement, her first job this morning was to check the basement, especially the room only she and Dee knew about. A quick check on the app confirmed that the hell gate was still stable and got her wondering again what all the *Macbeth* fuss had been about.

Her dream nagged at her as she flipped the lights on in the

workshop. Theatres could also be dangerous places, and Dee had drummed safety into her from her first memory. Soon the workshop would get busy with set builders and painters as they prepared the backdrop for *Macbeth*, and then Eddie would be run off her feet trying to manage them all and keep everyone's limbs attached to the appropriate body, but for now it was peaceful, and sleepy dust motes danced in the air beneath the benign hum of fluorescent lighting.

The room with the hell gate looked pretty much the same as it had yesterday, the gray-black smoky rings within rings languidly twirling around and through each other. No sign of her nasty little bug either.

In the dream, Shade had asked her what she'd done, and the only thing that came to mind was the auditions for the dreaded Scottish play. But what Shade had to do with that, she couldn't fathom. Still, she checked the room one more time before closing it and making her way upstairs. She needed to repair the tread on the stairs leading to the auditorium before an aging audience member took a header.

As a resident stage manager to a community theatre group, Eddie should have known better than to relax and think the trite old how bad can it get?

Answer: really fucking bad.

The callbacks had gotten to the appearance of Hecate when all hell—or the part that was coming through the theatre basement—broke loose.

"Get it. Kill it!" Whitney screamed from her onstage perch on a chair.

Armed with a bucket, Eddie darted around and through the actors on stage. Her target, a rather large and warty toad-like creature that ran instead of hopped and got some serious speed from its meaty thighs.

Right on Eddie's heels, Trina had tears streaming down her

face as she begged, "Please don't kill it. Everything deserves to live."

Barrie had dived off stage and into the auditorium at the thing's first appearance and was currently cowering between rows C and D. "Don't be ridiculous, Trina. It's vermin."

"Really, Eddie darling." Peter stood atop his table, which was precariously perched atop the seatbacks in the middle of the auditorium. "We cannot have these sorts of disruptions to the creative process."

"Weird looking toad." Patty peered over her crocheting from the first row. "Never seen a toad book it like that."

The toad shot under Whitney's chair and elicited a fresh round of screams and exhortations for Eddie to end its life.

Eddie dashed around the other side of Whitney's chair, ready to snare it when it emerged.

"Toads are very important to the ecosystem." Trina sobbed as she crouched behind Eddie with her hands cupped to catch.

"I don't care," Whitney shrieked. "Don't let it touch me."

From where she stood on seat E11, Lillian raised her hands like their resident prophet. "Everyone calm down. Edsie will deal with the nasty creature."

"It's not nasty." Trina dropped to her knees. "It's part of the living wonder."

"It's a bloody toad," Peter bellowed.

"Loving space, babe," Lillian called. "We create positive spaces."

Kathryn ducked into the wings on stage left and clambered onto the stage manager's desk. "Are we still going to have callbacks?"

"Yup." Eddie lunged as the thing made an appearance.

It shot through her legs, deked past Trina's outstretched palms, and headed for the stage apron.

With a rebel yell, Barrie vaulted three rows back, his long legs spider walking as he made his escape.

Trina ripped off her T-shirt and tossed it over the toad.

Barrie's head popped up from behind the seats as he ogled Trina's bra-clad torso. "Well done."

The thing stopped moving beneath Trina's shirt, and Eddie lunged with her empty bucket and trapped it.

"You got it, Edsie." Lillian clapped and looked at the rest of the occupants. "I told you she would deal with it."

Inside the bucket, the thing had recovered from its momentary paralysis and thumped against the side.

"Have you got it?" Shirley wandered back on stage, having used the toad as an opportunity to take a quick smoke break.

"Get it off the stage." Whitney pointed an imperious finger to the stage right wings. "I'm not getting down until that thing is out of here."

Trina crouched beside the bucket and whispered, "Please don't hurt him."

"I'm not going to hurt him." Eddie slid a piece of plywood between the bucket and stage floor. "And I'm getting him out of here now."

The toad went crazy, flinging itself against the side of the bucket. That was no ordinary damn toad, and Eddie was relieved nobody had taken a closer look at the thing. From what she'd been able to catch, other than its strange way of moving, it had horns and sharp teeth as part of its allure. Along with an odd blue underbelly. Regardless, the thing was going back through the hell gate.

She needed to get ahold of Dee. Grasshoppers and toads were no reason to panic, but they were raising a very decided prickle of alarm.

"It's escaping," Whitney screamed.

Folding her long, elegant legs, Lillian held up one hand. "I have total faith in Edsie."

Shirley's daisy patterned Doc Martins appeared beside the bucket. "What are you gonna do with it now?"

Trina's big blue eyes implored her.

"Put it outside," Eddie said. Outside this realm.

"Thank you." Tears spilled over Trina's lids. "I can help."

That was the last thing she needed, and Eddie pulled back on her yelp and modulated her tone. "No, that's fine. You carry on with your callbacks."

"Indeed," Peter thundered. "Eddie, if you would be so good as to remove the distraction, we can continue." He pinned her with a censorious look. "The show must go on."

If Eddie had a dollar for every time she'd heard that old workhorse, she'd...well, she'd still be here, but she'd be able to renovate the living quarters above the theatre. One hand on the top of the bucket, she slid the other under the plywood.

Hell toad lost his shit, and through the plywood she could feel him going for broke as he tried to bust his way out. The jostling motion jarred the grasshopper's parting gift on her hand.

Kathryn, now standing beside the stage manager's desk, reeled back as Eddie carried her bucket and wood trap past.

Through the workshop, she took her protesting captive. An odd yowling from the bucket got Eddie moving faster. She didn't want to answer the questions that would follow if anyone heard that noise.

Down in the basement, the door to the hell gate room stood ajar. Thus answering her question as to how the toad had got into the theatre in the first place. Why the door was open when, as far as she knew, the app was the only way it could be opened, remained a mystery.

Dee had more 'splainin' to do.

Putting the bucket on the floor, Eddie toed it closer to the hell gate.

Disturbing reds and yellows colored the gray-black swirl. Grasshopper's bite in mind, she got her trap as close to the hell gate as she dared, using a broom handle to place it right at the edge.

The hell gate swirled faster, silvery tendrils of smoke rising and dissipating as they hit the air. Not dissimilar to the vape smoke Shirley generated.

"Right." Eddie got her broom handle ready for the final push over the edge. Who the hell knew what would happen to the bucket. "One, two…" Eddie shoved the bucket into the hell gate. "Three!"

The hell gate emitted a loud sucking noise, then a guttural burp.

The bucket came flying back, smacking into the wall behind Eddie. The plywood seemed to be now fueling the fires of hell.

Whelp! That was that.

Rodney was standing in the workshop when she emerged from the basement.

"Edme." He gave her a tight smile. "About this morning's incident." He stroked his mustache by splitting his forefinger and thumb over the two sides in a neat, practiced movement. "We cannot have vermin in the theatre." His gaze took on a portentous cast, and he lowered his voice. "Particularly with the…er…financial difficulties we are facing and our need to attract donations."

Eddie gritted her teeth. "I'm dealing with it, Rodney."

"Excellent." He clicked his heels together. "I know I can rely on you to ensure future donors do not see a repeat of this morning."

FOUR

"Eddie." Jean-Claude sounded even happier than the last time she'd called to hear from her that night. *"Bonjour."*

Callbacks had gone without another hitch. The app showed the hell gate as stable. For whatever that was worth, because the damn thing hadn't flickered when the toad had appeared. "Hi, Jean-Claude. Is Dee there?"

"Dee?" He sounded as if the idea of Dee being at the end of her phone was an unusual request. "Dee is at dinner now." The phone crackled, and background noise changed to the gentle chatter of numerous voices. "Dee, she is eating now, and I will join her."

Eddie sank on her bed and pressed a hand to the headache threatening between her eyes. She could not have this conversation in a ship's dining room. "No, that's fine Jean-Claude. Could you please tell her I called and that it's urgent she call me back?"

"Everything is all right?" Jean-Claude's voice clouded with concern.

No, it wasn't but she couldn't get into it with him. "If you could just tell her to call me as soon as she can."

"But of course." Jean-Claude's cheery chirp was back.

She hung up and sent Dee their codeword text: WHAT THE HELL!!!

Dee had been the last official hell gate guardian, a position that Dee's grandmother's grandmother had first taken. When Dee retired, Rosebella, as the next woman in the family line, should have taken over. However, Eddie's mom had envisioned an entirely different future for herself and disappeared with her boyfriend *du jour*—Eddie did a quick mental calculation— six years ago now. Not that she'd been a constant presence in Eddie's life before that. Her mother believed in fly-by check-ins generally around the time she ran out of money or male companionship. The two events often coincided. Eddie had long ago given up on expecting more from Rosabella. Dee had been the constant presence in her life, her de facto mother as it were.

To be honest, the biggest issue with Rosabella not being around was the guardianship. Rosabella had been trained for the job, disappearing each summer of her childhood to a special camp for young guardians. Dee had never let Eddie go, for reasons that now that she really examined them seemed sketchy. Eddie was firstly too young, and then not following the chain of inheritance, and finally, too old to start now. In fact, Dee had been annoyingly vague about the guardianship, and it begged the question as to why. For as long as the hell gate lay dormant, which had been most of her life, she'd never bothered to ask. But she was asking now. Or she would as soon as Dee answered her damned phone.

The guardians had no idea Dee had passed the baton to Eddie and not Rosabella, and the only thing Dee had been forthcoming about was that the guardians would have very strong opinions on the matter. Probably life or death status issues that had a lot to do with Eddie not having been trained to take on what—and Eddie had to face it—was a serious job. Guarding a gate to the underworld did seem to be important.

All her life, and long before that even, the hell gate had been in the theatre basement. She'd grown up knowing it was there, and she was not to go near it and not tell anyone about it. In fact, she'd been five or six before she realized not everyone had a hell gate in their basement. And the thing had been a silent, trouble-free presence. Most days she didn't even know it was there. Dee had been away before, and nothing like this had happened. Then Bianca had suggested *Macbeth*, and now all hell was breaking lose in her theatre.

After a dinner of a peanut butter sandwich and a bowl of popcorn—made the old-fashioned stovetop way, thank you very much—Eddie indulged in a long, relaxing bath before climbing into bed.

She read until her eyes were crossing, and she was in peril of braining herself with her e-reader. She was stalling going to sleep. The last dream had disturbed her, and she was less than keen to visit another war zone. After a last check on the app and another trip to the basement to make sure the hell gate hadn't spit out another unwelcome guest, she took the chance on sleep.

WHEN SHE CONNECTED WITH HIM, Shade was running through a mist shrouded jungle. Yips, howls, and grunts pursued him as he wove through the trees. Sweat and blood smeared his face, his jaw set in a grimly determined line. Around him, shadowy figures kept pace with him, but whether they were with him or pursuing him, Eddie couldn't tell.

Her heart rate accelerated to match the pumping of his strong legs.

He burst out of the jungle into a meadow lush with wild-flowers.

"Shade!" A deep bass voice resonated behind him.

Increasing his pace, Shade gathered his muscles and leapt. Giant wings burst out of his back and swept him into a murky sky. Light played across the midnight black of his wings and caught iridescent bolts of gold and blue buried in the silky feathers.

This was definitely new, and Eddie stood as an enthralled dream bystander as those powerful wings dipped and swept, gaining altitude.

A second figure, large and muscular, hit the edge of the jungle and bellowed at the sky. He unleashed a set of wings as well and shot into the sky after Shade.

The second winged man faltered, and he turned his head. Piercing blue eyes in a roughly hewn face stared right at her. He frowned and hovered, as he cocked his head and studied her.

Shade streaked toward him, broadsiding the second man and sending them both tumbling for the ground.

Eddie screamed.

And got a poke in the eye.

A real poke in the eye. As in one not happening in the dream but coming from her real world.

The poke came again and ripped Eddie out of the dream.

She reared back for the sake of her watering eye.

And screamed.

The creature squatting on the bed beside her started and screamed. Still shrieking, it shot off her bed and disappeared beneath it.

Scrabbling away until her iron bed frame bruised her spine, Eddie snapped on her bedside light.

A pair of pale-yellow horns stuck up from the side of her bed. The creature's ear-splitting screams got louder.

Eddie felt cheated of her reaction, and she shouted, "Stop."

The screaming stopped. The horns quivered, and a soft voice said, "You stop."

"I have stopped." Eddie pushed her hair off her face with a shaky hand. Her heart was beating so hard it pounded in her ears. She wanted to grab her phone and check the app, but she was certain she didn't want to take her eyes off whatever was lurking next to her bed. She hefted her bedside lamp, throwing careening shadows across her room. Mastering her best in command voice she said, "Show yourself."

"You show yourself," the creature lisped.

"I'm sitting right here." She might still be asleep, so Eddie pinched herself. It hurt. Not doing that again.

The horns edged up. "And I'm sitting right here."

A bald creamy head appeared over her duvet.

So many questions.

It took a long time before two almond shaped, black eyes peeked over the duvet at her.

She opened her mouth and let the first of her clamoring questions out. "Are you real?"

"Yes." It cocked its head, tiny pointy ears twitching. "Are you real?"

Its gaze locked on the lamp in her hand, and with a squeak, it disappeared again.

Lamp at the ready, Eddie scooted closer to the creature. Taking a deep breath, she peered over the side of her bed.

About the size of a medium dog, the creature crouched beside her bed, chubby little arms shielding its pate. It was kind of cute and like nothing she'd ever seen. "What are you?"

"What are you?" It shot her a quick glance.

Eddie's sense of the ridiculous won the battle over her fear. "I asked you first."

It lowered one arm and glared at her. "I'm an imp."

Of course it was, complete with duckling yellow wings flaring from its back. It was kind of cute, in an adorably *Gremlins* sort of way. Round little face and wide mouth, with a tiny button nose and bright black eyes staring at her without blinking. Eddie lowered her lamp. "What are you doing here?"

"What are—"

"I live here." The mimic game was getting old, fast.

"Here?" The imp looked around it with that unblinking stare. Its pink tongue shot out as if tasting the air. "Are you the hell guardian?"

In a manner of speaking, and not officially if anyone official ever asked. "Yes."

"Huh?" It eyed her critically. "I thought you'd be bigger." Its ears twitched, and one moved ninety degrees to the right. "You should be bigger."

Eddie didn't like the sound of that. "Why?"

The imp started. "Why what?"

"Why should I be bigger?"

Its ear shifted all the way around until it was facing backwards. "No reason."

Now Eddie was no imp expert, but that seemed like a tell to her. "You're lying."

"Probably." The imp shrugged. "I'm an imp; we lie."

Well, that fit with what she knew of imps, admittedly not much. Actually, very little. Okay, nothing at all. Eddie put the lamp back on her bedside table. "Why don't we start with why you're here." Then she added a proviso. "And without lying."

"Hmm." The imp gave that some thought, little horns

vibrating. "I could try not to lie. If given the right incentive." Its button eyes fastened on her with unnerving intensity.

"What sort of incentive?" Eddie wasn't promising her first born or any such shit. She'd read fairytales, she had a suspicion where this was going.

Its face crumpled into a truly pitiful expression. "I'm hungry." It glanced at the empty plate from her peanut butter sandwich. "And that smells like the sort of food for a hungry imp."

Peanut butter? That she could do. Still keeping a respectable space between them, Eddie slipped her legs over the side of the bed.

The imp scrambled back, horns straightening like arrow points.

Moving slower, Eddie stood.

Cocking its head, the imp studied her from toes to top. "Hmm."

Feeling suddenly exposed, Eddie grabbed a sweater and hauled it over her pjs. "What?"

"You might be big enough," it said.

Peanut butter sandwich and truth it was. Eddie padded through to her kitchen.

The imp followed, its tail dragging on the ground behind. It watched her as she went through the motions of making a sandwich.

She handed the sandwich to him.

Snatching it from her, it opened its mouth, which split the bottom half of its face in two and tossed the sandwich in. Swallowing, it blinked at her.

Eddie made another sandwich. The size of its mouth made her regret her lack of a threatening lamp.

The second sandwich went the way of the first. Scratching behind an ear, the imp belched and nodded.

Dragging out a chair, Eddie sat at the kitchen table. The microwave clock announced the ridiculous hour of three a.m. "Do you have a name?"

"Yesterday." The imp dragged out a second chair and scrambled onto the seat.

"Your name is Yesterday?"

The imp nodded and examined the kitchen.

"I'm Eddie," she said. It only seemed polite at this point. "And I'm guessing you came through the hell gate."

"What is this place?" Its eyes locked on the oven.

"It's a kitchen." Which probably meant exactly nothing to an imp. "It's a room in which I make food."

The imp grunted. "This is a good room." He sniffed and glared at her. "You smell of rakshasa."

The name sounded familiar. "Who's Rakshasa?"

"A demon." The imp sneered. "A hell guardian knows rakshasa demons."

From which she gathered there were different types of demons, and that fit with her sketchy mythology knowledge. Whether it was the toad or the grasshopper she wasn't going to reveal her ignorance. "There have been a couple of...er... demons coming through the hell gate in the last couple of days."

"Hmm." Yesterday scratched his horn. "That makes sense."

"Why?" And should she expect more otherworldly visitors? How to stop them might also be a good piece of information.

It blinked at her. "The gate is open."

Putting two and two together, because she was quick like that, she linked the open gate with the dreaded Scottish play. "Which is why you came through it?"

"It was open." The imp shrugged.

A nasty follow-up thought chased through her mind. A grasshopper, a toad, and an imp she could handle, but Dee had always warned her of the apocalyptic consequences of the gate being open, so it stood to reason that there were more threatening things that could come through. Mind like a steel trap, that was her. Dee needed to get her ass off her Alaskan cruise and back here, and close that fucking gate. "We need to close the gate."

"No problem." Yesterday sniffed and twitched his ears. "For another of those magic yummies, I can lend you my assistance."

A peanut butter sandwich to close the hell gate seemed like a hell of a deal to her. Then again, maybe too good of a deal. "Are you lying to me?"

The imp snorted.

Not an answer, but Eddie made another sandwich anyway.

The imp didn't even chew them. He pointed to her arm. "The rakshasa bit you?"

The wound on her hand was even bigger and red and swollen. "It's getting worse."

"Bad." Yesterday made a clicking sound. "Very bad. Rakshasa bites."

Her bite looked like it was infected. "What do I do?"

"No problem." Yesterday blinked. "Rub some salt on it."

"Salt?" She was thinking more in the antibiotic direction. Then again, didn't salt block demons and witches and crap?

Yesterday nodded and eyed the bread on the counter.

For a small little bugger, he could pack it away, and Eddie made him another sandwich. Grabbing the box of kosher salt, she poured a handful on her bite.

"Motherfucker!" It stung, like a whole helluva lot, like her leaping around the kitchen and swearing a lot.

Yesterday belched and hopped off his chair. "And now we close the hell gate."

Well, that was easy.

FIVE

For the second morning in a row, Eddie woke to being poked in the eye. This time, she spoke before opening her eyes. "Stop it, Yesterday."

Despite his declaration of helping her close the gate, when they'd gone downstairs, he'd bolted into the depths of the theatre and disappeared. Eddie had spent the morning hours in which she should have been working at her real job trying to find him. No luck until now.

It would also be super if the gremlin looking little fucker let her sleep until sunrise. She'd dragged her ass through a full day of diva wrangling and stumbled into bed late. Yesterday had appeared just as she was locking up for the night. A quick chant, a bit more salt tossed at the hell gate and no more demons would be arriving to spoil her day.

Poke.

Hard enough this time to make her eye water, and Eddie batted him away.

A *thump* followed by a yelp got her eyes open.

Yesterday was struggling back to his feet. "Open them." He pointed to her face. "Open them and come with me."

That sounded like a thing she really shouldn't be doing. "Why?"

"Why what?"

Jesus, not this again. "Why should I follow you?"

"Why not?" Yesterday blinked at her.

Clearly, yes, this again. They needed a more effective communication technique if Yesterday was going to hang around. Then again, the suggestion of efficient communications might encourage him to stay longer. She'd been so grateful for his help in closing the hell gate, she hadn't thought to ask how he was going to get back through if it was now closed. It was another problem Eddie laid in Dee's growing pile. God, she wished Dee had sent her for that guardian training. She might have some idea how to deal with her current predicament if she had. All Dee would say about that was that it had to be Rosabella. And it had been working fine for them, until Bianca had given play selection a go.

The more she thought about Bianca, the more Eddie got the idea that Bianca had manipulated the bored meeting to get her way. Was *Macbeth* just an inconvenient coincidence, or had Bianca wanted that specific play to be staged?

Recent events had her getting suspicious.

After hauling her reluctant ass out of bed, Eddie found her robe and slippers and pulled them on. Managing a theatre had the unfortunate side effect of being pulled out of bed at all hours, and wandering around in panties and a T-shirt didn't work for her. By the constipated look on Rodney's face, the one time it had happened, it hadn't worked for him either. And Eddie refused to think about what that said about her ass.

"Come, come." Yesterday hopped from one stubby leg to the other. "It is bad, very bad."

Bad like the rakshasa bite? Which was looking nastier this morning. The skin on either side of her bite was puffy and shiny, and it hurt like shit. "Are you sure about the salt on my bite?"

"No problem." Ears twitching, Yesterday puffed his chest. "I am an imp; I know these things. These are things I know."

He did come from hell, and given the resounding silence from Dee, was pretty much her only source of information.

Yesterday leapt and opened her door. "Come now."

Eddie flipped on the light switch over the stairwell leading down to the theatre. Yesterday didn't seem to struggle with the dark, but she wasn't compounding her wee hours meanderings with a faceplant down the stairs.

As expected, he led her into the basement and through the secret door, which was open. Again. Dammit! What was the point in having a fucking app if it never—

Eddie stopped in the doorway and blinked. "Um, Yesterday."

"See." Yesterday pointed to the problem.

Not that pointing was necessary. At all.

A naked man lay beside the hell gate. He was lying on his side, facing away from her. Broad shoulders topped a muscular back, which tapered into a slim waist. Eddie tried not to look at his tight, muscular ass. Powerful thighs were tucked up in a near fetal position. Rust streaked his biceps and forearms.

"Very bad," Yesterday whispered. "And you are definitely not big enough."

This was the problem she had to be big enough to handle. Total fail! Even lying down, naked guy was a big 'un. "Who is he?"

The man groaned.

On a squeak, Yesterday scuttled out the door and it

slammed shut behind him, trapping her in the room with a naked guy.

Moaning, he rolled to his back.

Now Eddie definitely looked away. Her eyes threatened a mutiny and kept trying to sneak a peek. Digging in her robe pocket, she grabbed her phone to open the door. She and Yesterday were going to have words about his dash and door close.

"You," the man rasped.

And Eddie's head snapped up. She would know that voice anywhere. It had been whispering that one word in her dreams for weeks now.

His eyes were open and looking at her. Those eyes were so much more potent in real life, a perfect silvery gray ringed by thick, dark lashes. And judging by the gleam in them, he was pissed as...well, hell. Had he come through the hell gate? The same hell gate which now shone purest silver and swirled like liquid metal. The same hell gate Yesterday had helped her close.

Her gaze locked with Shade's. For some inexplicable reason, her right hand raised itself and waggled its fingers at him. "Hi."

She wanted to punch herself in the face.

The chiseled planes of his face stopped a hair short of being harsh.

"You," he said again. "What have you done?"

Okay, as far as verbal variety went, he was not doing well. Her lame hi didn't seem quite so inane now. Nope, it had still been dumb as fuck. And she would ask the questions here. Her basement, her hell gate, her rules. "Who are you?"

Those gray eyes stripped past her defenses and left her feeling naked. He took a slow perusal from her face down to her toes and up again. "You are not the hell guardian." His voice was pure sex. Raspy, deep, and gritty.

Also, hold the phone there, Hotness. "Yes, I am."

"No." He narrowed his gaze at her. "You are something, though."

She'd like to take that as a compliment, as in *you are something else, woman,* but she wasn't getting the warm and fuzzies from the calculating gleam in his eyes. The horrible idea that she might be talking to a guardian pierced her brain. Going on the theory that a good offense was the best form of defense; she summoned all her sass. "I think the more relevant question is what you are doing in my basement."

On a scoff, he shook his head and got his feet under him. He crouched, thigh muscles bulging, as if getting his bearings. "I am in your basement because you opened the hell gate and summoned me." He locked those steely grays on her. "You're a witch?"

"No." Eddie was unclear on many details about the hell gate, but she was clear on not being a witch, and also not doing any summoning. Might not be the best time to mention *Macbeth.* "I didn't summon you."

"And yet, I am here." He rose to what must be six three or four and worked a crick out of his neck. "I am here, and therefore I was summoned. I don't journey to this realm for shits and giggles." He sniffed. "Treacherous, miserable place that it is."

On behalf of humanity, Eddie felt obligated to say, "I don't think it's that bad."

"You don't think." His wintry gaze locked on her as he sneered. "How surprising."

Well now, hot or not, the man was just rude. Eddie gathered her own frost as she said, "Is there a reason you're hanging around naked in my basement?"

And there's a sentence she'd never thought she'd say. Did that make her life pathetic or really narrow?

"We have covered this." He examined a nasty gash on his forearm. "And you have, as yet, to supply a reasonable answer." Cocking his head, he studied her. "No, not a witch. And yet, I walked in your dreams."

"Uninvited, I might add." She had definitely liked him better in her dreams. This new and verbal version of her dream lover—still maybe a tiny bit wishful—was a disappointment. Despite what he said, she was the hell guardian, or as near to it as either of them had right now and it was time to do her job. Hauling out every ounce of authority she had no right to use, she pointed to the hell gate. "You have no business here. You need to go back."

He stilled and studied her. A smirk tilted his full, pouty mouth. "Are you giving me orders, little human woman?"

"Yep." At five eight, Eddie didn't hear little applied to her often, if at all. "And you need to hop through that gate again," she couldn't resist adding, "to wherever you left your pants."

Speculation gleamed in his eyes. "Do you know who I am?"

Eddie had read too many memes and jokes not to answer that one. "Nope, and if you don't, we can always ask someone."

"Intriguing," he drawled. "A being, who is not the hell guardian, but not entirely human either, who has the power to summon me, but has no idea who she has summoned. And a woman whose dreams I walked."

Listening skills were clearly not one of his strengths, and did he call her not entirely human? "I don't care who you are, but you need to get back to wherever you came from. I'm assuming hell."

"What do they call you?" He stalked toward her, and Eddie backed up. Whoever he was, he was big. And in her dreams, he had wings. There was no evidence of them now, but she recalled how they'd sort of popped out of his back.

"Look." Her back hit the wall, necessitating her taking charge of the interaction. A firm, no-nonsense tone was vital when dealing with winged whack jobs. "I'm going to need you to stay where you are."

"Need?" The word rumbled through his voice and came out like a stroke over her senses. "What an interesting word to use."

He kept coming until he was barely three inches away. Looming over her, muscular body radiating heat, he lowered his head and whispered in her ear. "Tell me what you need?"

Eddie was horrified when arousal tingled through her, peaking her nipples and pooling between her thighs. She clenched her jaw to keep from heavy breathing. She wanted to touch him, wanted to press against him, rub herself over him like a cat. "I'm really not comfortable with your behavior."

"What are you then?" Raspy and deep, his voice stroked her desire like he was blowing on flame.

"Scared." That had to be it. She couldn't be turned on by this dickwad. She didn't like overbearing men.

He chuckled, his breath puffing hot against her neck. He was so close, yet no part of him actually made contact with her. She wanted to melt like hot toffee and glue herself to him.

"Shall I tell you what you are?" he rasped.

"N-no." She couldn't seem to make her mouth form words. A moan built in her throat, and she clamped her jaw before it escaped. Heat prickled over her skin, sunk into her muscles, and settled deep into her cells. She needed him to touch her, to touch him, to have him, for him to possess her. Use her. Take her.

"There is a name for what makes your breasts throb for my

hand and my mouth. There is a reason why your pussy is hot and wet for me."

Dear God, he was right. Her panties felt uncomfortably constricting against the molten heat. Every sound he made increased the pressure on her clit. If she wasn't so aroused, she might find her condition embarrassing.

"Shall I make you feel better? he whispered. "Shall I make you come?"

"What?" she breathed, part of her wanting to shove him away, but an even bigger part wanting what he promised.

"I can do it," he murmured, still no contact but his mouth so close her skin tingled from proximity. "I can make you come without touching you."

He was too close, not close enough. "Please," she whispered, not sure what she was begging for.

Heat built inside her, burning her up from the inside out. She felt like she would go up in flames and glory in the conflagration.

"I can do anything I want with you." He blew on her neck. "Your body is mine to play with."

A voice screamed inside her, trying desperately to be heard over the clamor of her desire. She didn't want this, didn't want him. Oh, but she did. She needed him. She needed him to make her feel so good.

"Remember, little human," he whispered. "I can own every part of you."

No, she refused. Her protest begged to be heard, and she tugged desperately for some semblance of sanity. "No."

"No?" He met her gaze. Surprise flickered in his eyes.

"No." She didn't know how she could ever have thought his eyes cold. They blazed with heat as he gazed down at her. Not even she could believe her as she whispered, "I mean yes."

He raised one darkly slashed eyebrow at her. "Is it yes or no, little human?"

"Definitely no." She dragged a deep breath into her starved lungs. "Step back."

For a long, charged moment, he stared down at her.

Eddie battled her traitorous body into submission. Already the words to take back her refusal gathered behind her teeth and begged to be spoken.

"Lust." He finally nodded. "Do not summon me again unless you want to feel it consume you."

He stepped away, taking the heat with him, and stepped through the hell gate.

The gate flared bright enough to sear her retinas and then returned to its normal gray-black slumberous spiral.

Desire drained from her as fast as it had risen. Clammy sweat coated her skin and made it prickle. Her damp panties clung uncomfortably, and her breasts felt achy and sore.

With shaking hands, Eddie located the app, opened the door, and threw herself into the cool, quiet basement. The steady hum of mechanics was reassuring in its familiarity. She stumbled up the stairs to the main part of the theatre. Only once the comforting dark surrounded her, did she whisper, "What the fuck was that?"

PERCHED in one of her favorite places in the theatre, Eddie let her legs hang over the edge of the catwalk. Concealed by the dark above the auditorium, she finally allowed herself to think about what had happened this morning. On stage, Peter was fumbling his way through choreographing a sword fight.

The hell gate was not closed, and that was problem number one. In the dream, the other flying man had called him

Shade. Perhaps Yesterday could tell her who he was. Then again, she was thinking about asking the same being for information who'd had her put salt on a bite that was even bigger today than before, and who'd also told her they'd shut the hell gate.

Yesterday popped up beside her. She hadn't seen him since she'd encountered naked Shade in the basement. Part of her had been hoping he'd hopped through the hell gate with dream man. Except, not so much dream man anymore. He was an asshole. An extremely hot asshole, but also scary and a dickhead.

"Where did you go?" Eddie had no idea how she would explain an imp running around the theatre. Beasties that looked like toads and grasshoppers she could explain away, but Yesterday—not so much.

"Dave!" Peter bellowed from the stage. "It's a sword not a bloody baseball bat. Swing it like you mean to do some harm."

"Um...Peter?" Barrie lowered his sword. "Do we really think it's right for Dave's character?"

"He's playing Macduff," Peter thundered with the kind of projection actors dreamed off.

Dave took the opportunity to practice a couple of thrusts and parries. "*En garde,*" he yelled and lunged at the drapery.

"What are they doing?" Yesterday took a seat beside her, his stubby legs sticking straight out in the air.

"Acting." Reliable or not, Yesterday was her only source of information, and until Dee contacted her, he was the best resource she had. "Where did you go?"

"Acting." Yesterday tested the word out as if sampling it for the first time. "What is that?"

Eddie didn't have time or energy to go into the explanation. What had happened in the basement had shaken her to her core. She had a normal sex life—current dry spell aside—

and liked to think of herself as having a normal sex drive, but what she'd felt this morning had been beyond her experience. "Acting is like a game of pretend."

"Hmm." Yesterday wrapped his arms around the safety bar on the catwalk banister. "Are they warriors?"

Eddie had to chuckle at that one. "No, but they're pretending to be."

"Not very well." Yesterday snorted.

"I understand that, Peter." Barrie jammed his hands on his hips. "And correct me if I'm wrong, but it always struck me that Macduff was more cerebral than Macbeth."

"Where did you go this morning?" Eddie asked. Yesterday had disappeared faster than ice on a summer day.

Yesterday kept his focus on what was happening onstage. "They do not know how to fight."

"When you left me in the basement." Eddie spent her life around people who dodged answering questions. "Where did you go?"

"Macduff defeats Macbeth." Peter threw his hands up. "He kills him." Getting nose to nose with Barrie, Peter yelled. "He cuts his head off."

"I realize that, Peter." Barrie got snippy. "I've read the script. In fact, I've done *Macbeth* at least five times."

Dave got tired of swishing his sword around. "Are we going to, like, choreograph this fight or what?"

"Dave!" Barrie and Peter yelled at once.

"We are discussing your character." Barrie sniffed.

"Those swords do not look real." Yesterday inched away from her, ears twitching in all directions and looking shifty as hell.

Eddie pinned him with a stare. "You left very quickly. And you left me alone with Shade."

"Of course I left." Yesterday looked at her as if she'd lost the plot.

"Artistic differences are part of the creative process," Peter said from onstage.

She kept her eyes on the lying imp. "Why of course?"

"I have good news." Yesterday's mouth split in a huge grin and he looked like a frog about to zap a fly. It was more unsettling than comforting. "The hell gate is now closed."

"Really?" She'd tried to reach Dee again after the incident in the basement. Apparently, Dee had been taking dancing lessons that morning. At least, that's what she could decipher from another frustrating conversation with Jean-Claude. "Like you said it was yesterday?"

"No." Yesterday scoffed. "This time it is truly closed."

She'd believe that when nothing more came through it. "Who was the man in the basement?"

"There was a man in the basement?" Yesterday failed that round of lies.

Eddie stared him down. "Yes, I think his name is Shade."

Yesterday muttered something she didn't catch.

"I have more peanut butter." She went with the carrot not the stick.

Yesterday's entire face twisted like a wrung-out dishrag. "You do not know?"

"Crunchy peanut butter," she said.

Taking a deep breath, Yesterday dropped the name in a rush. "Asmodeus."

"Who?" The name rang a bell of the tolling, warning kind.

"Asmodeus." Yesterday checked behind him as if waiting for the guy to appear behind him. When the dark catwalk remained empty, he looked relieved. "Asmodeus. The hell prince."

"As in the prince of hell?" This was taking a disturbing turn. "Like Lucifer."

"No." Yesterday scoffed. "Lucifer is Lucifer. Asmodeus is Asmodeus."

Eddie dug deep for her Christian theology. "So he works for Lucifer?"

A hissing cackle came out of Yesterday. "I would not say so to Asmodeus."

"Why not?"

"One hell prince cannot work for another." Yesterday nodded as if the matter was now clear.

Eddie rather thought not. "There is more than one prince of hell?"

"Of course." Yesterday snorted. "How can a hell guardian not know this?"

It was an excellent question, and not one she intended to answer. "How many hell princes?"

"Seven." Yesterday leaned forward as the clang of swords came from the stage.

"Seven?" Dee should have told her this stuff. Or maybe Dee didn't even know.

"Indeed." Yesterday glared at the stage. "They are not even good pretend warriors."

Eddie agreed on that point. "Why seven?"

"Because there must be seven," Yesterday said. "There are seven seals and seven hell princes who guard them."

Yesterday must be making things up, because it was nothing like she'd heard. "When you say hell princes, you mean demons, right?"

"No." Yesterday jabbed a thumb at his chest. "I am a demon."

"You said you were an imp."

Yesterday rolled his eyes. "An imp is a type of demon."

"And a hell prince is not a demon?"

"No." Yesterday made a rude noise. "A hell prince is a hell prince."

God, she wished Dee would return her damn call and she could get some straight answers. "I thought there were only demons in hell."

"Demons are vassals to hell princes." Yesterday counted his points off on his sausage fingers. "Hell princes guard the seals and keep what's in them from leaking onto earth. Asmodeus is a hell prince. One of seven."

"What are the seals...er...sealing?"

Yesterday screwed up his face. "The things." He made an impatient gesture with his stubby arms. "You humans call the things behind the seals something." He tapped his head. "Something like dangerous or fatal...um...sins?"

"The deadly sins?"

He slapped his scalp. "That's them."

"So, the seals are containing the deadly sins?" Unless she had missed a secret part of theology, this was nothing like how she'd understood hell to work. "And the hell princes guard the seals?"

"Yes." Yesterday patted her shoulder and beamed at her like a proud parent. "Now you understand."

Eddie went through a mental catalogue of the deadly sins. "And Asmodeus guards which seal?"

But she kind of worked out the answer before Yesterday said, "Lust."

SIX

Eddie was in a castle, or as near as she could tell, it was a castle. Massive wooden beams marched in symmetrical rows down each side of an expansive hall and crisscrossed a ceiling that made her crane her head up to see. A gleaming stone floor reflected light from a roaring central fire pit. Her footsteps echoed on the floor as she crept forward. Outside soaring arched windows, a grassy expanse sloped gently away from the hall she stood in.

Despite its beauty, she didn't feel safe. An air of menace hung about the gorgeous hall as she crept deeper into the space.

A pair of towering wooden doors burst open, and creatures swarmed the hall.

Eddie shrunk behind a pillar. Heart drumming, she peered out.

None of the creatures was paying any attention to her. Their aggression was focused on one being they tossed to the gleaming floor.

The second winged being, the one who had chased Shade

in her last dream, strode through the teeming creatures. Many of them sported wings, or horns, strange variations of basically humanoid figures dressed in a variety of warrior garbs. Most of them carried weapons: swords, clubs, flails, whips, and daggers.

A huge bull-like creature lunged forward and kicked the one they had thrown to the floor. His steel capped boot connected with the poor being they were torturing and flipped him to his side so that he now faced her.

Shade.

Blood and saliva dribbled through broken teeth over his lacerated mouth. His nose canted at a painful angle and blood coated his nostrils.

Eddie wrapped her hands over her mouth to stop herself from crying out.

One eye was entirely swollen shut. Shade's unharmed gray eye met hers. Recognition flashed in its depth, and then he frowned. "Leave."

As if she had any choice in being here, and given what she'd encountered of him recently, she'd rather not be.

Piercing shouts and whistles rose from the enraged mob.

Fury and hatred rode the air in a palpable cloud, and Eddie shrunk farther back against her pillar. Shade had been an asshole to her, but seeing him bloodied, broken, and bleeding yanked something visceral in her, and she needed to get him out.

Oh God, she couldn't believe she was even thinking of rescuing him. She wasn't brave, didn't have any special skills, didn't even know if she was here or dreaming what was happening.

"Go," Shade whispered as he stared at her. "You have no place here."

"Shade." The winged man crouched beside Shade and

gripped his hair in a big hand. Yanking Shade's head back, he leaned down and whispered in Shade's ear.

The same pulsing energy that Shade carried emanated from the one crouched beside him. Another hell prince? Yesterday had said there were seven of them. He shrugged, and his enormous red and black wings disappeared. He stood and stared down at Shade, contempt tightening the strong, uncompromising lines of his face. There was something familiar about him, other than her dream. Eddie had a feeling she knew this being. Was that the way of all the hell princes?

"You tried to end me." He spat on Shade. "And now you pay for what you've done." Stilling, he looked up suddenly and right at her. His blue eyes blazed. "Who—"

"Hey, you!"

Eddie felt a tug at her hair.

Another yank made her hair roots object strenuously. "Hey, girl. Eddie!"

Frowning, the big being over Shade took a step toward where she was hiding.

The hall blurred and swirled, and her eyelids were forced open.

Yesterday's saucer-like, black gaze bored into her. "You need to wake up."

"Shit." The dream followed her into wakefulness. They were going to kill Shade, and everything in her objected to that. Trying to catch her breath, she shoved Yesterday's face out of her own. The image of Shade's battered face velcroed itself to her mind. She was surprised to find she was crying, and she scrubbed her palms over her cheeks. "Can a hell prince die?"

Blinking at her, Yesterday scrabbled back on the bed. "Yes." He nodded his oversize head three times. "But only one hell prince can kill another." His face grew thoughtful. "And an archangel. They can kill a hell prince. And I suppose that means a hell prince could kill an archangel, but none of them have ever tried, so nobody can be totally sure."

She tried to make sense of her dream. It was a dream, just a dream, despite how real it had felt. "And demons serve hell princes?"

Yesterday nodded and then pulled a face. "Most demons serve hell princes."

"Can you tell me about the other hell princes?" Eddie pushed her legs over the edge of her bed.

Yesterday averted his gaze. "Why?"

The little guy was hiding something, and she was equally sure she wanted to hear what that something was. Needed to hear what he was squirreling about. She pinned him with her best no-bullshit stare. "Why not?"

"Hell princes are bad business." Yesterday hopped off her bed and scuttled to her bedroom door. "You don't want to know about hell princes."

Clearly her no-bullshit look needed work, but it was the best she had, so she gave it another go. "I need to know everything you know about the other princes."

Images in her mind kept trying to make a comeback. God, the violence, and the anger were terrifying. The other winged one had looked ready to kill Shade.

"What prince?" He opened the door and made shooing motions to her. "And you really do have a bigger thing to worry about."

Bigger than hell princes killing each other and somehow looking into her head while she dreamed? What a super way to get her day started.

"A tall, muscular man." Was that the right term to describe the winged man...er....creature? "Well, he looks male."

"Lots of male hell princes." Yesterday flapped a dismissive

hand. "Don't need to worry about them. You have the thing to worry about at the hell gate." He winced. "Actually, two somethings."

Not ready to let the hell princes go, but also not about to wander after Yesterday in her panties, Eddie hauled on a pair of track pants. "You said there were seven hell princes. How many of them are male?"

"You don't have time for chattery now." Yesterday's sweet face folded into a frown that almost made her laugh. He looked like a wrinkled little old man. "You have two big problems in your basement."

Two big problems was way light in Eddie's estimation. Dee still hadn't called her back. The hell gate app—and there really was an app for everything—had so many power fluctuations it was looking bipolar. Shade was being beaten to death, she hoped only in her dreams. And worst of all, Lillian was due at rehearsal today as Lady M. There would be great disturbances in the force. It almost made her want to go back to bed.

Her entire forearm now looked red and swollen, the bites oozing a shiny, yellow fluid. A trip to the doctor was definitely in order.

She threw a sweatshirt on and stuffed her feet into her Converses. Whatever bug had got out of the hell gate and up Yesterday's ass needed dealing with first. One problem at a time. Or two, according to Yesterday.

She followed him down into the dark backstage area of the theatre. On their way, she snagged a broom and pan, then a pair of gloves. As she had discovered, hell grasshoppers bit.

She didn't bother with the stupid app. Damn thing was as useful as tits on a tortoise.

"Hey." She suddenly thought of a solution to one of her concerns.

Yesterday stopped and glanced at her. "Hey what?"

"You're from hell, right?"

He rolled his eyes. "Obvi."

Okay, he could drop the Gen Z 'tude right now. "If you came from hell, it means you can go back there."

"No, no, no, no, no." Yesterday backed away from her with his palms up. Then, in case she hadn't gotten it the first time, he said, "No, no, no, no, no."

"Why not?" She flung his crap right back at him.

Yesterday went an alarming shade of mustard. "You understand nothing."

"And you're deflecting." Eddie folded her arms and returned his scowl. Her bite hurt enough for her not to give a shit about a grumpy imp. "You could go back and check on Shade."

"Check on Asmodeus?" Yesterday's voice rose to a shrill chirp. "You do not check on a hell prince."

"Even if they're in trouble?" And Shade had definitely been in trouble according to her dream.

Yesterday snorted, and his color returned to duckling yellow. "Hell princes don't get into trouble. They are immortal, powerful beings who hold the fate of the universe in their hands."

"But they can kill each other, right?" The other one gave off the same level of power aura as Shade, and he hadn't looked happy.

"Eh." Yesterday grimaced. "You humans have such a limited view of life and death."

This limited human was getting pissed off. "So, explain it to me."

"We have no time." Ears twitching, Yesterday drifted back toward mustard yellow, and not the attractive shade of mustard either, but more the cat-sick yellow side of the spectrum. "You have a problem you need to deal with."

She was smelling the earthy waft of bullshit from the little yellow fucker. "Why don't you handle it?"

"Pah!" Yesterday flung his stubby little arms into the air. "Because you are the hell guardian."

Welp, he had her there. On that point at least. "You still haven't given me a reason why you can't go and check on Shade."

"As. Mo. De. Us." Yesterday punctuated each syllable with his jabbing forefinger. "The hell princes demand respect."

The hell prince who had been hanging around stark-bollock nekkid in her basement had demanded something, respect not being top of her list. "None of which explains why you won't go back through the hell gate."

"I do not have to tell you." He folded his arms, or tried to. With arms that short, it was more wishful thinking than performance, and he ended up clasping his wrists with opposite hands.

Eddie was no stranger to hard ball, and she folded her arms. "And I don't have to deal with whatever has your impy panties in a wad in the basement."

Yesterday gaped at her, pshawed, and gaped some more. "Impy panties?"

Staying strong, she stared him down. These midnight wakings and problems were getting old—fast.

"Rwthizgngtkylme," Yesterday got super interested in the laminate beneath his feet.

Eddie cupped her ear with her palm. "What was that?"

"Wrathisgonnakillme." Yesterday took a deep breath.

Eddie took a minute to decipher his burble. "Wrath is going to kill you?"

Startling, Yesterday glanced around them. "Shhh!"

"Why?"

"Why no—"

"I'll say his name louder if you don't stop answering questions with questions."

Yesterday groaned, did a quick circle around a cleaning bucket, took a deep breath, and said, "I may have annoyed a certain hell prince of changeable temperament."

"Wrath?" she whispered. Now she had names for two of the hell princes. At this rate, somewhere around the turn of the century, she'd have the full picture.

"I told you not to say his name." Yesterday glowered at her. He waggled his hands above his head. "They hear everything."

"Uh-huh." His dramatics also needed to make like Elvis and leave the building. She'd lived her thirty-two years without the hell princes hearing her and acting on what they heard. At least, she thought she had. Yesterday's pronouncement raised some unsettling possibilities. Most of them about creepy, listening men with zero social skills.

"I was born of...his...court." Yesterday sighed and rolled his eyes. "And then I did a thing, which he did not like, and now he searches for me."

Way to go on the information. "What did you do?"

"Does it matter?"

"What did I say about answering questions with questions?"

Yesterday stamped his foot. "Ugh! Humans are so annoying."

"Still waiting." Eddie tapped her foot.

"Fine." Yesterday quasi-folded his arms again. "I may have said a thing to some of Asmodeus's demons, which might or might not have made...Asmodeus angry with him and led to a spot of trouble in hell."

Slippery little fucker. Eddie could well believe that. "Still waiting for more details."

Actual steam escaped in enthusiastic puffs from Yesterday's ears. "There is a war in hell."

"Keep going."

"But there is always a war in hell." Yesterday raised his hands—an innocent soul tossed about by the vagaries of fate. "They're hell princes. They fuck and they fight."

Eddie wanted to hear less about the fucking and more about the fighting. "Why do they fight?"

"Because they're hell princes." Yesterday shrugged. "It is in their nature to war."

That tracked, so Eddie shifted her focus. "So if they're always making war, why is...he...mad at you about this war?"

"This war is different." Yesterday frowned as if trying to puzzle it out. "This time they are trying to end each other."

SEVEN

Eddie stopped outside the concealed door to the hell gate. She'd done grasshoppers, toads, and naked beings from hell, she had this. Gripping the handle of her broom tighter, she eased the door open.

Fangs, fur, saliva, and glowing red eyes lunged for her.

"Christ!" Slamming the door shut, Eddie leapt back from it, broom at the ready.

Yesterday scuttled behind the propane tank. "Told you."

"What the fuck was that?"

Something large hit the door hard enough to rattle it in its frame.

Eddie's mouth went dry. The broom quivered in her hand. Fear made her voice wobble. "What the fuck was that?"

Poking his head out, Yesterday scrunched up his nose. "Your problem."

A vicious snarl came from behind the door, followed by loud snuffling at the bottom. Whatever was in there was bigger than a hopper or a toad, and she was not opening that door again.

More snuffling that sounded like it came from huge, terrifying nostrils. Nostrils big enough to match those gargantuan snapping teeth that had come for her.

Silence.

Snuffle, snuffle, snuffle—whine.

"Get out here," she spat at the cowardly yellow bastard cowering behind her propane tank.

"Uh-uh," Yesterday said and ducked out of sight.

AWROOOOOO!

Howling? That thing behind the door was howling now? Fur, fangs, sniffing, whining, and howling all pointed to… "Was that a dog?"

"Kinda." Yesterday sniffled. "Mostly."

Dogs and hell, look at her mathematical genius putting two and two together and dragging them through all the seasons of *Buffy the Vampire Slayer*. Cringing that the idea had even entered her mind, she asked, "Is that a"—she couldn't believe she was going to voice this—"hell hound?"

"Yep." Yesterday smoothed back the single wisp of hair on his head. "Two of them."

"Two." Hysterical laughter clogged her throat, and she had to lean against the wall before her knees gave out. "Two hell hounds. In my basement. I didn't even know they were a thing."

"Oh, yes." Yesterday strutted out from behind the propane tank. If he'd been wearing pants, he would have hitched them. "Asmodeus created them."

Asmodeus. Shade. Well, wasn't he a candidate for charm school? "Why?"

"The ways of the hell princes"—Yesterday waved his hands around like a cheap conjurer at a carnival—"are not for us to know."

AR AR AWRWOOOOO

She better find out about the ways of hell princes before those things brought animal control down on her. "Why are they here?"

More hand waving. "The ways of hell hounds—"

"I will punch you."

With a yelp, Yesterday darted behind the propane tank again. "They must be looking for Asmodeus."

"He's not here," Eddie stated the obvious as louder sniffing punctuated the low hum of the mechanical equipment. She pointed to the closed door and mustered as much authority as she could manage in her voice. "Tell them he's not here and they have to go."

Call her a pessimist but in the brief flash she'd gotten of the hell hound, she didn't rate her chances with a broom.

"Can't," Yesterday replied, far calmer than the situation warranted. Not that she had enough experience to guess at what tone would suffice. Edging out from his hiding place, Yesterday said, "They respond only to Asmodeus."

"Who isn't here to tell them to go back." Despite a lifetime of Dee's warnings to never contact the guardians, that was looking like a much better option than hell teeth at her throat.

"No." Yesterday got his swagger back as he approached her. "There really is only one thing we can do."

Options? She had options? Relief coursed through her. She had options. "Which is?"

Yesterday threw her a look of unadulterated scorn. "Summon Asmodeus."

Nope. No options. Not a one. "I'm not doing that."

"You must."

Not to mention she wasn't quite sure how she'd summoned him in the first place.

Some hell hound part thudded against the door.

Eddie and Yesterday jumped back.

More door thumping, in a rhythmic pattern like the damned thing was trying to pound its way out.

She dug her phone from her pocket. "Maybe Dee—"

An ominous crack came from the door frame. You would have thought they would have built the door guarding a hell gate strong enough to withstand assault by hell hound.

"Summon him," Yesterday hissed. "Before they break that door down and kill us."

Not Dee then.

A second set of pounding made a counterpoint to the first set. Both hell hounds were trying to bust their way out now.

"I don't know how to summon Asmodeus." She joined Yesterday behind the propane tank as she scanned the area for a weapon. "Do they like meat?"

"Not unless it's attached to a soul they want." Yesterday's eyes were the size of dinner plates as he watched the door jump and judder in its jam. "You have magic, summon him."

"I don't have magic."

"Yes, you do."

Craaack.

"Asmodeus," Eddie shrieked. "Shade! I summon you."

Yesterday gaped at her. "Not like that."

"I told you I don't know how."

The door pounding increased in pace.

Yesterday pinwheeled his arms frantically. "Summon him like you did before."

Like she had before? She hadn't summoned him. She'd only dreamed about him. "I dreamed about him."

"Do it again," Yesterday squeaked as the door gave an ominous groan.

"I'm not sleeping."

"Imagine you are."

Oh, this was a fucking horrible idea. Eddie squeezed her

eyes shut and tried to picture Shade. The assault the door was taking kept breaking her concentration. "I can't."

"Try harder."

The door warped in its frame, and a series of excited yips came from the hell hounds.

"Asmodeus," Eddie bellowed.

The door flew open.

Yesterday screeched and made it to the top of the propane tank in a single bound.

Two pony-size furry bodies lunged through the shattered door. At her.

Eddie didn't make it two feet before four glowing red eyes locked on her.

She backed up.

The hounds lowered their heads, hackles rising and closed on her.

The water heater pressed into her spine, warm but in no way reassuring.

"We're dead." Yesterday sobbed.

It very much looked that way as the hounds peeled lips back from canines longer than her arm. Low growls made her nape tingle, and she might have peed a little. Their heads on a level with hers, they looked like a pissed off cross between pit bulls and panthers. Red eyes glowed scarlet at her, and they stank of rotten eggs and farts. Lethally sharp spikes fanned behind their stubby ears.

"Sit," Eddie whispered. She'd watched Cesar Milan. She liked dogs, had wanted one since she was a child.

The closest hound snarled. Long strings of saliva stretched between its fangs and lips.

Oddly enough, the reason she'd never been allowed a dog was because of the hell gate. Lucky her, now she had two. Unlucky her, those two were going to eat her.

The second hell hound took a long, strong exhale, his nostrils quivering at the force with which he pulled air into his lungs. His barrel chest expanded and the spikes around his neck quivered and lowered. Both hounds stopped.

The front one cocked his head and made an odd little mewl, a sound so at odds with his fearsome appearance that at first, Eddie thought it had come from Yesterday.

"What are they doing?" Yesterday whispered.

"Don't know." Eddie kept her eyes on the paused hounds.

The front one also hauled air into his lungs. The spikes around his neck lowered to lie against the powerfully bunched muscle of his shoulders. He padded closer.

Eddie shrank back as far as the water heater would allow. Not nearly far enough.

The hell hound's searingly hot breath chuffed against her hand. His nose traveled up her arm and blew hot steam against her neck.

Eddie yelped.

The hound jerked back and sat.

The other one sat as well, head tilted and studied her.

Oh-kay.

"Do something," she ground out to Yesterday.

"Not that kind of demon," he hissed back at her.

The front hound whined and pawed her leg. Claws like three-foot daggers shredded her track pants but didn't pierce her skin.

Yesterday's head appeared from the dark recesses above the propane tank. "Command them."

"What?"

"Command them," Yesterday instructed with all the confidence of a demon not huddled atop a propane tank. "They're not eating you. I think they're waiting for you to tell them what to do."

She would have felt a lot better if he hadn't had to drop the *I think* at the start of that sentence. Still, she had nothing better to offer. Channeling her inner Cesar, she said, "S-ii-t."

"They are sitting." Yesterday scoffed.

"Right." Calm, dominant energy. *Don't reason with it. Don't argue with it. Just dominate it.* "Down." Her voice shook.

Glowing red eyes tracked her every wince and flinch.

Eddie cleared her throat and grabbed her dominant— albeit quaking—energy. Her voice ricocheted around the basement. "Down!"

The hounds grumbled and lay down.

"Dude!" Yesterday leaned over farther from his perch. "It worked. Nobody but Asmodeus can command them. Ever." He made an impressed face. "Not even Wrath, and he can command anything."

More questions, but so not the time to ask them. "What do I do with them now?"

"Send 'em back." Yesterday sniffed and scrabbled down the propane tank. He strutted closer to the nearest hound.

A low growl sent him yelping back again.

An unworthy idea wormed into her brain. Yesterday was an annoying little prick. A tiny nip from one of the hounds—the merest nibble—would get him answering all her questions, right quick. She couldn't do that. Could she? No. Okay, maybe she'd hold that one in reserve.

Cesar was fitting much more comfortably under her skin as she held her hand out and said, "Go home."

The second hound eyed her, yawned wide enough to display acres of orthodontics, and lowered his head to his paws.

"Home." She shooed them with her hands. "Go home."

Yesterday picked his ear with a curved fingernail. "They probably don't speak English."

"*Allez! Chez! Nous!*"

"Or any other human language." Yesterday rolled his eyes.

The biting idea got a lot more attractive.

He dug something out of his ear and slurped it down. "You should probably try mental compulsion." He went at his other ear and Eddie couldn't watch anymore. "You know, like think a thing at them."

Images of Yesterday getting nipped swarmed her mind.

Hound number one perked up and looked at Yesterday.

Interesting. And not worthy. But, oh so tempting. Instead, Eddie forced that mental movie away and pictured flames and glowing pits of sulfur and sent the mental intention for the hounds to return there.

Number two whined and studied her with an almost comically confused look.

She risked a step away from her water heater haven.

Both hounds stood.

Eddie stopped that idea right along with her feet. "Return," she thundered with as much authority as she could. "*Retourne!*" And dredging up her best French from school. "*Vous.*"

Should she have used *retournez*? Definitely, but as they couldn't see her French workbook in their minds, probably not that relevant to the hounds. "Can you guys please go back where you came from?"

"Command them." Yesterday thrust his bony chest out. "Be firm."

The first hound whimpered and looked heartbroken. The second inched closer to her with a pleading expression.

"They don't seem to want to go back," she said.

"That is neither here nor there." Yesterday slashed the air with his hand. "They are to do as you command."

"But they look upset." Heaving muscle, razor claws, and

sword teeth aside, they did look...disappointed. Some half-mad inner voice had her crouching down in front of them. "Don't you want to go home?"

"Pfft." Yesterday tossed his stubby arms in the air. "You're useless at this."

And now that they weren't trying to kill her, the hounds were kind of sweet. Well, sweet adjacent at any rate.

Both hounds lunged to their feet.

Eddie scrambled back on her butt.

"Edme?" Rodney called from the other side of the basement door. "Are you down here?"

Hound two growled deep in his throat, the sound rattling Eddie's bones.

"Stay," she whispered to the hounds and Yesterday, all of whom had locked on to the closed door. "Yes," she called to Rodney. "Do you need something?"

"The toilet is blocked in the makeup room," Rodney called, and she could hear the censure in his tone. "Could you deal with it, please?"

Theatre! Such a glamorous business.

EIGHT

An energetic plunge solved the toilet in the makeup room. Perhaps a plunger big enough for the hell gate would send all the nasties flushing back down to hell. And speaking of large plungers, she wished she had one large enough to plunge the shit out of this rehearsal.

Lillian and Barrie were facing off over act one, scene seven, and neither had any interest in giving ground.

"I just feel, Bazzer." Lillian fluttered her lashes at an arms-crossed, legs-akimbo Barrie. "That she's not so much manipulative as misunderstood. She's a woman in her prime, flexing her power."

"Lovely internal work, Poppet," Peter called from the safety of his director's desk in the auditorium.

Lillian simpered. "Thank you, babe. I love working with you." She pressed her hand to her chest. "You're so respectful of the actor's process."

"She's a bitch," Barrie announced.

"Bazzer." Lillian's eyes flashed a woman's wrath. "We don't

judge our characters. We pay humble tribute to them through allowing them to speak through us."

"So true," Peter intoned.

Eddie hadn't seen much humility on or off this stage in more years than she could count. If ever. She also had the lighting technician scheduled to take over the auditorium in fifteen minutes. "Perhaps we can take this conversation to the greenroom?"

"There's absolutely nothing to discuss." Barrie scoffed. "The bitch makes him kill the king."

"Um...Barrie." Matt, the actor playing Macbeth's sidekick, Seyton, put his hand up. "Positive space, man, positive space."

Matt, who'd just returned from his immersive method acting class in Toronto, gave them all a positive smile. "We need a safe place from which to create. A womb of creativity, if you will."

Barrie threw up his hands. "Oh, for God's sake."

Eddie looked warily for the godly bolt of lightning that might follow using the Lord's name in vain. Given that she now housed two hell hounds and a small demon in her basement, it didn't auger well for her in the heavenly department.

"Lady Macbeth manipulates Macbeth into killing the king." Barrie glared at Matt. "Everybody knows that."

"Um...Barrie." Matt grimaced. "There is more than one way to play a role. If you've ever seen Patrick Stewart's interpretation—"

"Captain Picard!" Barrie glowered. "We're using the captain of the Starship Enterprise as our guide here?"

"Actually, Barrie, respectfully, it was the USS Enterprise NCC-1701-D, or Enterprise-D in *The Next Generation*." Matt looked pained. "And you really should see Patrick's Macbeth." He chef-kissed his fingers. "Masterful."

Barrie pressed his forefinger and thumb into his eye sockets. "I don't care."

"Yes, you do, Bazzer." Lillian stroked his arm. "You just don't know that you care yet. You haven't processed your resistance to our exploration of the traditional dynamics between Macbeth and his lady."

"I tell you what I'm processing." Barrie yanked his arm away. "I'm processing the Huge Burrito with extra beans from Fat Bastard that I had last night."

Ooh, Fat Bastard burritos. It had been a while since Eddie had eaten one of those. And still she had basement hell hounds and a grumpy lighting technician. "All right, then." She clapped her hands and pulled another Cesar Millan—say what you will, that shit had worked on the hounds. "Lighting is due in any minute, and we don't seem to be reaching resolution." Summoning her inner calm dominance, she pointed. "Greenroom."

Lillian teared up, and Peter turned on her. "Really, Eddie, this is not your place—"

AWROOO. ARH-ARH-ARH-AWROO.

Everyone on stage and in the auditorium froze.

"I fucking love dogs," Patty muttered as she changed needles. "We need more dogs around here."

"Edme." Rodney popped up from the dim back of the auditorium like the ghost of Hamlet's dad. "Is there a dog on the premises?"

"Of course not." Eddie met him eye to eye. There wasn't, in fact, a dog on the premises at all.

"Because I feel I need to remind you"—Rodney continued as if she hadn't spoken—"that other than service animals, pets are not allowed in the theatre."

"Oh, Rodders," Lillian purred. "We should get an emotional support dog."

Eddie didn't think any dog was up to that task. Or deserved it. "I can assure you, Rodney." And she honestly could. "There isn't a dog in the theatre."

Two hell hounds, totally. Dog, absolutely not.

A flicker of movement in the flies caught her attention as Yesterday popped his swollen duckling-yellow mug out from behind a light. He made urgent gestures at the basement, as if she hadn't already assessed the problem quite nicely, thank you. "I think the house down the road just got a pit bull," she said. "It must be upset."

"The house down the road?" Rodney frowned and reached in his pocket for his iPhone. "As far as I know, that property is still vacant."

"Such a lovely house." Lillian sighed and clasped her hands under her chin. "So moody, and atmospheric."

"It would make a fantastic venue," Matt gushed. "We could stage an Agatha Christie there, or some late-night theatre."

"Oh." Lillian's mouth made a perfect oval as stars glittered in her eyes. "Theatre in the dark."

"I need to program the lights," Dean, their resident lighting technician said. "Need the theatre." A tall, slim man with the tortured face of a Goya subject, Dean strode across the stage and took the stairs to the lighting box.

"Hello, Dean." Lillian, always conscious that every actress needed to befriend the lighting guy, simpered and fluttered. "It's so lovely to see you."

"Surprise Pink," Dean yelled from the stairwell. "Use it to light you. Got it." He popped onto the gantry above them. "Makes you look younger."

"Well." Lillian almost frowned through her Botox. "Not that I need it, or anything."

"Absolutely not, poppet." Peter rose to the occasion with a scoff. "You are a vision. A vision of youth and beauty."

"Fifty-three if she's a day," Patty said.

"Not only is she physically beautiful." Matt made his bid for more lines. "She portrays youth and loveliness every time she steps on the stage."

"Matt." Lillian giggled and slapped his arm. "You're such a flirt."

Aroogah. Peter brayed his positive spaces laugh. "Are you flirting with my lady, Stripling?"

"Peter." Matt drew himself up and looked censorious. "I'm gay. You know I'm gay."

"Of course." Peter tripped over a seat as he made his way down the aisles. "Just joking around."

"We need to recognize our internalized misogyny as men." Matt smoothed his crisp cotton shirt. "Nice guys." He deployed finger quotes. "Often use humor to deflect from their deeply seated prejudices."

Eddie was losing track of the conversation. "Greenroom," she ordered. "Lighting bars are coming down and I need to clear the stage."

"Theatre safety code section two, paragraph twelve," Rodney murmured.

Whatever!

"Excuse me." A melodic female voice floated into the theatre like the scent of apple pie on a crisp autumn morning. A woman stepped into the light of the working lamps overhead. It struck her golden blond hair and made it gleam.

Everyone gaped.

AWROOO. AWROOO. AWROOO.

The hell hound's howling drifted away, lost in the thrall of the woman now standing in the auditorium.

She smiled—and holy baby Jesus—Eddie was ready to hand over her wallet, her heart, her life, and her soul. Curved, pillowy ruby lips parted over crystalline white teeth. "I didn't mean to interrupt."

"Not at all." Peter nearly face planted into H1 in his rush to reach her. "We were just about to take a break."

"Actually." Lillian got tightlipped. "We were in the middle of a very important creative conflict."

"No, we weren't." Barrie adopted his matinee idol drawl. "Woman in her prime. Flexing her power." He strode across the stage and niftily vaulted the three steps leading from the stage to the auditorium with his hand held out. "Barrie Vermark." He flashed a toothy grin. "Currently, Macbeth, and at your service."

"Hello." The woman giggled and returned the handshake. "Sophia."

Peter shouldered Barrie out of the way. "Peter Hampstead, resident director, and board member. How can we help you?"

Patty snorted.

"Are we going to the greenroom, or not?" Lillian jammed her hands on her hips.

"Apparently, not." Matt sniffed and leaned closer to Lillian and whispered, "You're so much hotter."

Lillian was beautiful, no bones about it, but this woman was next level. Iris-blue eyes glowed at Peter and Barrie as she smiled and explained she was new in town.

"What brings you to Clayton, Ontario?" Barrie flexed a bicep as he smoothed back his hair. "Not exactly on the beaten path."

"Oh." Sophia smiled. "I love it here. So charming, and everyone is so friendly."

Yesterday had launched into what looked like a St. Vitus dance behind his light. Eddie couldn't drag her gaze off Sophia. It was almost as if a golden glow surrounded her, and it made Eddie want to get closer to its warmth.

"We are super friendly." Peter oozed close enough to qualify as a physical threat.

Lillian stalked to the edge of the stage. "You didn't say what you were doing here."

"So true," Matt whispered.

Sophia turned those hyacinth blues on Lillian. "Are you Lillian Hampstead?"

"Y-e-s." Not eager to offend a possible fan, Lillian brought her hostile down from DEFCON four.

"I'm such a fan." Pretty pink stained the perfect peach of Sophia's cheeks. "I saw you at the NAC and I..." She gave a helpless little hand flutter. "I've been a fan ever since."

AWROOO. AWROOO. AWROOO. ARGGGGOOOOOO.

What the...well, hell...were the hounds getting so antsy about?

Lillian crumpled like a paper napkin at a rib fest. "The NAC?"

"Three times." Sophia held up three precisely manicured, pink-tipped fingers. "Your performance was so...compelling."

Lillian giggled and curled a lock of hair around her finger. "Oh, that." She waved a dismissive hand. "I was so much more inexperienced then."

"I didn't know you were part of the Paradise Players." Sophia's giggling was like tinkling bells on a Christmas tree. "It's almost like fate that I wandered in here."

"No lights, no play," Dean bellowed from the lighting booth.

"Shall we take this to the greenroom?" Lillian waved her arm like a benevolent dictator casting money to the masses. "And take this conversation further."

"Quite right." Peter cleared his throat. "Perhaps you can tell us how we can help you."

"We'd love to help you." Barrie flexed the opposite bicep as he motioned the way. "We're a very inclusive theatre company."

Rodney seemed to shake himself out of his reveries. "Are we certain that dog is down the road? I felt sure that sound came from inside the building."

"There are no dogs in the building." Eddie brazened it out. "What, do you think I have a dog chained in the basement?"

Sophia cut a sharp gaze at Eddie. It made her want to confess her lie and beg for forgiveness. "Greenroom?" she managed weakly.

"Splendid." Peter rubbed his hands together. "And perhaps Sophia can tell us her areas of interest."

Patty gathered her wool. "Hehehe."

Ugh! He made it sound dirty, and Eddie hurried off to deal with her noisy hounds.

NINE

Yesterday met her at the basement entrance, his face creased up like an old shoe. "Not good. Not good at all."

Just once, it would be great if the little shit had good news for her.

Eddie followed him into the basement, conspicuously empty of hell hounds. "Where are they?"

"With their master." Yesterday scuttled, rotating his arms like helicopter blades in a way she guessed meant he wanted her to hurry up.

"They went back to hell?" That was good news. Maybe that last howl had been a kind of so-long-see-ya kind of howl.

"No." Yesterday blinked at him. "Why would they be back in hell?"

"Because—" And a horrible thought struck her. If the hell hounds were with their master, and their master happened to be the same being who created them. Following that golden line of fuck no—and the hounds were not back in hell, but in her basement—

Her brain stalled as Eddie outran Yesterday to the hell gate.

At first, all she could see was two large, furry bodies. Then one hound turned to her with a mournful expression, whimpered, and shifted aside.

And Eddie saw Shade.

Only so much worse than when she'd seen him in her vision. Both eyes were swollen shut, his face distorted and bruised. Gashes across his torso and thighs that looked like claw marks oozed blood on the floor. One leg jutted at an angle that made her queasy, and his beautiful wings lay like broken, plucked birds beneath him.

Nope, not good at all. Her stomach in knots, her heart thumping uncomfortably, Eddie hurried forward. "Is he dead?" The idea tugged at something in her chest and made her breath catch.

The other hound nuzzled Shade's side.

She was not good with blood. It kind of made her light-headed, and Eddie took deep breaths as she knelt beside Shade. She needed to help him, put his broken pieces back together.

Basic first aid. Check for a pulse.

Gingerly, she pressed her fore and middle fingers to his neck. His skin was hot, but a faint flutter beat beneath her fingers. Relief washed over her. "Okay, so not dead."

The hounds watched her.

"Fix him." Yesterday stuck his mug in hers. "You need to fix him."

"I'm not a doctor." Eddie pressed him back. "He needs a doctor."

"No, no, no, no, no." Yesterday shook his head. "No doctors. Not ever. Never."

"He's hurt." He was so battered; Eddie didn't know where to touch him. Her heart squeezed. "Badly."

"Yes." Yesterday's face folded into a frown. He pointed to a twelve-inch gash pumping blood from Shade's side. "He has a mortal wound, and you must fix it."

Mortal wounds sounded bad, like they needed a hospital bad. "We have to take him to a doctor. I don't know anything about serious injuries or how to heal them."

"I said, no," Yesterday yelled, his voice going a deep, reverberating bass that transfixed Eddie for a moment. She wanted to ask where he kept that sound tucked in his little body. "You must fix him." Yesterday paced the room, his arms circling again. "There must always be seven princes. Seven princes, seven archangels, seven guardians. Balance." He glowered at Eddie as if his words should mean something. "Must always be balance or the whole thing goes bang."

"What whole thing?" She was almost afraid to hear the answer.

"Everything." Yesterday quickened his pacing. "Heaven, earth, hell, all of it goes up in smoke if we don't have balance." He leaned closer to her. "I do not want to cease to be, so you must fix him."

Eddie didn't want Shade to cease to be either. When he wasn't bleeding to death in her basement, she would think about why. For now though, he needed more help than she could give him, and she eyed the half a meter between Shade's prone form and the hell gate. "What if we shove him back? There must be someone or something in hell that can help him?"

Both hell hounds moved as much of themselves as they could wedge between Shade and the hell gate. One lowered his head and bared his teeth at her. Eddie was going to go ahead and take that as a no on the tossing this big fish back.

"You can't shove him back." Yesterday gaped at her. "First, he's a hell prince, and nobody shoves him anywhere. And second, he has a mortal wound."

She was missing something. Like the part about how she was going to be of any use in the situation. "And?"

"And only another hell prince wielding an obsidian blade can give him that. Or an archangel with a heaven wrought blade, but that is neither here nor there." Yesterday let the full weight of his scorn for her intelligence show. "Whoever gave him the mortal wound is waiting for him to go back. In fact"—Yesterday winced—"if we don't move him away from the hell gate, they might be able to track him here."

Way to bury the lede about another hell prince. "Right." Eddie forced her mind to start working in a useful direction. She had an injured man...person...prince lying on the floor of her basement. Doctors and hospitals were out; sending him back was out. First aid. It was the best she could come up with. "Wait here," she told Yesterday.

"Where are you going?" Yesterday scrambled after her.

"To get the first aid box." She gestured to Shade. "I can try and patch him up a bit." Not that a slap of Polysporin and a Band-Aid held much hope against his multiple injuries. This was so fucking out of her wheelhouse.

A hound blocked the door, red eyes looking redder than usual, filling the doorway with his sheer size.

It didn't seem right to yell at it. "You need to move?"

The hound tilted his head.

"I need to get the first aid box." She pointed to the area beyond its hairy shoulder. "It's in the greenroom. Actually, there's one in the rehearsal hall as well."

"He's nearly dead over here," Yesterday yelled. "Command it to move."

Yesterday was getting entirely too comfortable with the idea of her commanding things. She'd like to command his ass right out of here. "You wanna come over here and give that a try?"

There was definite intelligence in the hound's gaze, like it was trying to understand her and convey meaning.

"I'm trying to help him," she said to the hound. She then tried sending inner pictures of her tending Shade, but as that wasn't exactly her thing, it could account for some of the confusion currently playing across the hound's face.

A low groan sounded from Shade's general direction. Eddie had once heard a cop say it was always the quiet ones at an accident scene you had to worry about. She was taking the groan as a positive sign. She was also reaching for any sliver of hope and mentally babbling. "I will help him," she said.

On a grumble that sounded vaguely threatening, the hound eased out of the way.

Shutting the door behind it, Eddie took a moment to center herself. She leaned back against the door and tried for a deep breath.

Phenomenally stupid idea, as it turned out. The moment she closed her eyes, she was beset with images of Shade's broken and bleeding body. Action it was then, and she took the stairs to the theater three at a time.

From the stage, it sounded like Lillian and Barrie had solved their artistic differences.

"Edme." Rodney emerged from the door to stage right. "I've been looking all over for you."

Were hell princes like vampires and needed human blood to heal? In which case she might consider tossing Rodney on the cause of saving Shade's life. "Yup. Here I am."

"I have looked into the matter of the dog down the road." Rodney frowned.

Here it came.

"And you're quite right." He gave a stiff nod. "The house was recently rented, and they do own a large dog. I wanted to assure you that I will be sending them a firm email in which I insist they maintain control of their animal." He shook his head, the only man capable of seeing reason in this world. "We cannot have all that howling. Especially not during performances."

"Great idea." She decided a hasty retreat was in order. She'd been taking a complete flyer on there being a dog down the road. Also, she really wouldn't feed Rodney to a vampire. At least, not to the death.

Rodney stood between her and the door to the greenroom. "I also wanted to speak to you about the box office."

"Right." She didn't have time for this. Any moment now, one of the hounds might take it into its head to bust out of the basement and come looking for her. "Actually, Rodney, I don't have time right now to talk about the box office, but we can meet early next week."

Rodney's eyes narrowed suspiciously. "You don't have time?"

"No, Rodney." This commanding thing was getting contagious. "I have a lot of responsibilities in this theatre, and I need to schedule my time carefully."

"Really?" He flushed as if she'd slapped him. "If you find your responsibilities too onerous, we can always find someone who can manage them."

Eddie nearly laughed in his pompous face. Yeah, good luck getting someone else to manage this theatre in rural Ontario on what they paid her. She flashed him a smile. "You're welcome to look."

"Well." Rodney straightened the pens in his top pocket. "I don't think we need to start that process just yet." Then he found his balls again. "Did you fix the clogged toilet?"

"All done." She smirked and ducked past him. "Next time use less paper to wipe."

It was a good thing you couldn't slam stage doors, because Rodney gave it his best as he stomped off.

Matt was in the greenroom studying his script and making notes. As Seyton only had five lines, Eddie gave him points for enthusiasm. He smiled when he saw her. "Hey, Eddie."

"Matt." She found the first aid kit on the small bookshelf beside the couch and hauled it out.

Eyes glinting as his gaze locked on the first aid box, Matt jumped to his feet. "Is somebody injured? Is it Barrie? Because not to worry if it is, I've been studying Macbeth's lines, and I can easily step in."

"It's not Barrie." Eddie tucked the white metal box under her arm. "And it's a fantastic idea to understudy the lead. Because this is live theater, and you never know."

Matt flushed and gave her a shy smile. "You think? Because Macbeth is such a wonderfully, complex character." He pounded his chest with a fist. "I really feel like I can relate to him on such a visceral level." Moisture gleamed in his large brown eyes. "His struggle for identity, his desperate need for affirmation, his profoundly held belief that he is not good enough."

He was such a sweet guy and deserved a chance to do more than shadow Barrie. Eddie squeezed his shoulder. "I'm sure you'd make a great Macbeth."

"Hey, Eddie." Bianca's raspy, hot coals voice came from the doorway.

Eddie turned and was hit by The Smile. She held firm against its charm. Nearly dead hell prince in her basement trumped all other distractions. "Hey, Bianca." She moved to slide past her.

Bianca somehow got between Eddie and the greenroom door. The Smile gained intensity. "How are you, Eddie? I wanted to check in with you. You were pretty upset at the board meeting the other day."

"I'm good, Bianca." Eddie tried for a light tone but came out sounding more like she was running to catch the last bus of the day. "I really need to get on."

"Oh, dear." Bianca clocked the first aid box under her arm. "Is somebody hurt?"

"Nope." Eddie was proud of the evasion she produced. "I just need to check the contents and make sure the box is up to date."

Bianca looked at her and drawled, "Right." Then she curled her ruby-painted mouth into her secret weapon. "It's only that Dee was worried about you before she left, and I promised I would check in with you." She leaned closer, enveloping Eddie in a cloud of juniper. "I know things are not always"—she grimaced—"easy here. What with all the personalities. And I want you to know that if anything is worrying you." She touched Eddie's shoulder and comforting warmth radiated from the contact. "Anything at all. I'm here for you."

"Thanks?" Eddie didn't think they were that kind of friends, and Bianca had been the one to get *Macbeth* vomiting its curse all over her theatre. She had to wonder how well Dee really knew Bianca and how she would feel about her once Eddie caught up with her grandmother. "But I really am fine." She flashed her, admittedly less effective, smile. "Just busy."

"Hello, Bianca." Matt scuttled closer. "Have you got a minute? I wanted to talk to you about my role in the play."

Eddie took the gap and slipped through the door. Hurrying down the corridor, she almost made it to the basement door when Sophia materialized in front of her. "Hello." The woman was even more stunning up close. There was not one visible pore on her skin, and her blue eyes hit Eddie like an arc light. "It's Edme, isn't it?"

She hated that name. "Yes, but everyone calls me Eddie."

"Eddie." Sophia made her name sound oddly exotic. "It like it; it suits you."

"Thanks?" Man, was she ever gathering new friends this morning. "Can I help you, Sophia?" And she really did want to help Sophia. Something about the woman made you want to move mountains on her behalf.

"Oh, no." Sophia laughed like the chiming of crystal bells. "You looked a bit harried, and I wanted to make sure there was nothing I could do to help you." Her eyes grew bluer and brighter. "Is there anything I can help you with, Eddie? Anything at all."

Eddie opened her mouth and the truth damn near came pouring out. She wanted to tell Sophia all about the unstable hell gate, the hoppers and the toad, the hounds and Yesterday, and most of all, about the nearly dead hell prince bleeding out on the basement floor. "No." She forced the word past her jaw. "Everything is A-okay."

TEN

uch sweating and cursing, and creative use of a scene moving dolly got Shade out of the basement and into Dee's room. She couldn't leave the man... hell prince...being down there on the cold basement floor while he was so badly injured. Well, she could have, but she was a nice person. At least, that was what she told herself. It had nothing to do with the sheer mind-boggling beauty of the man...hell prince—screw it. Until another option presented itself, Shade was getting the pronouns him/he and identifying as a man.

If the fucker ever woke up, he could correct her. Fucker seemed to work pretty well as a moniker too. It had taken several warm towels to clean away the blood, and every bandage in the first aid box to deal with his various wounds.

The hounds had insisted on following her up to Dee's room and had even put their muscular necks against the dolly to help heave him up the stairs. At least they were now not howling the theatre down.

They were kind of sweet, curled up on either side of the bed like massive, furry, fanged, fatal bookends. Realizing she hadn't eaten all day, she popped into the kitchen for a depressing inventory of the sixty's fridge that neither Eddie nor Dee had the heart to toss.

Her options were suspiciously old cold cuts, a dried-out block of cheddar, or limp celery. She grabbed her trusty bag of popcorn, tossed some oil into a pot and cranked up the heat on her stove. Today she was really regretting her elitism about microwave popcorn.

The hounds watched her, red eyes glowing faintly through Dee's bedroom doorway. Now that she wasn't afraid they were going to tear her apart and gobble her parts, she found their eyes a rather pretty shade of cherry. They hadn't eaten either. "Are you guys hungry?"

Eddie winced inwardly. Asking them that might be a question she regretted, because if the answer came back as the souls of the living, or the flesh off your bones, she was the only feeding option.

One of them yawned and provided a fang-size reminder of why she shouldn't have asked.

Shade looked like he was sleeping peacefully now. Was he like other supernatural creatures she'd read about or seen on television that could heal themselves?

"Yesterday?" The little yellow bastard had disappeared around about the time the hard work of heaving a six four, muscular man up the stairs had begun. She added a bit more volume. "Yesterday!"

He appeared with suspicious speed. "What?"

"Where have you been?"

His huge eyes grew shifty. "I was here."

"No, you weren't."

"Yes, I—"

Hound two growled and raised his head to glare at Yesterday.

"Fine." Yesterday pouted. "I am not good at lifting and carrying."

Hound one added a growl to two's.

"All right." Yesterday huffed. "He's a hell prince, and they're scary. Demons get dead when hell princes get angry."

Eddie gaped at him. "He's nearly dead. What possible danger could he be to you?"

"He's a hell prince." Yesterday glowered at her. "They're just about immortal."

She had thought Shade looked better since she'd brought him up here, but that could have been wishful thinking on her part. "What about his mortal wound? Can he heal himself?"

"Oh, yes." Yesterday nodded.

Information that would have been useful before she'd dragged him up the stairs. "You could have told me that."

She probably would have dragged him up the stairs anyway. Leaving him down there in his condition didn't sit right with her.

"You didn't ask." Yesterday smirked. "I did tell you that only a hell prince could kill him."

"Yes." Eddie reached for her diminishing patience. The popping against the pot lid pulled her attention back to the stove. About thirty seconds later, she was adding melted butter and salt to a large bowl of hot, freshly popped corn. "But you also said he had a mortal wound and only another hell prince with an obsidian blade could give him that."

"Did I say that?" Yesterday's googly eyes locked on her popcorn, and he licked his lips.

No way she was sharing her popcorn with him. She tossed

a kernel into her mouth. "Yup." To up the ante, she shoved a fistful in her mouth. "That's what you said."

"Well." Yesterday sidled closer, a droplet of drool forming at the corner of his mouth. "It's hard to tell a mortal wound from the regular kind."

"Oh, yeah?" Eddie took childish pleasure in her next fistful of popcorn. Her aching back muscles had a bone to pick with Yesterday if he had been stretching the truth. "So, what made you say Shade was mortally wounded."

"Eh?" Yesterday shot her an aggravated look before going back to ogling her popcorn. "Well, look at him. Doesn't he look like he's mortally wounded?"

"You see, that's the thing." Eddie sucked butter and salt off her fingers. "I don't know anything about demons, hell princes, hell hounds, or mortal wounds. I'm relying on you for my information."

"Of course." Yesterday sidled closer. "And I have all the information for you." He got even closer. "All the information you need." He puffed up his chest and waggled his ears. "I am a demon. I know all about hell."

His bombast annoyed her. "You're an imp."

"An imp is a demon." He smirked.

He made a grab for her popcorn.

Eddie snatched the bowl back before he could grab a handful. "Answers first."

"Aww." Yesterday's face fell into pitiful pleading. "I am hungry."

"No, you're not." Eddie chowed down on another fistful. "You ate three jars of peanut butter today."

"Did not." Yesterday pouted.

"Yup." Eddie tossed a kernel into her mouth. "I bought three jars yesterday. Today there are none left." She carefully selected her next kernel and ate it. "I didn't eat them. So, you do the math."

Yesterday harrumphed. "Why are we talking about this?"

"Agreed." Eddie had him now. "What I want to talk about is hell princes."

Yesterday glared at the popcorn bowl. "It is dangerous to talk about hell princes. Hell princes are powerful."

"How powerful?" She grabbed another handful and held it in her hand.

Yesterday drooled. "Very powerful. Very, very powerful." He wiped saliva off his chin. "Very powerful."

Yeah, he wasn't getting popcorn for that. "What can they do?"

"Everything." Yesterday growled.

She waggled her fingers at him. "Details."

"Ugh!" Long lines of spit trailed from Yesterday's chin. "They fly."

"Already knew that." She ate her handful of popcorn with an extra crunch. "Do they have magical abilities?"

"No." Yesterday gave her a scornful look. "They don't do magic."

"So what makes them powerful?" She took her time eating another mouthful.

Yesterday stared at the bowl. "It's nearly gone."

"Got more in the packet."

"More." Yesterday licked his lipless mouth. "They are power."

"What does that mean?"

"Do you have more than one packet left?"

"Maybe." She crunched through a couple of kernels. "Depends on how many details I get." Her attention snagged on her now swollen left arm. "Let's start with why the hell this thing hurts so much."

Yesterday wailed. "I don't know that one."

"Then why did you make me put salt on it?" That had hurt like a bitch.

Yesterday was nearly sobbing as she ate another mouthful. "It seemed like the right thing to say."

She didn't trust the yellow scumbag, other than when peanut butter—and apparently popcorn—was involved.

She tossed him a few kernels.

His tongue shot out like a chameleon and slurped them out of the air.

"Back to the they are power thing." She held a handful out.

"They are woven into the fabric of creation." Yesterday's eyes didn't stray from her hand.

"More."

"Argh!" Yesterday twisted like he was made of Play-Doh. "You have heaven, earth, and hell. The three live in balance. Hell princes rule hell. Archangels rule heaven. Humans..." He grimaced. "I don't know what the point to humans is."

Eddie had days when she wondered that herself. "So hell princes are evil?" And one of them was sleeping in Dee's bed. "And archangels are good?"

"Eh?" The question shook Yesterday enough to drag his gaze up to hers. "I don't understand."

"Hell is for sinners, and heaven is for the worthy." She tossed the popcorn.

Yesterday snatched it out of the air again.

How long was his tongue exactly?

She took her clarification slowly, accompanied with another handful of Yesterday's crack. "Bad people go to hell. Good people go to heaven." He still looked confused. "After they die."

"You mean humans?" Yesterday frowned.

"Obviously."

Yesterday went back to lusting after the corn. "There are no humans in hell.

Say what now? "So who is in hell?"

"Demons." Yesterday glanced at Shade. "And the hell princes."

Eddie tossed the handful while she thought that through. "But hell exists?"

He rolled his eyes. "Obvi."

"Why?"

"What?"

"Why?" Eddie dragged the word out. She was kind of enjoying the power. "If hell is not there for sinners' souls, then why does it exist?"

Yesterday sniffed and looked superior. "You don't know anything, do you?"

"I know lots of things." But none of them relating to heaven or hell apparently. "But carry on."

Yesterday scowled at the bowl. "There's none left."

"More in the bag." She stood and sauntered over to the stove. Maybe she had a little evil queen in her after all. She added more oil and kernels to her pot.

Yesterday scuttled up and stood beside her, his gaze locked on the pot. "It's taking too long."

Eddie nudged him. "Keep talking, short stuff. It'll take your mind off the wait."

"I don't have all the information on heaven and earth." He gave her a wary glance.

"Fair enough." A popped kernel pinged against the pot lid. Several more pings followed "No more drooling." She snatched up some paper towel and handed it to him. "It's gross."

Yesterday mopped himself up. "Hell guards the deadly sins."

Eddie shook the pot so the bottom kernels didn't burn.

What Yesterday was telling her couldn't be right. "No, the deadly sins come from hell."

"Technically, yes, because the seals to the deadly sins are there, and the hell princes guard them and stop them from escaping." Yesterday pressed his button nose against the oven. "But the seals are breaking now. Hell princes are warring. Very bad."

Now she had more questions. "What do you mean the seals are breaking?"

She snatched the pot off the stove and tipped the contents into the bowl.

"Breaking." Yesterday lunged for the bowl, grabbed it, and scuttled off with it. Popcorn flew as he two-fisted it into his mouth. Any escaping kernels were quickly swiped up with that prehensile tongue.

"What does—"

Dee's distinctive *Bat Out of Hell* ringtone came from her phone, and Eddie forgot the popcorn, forgot the demon scarfing it, almost forgot the near-naked hell prince making Dee's bed look like a place she wanted to be. She answered the call. "Dee?"

Forgot Yesterday and his answers that just led to more questions.

"Eddie?" Dee's familiar sweet tones came down the line, and Eddie wanted to sit on the floor and weep. "Is that you, Eddie? It's Deandra. Your grandmother. Dee."

Yeah, cell phones and caller ID had pretty much bypassed Dee altogether.

"I've been calling you for days." And had more conversations with Jean-Claude than she cared to. Not that he wasn't a sweetheart, but...a lot escaped Jean-Claude. 'Nuff said.

"I'm so sorry, Eddie-girl," Dee said. "I thought I'd lost my phone and Jean-Claude only told me he was keeping it in his suitcase about two minutes ago." Jean-Claude murmured something in the background that sounded apologetic. Dee sighed. "I would have called the moment I got your text."

When she was around eight, Eddie had overheard Rosabella telling Dee that Eddie's nickname made people think she was a boy—the insurmountable horror! Dee had solved that by calling her Eddie-girl, and then taking her for the short haircut Eddie had craved. "Didn't he tell you I've been calling?"

Dee made a soft noise of distress. She moved, and a door closed. "Jean-Claude is a dear, sweet man with some impressive skills. Unfortunately, remembering things is not one of them."

Eddie for damn sure didn't want to talk about Jean-Claude's skills, and she had Dee on the line now. "We've got a problem, Dee."

"I guessed that from the text. Tell me."

Eddie kept it short and to the point. *Macbeth*, hell gate, hoppers, toads, Yesterday, and now hell princes.

After she'd finished, Dee fell silent long enough for Eddie to ask. "Dee?"

"Did you call the guardians?"

That was Dee's first question? "No, Dee. You told me to never call them, but I have to say with all this going on, I was sorely tempted to call them."

Dee took a deep breath. "But you didn't?"

"No, I didn't."

Dee let out a long exhale. "Thank you, baby Jesus, for that."

"Did you miss the part about the hell prince sleeping in your bed and the demon gobbling popcorn in my kitchen?"

"Okay." Dee sighed. "Firstly, if what you tell me about his injuries is true, there's an excellent chance an obsidian or heaven wrought blade was involved. But anyone can wield those and it's unlikely another hell prince injured him."

Eddie turned to throw Yesterday the stink eye. For an imp who claimed to know all about hell, he got a number of details wrong. "So, I could wield one if I wanted to?"

Yesterday shrugged and trotted out of the kitchen with his bowl of popcorn.

"It's a weapon, Eddie," Dee said. "It's only fatal to a hell prince or an archangel when used by a hell prince or an archangel. That doesn't mean it can't deliver a nasty wound when used by another being. And for humans, they're fatal regardless of who or what is doing the stabbing."

"So Shade...er...Asmodeus might not be mortally wounded?" Her relief had nothing to do with Shade, but everything to do with her not having to get rid of a dead body. And yup, she was sticking with that story.

"If he's still around, the chance of the assailant being a hell prince is slim. It's bad, but it's not hopeless."

Funny Dee should say that, because hopeless was sounding pretty apt right now. "What do I do?"

"One thing at a time." Dee's take charge tone lifted the weight off Eddie's shoulders. "You said the thing that bit you looked like a grasshopper?"

Eddie was struggling to find the conversational connection. "Ye-e-s."

"And other than your arm being sore, you're feeling okay?" Dee was really focused on the hopper.

"I feel fine," she said. "Could we get to what I do about Asmodeus?"

"It's very clear to me what you should do," Dee snapped. "Send him back to hell."

"Send him back to hell?" Eddie lowered her rising voice. "He could really die if I send him back."

"Not your problem, Eddie." Dee didn't even falter. "Asmodeus is a prince of hell. He can take care of himself. You, on the other hand, are human." She took a deep breath. "And I know you're already freaked out, but we can't ignore the possibility that now the gate is open that whoever injured Asmodeus may decide to hop through and finish the job."

"Shit, Dee." She moved closer to Dee's bed. "That had definitely occurred to me, but did you miss the part about the possible end of the world if he dies?"

Shade lay on his back with the sheet tucked under his armpits. His clean, strong bone structure didn't even look vulnerable in sleep. It was a bit like having a sleeping tiger on your bed. It might be wishful thinking, but he didn't look quite as pale as he had. The blood that had seeped through his bandage didn't look fresh.

"I think you're the one who missed that part," Dee said. And really with the sarcasm? "Someone has it in for Asmodeus, and that can only be a demon or a hell prince. Both of those options are deadly, and they don't like us." Dee's voice gentled. "Listen to me, Eddie. They are not like us. They exist in a different universe to us, and we don't know the rules to that universe. Send him back to hell."

"Send him back to hell," she said. Even as she said it, some elemental part of her rejected the idea. He'd crawled out of the hell gate searching for safety. He must have. "He is a bit of an asshole." She hadn't forgotten that first incident with Shade.

"He's not a bit of an asshole, Eddie-girl, he's a total asshole, and don't forget it. Not for a moment. It will cost you your life if you do." Dee paused and then said, "I'm coming home."

As much as Eddie would love that, she felt guilty about dragging Dee back from her vacation. "Maybe that's not necessary. I'll haul him back downstairs and toss him back like a bad fish. That should fix the problem." She stamped on the niggle of objection squirming around in her brain.

"Hmm." Dee's tone was not at all reassuring. "I don't like what's been happening there, and I think I need to come back."

"You don't have to do that," Eddie replied in a tone that convinced nobody.

Dee hummed and said, "Push him back through the hell gate, Eddie. Do it now."

ELEVEN

Eddie stood by the side of Dee's bed over the unconscious Shade and tried not to feel like a total creeper. Dear God—please no lightning bolt for using God's name over a hell prince—but he was beautiful. His perfect bone structure would have made Michelangelo toss in his chisel. Nothing human could be that perfect.

His skin was like warm honey and made her itch to touch. Her hand was halfway to doing just that before she yanked it back. A full mouth rested beneath the strong blade of his nose. It was the sort of mouth that made a smart woman want to do very stupid things.

Of course he made a woman want to toss wisdom and inhibitions out the window. He was Asmodeus, hell prince of lust. Not the sort of résumé that would leave a woman feeling meh. His body had been sculpted by the same master who'd done his face. Not overly muscular but cut and defined and quintessentially male. If the hell prince gig didn't work out for him—and right now it didn't seem to be—he could make bank at selling men's underwear to the masses.

"Okay." Her voice sounded loud in the silent room. "Dee says I need to put you back in hell. That whatever is going on down there needs to stay down there."

Where, according to Yesterday, something nastier was waiting for him. She shouldn't care as much as she did, particularly not after the shit he'd pulled on her. She'd seen this being in action, and the experience had left her feeling violated and shocked. Dee was right; she couldn't risk whoever had done this to him coming to find him. And she certainly didn't want to be the poor sucker standing in the way if that did happen.

The hounds lying on either side of the bed guarding their master looked up at her, and one of them grumbled.

"He can't stay here," she said. "This is not his place."

Hound two's top lip quivered and it flashed fang at her.

"Don't give me that." Eddie stared it down. "We both know you're not going to eat me."

The hound sighed and dropped his head to his paws.

"You're dangerous." She took the argument to Shade. "And you need to go back where you came from." She added a bit more conviction to her tone. "It's for the good of the world."

But can't we keep him? whispered her hormones.

"No," she said.

Yesterday poked his head around the door. "Who are you talking to?"

"Him." Eddie pointed to Shade. No way she was talking about her unruly hormones with Yesterday.

Yesterday squealed. "He's awake?"

"Not as far as I can see." She leaned over and peered closer.

Shade lay still as the pillow he was resting on. His chest rose and fell on deep, even breaths.

"Do hell princes sleep?"

Yesterday scoffed. "Hell princes can do everything you can do, only better."

The absurdity of his statement made her laugh. "You're saying he sleeps better than me?"

"Of course."

The bizarre was lost on Yesterday. She really needed a sidekick with a better sense of the ridiculous. "Anyway, time to get this show on the road." She motioned Yesterday closer. "We need to get him back through the hell gate, and I'm going to need your help."

Judging by the way they were both glowering at her, she wasn't getting any help from the furry contingent. Would they try to stop her?

Yesterday leapt back. "I can't help you."

"Why not?" He might be small, but any help would be welcome.

Yesterday looked at her askance. "He's a hell prince. I'm a demon."

Which explained exactly nothing. She waited for more, but Yesterday stared at her.

At least she had the dolly. Just thinking about dragging Shade back down three flights of stairs to the basement made her muscles ache. He had to go back, that much was clear, but it was late, and he wasn't going anywhere. Shade had done nothing but breathe since he'd lain there.

"In the morning," she said to the hounds. "You guys watch him, but in the morning, I'm sending him back." And it wasn't like she would be sending him there alone. "And you guys will go with him and make sure he's okay, right?"

Hound one gave her a derisive look as if she got precisely nothing about this situation. She was getting tired of being the idiot in the room. "What?"

It closed its red eyes and sighed.

Time for bed.

⌇

SHADE FELT her presence recede along with the faint wafting of roses. He knew it was her without having to open his eyes. He'd felt her in his mind, seen her wideset blue-green eyes and the elegant, fine lines of her face when she'd done so. The human woman was beautiful, but he couldn't allow that to distract him. Somehow, she had dream walked into his mind and summoned him. Yet, she wasn't a witch.

She also intended to toss him back through the hell gate in the morning. Humans were notoriously treacherous and self-serving. He shouldn't be surprised that she had proven true to her species. He'd allowed her sweet face to lull him into complacency.

The wound in his side throbbed with each strengthening beat of his heart. He remembered two things about the demon who had jumped him. One, the fucker's face, and as soon as he was healed, he would be hunting the son of a bitch down. And secondly, that demon had come from Wrath's horde and nearly gutted him with an obsidian blade. After he'd ended the demon who had stabbed him, he was going for Wrath. No demon acted without its master's instructions or had access to an obsidian blade without their master giving it to them. Wrath had wanted him badly injured, and the only motive for that Shade could fathom was Wrath had given the command and hoped to finish him off in his weakened state.

Shade didn't get it. Why would Wrath be seeking to end him? It made no bloody sense. If he ended, so did Wrath. Shade wanted answers, and he wasn't going to get them lying here. He needed to heal and do it fast.

~

A TAP to her cheek woke her from a deep sleep. Fucking Yesterday and his need to wake her up all the time. She shoved his hand away. "Go away, Yesterday. I'm tired and I want to sleep."

"Wake up, little human."

That voice that didn't belong to Yesterday.

Shade's slate blue eyes hovered about two inches above her face.

He was even more gorgeous awake.

He was awake? "You're awake."

"Indeed." His eyes glowed more silver than gray. "And you're going to help me heal."

Heat coursed through Eddie, prickling over her skin, and turning her muscles to water. "I am?" she whispered.

His mouth was so close, and she wanted to taste him. Feel the press of his mouth against hers, have him push his tongue past her lips and mouth fuck her.

Shade closed his eyes on a deep, rough purr. "Give me more."

Eddie would die if she didn't give him more. She wrapped her arms around his neck. Her fingers dug into the silk of his hair and tugged him closer.

"Yes." His hoarse whisper stroked between her thighs. "Give me your lust, little human."

"I need you." If he didn't kiss her, she might explode. Between her thighs, she was hot and slick. Her nipples ached with her need for him to touch her.

He chuckled, a warm, husky sound that ramped up her desire. "That's my line."

"Kiss me." She didn't want to talk. Mouths were made for much more interesting things than talking. "Please."

A brief flash of confusion crossed his face. His eyes blazed silver, and he pressed his mouth to hers. "So sweet," he murmured, sucking her bottom lip into the searing hot cavern of his mouth. "You make me greedy for more."

Eddie tightened her grip on his hair and slid her tongue into his mouth.

He tasted incredible, like honey and musk, and she wanted all of him. But he wasn't kissing her back, just letting her kiss him.

Eddie ached for him. She pulled her mouth away. "Kiss me back." Her voice came out as a plea. "I need you to kiss me back."

"Eddie," he purred. "That's not how this works."

The heat of his body burned through the thin cotton of her T-shirt. She spread her hands over his silken, hot back. She wanted to absorb him into her. Her hard nipples rubbed against his chest, and she undulated to increase the pressure.

"Hmm," he rumbled. "I can smell how much you want me."

Eddie was way past caring. She wanted his hands on her, wanted his body on hers—inside her. She would explode if he didn't fuck her.

Wrapping her thighs around one of his, Eddie pushed her core against the hard muscle. She was swollen, wet, and needy.

She gripped his ass and pushed him against where she needed him most.

"Easy, little human." He gripped her hips and controlled her frenetic pace. "Give me all that desire."

Eddie fought against his control. She would go up in flames if she didn't get relief soon. "No." She panted. "Let me come. I need to come."

"And you will." His silver eyes met hers. "But not yet."

His gaze burned into her, and a warning bell sounded in the back of her mind. She wanted him so badly, but something wasn't right here. From a place way deep inside, Eddie dredged up her good sense. "What are you doing to me?"

He looked surprised, and then intrigued. "You deny me?"

God, she was going to hate herself for this when he left her in this state. "This is not right."

"Shh." He feathered his mouth over her jawbone. "You're going to feel so good, Eddie. Let yourself feel."

She was ready to rub herself against him to orgasm, but his detachment penetrated her lust haze. As much as she lusted after him, he wasn't feeling it. "Stop." She dredged up her last ounce of resolve. "I don't want this."

"Yes, you do." His eyes glowed silver. "Let yourself feel."

"No." Eddie shoved at his shoulder. She didn't know how he was doing it, but he was making her desire him. And he was not feeling the same. It made her feel cheapened, and also dealt very neatly with the situation between her legs. "Get off me."

Shade frowned and pulled back.

Eddie drew a deep breath and shoved him the rest of the way off her.

He rolled to his feet smoothly, an unreadable expression on his face. Shadowy wings rose behind his shoulders. "Go to sleep, Eddie."

And amazingly, she did.

CURIOSER AND CURIOSER. Shade was intrigued. Moonlight played lovingly across her high cheekbones and full mouth. Her eyelashes lay in thick halfmoons against her creamy skin. She had resisted him.

He couldn't remember the last time that had happened, and never with a human. Leaning down, he studied her closer.

The hounds pressed against him and whined softly.

Shade stared at them.

They liked her, and they felt the compulsion to obey her.

Eddie shifted in her sleep and threw one restless arm out of the covers.

She had strength this one, and her lust had carried a potent punch that had almost drawn him in and mired him in its allure. He was lust; he didn't feel it. And yet with this human woman, he had wanted to taste her, touch her, press his heated flesh against hers and lose himself in the temptation of her.

His body ached, and he needed to rest. Her lust had also been so much more potent than any he'd ever experienced, and already his muscles, bone, and skin knit themselves together. She was one mystery wrapped within another, and he needed to watch her carefully.

Which was the only reason he pulled back the covers and slid into the bed beside her.

His first hound raised its head and stared at him. Did it think to challenge him?

Over a human woman?

Her body heat drew him closer, and he eased her back against his chest. She fit him like a key in a lock, and he took a moment to draw her scent into him, feel the press of her silky skin and strong body against him.

Not a witch, yet powerful in her own right. The only answer that came to him was so nonsensical that he dismissed it out of hand. Such a being could not possibly exist.

EDDIE WOKE with her back pressed against warm, smooth skin that smelled amazing.

A huge furry head appeared beside her bed, as one of the

hounds propped his chin on her bed. The hounds she'd last seen lying beside Shade, who was apparently sleeping in her bed with her.

Eddie leapt out of the bed as if he'd scalded her. "What the fuck are you doing here?"

Flashing straight, white teeth, Shade yawned and rolled to his back. He stretched his arms above his head in a thoroughly distracting snap and ripple of muscle. The bandages she'd wrapped around him were gone, leaving only small cuts and abrasions to mar his perfect skin. "I was sleeping." His slate eyes opened and fastened on her with disconcerting intensity. "You intrigue me, little human."

What the hell was this little human business? Last night, lost in desire, she'd not had any interest in bringing it up. But now that she was awake and not trying to dry hump him, she was laying down her issue. "Stop calling me little human. It's demeaning and pejorative."

"Big words, little—Eddie." He tucked his hands behind his head. Biceps bulged in a way his smug expression declared he was all too well aware of.

Dragging her gaze away from the view, she snapped, "How do you know my name?"

"I know all." His eyes twinkled, and she hardened herself against the effect.

Her knees rejected the suggestion, and she had to hold on to the bedpost.

He jerked his head toward the side of the bed. "And the lads told me."

"They speak to you?" Eddie felt oddly let down.

He shrugged. "I created them."

Right, well, she'd forgotten that. But hang on a hot second here. "None of which explains what you were doing in my bed."

"It's a good bed," he said. "And I don't like to sleep alone."

Words vaporized and left her brain empty. She stood there gaping like the village idiot.

"A more interesting topic is what else the lads told me." He rubbed one large, square hand across his chest, and then kept going down his abdominals and stopped halfway beneath the sheet draped over his hips.

Thank the lord for that, because she couldn't seem to tear her gaze away. Spit dried in her mouth, and prickles of desire unfurled through her. "Stop doing that."

"Doing what, Eddie?" His eyes glowed silver.

"That thing." She jabbed a forefinger at his face. "Whatever the hell that thing is that you do that makes me...experience certain sensations."

"Sensations?" He raised one brow. "Let's talk about those sensations."

"Nope." She grabbed her trusty bathrobe and slipped it on. Armed with terrycloth, she felt much more capable of having this conversation. Coffee would be good, but she wasn't taking her eyes off that tricky son of a bitch.

"Fair enough." He sat up, not quite suppressing his grimace. The sheet pooled in his lap.

It begged the question that if the man was the personification of lust, did the equipment match the reputation? No, it fucking didn't. She needed to stop this shit. "You're doing it again."

His gaze hadn't gone silver. "I'm really not."

"So not the point." Eddie folded her arms over her breasts. She didn't want him to see her disobedient nipples.

"Let's discuss what else the lads told me." His expression hardened. "The lads also told me you were going to toss me through the hell gate again." His eyes went glacial. "You were going to push me through the hell gate to fend for myself in my weakened state."

"You're still here, aren't you?" She glowered at the traitorous hounds. They'd hurled her under the bus, backed it up, and ridden over her again.

Shade moved so quickly she didn't have a chance to evade him. He grabbed her sore arm and made her yelp. Then he sniffed it. "When did you get bitten by a rakshasa?" His expression turned thoughtful. "And how the fuck are you still alive?"

TWELVE

"What the hell does that mean?" Eddie yelled. "What do you mean why am I still alive?" Yesterday had told her to put fucking salt on her bite. Her bite that apparently should have killed her.

"You were bitten by a rakshasa demon." Shade rearranged pillows behind his back and leaned back, as if he hadn't announced her narrow brush with death. She might be dying right now.

Had her heart just missed a beat? Was her breathing becoming labored? Yes and yes, but that was outrage not imminent death. "Yesterday!" she bellowed.

Shade studied her like a culture on a slide. "It bit you yesterday?" He looked thoughtful. "I've never heard of a human surviving a rakshasa demon that long."

"It bit me days ago." She shoved her injured arm closer to him. "And it's getting worse. Yesterday is a little yellow scum sucker who has some explaining to do."

"Scum sucker?" He tilted his head. "Is that an actual description or colorful human invective?"

"You know what?" She was done with these assholes from hell. "I'm over the way you say human like it's a bad thing." And more importantly. "What's going to happen to me?"

"I'm not sure I take your meaning." A smirk tilted his sultry mouth. "I have a couple of ideas, but now might not be the best time to suggest them."

"Rakshasa bite." She shoved her arm right under his nose. "That should have killed me. Am I dying?"

"Ugh." He recoiled from her arm. "You stink."

"And you suck," she snapped. "But answer my question."

"I don't know." He shrugged. "As I said, I have never known a human to last more than an hour after a rakshasa bite. The fact that you are still standing is unprecedented."

She was getting nowhere with this one, so she yelled again, "Yesterday!"

"You're calling the little yellow scum sucker?" He glanced at the hounds, and they both stood.

Eddie eyed the traitors with misgiving. "What are they doing?"

"They're going hunting."

The hounds slunk out the door.

Eddie was suddenly nervous for Yesterday. She wouldn't really have set the hounds on him. Shade had no such compunction. "Will they hurt him?"

Shade chuckled. "They're hell hounds."

Not reassuring. Not even a teeny bit. She rushed after the hounds. "Don't hurt him."

Both hounds turned to stare at her.

"Please?"

One of them sighed and raised his head and sniffed. It sounded like the suction on a vacuum hose. Then both hounds shot off together.

"Eddie?" Shade called from the bedroom. "There is something else we need to address."

Never mind address, one of them had to get dressed. Still, she found herself heading back into the bedroom and saying with as much grace as she could muster. "What?"

"The hounds." Shade jerked his head in the direction they'd disappeared. "You speak to them."

"I don't think they understand me." God, she hoped they didn't rip Yesterday into tiny pieces. And also, people would be coming into the theatre any moment now. People who she did not want to see ripped into pieces—at least, not every day. "You need to call them back. We have rehearsal today."

"They can take care of themselves." Shade smirked.

So not the fucking point. "They can't rampage around my theatre killing people. Yesterday said they feed on human souls."

Shade's expression grew annoyed. "Tell me more about this Yesterday."

"Like what?" She hadn't even had her coffee yet, and now she was dealing with all this hell crap. "I need coffee."

"You may fetch me a cup," Shade announced.

Ah, hell no. Someone had to bring a dose of reality to this motherfucker. "You can get off your ass and get your own coffee."

Shade laughed, a full-bodied sound that came from his belly and crinkled his face in a way that made him dangerously charming.

"Stop it!"

"Stop what?" He looked genuinely confused.

"Doing that thing." She waved her hands about as she ran out of words. She wasn't sure exactly what it was he did, but she knew she didn't like its effect on her.

"Ah." He grinned and folded his arms. Pectorals and biceps

bulged and made her lose her thoughts. His eyes glowed silver. "You mean this thing?"

And she wanted to leap on his naked self and ride him like a wild pony. Caffeine! Lots of it. Right now. Eddie whirled and stomped into the kitchen.

She loaded grounds into her coffeemaker and pressed the button that would make the magic black elixir. Her life had taken such a weird fucking turn lately. And now she could be dying.

Whatever!

Her arm looked bad, purple and distended and oozing. She grabbed the salt and slapped a handful on her bite. "Mother. Fucker." It hurt enough to bring tears to her eyes.

"Did you just put salt on a rakshasa bite?" Shade spoke from the kitchen doorway. Where he was standing buck assed naked.

And Shade did naked well. Oh boy, did he do naked well. She caught a glimpse of the most perfect cock she'd ever seen before she dragged her traitorous gaze away. "You're naked."

"Yes," Shade drawled. "I don't subscribe to your human obsession with modesty."

Eddie hit her limit. "Just put some pants on."

"I don't have any pants."

That was a problem. And she had the solution. "Wardrobe room." She pointed down the corridor. "Third door on the right. Find some pants."

"Does my nudity bother you, Eddie?" His voice grew smoky.

"Everything about you bothers me." Eddie sighed. She was so out of her depth. She needed Dee to come home and do it now. Then she could unload this entire mess on her grandmother. If Dee had the energy for men thirty years her junior, she could take on the hell contingent currently taking over her theatre.

Shade vanished in the correct direction, and the coffee machine beeped that it was ready to deliver its magic. Eddie grabbed two mugs and poured. She gave hers a life affirming load of French vanilla creamer. Wrapping both hands around her mug, she breathed deep. Coffee. Pure heaven.

A loud squeal startled her and almost caused her to spill a drop. Survival instinct stopped that from happening.

The hounds slunk into the kitchen, a squirming, squealing Yesterday trapped in one's jaws.

At least he was alive. Eddie took a sip of her coffee before she dealt with the newest crisis. "Put him down."

The hound opened its maw and Yesterday tumbled to the kitchen floor.

Eddie took a second sip—earth, chocolate, nuts, and vanilla. Life.

Yesterday tried to bolt.

The hound stretched out one massive paw and pinned him to the floor.

"Make them stop," Yesterday shrieked.

Bitter bite followed by a burst of sweet. "Don't break him."

The hound threw her a loaded glance.

"Yeah, I know." Eddie got it. "He's annoying."

Yesterday gasped and glowered at her. "Really?"

"Ah." Shade strolled through the door. His lovely bits mercifully concealed by denim. He'd taken the time to find a T-shirt with the jeans. A faded pink smiley face stretched over his broad chest and somehow managed to look sexy.

It could have been him being covered up, or the coffee, probably the combination of both, but Eddie's brain finally clicked into action. "This is Yesterday."

"An imp." Shade sauntered closer to Yesterday and nudged him with his foot.

Shade even had perfect toes. It wasn't right.

He closed on her and pried the mug from her fingers. He risked his life by taking a long sip. He swallowed and sighed. "Of all of your human creations, coffee might be my favorite."

They might have found a tiny patch of common ground, but that didn't mean she was prepared to share her coffee. "I poured you a mug." She pointed. "Creamer's in the fridge."

Shade grinned and turned back to Yesterday. With her fucking coffee.

Growling, Eddie snatched up the other cup and doctored it as she liked it. "Don't get comfortable here."

"Here?" He smirked. "This realm? Your kitchen?" His eyes smoldered. "Your bed?"

Done with words, she snapped, "Yes."

Shade laughed and strolled closer to where the hounds were keeping Yesterday pinned. Tilting his head, he studied Yesterday. "What is an imp doing here?"

Yesterday wriggled and squirmed beneath the hound's paw. He tossed Eddie a pitiful look.

She'd step in if it looked like he was in real danger, but it hadn't escaped her caffeinated brain that Shade might get her the answers she wanted. It struck her that despite all Yesterday had told her about hell princes, she didn't seem afraid of this one. And maybe she should be. A being described as power might be one to stay on the right side of. Screw it! He'd pissed her off, and she had a temper of her own.

Shade crouched down closer to Yesterday. "Speak, imp."

"I didn't want to," Yesterday whined. "I didn't mean to."

Leaning closer, Shade took a deep sniff. "You stink of Wrath. You are of Wrath's court."

"He said Wrath wanted to kill him," Eddie said, deciding to hurry this along before the risk of torture rose.

"Why?" Shade pinned Yesterday with a stare.

"I don't know," Yesterday blubbered, tears snaking down his cheeks.

"He told me he might have said something to some demons to make you angry with Wrath."

Shade gripped Yesterday by the throat. "What did you do?"

"I did nothing," Yesterday squealed.

As his fingers tightened around Yesterday's throat, Shade's voice went deep and resonant. "You will regret your trouble-making, imp."

And Eddie believed him. Intervention time. "You're frightening him," Eddie said.

"He's an imp." Shade gaped at her. "His entire purpose is to make mischief."

Yesterday certainly seemed to be fulfilling his purpose, but still, she didn't want Shade hurting him, or worse. "That doesn't mean you can torment him."

Shade shook his head and stood. "I'm a hell prince." He scoffed. "According to you humans, that is my purpose."

"I don't care." Eddie nudged the hound pinning Yesterday with her hip. "There will be no tormenting in my theatre."

Yesterday scrambled free. "It's not entirely my fault." He glanced at Shade and shrugged. "You know what Wrath's like. It doesn't take much to make him angry."

"This is true." Shade weighed this up. "But imps are always known to lie."

"Edsie?" Lillian's fruity tones floated up the stairs. "Are you up there, Edsie-darling?"

The last thing she needed was Lillian in her kitchen. "Hi, Lillian," she called back. "Did you need something?"

"I need to talk, Edsie." Lillian sounded piteous. "Can I come up?"

That would be a hard no. "Give me a second to get dressed, Lillian, and I'll be right down."

"I don't mind coming up."

Shade leaned his hips against the counter and grinned at her. "Want me to do my thing? I can make her forget her own name."

"Stay right here," she hissed at him. She did not want Shade doing his thing with Lillian. She did not want Shade anywhere near Lillian. She jabbed her fore and middle fingers at the hounds. "And that goes for you two as well." She almost forgot about Yesterday. "And keep that one here too."

THIRTEEN

Eddie handed over her fortieth Kleenex.

"I'm desperate, Edsie." Lillian sniffled and daintily blew her nose. "I didn't know where else to turn."

As they huddled in the greenroom together for the past twenty minutes, there had been a lot more in that vein, and as yet, no reason for Lillian's distress. If Eddie had to guess, she would say the trouble started with an S and ended with an ophia. "What's wrong, Lillian?"

"I can't work like this." Lillian pressed a trembling hand to her heaving bosom. "I have an artistic soul, and all this doubt stunts my creativity."

"Is there a problem with your role?"

"N-o-o." Lillian drew a shaky breath. "I really feel like I am becoming one with Lady M."

"That's good." Eddie palmed another Kleenex in case the tears started again. "I know you'll do a wonderful job."

"Really?" Lillian's green eyes filled with tears. "Do you really think so?"

"I know so." Eddie handed her the Kleenex. Whatever else Lillian was, she was a good actress.

"You see." Lillian exhaled and dabbed her cheeks. "This is why I knew I had to talk to you." She grabbed Eddie's hands and squeezed. "We are simpatico souls."

Eddie was less sure of that. "So, what's bothering you?"

"I feel terrible." Lillian sighed. "Because she's such a sweet and wonderful person."

Here it came.

Lillian's tears dried, and her face hardened. "It's that Sophia."

Was she clairvoyant or what? "What's wrong with Sophia?"

"She's cold, Edsie." Lillian clasped her hands to her chest. "She's calculating. Beneath that honeyed smile lurks a viper."

A very beautiful, younger viper. "Did she do anything specific?"

"Not yet." Narrowing her eyes, Lillian hissed, "But I see her. I know what's she's up to."

"Which is?"

"She wants my part." Lillian's grip on Eddie's hands increased to a painful level. "She's working to get me out of the Paradise Players."

Eddie didn't know about that, but a jot of logic wouldn't go amiss right now. "But she only arrived here yesterday morning."

"Ha!" Lillian gave a bitter chuckle. "I knew what she was about the moment I clapped eyes on her."

It hadn't looked that way to Eddie, but she knew better than to go down that road with Lillian. "What happened at your greenroom meeting?"

"That's when her true colors emerged." Lillian scowled. "Working her wiles on Peter and Rodders. Even Patty was lured under her spell." Her eyes teared up again. "And Barrie hates me, so he was sucking up to her to hurt me."

That must have been quite some meeting. "Did Peter say anything about her?"

"That's all he could talk about. All night long." Lillian's face crumpled back into woeful lines. "All night, he went on and on about how beautiful she was, and how much he wanted to see her read for a part."

"Is she interested in acting?" Eddie trod carefully forward. She wanted to smack Peter. He should know his wife better than to talk about another woman in front of her.

Lillian reared back as if Eddie had struck her. "You think she's trying to get me kicked off *Macbeth*?"

"No." Eddie still had to suppress her wince when the Scottish play was mentioned. Which was pig stupid, because in terms of the worst happening, they'd pretty much blown that bridge to shit already.

"Good morning." Shade's honey and whisky voice spoke from the doorway.

It was assuming that the worst had already happened that did it every time. It was like showing the universe the finger, and it came back with a throat punch.

Lillian's eyes went huge, and her mouth dropped open.

He sauntered into the room like he was on the catwalk, sexy half-smile in place, eyes glinting silver. "I'm Shade."

"Shade." Lillian snapped her mouth shut and flushed. "Lillian. Lillian Hampstead."

"Pleased to meet you, Lillian." Taking Lillian's elegant, pale hand between his palms, Shade stared into her eyes.

Lillian's flush deepened, and her eyes grew brighter. Her chest rose and fell as her breathing changed. Leaning toward Shade like a tree in a tall wind, she whimpered.

Color flooded Eddie's cheeks at the signs of Lillian's arousal.

Rising from her chair, Lillian moved closer to Shade. She wrapped her arms around his neck and pressed her breasts into his chest.

Eddie scrambled to her feet. She had to stop this. "Lillian."

"I need you," Lillian whispered. "Fuck me, please. Fuck me hard."

Oh sweet fuckery. The son of a bitch was doing this to Lillian.

Eddie pinched his arm. "Stop it. Stop doing that to her. You have no right."

"Ouch." Shade snatched his arm away. "I have to," he gritted out. "I need the lust to heal."

"I don't care." Eddie yanked on his arm. "What you're doing to her is wrong, and it needs to stop." This was so wrong. He was using Lillian in a horrible way, using her body's reaction against her. Eddie was disgusted. "Stop it." She punched his arm. "You fucking stop that now. You're abusing her."

"I have to heal." He tightened his jaw and glared at her. "If I don't, I won't stand a chance against Wrath."

Gathering every ounce of her strength, Eddie shoved him away from Lillian.

Whimpering, Lillian scuttled along the floor after him.

Eddie lunged for him. She'd rip him apart with her bare hands. There was no difference between what he was doing and some asshole trying to roofie a woman in a club. "You fucking—"

"Asmodeus!" Sophia appeared in the doorway. Only not the Sophia Eddie had last seen. Her eyes blazed with an inner fire, her hair floated in a gleaming mass around her head, and a dazzling white light surrounded her. "You have no place here."

Shade whirled. Black wings sprang from his back.

A matching pair of white wings materialized on Sophia.

They both pulsed with energy and swelled to twice their size.

Holy shit! Or unholy shit! Whatever the fuck was going on here, Eddie was certain she didn't want to get caught in the middle of it.

The two huge, powerful beings circled each other.

Grabbing Lillian by the waist, Eddie dragged her as far away from the scary supernaturals as she could and tugged them both behind a sofa.

"Asmodeus," Sophia called in a voice that rang in Eddie's head. "You are trespassing in this realm."

"Uriel." Shade's voice had grown deeper and more resonant. "I could say the same to you."

Uriel? Who the hell was Uriel?

Eddie risked a peek over the top of the sofa.

Gazes locked, Shade and Uriel/Sophia squared off against each other. Light brightened around both of them.

Uriel moved so fast she blurred. Rising in the air, she rotated and landed a kick to Shade's middle.

The blow threw him across the greenroom and into the mirror on the wall. Glass shattered and rained down on him, but Shade was already up.

With a roar, he flew at Uriel.

She met him halfway and they crashed in midair. White and black feathers fluttered around them as the two beings locked hands. Three feet in the air, they continued their bizarre wrestling match, both faces intent and deadly. Muscles and sinews straining, gazes locked, neither of them gained or gave ground.

"What's happening?" Lillian whimpered.

Eddie shielded Lillian's body with her own. "Just keep down."

Shade kicked out and sent Uriel careening into the wall behind her. She landed with an *oof*, plaster dust coated her hair and shoulders, and her body left a giant hole in the sheetrock. Without so much as a flinch, she launched herself back at Shade.

The coffee station mugs shattered. Water gushed from the broken tap.

"Enough." Shade shot to the side. "Your point is made, Uriel!"

Her face a mask of fury, Uriel nearly crashed into the wall, spun in the air and bellowed.

Closing on Shade again, Uriel wasn't in a listening kind of mood. Her arm shot out, and she rammed her elbow into Shade's face.

His head snapped back. Blood streamed from his mashed nose. "That fucking hurt."

With a feral grin, Uriel executed a bad ass flip through the air, and came up behind him. Her arm locked around his throat, a gleaming crystal dagger was in her hand and pressed against his jugular.

Shade froze.

Uriel's arm muscles flexed as she tightened her grip around his throat. Her legs gripped his waist.

Shade's wings fluttered. Strain showed on his face, and then he dropped them both to the floor.

Uriel leapt clear, rolled, and came up in a fighting crouch, her dagger held before her. "You know the rules, Asmodeus."

"Who's Asmodeus?" Lillian popped her head out and peered around the side of the sofa.

Eddie let her go. She had a broken mirror, a busted wall in her greenroom, and water pouring over the greenroom floor. The water mixed with blood and feathers and crept closer to the couch. Three lone intact mugs sat on the shelves. And

Eddie had no budget and no explanation to make any of that go away.

These flying fuckers could fix this. All of it.

Shade stumbled to a kneeling position. His wings drooped, his head dropped forward, and his chest heaved. "Yes, I know the fucking rules. I was waiting for you to show up."

"And amusing yourself with the human woman while you did." Sophia's teeth flashed in a vicious snarl. "Humans are forbidden. Another rule you conveniently forgot?"

"Christ, Uriel!" Shade swiped blood away from his face with the back of his hand. "Do you think I would have done that if I had a choice?"

Eddie absolutely wanted to yell yes to his question.

Uriel didn't look so certain. Then again, Uriel hadn't been the victim of Shade's little game of head rape. "Why?"

"I needed her lust." Shade raised his head and locked on Uriel. "I have received a wound from an obsidian blade."

"From who?" Uriel blinked at him.

"One of Wrath's horde," Shade said.

"Wrath?" Uriel looked taken aback. "Wrath gave you a mortal wound?"

"Not Wrath himself." Shade pushed himself to his feet. "But his horde ambushed me, and they had an obsidian blade."

"Wrath would never give an obsidian blade to his horde." Sophia's eyes flashed, and she pulsed with light. "You're lying."

"Stop." Shade held his hand up. "I am in no condition to fight you. And I am also well aware that demons should not possess an obsidian blade. But these did, and they used it on me." He shrugged. "I used the hell gate to escape them."

"Why here?" Sophia stopped pulsing, but her eyes still glittered.

"I had been here recently." Shade indicated Eddie. "She summoned me."

From her hiding place, Eddie shook her head. "I didn't summon him."

"But she's not a witch." Sophia frowned at her. "I also sense the hell gate is open. Did you open it?"

"No." If she had, Eddie would kick herself. And also, probably more importantly, close the crappy thing.

Shade shook his head. "Then how—"

"*Macbeth*." Sophia scoffed. "They were rehearsing it when I arrived. The witch's curse opened the hell gate." Then she grew thoughtful. "But even with the curse, there would need to be a witch to cast it."

Lillian held her hand up. "I'm not one of the witches, but I am Lady Macbeth."

Nails skittered on laminate and the hounds rounded the corner into the greenroom.

Shrieking, Lillian ducked behind the sofa.

Leaping back, Uriel raised her dagger. Her wings flared behind her and started glowing. "I thought something stank."

The hounds smelled a bit, but Eddie thought stank was rather strong. She eased out from behind the sofa, not taking her eyes off Asmodeus or Uriel. "They came through the hell gate before him."

Uriel glanced at her. "Yesterday?"

It took Eddie a moment to catch on that she meant the time and not the imp. "Yes."

Now Uriel turned and stared at her. "And they didn't rend you limb from limb?"

"She might not be a witch, but she's different." Shade jerked his head in her direction. "They heed her."

As if to prove his point, both hounds moved to Eddie and flanked her.

Gaping at the hounds, Uriel lowered her dagger. "I thought they'd bitten her. I smelled hell on her yesterday."

"Not them." Grimacing, Shade bent over and rested his hands on his knees. "Rakshasa demon."

"Bullshit!" Uriel—who was looking more like Sophia now —glanced from her to Shade and then the hounds. "No human survives a rakshasa bite."

"I was once bitten by wolf spider." Lillian poked her head around the sofa. "My hand swelled right up and went all red and nasty looking. I had the worst headache as well, and I was really rather queasy."

Uriel's expression softened. "That must have been awful for you."

"It was." Lillian nodded vigorously enough to send her hair flying. "But I have a very strong immune system. The doctors said so." She preened and giggled. "I may look like a delicate flower, but I'm very strong."

Shade kept his gaze on Eddie. "She can also resist my lust."

Frowning, Uriel turned back to her. "You can?"

"If you mean that disgusting thing he does, then I suppose so." Eddie didn't want to get into the fact that it hadn't been exactly easy. The temptation to go full Lillian on him had been hard to shove aside. She shuddered as she remembered Lillian's reaction. "He's a fucking asshole."

"You'll get no argument from me on that." Uriel chuckled. "But he's a very powerful asshole, and you should not have been able to resist." Uriel cocked her head and studied her. "What are you?"

As that was patently obvious, Eddie didn't bother to reply. "I think a better question is what are you?"

"Meet Uriel." Shade groaned and levered himself to standing. Pressing his fist into the small of his back, he stretched and hissed. "Archangel and my balancing force."

"Uriel?" Lillian wrinkled her nose. "You said your name was Sophia."

"I hate Uriel." Uriel threw a glare at Shade. "Which is why I go by Sophia. Only assholes call me Uriel."

She had a point, and Eddie mentally erased Uriel. "You're an archangel, Sophia?"

"See." Sophia gave Shade a pointed stare. "It's not that hard to remember."

"Uriel is a name that happens when a bunch of senior middle eastern men get to name angels and demons." Holding his shoulder, he carefully rotated his arm.

"You go by Shade," Lillian pointed out. "Isn't that also a stage name?"

"She's got you there." Sophia smirked.

"Yeah, well." He grimaced as his rotation hit a tender spot. "Asmodeus is no party either."

They had drifted so far off the point. Eddie needed them back on topic. "You're an archangel and he's a hell prince. And you guys are opposites?"

"Something like that." Sophia held her hand out to Lillian. Her eyes blazed electric blue. "Nothing happened here today," she crooned. "You came to the theatre and went to rehearse your monologue on stage."

Lillian nodded and traipsed out of the greenroom.

The door to stage right opened and whispered shut again.

"I have questions." Eddie faced down both beings. "Not the least of which is who is going to pay for the repairs to my greenroom."

"So." Shade kept his senses wide open for Uriel reaching for her power as he took a seat on the battered old leather couch. He barely suppressed a wince as he sat. Combined with his former injuries, the showdown with Uriel had him wishing he could plug into Eddie's delicious lust again. But she'd probably stab him if he tried, and Uriel would hold him down while she did. "It's been some time since I last saw you."

Uriel narrowed her eyes and studied him. "You look awful."

"Why, thank you very much." He grinned just to irk her. "You'll be super concerned to know I feel even worse."

"What happened?" She perched on the table. "How did Wrath's horde manage to ambush you?"

Admitting a weakness to another supernatural was a dangerous proposition, but he liked Uriel. Or came as close as he could to liking any archangel. Uriel was all right. She didn't molt feathers over the insignificant and inconsequential. As his balancing force, she was as near as he had to an ally. "Wrath's been growing more aggressive."

Uriel raised an eyebrow.

He understood her skepticism. Wrath had come into being with fury and vengeance pounding through his veins. "His horde have been attacking settlements throughout my demesne. They've been growing steadily braver too, and I've had to deal with several incursions into my palace."

"To what end?" Uriel frowned.

"That, my dear Sophia, is what I would like to know." Their normal wars were one thing, business as usual. "It defies logic even for Wrath."

She tapped her hand against her thigh. "Not even Wrath is angry enough to end himself to end you."

"Exactly." Shade shifted to ease the pain in his ribs. "But he seems determined to end me. If he persists in this vein, it can only result in one of us ending the other."

"Hmm." Uriel stood and paced the room, her shoes sloshing through the mess on the floor. "That's why you breached the hell gate?"

Shade would love to take the easy explanation, but the

stakes were too high for lies and half-truths. "To be honest, there wasn't a lot of thinking about it. I acted on instinct in coming here."

"Which brings us back to Eddie." Uriel's gaze sharpened on him. "She dream walked you?"

"More than once." So many times that he'd almost become accustomed to her popping into his awareness.

"You know that humans can't do that," Uriel said. "Even witches who can summon us cannot dream walk us."

Shade didn't dignify that with a response and waited while Uriel reached the same conclusion he had.

Her eyes clouded and she frowned. "You know what that means."

Shade nodded. Tension coiled into a knot in his belly. They understood each other perfectly. Where they could differ was in how they wanted to handle the truth about Eddie. And Shade was not about to step aside and let Uriel do what the rest of her angelic assholes would demand.

"You haven't told the others?" Sophia studied him as he shook his head. Then she surprised him by saying, "Good."

"Good?" They were in dangerous territory here, and he needed to move carefully.

"Yes, good," Uriel said. "That gives us time to come up with a plan to keep her safe."

FOURTEEN

How exactly was this her life? Eddie left the two feathered dickheads to it and stormed out of the greenroom. She had shit to do. This theatre didn't run itself. Snatching up her script for *Macbeth*, she stomped into the lighting box and fired up the system. Somebody needed to program the lights Dean had set up for this cursed show, unless Tweedledum and Tweedledummer still glaring at each other and looking like they might start on her greenroom again, could go full lightning bug and shine their asses at the stage.

She sent Dee a text to update her. Dee needed to know what she was walking into.

"Edme," Sophia spoke from the lighting box door. How she'd gotten there so silently, Eddie added to the growing list of shit she didn't get and didn't care to.

Eddie grabbed a plot sheet. Peter and Dean wanted to open with a moody, cold atmosphere. For *Macbeth*. Revolutionary. Not! "I'm busy, Sophia. And unless you're here to tell me you're going to pay—"

"Shade and I have repaired the damage we did."

Okay, well that was good.

Eddie jotted down some notes. LX 1.1, preset.

Sophia moved beside the lighting board. "May I see your arm?"

"It's fine." By which she meant hurt like a son of a bitch and might be the death of her, but whatever.

"Edme—"

"I hate that name," she snapped. "Call me Eddie. Or better yet, leave me alone." And by this she meant in the broader sense as in get the fuck out of her theatre. Perhaps getting mouthy with an archangel wasn't her best move, but she was past caring.

Sophia's gaze went gentle and understanding as she put her hand on Eddie's arm. "I know this is a lot to take in. But I might be able to help with your bite."

The desire to be a hard ass was tempting, but the possible death from rakshasa demon bite scenario had her swinging her chair around.

"You're not the real guardian." Sophia took her arm carefully.

"You don't know that." As far as Eddie knew, she and Dee were the only two people privy to that information. Other than Rosabella, and as she was the reason for the lie, Eddie would bet her best pair of vintage Chucks, she wasn't going to say anything either.

Sophia chuckled and bent to examine her bite. "Yes, I do, Eddie. I know it the same way I would recognize another angel, or a demon disguised as a human." She sniffed at the wound with her adorably upturned nose. "Ugh! That stinks."

"Thanks." Eddie tried to snatch her hand back. "Nice of you to notice."

Sophia pulled out the sound operator's chair, put Eddie's

arm back on the desk, and sat. "Also, if you were the guardian, you would have realized what I was the moment I stepped into the theatre."

It struck Eddie that here might be the answers she craved. "You going to tell me what's going on?"

"We both are." Shade stood in the doorway, looking like every girl's dirty dream with his ankles crossed, his shoulder propped on the jamb, and his low-slung jeans.

So, now the shithead wanted to talk. She wasn't going to forget what he'd done to Lillian in a hurry. No amount of drop dead sexy was going to mitigate that.

"I need to make sure Uriel tells you the full story."

Sophia bristled. "I do not lie."

"We both know you just did."

"No fighting in here." Eddie slammed her hand down on the desk. "There's a lot of expensive equipment in here." And Eddie had pretty much reached her limit, sailed right past and landed on the dangerous end of pissed off.

"We've got a big problem, Eddie." Sophia's beautiful face invited her trust.

"We?"

"Well..." Sophia shrugged prettily. "All of us. Heaven, earth." She jerked her head at Shade. "Hell."

Eddie resisted Sophia's charm. "You just got through telling me how I'm not the guardian, so how is any of this my problem?" She jabbed her thumb at Shade. "Him and his shitty tricks can go right back to hell." She held her hand up to stop Shade from speaking. "And I really don't care if Wrath wants his head on a stick. After what he pulled with me and then Lillian, I'm not going to stop another hell prince from slapping down some harsh justice."

The hounds shoved past Shade and flanked Eddie.

"Wow." Sophia eyed the hounds. "They really do listen to you."

"Ungrateful sods." Shade snorted. "I created them, and now look at them."

"They can stay." Eddie touched the left hound's ear. "They don't break stuff."

It leaned into her caress with a cute purr.

"Eddie." Sophia leaned her elbows on her knees and scooted her chair closer. "As much as Shade annoys me." She scowled at him. "We can't let Wrath kill him."

"Why not?" Six hell princes sounded like enough to her. If they are all like Shade, it was probably six too many. She wasn't putting any faith in what Yesterday had told her about how the whole thing worked.

"It's a good question." Sophia giggled. "And as much as I'd like to get rid of all the hell princes, we do need them."

To spread more of what Shade gave out. Eddie didn't think so. "For what?"

"They keep the system in balance." Sophia pulled a face. "Without Shade, there can be no me."

As Sophia had lied to her, broken up her greenroom, and now knew her greatest secret, Eddie wasn't seeing a total downside there either. "And?"

"Without heaven, there can be no hell. Without heaven and hell, there can be no earth."

Dee had clearly been very skimpy on the details of what being a hell gate guardian meant, but what Sophia said did line up with Yesterday's explanation.

"A deal was struck millennia ago," Sophia continued. "The battle is for ascended souls, and human souls are the ones we're guiding to ascension."

"Why?"

Shade chuckled and folded his arms. "Another excellent question, Eddie." He smirked at Sophia. "I look forward to your answer."

"You're an asshole," Sophia snapped.

The whole angels swearing thing was messing with Eddie's mind, but she tried to focus on the answer to her question.

"Nobody knows." She gestured Shade. "Well, none of us in any case. We were created for a purpose, and we follow that purpose."

Any moment now, somebody was going to pinch her, and she'd wake up in the middle of that fateful Wednesday bored meeting, and all of this would poof away.

"The universe is a constantly evolving thing." Shade strolled closer. "Souls are created, they learn through a long series of lifetimes, and then they ascend." He brushed his fingers over the buttons on her lightboard. "Over time, humans have distilled the explanation of that process into a simplistic good and bad equation."

Eddie slapped his hand away. "Is this where religion comes in?"

"Yup." He gave her an amused glance. "The mortal mind is limited by the notions of life and death. You are not capable of absorbing the breadth and enormity of the truth."

"And you are?" She glared at him to let him know being patronizing was not the right tack to take.

"I have a greater understanding than you, little human." He leaned down and put his face inches from hers. "I have been around for millions upon millions of your human years. I have seen the sun born and the creation of your species. I have watched every time your pathetic attempts have nearly destroyed you."

"That is not helpful, Asmodeus," Sophia said. "We all have our parts to play, and none is more important than the other." She tilted her head and studied Eddie. "And she's not human."

"And there are no accidents or coincidences," Shade said. "If she didn't summon me, and I still appeared in her dreams, then I am here because she has some part to play in all of this."

"Shade and I have been speaking," Sophia said. "When he was injured, he came through the hell gate nearest to you. There is some connection between the two of you, and he responded to that instinctively."

Eddie snorted to let them both know what she thought about that.

"It's true, Eddie." Shade grinned at her. "You dream walked with me, which is extremely rare."

"Great." She couldn't have been born with a widow's peak, or something else rare. Nope. She had to stalk a hell prince in her dreams.

"And those demons did try to end me." Shade grew serious again. "That can't happen, Eddie."

"No, it can't. For all our sakes," Sophia said. "For now, we need to ask you to keep Shade here." She pulled a face as if she understood exactly how much of an ask that was. "There must always be seven hell princes and seven archangels. There are also seven hell gates and seven heavenly portals. The guardians will not be happy either of us are here." She glanced at Shade. "And we are going to have to ask you to also keep them from knowing."

"Why seven?" Keeping shit from the guardians was pretty much the title of her autobiography at this stage. It was probably not the question she should be asking but she was spoiled for choice.

"Humans got that part right." Shade sneered. "Seven

deadly sins, seven virtues." He motioned himself. "I guard the lust seal. Uriel over there is responsible for keeping chastity under control."

"They're all part of a soul's journey." Sophia took up the explanation again. "If a soul has too much of one—even the virtues—it gets thrown out of harmony and must reincarnate again. And again. Until it finds the balance."

"Your soul, however." Shade took her hand. "Neither of us can read."

Eddie yanked her hand back. She didn't want this son of a bitch touching her.

"Which is another reason we believe you are not entirely human."

The right-hand hound laid his huge head on her knee as if offering her comfort.

Her mind refused to process the not human thing. They had to be wrong about that. She had memories from being a child. Dee had countless photos of her as a baby. She was as normal as the next person. She couldn't entertain even the possibility that they were right on the non-human thing. Her brain kicked that out and chose to focus on all the other stuff.

"Why does Wrath want to kill you?" Not that she cared.

Sophia beamed at her like a proud parent. "You keep asking all the most important questions."

"Yesterday—he's an imp—said they fight all the time." Actually, he'd said they fucked and fought, but she wasn't bringing that up around Shade. "Don't they always try and kill each other?"

"No." Sophia frowned. "They war for power, and because it's in their nature, but trying to kill each other would end all of them." She gestured around them. "All of us as well." She smiled, and Eddie struggled not to melt. "The problem is bigger than Wrath and Shade however."

Bigger? Oh, that's exactly what she needed. For this shit show to get worse. "Define bigger."

"Wrath is not behaving as he usually does." Shade propped his hips against the desk and dropped his chin to his chest. "His seal is breaking, and wrath is out of control."

Sophia sucked in a sharp breath. "And your seal?"

"The same." He cleared his throat. "It's hard to control the leakage."

Sophia stood and paced the three by eight foot lighting booth, somehow managing to dodge the two huge hell hounds, three chairs and a couple of boxes filled with gels lying against the back wall. "Ramiel will have to be told." She heaved a sigh. "And Gabriel."

Shade scowled. "Not that uptight ass."

With a pained expression, Sophia nodded. "I know. She is uptight, but we need her."

"Gabriel is a woman?" That was her question? And Sophia said she asked good questions.

"Gender is fluid." Sophia waggled her hand. "We are what we choose to be."

"You humans." Shade scoffed. "You always have to over-simplify everything."

"Oh yeah?" Eddie'd had a gut load of his crap. "And yet we puny humans are going to hide you here to keep you safe from your homicidal buddy."

"I'm sorry, Eddie, but we are going to have to ask you to keep him here." Sophia winced. "At least until he is healed enough to face Wrath."

Eddie had no doubt on this score. "No."

"We have no choice." Sophia gave her a look of unadulter-ated pleading.

"I like it here." He grinned at her. "And I like you."

"Yay, me." Eddie rolled her eyes and made sure he saw.

"Does that mean you're going to do that mind fuck thing with me again? Because I'll rip your balls off if you try that again."

"He won't try that again," Sophia said with enough steel in her voice for Eddie to fear for her lighting booth.

"I won't do that again." Shade looked from her to Sophia and back again. Then he smirked. "Mainly because I don't need to. You managed to resist my full impact but you're like plugging into a nuclear reactor."

"Really." Sophia seemed to consider this seriously. "She is getting more and more interesting."

"I know." Shade looked smug. "For that alone it's worth staying here."

"You're not staying." Eddie scowled at him, so he knew she meant it.

Both hell hounds gave her pitiful, pleading glances.

"He's a prick," she said to them. "And I don't trust him."

The one on her right whined.

"I do trust you." Eddie didn't question why she knew what that whine had meant. "You guys have given me no reason not to trust you." Honesty compelled her to add. "Other than when we first met, and you tried to eat me."

Left hound nudged her hand with his snout.

"Yeah, yeah, yeah." She patted his giant head. "But just because you thought I was human, doesn't mean it's okay to eat me."

Righty chuffed.

"I mean it." Eddie gave his ear a gentle tug. "And if you're going to hang around here, you both need to understand that there will be no more eating of humans."

"Remarkable," Sophia murmured. "I can see why you like her."

"The question remains what to do about her," Shade said. He gave Sophia a hard look. "And I trust we are in agreement."

"We are completely in agreement." Sophia nodded and then clapped her hands. "It's so long since we've had a good challenge."

CHAPTER

FIFTEEN

Eddie spent the day ignoring the shitshow that had taken over her theatre. Fortunately, Lillian and Barrie managed a three-hour distraction with a screaming match, through which Peter drank steadily from his "water" bottle. Now, Eddie was not a woman to cast aspersions, but Peter before his water was a lot less cheerful than Peter on a steady three hours of water.

She watched it all from the catwalk as she slipped gels over lights.

"I don't care if you spent twenty years at the NAC," Barrie bellowed. "And even if you had, you would still be the largest ham I've ever seen on stage."

"Ham?" Lillian screeched. "You're a geriatric Macbeth. How the hell am I supposed to behave like I desire you?"

Barrie took a deep breath and flushed. "It's called acting, you tart."

"How would you know?" Lillian shook with rage. "You wouldn't know acting if it bit you on your wrinkly old ass."

142

"People." Peter was lounging in the auditorium with his water bottle clutched in his hand. "Positive spaces."

Lillian and Barrie ignored him and got steadily more vitriolic.

"Psst." Yesterday popped his head out from behind a light, and startled Eddie so badly, she nearly slipped off the catwalk.

She pressed a hand to her thundering heart. "Jesus! Don't do that."

"Are they gone?" He peered around the theatre.

Eddie hadn't seen him all day. "Where have you been?"

"Here and there." He averted his gaze, looking everywhere but at her. "I can't be around Uriel and Asmodeus."

As much as Eddie wanted to ask why, she did not want to discuss those two. Of course she was fucking human. She had been human her entire life and she didn't need those idiots messing with her head. "Yesterday?"

"What?" He started.

"I'm human, right?"

Scoffing, Yesterday twitched his left ear. "What else would you be?"

See there! She knew exactly what she was. Yesterday probably only had a fly on his ear. "So, apparently there is big trouble in hell."

"I told you that." Yesterday looked affronted.

"Yes, but you didn't tell me how big that trouble was." She picked up the discarded gels from the catwalk. Her day would be totally complete if she managed to slip and throw her human body off the catwalk. Because humans couldn't crash into walls and shake it off as if it had barely even hurt. "People see hell princes in their dreams all the time, right?"

"Who said that?" Yesterday slunk behind his light again. "I didn't say that."

For the sake of her sanity, she came clean. "Shade has been

in my dreams. Also, it seems like Wrath could see me in those same dreams."

"You dreamed walked with Shade and Wrath?" Yesterday sprung out from behind his newest hiding place. "You never told me that."

"I'm telling you now."

"Are you sure it was Wrath you saw?" Yesterday followed her down the catwalk.

Verification couldn't hurt. She had no way of knowing it was Wrath she'd seen beating the crap out of Shade, but all the other information that was being thrown at her would make it a logical assumption. "Big guy, brown hair, pale blue eyes, muscular. Oh, and red in his wings."

Yesterday grumbled behind her. "Sounds like him."

"He doesn't look like a nice guy." Eddie was tired and hungry, and she wanted the yell-a-thon onstage to end. Leaning over the catwalk, she called down to Peter, "Rehearsal is over, Peter. I need to shut up for the night." And pray that she had no more midnight visitors. She might not have met Wrath, but from what she'd seen, she'd really rather not.

As she waited for the theatre to empty, she ordered pizza to be delivered. With Yesterday hanging about, she ordered more than her usual. While she waited, she cleaned up the auditorium, and checked the greenroom. It had been repaired, and there was no sign anything untoward had happened in there. The tired old couches looked better than they had in years.

At least Uriel and Shade were good for that much.

Pizza boxes in hand, she dragged her tired ass upstairs. Noises from her bathroom dragged her that way. She prayed it was the plumbing.

Clearly, her prayer did bugger all, because Shade was stepping out the shower as she peered around the door. He snatched up a towel and rubbed it over his hair. "Hey."

"What are you doing here?" She was way past polite at this stage. Because she was human and hangry, and that happened to humans.

Shade blinked at her. "Having a shower."

Eddie breathed deep to keep her patience with him. "I meant, why are you still in the theatre."

"I have to stay here." Shade looked genuinely confused. "Sophia and I explained it to you. I can't go back to hell until I regain my full strength." He hung the towel around his neck, leaving much skin real estate uncovered if she were so inclined, which she was not. "If I'm not at full strength, Wrath will end me."

"I never agreed to you using my personal space." She refused to let her gaze wander south of his face. "In fact, I was quite clear on my feelings about you staying."

He grimaced. "There's nowhere else I can stay, Eddie, and I can't go back to hell yet, because the consequences made the decision for both of us."

That would be the end of life as they knew it category of consequences. *Whatever.* "Don't leave water all over my bathroom floor." And then because she had a feeling she would need to explain politeness to him. "And hang up your towel when you're done."

Shade cocked his head and grabbed the dangling ends of his towel. His smile was pure sex.

And wasted on her. Eddie wasn't going to get all flustered by that incredible body and perfect cock. She'd seen all that before anyway. Before her gaze made a liar out of her, she stomped off to her kitchen. And he needn't think she was sharing her pizza with him. She was going to eat the whole thing, all by herself. She opened a bottle of wine and poured herself a glass.

Shade wandered into the kitchen in a virulent purple pair

of satin harem pants that had been used in the Christmas pantomime. He should have looked ridiculous. Instead, he looked like a sexy Aladdin. She had the insane urge to stroke his bare, cut chest and slide her hand into—"You said you wouldn't do that lust thing anymore." She grabbed a slice of pizza and jammed it between her lips.

"I'm not." Shade leaned his shoulder against the doorjamb and jerked his head at the pizza. "You gonna share that?"

"Nope." She took another huge bite.

Chuckling, Shade strolled into the kitchen and grabbed himself a glass. He poured wine and took a sip. Shutting his eyes, he groaned. "Humans do have some redeeming qualities."

"Yes, *we* do." Eddie glared at him to drive her point home.

"Eddie, Eddie, Eddie." He shook his head. "You're not human."

"Just because I survived some stupid bite?" Eddie shoved her hand at him. It didn't look as swollen as it had this morning. Come to think on it, it hadn't been hurting as much today. Maybe she'd gotten used to the pain.

Shade sipped his wine and studied her over the glass. "And you are more immune to my lust." He smirked. "When I'm using it, which I'm not at this moment. So it begs the question as to why you thought I was the one spreading lust." He quirked an eyebrow. "Could there be someone else in this scenario having lustful leanings?"

Eddie knew a conversational bear trap when she saw one, and she wasn't tripping that behemoth any time soon.

As if he'd heard her thought, Shade gave her a dirty grin. "Nothing to say?"

"Here." To shut him up, Eddie thrust the pizza box at him. She couldn't eat all of it anyway. And Dee had brought her up right. Which reminded her that she wanted to call Dee tonight and share the latest tidbit with her. Dee would laugh and tell her they were full of shit, and that would be the end of that. "I need to make a phone call."

"Eddie?" Shade helped himself to a slice. "There's another reason we don't believe you're human."

Oh, Eddie couldn't wait to hear this, and she stared him down as she waited for the answer.

"I can't read your soul." Shade bit down with his gleaming, straight white teeth. "And neither can Uriel."

"So?" Whatever the hell that meant.

"I'm a hell prince. She's an archangel." He shrugged. "It's kind of what we do."

"Don't get pizza sauce on those pants," she snapped as she stalked out of the kitchen. She was done with this crap. Time to let Dee settle it. She took her phone and her wine to her bedroom and perched on the end of the bed.

"Eddie-girl," Dee answered her call. "Don't worry, I'm on my way."

"Good." She needed to give Dee the latest. "And apparently we have the archangel Uriel here as well."

Dee sighed. "Well, that's to be expected. If Asmodeus is on earth, Uriel would know and want to check it out."

Resentment made Eddie want to snap at her grandmother, but she wrestled it back down to a low grumble. "You couldn't have warned me?"

"Sorry, Eddie-girl." Dee's voice softened in a way that melted Eddie's resentment. "I should have warned you of the possibility. Did they fight?"

"Yup." She wanted another slice of pizza, but that would involve going back into the kitchen and dealing with Shade again. "They tore up the greenroom."

"Idiots," Dee snapped. "Did they fix it again?"

"Yup." Pizza might be worth running into Shade. It was

pizza after all. *Pizza.* "And according to them, Wrath is trying—"

"Wrath?" Dee's voice sharpened. "Is Wrath there?"

"No, but—"

"Good." Dee exhaled. "That's good news."

Dee's reaction to Wrath bothered her, but they'd get to that. "So, Wrath is trying to end Shade, and Uriel and Shade decided he should stay here."

Dee scoffed. "He can't stay there."

"When you get here, you can tell him that." And maybe tell him to back off her pizza at the same time.

Shade wandered into her bedroom with a plate in his hand. Winking at her, he put it down on the bed beside her and sashayed his fine ass out of there again.

He'd brought her a few slices of pizza.

"Eddie?" Dee shook her back to the call. "Are you there?"

"Yes. Shade just—never mind." Never one to look a gift horse and all that, Eddie took one of the pieces and bit into it. "They say they can't take the risk of Wrath ending Shade. And until Shade is at full strength again, he can't go back to hell."

"Hmmm." Dee went silent for a while. "I suppose that makes sense, and we'll just have to hope that the guardians don't pick up that he's there."

"What would they do if they found out?" She was beginning to realize how sparse Dee had been on the details around the hell gate. If she'd known more, she might have been better prepared for what had gone down.

"They can't be on this plane without informing the guardians," Dee said. "It's a deal the three factions struck. And for the sake of peace, everyone makes sure they keep it."

Eddie's head ached. One fucking problem at a time was about all she had capacity for. "Dee there's something else." She tried to keep it light. She didn't believe a word of what they'd said to her, but it was needling at her mind, and it was best to put it to rest sooner rather than later. "Shade and Uriel said the weirdest thing to me today."

"Oh?" Dee sounded distracted.

Eddie went through the story as quickly as she could and made sure to include all the details. When she was finished, she waited for Dee to laugh, or scoff. Instead, a heavy silence came down the phone. "Dee?"

"I'm on my way, Eddie." She took a long, slow exhale. "Just hang in there."

Then, to Eddie's astonishment, Dee hung up. Eddie sat on her bed and stared at her phone.

"Was that the real guardian?" Shade strolled in and draped himself on her bed.

"What are you doing?"

"Your mother?"

"What?" she snapped going cold inside.

Shade grinned. "Was that your mother on the phone?"

"Grandmother." Eddie shoved his leg. "And you may have to stay here, but that doesn't give you the right to make like my bedroom is yours."

"I like it better in here. It smells like you." Shade crossed his ankles and tucked his arms behind his head. "Where's your mother?"

No way she was getting into that story. "Not here. And get off my bed."

"Where is she?" Shade's gaze grew intent. "Why is your mother not the guardian?"

"She didn't want to be." And oh, my god, could he not stick to the subject. "This is my bed. Yours is down the hall."

"This one is more comfortable." Shade looked thoughtful. "Is that the reason you're not the real guardian, because your mother is not here?"

"I'm not talking about my mother." That was a sore spot she was not showing to Shade. "You need to get out."

He grinned at her. "And you need to relax."

With him on her bed? Fat fucking chance. "You need to leave."

"This plane? This theatre? This bed?" He cocked his head and smirked at her.

"All of the above." She needed a drink. Nobody could handle this...him...it sober.

Shade patted the bed beside him. "Come here, Eddie."

"Does that work for you?" Looking all gorgeous and ripped and sexy and patting the bed with a warm look in his eyes. Ridiculous! Eddie snorted and sent a swift mental *quit it* to her lady garden. She'd done it again. It was a vagina, not a lady garden or a downstairs, or a foof, or her bits.

His grin widened. "It's story time." He stroked the covers. "And I'll answer your questions."

And Eddie sat. Because he was going to answer her questions. Not because the invitation tugged a visceral part of her that wanted to toss herself next to him. "Uriel and I have been talking about you."

She stayed on the edge of the bed, spine straight. "Is this the non-human thing again?"

"Your grandmother didn't deny it, did she?" He looked so understanding, it was tempting to confide in him. Then she remembered the lust thing and that he couldn't be trusted.

"That proves nothing." Eddie wished she felt better about the fact that Dee hadn't responded in the way she'd wanted her to. "She didn't say anything to prove what you said either."

"Right." He nodded. "Come closer."

"I'm fine where I am." She was not getting within touching distance of him. Disastrous things happened when she made physical contact with him. Her skin prickled with his proximity, and her muscles wanted to cleave to him.

"Eddie." He sounded disappointed in her. "You don't trust me."

"I have no reason to trust you." If he was going to hang around on earth, then he needed to learn a few things about how to behave here. "Need I remind you what you did to me and Lillian?"

"I explained that." He frowned as if she'd said something stupid.

"And you think that justifies what you did?"

He shrugged. "Of course."

"It doesn't," Eddie yelled. She hauled her temper back. Shouting at people never got the desired result. "You took advantage of both me and Lillian and used our natural instincts against us."

Pursing his lips, he appeared to mull that over. "I am the hell prince of lust. I draw power from lust, and I needed that power to heal."

Eddie couldn't believe what she was hearing. "So, if your power was based on killing people, that would justify you ripping heads off left, right, and center."

"But it isn't." He spread his hands, trying to make it sound as if she was the unreasonable one.

Enough was enough, and Eddie shot to her feet. "Out."

"I'm not going anywhere, Eddie." He shook his head. "You really need to hear me out."

"Argh!" She was sorely tempted to stamp her foot. He was about 6'4", built strong, but she'd dragged his ass up the stairs. She would haul him out of here if he didn't leave voluntarily.

"It won't work." He raised an eyebrow at her. "Now, sit your pretty ass down and let me tell you a story."

"Don't call my ass pretty," she snapped. Under different

circumstances, she might not mind someone calling her ass pretty, but this shit was condescending and patronizing.

"Sexy?" He cocked his head. "Gorgeous? Lush? Irresistible?"

"I don't care what adjective you use." A baseball bat might get her point across succinctly. Despite her stance on nonviolence. "I don't want you looking at my ass, and it's totally inappropriate for you to comment on it."

"Hmm." He stroked his full bottom lip with a thumb. "It's been many years since I came to earth. Things appear to have changed."

"You bet your ass—life they have." And despite her annoyance, her perpetual curiosity got the better of her. "How many years?"

"Let me think." He narrowed his eyes. "We do not measure time as you do." He pulled a face. "We do not measure time at all. It serves no purpose."

Eddie's mind boggled at that idea. "Then how do you know when stuff is happening?"

"You measure time because your life has a beginning and an end. It is a completely human phenomena, and as we are immortal, we have no reason to measure time. But"—he held up a finger—"women were wearing long dresses and corsets."

Way to go on narrowing down a time period. "Never mind. Suffice to say women are no longer treated as objects for a man's pleasure."

"Now I know you still have sex." He scoffed.

"That has—" And this time Eddie did stamp her foot. "You know what? If you're going to stay here, we are going to establish some ground rules."

He nodded. "That's fair."

"No doing your lust thing."

"Agreed."

"No looking at my ass"—he opened his mouth—"or any of

my other bits and commenting on them like you have the right to do so."

He gave that some thought. "What if I look and don't comment?"

"Will I see you looking?"

He gave her a wolfish grin. "Never."

"Morally and ideologically gray area, but if you don't comment and I don't catch you, I won't know about it."

"Any more ground rules?"

"Yes." This was her theatre after all. "No fighting other supernatural beings and breaking my theatre."

His expression turned regretful. "I can't promise that."

"Why not?" Even if they had fixed her greenroom, she hadn't forgotten what he and Uriel had done.

"I cannot be responsible for the others."

She opened her mouth to tell him that was bullshit, but it kind of wasn't. "I want you to promise to control your...urges."

"Sure." He grinned and patted the bed. "Now can I tell you my story?"

"Oh-kay." Eddie folded her arms. No way she was sitting on the bed. "Tell me your story."

"There is only one creature that you could be, and that creature should not exist." He looked regretful. "In fact, that creature is such an abomination that the once or twice one has popped up, they were exterminated."

Eddie's veins iced over. She knew she shouldn't have stayed for story time. "You're saying I'm some kind of abomination that should be dead?" It's a good thing he had the lust thing, because he had bugger all charm to offer. His game needed serious work.

He nodded. "Eddie, Uriel and I are very much afraid that you are Nephilim."

SIXTEEN

Eddie grabbed another crate off the prop shelves and slammed it on the floor. Bottles clanked, and glass broke. "Shit!"

She'd undertaken a clear up of the prop shelves this morning. After Shade's announcement last night, she'd stormed off, and when she'd come back, he'd been out of her room. She didn't know where he'd slept last night, but it hadn't been in her bed, and she'd taken the win.

Nephilim. She snorted. She didn't even know what that was.

Inside the crate, fortunately only two of the bottles had broken. After picking out the broken glass, she tossed it in the recycling bin. The problem with community theatre is that nobody ever threw anything away. How many different bottles did one theatre need? She upended the entire crate into the recycling bin and took some enjoyment in the crash and shatter of glass.

"Whoa now!" Yesterday swaggered into the props room like he was toting a pair of six guns. "Where's the war?"

Great! He had jokes. "In hell, apparently," she snarled.

Both hounds raised their heads when Yesterday entered, their red eyes locking on him like he was lunch. She'd discovered this morning that hell hounds, like everyone else, loved pizza. When she'd woken this morning, there'd been no sign of Shade, and she had been peering around corners all morning. She did not want to run into him. His hounds, on the other hand, she was enjoying having around.

Yesterday hauled himself atop a stack of luggage and perched there. "What are you doing?"

Making a mess more than anything else. "Do you know what a Nephilim is?"

She could Google it, but why would she when she had hot and cold running hell creatures around the theatre.

"There's no such thing." Yesterday waved his stubby arms. "Any more pizza?"

"What do you mean there's no such thing? Shade says—" Given what Shade had said about exterminating Nephilim, she'd rather not take her chances on telling a demon anything. Even if she was pretty sure she could take Yesterday. "What do you know about them?"

"Nothing." Yesterday threw his arms in the air. "Because they don't exist. There is nothing to know about them. You know what does exist?" He looked crafty. "Pizza. Pizza exists, and I would like some."

"The hounds finished it." She didn't trust Yesterday. Then again, she didn't trust Shade either.

Yesterday glowered at the hounds. "Why did they finish it? They should be eating souls, not pizza."

"I'm not giving you any pizza." Eddie wanted to lie down on the floor and catch up on the sleep she'd missed last night. Would Dee never get here? Dee would sort all of this out. Eddie had so much riding on Dee doing just that. So much.

"Eddie?" Sophia stood in the doorway looking ridiculously beautiful with early morning light creating a halo around her pale hair. Or maybe that was a real halo. Eddie was getting the nasty sense that angels as she understood them had no interest in fitting in with her image of them. The Sophia/Uriel sending Shade sailing across the greenroom yesterday had as much in common with her image of an angel as a wolf with a Chihuahua.

Eddie had trouble facing her, so she grabbed a stack of prop books and sorted them.

Stepping into the room, Sophia said, "Asmodeus says he spoke to you yesterday."

Speaking of Yesterday, the little yellow fucker had disappeared again.

"Asmodeus and I have been speaking." Sophia picked up teapot and examined it. "He says you are having trouble with what you are."

Hang on now! Nothing had been decided, despite what Shade and Sophia said. She was human. "I'm not a Nephilim."

"Um...Eddie." Sophia gave her big, blue sad eyes. "We have discussed all the alternatives and that is the only one that makes sense."

Made sense to who exactly? "What is a Nephilim?" And then she couldn't resist adding. "And don't forget to mention the part about why they should be exterminated."

"Did Shade say that?"

He most certainly had, and Eddie nodded. It wasn't the sort of thing you forgot, especially not in conjunction with them saying you might be one those things that were exterminated.

"Nephilim are not supposed to exist." Sophia leaned down and examined an antique radio. "Congress between humans and hell princes is forbidden."

"And?" Eddie didn't like the direction this conversation was taking.

"And Nephilim are the product of a...er...relationship between what you humans call a fallen angel and a human." Sophia fiddled with the knobs on the old radio, looking everywhere but at Eddie.

"You mean my mother got freaky with a hell prince, and I'm the result?" Eddie didn't need any more bullshit in her life right now.

Sophia nodded and cleared her throat. "It is the only explanation that makes sense."

"Except for the teeny-tiny fact that if my mother had fucked a hell prince, don't you think I'd know?" Eddie wanted to slap Sophia's hands away from the props.

Straightening, Sophia met her gaze. "Are you sure you would know?"

Eddie would give everything she didn't own to be able to stare Sophia down and tell her that was ridiculous. Except Rosabella had always been unpredictable and had never bothered to explain herself. She'd left her daughter to be raised by Dee without a backward glance. Instead of opening that old wound, Eddie scoffed. "Yes."

"But the truth is, Eddie, that you cannot possibly be all human." Sophia looked so understanding, but it made Eddie want to rage against her. "A bite that kills humans within hours is currently healing on your arm. Not even archangels are totally impervious to a hell prince, and yet you resist Asmodeus."

The hounds stood. One of them flashed Sophia a fang as with a low menacing growl they both flanked Eddie.

Sophia gave them a meaningful look. "And then there is that."

Eddie patted their huge heads. Much as she was getting

fond of the guys, they were not exactly helping the cause right now. "So why are Nephilim exterminated?"

"Eh?" Sophia made a face and parked her perky ass on a sea chest. "The official answer is that Nephilim are unpredictable."

Not her. She was as predictable as they came. "I'm not—"

"In their power and how it manifests." Sophia winced as if she hated shooting Eddie down. "A lot of it depends on the human and what dormant power they might possess." Sophia frowned and tapped a forefinger to her chin. "In your case, your mother is of the guardian blood, so she must have some affinity to the hell gate." She shrugged. "But we have no idea what you can do or how strong you are." She seemed to think something over before nodding, and saying, "I'm not really supposed to tell you this, but in some cases, Nephilim are more powerful than hell princes and archangels."

"Well, I can tell you right now, I can't make people fall all over themselves trying to get into my pants." Not that Eddie would want that power. Much. It might have come in useful once or twice when she'd fallen for someone who didn't even know she existed. Eddie shook her head to clear her thoughts. What was she thinking? She was considering doing what she'd given Shade hell about.

"Shade is not your sire." Sophia shrugged and picked up a duster.

A truly nasty thought wriggled into Eddie's brain. "How can you be sure?"

"I can't." She got up and started dusting a collection of cameras. "But Shade would know immediately upon encountering you. His blood would call to yours."

That was one minor sop to her teetering reality. She addressed the bigger concern. "So why aren't you and Shade trying to exterminate me then?"

"Because the real reason Nephilim are not tolerated has

more to do with prejudice than anything else." Sophia applied her duster with the enthusiasm of someone who was either OCD or was finding dusting a novel experience. If it was the former, Eddie had plenty of places Sophia could work her compulsions out on. "Many of us"—Sophia moved on to some rotary dial telephones—"find the idea of relations with a human distasteful."

"Hey!" Eddie felt the need to defend her species. Human, dammit, she was human.

"Not because there is anything wrong with humans." Sophia held her hand up. "But more because...well, you saw what effect Shade had on darling Lillian. And although angels and princes are susceptible to him, we are not nearly as susceptible as humans." She cleared her throat. "Humans find themselves unable to resist a hell prince's powers. In Shade's case lust, but Lucifer is pride, Wrath is...fairly obvious. Then we have Leviathon and envy, Mammon and greed, Beelzebub is gluttony."

"That's six." Look at her killing the mental math.

"Oh, yes." Sophia flapped her hand. "Belphegor guards sloth. I always forget about her." She made a face. "But she's very quiet, and it's easy to do."

"There are female hell princes?" Although why anything surprised her at this point was beyond Eddie.

"Well...yes." Sophia looked at her as if that were patently obvious.

"But prince is a—never mind." So not the most important issue on the table. "And you say the hell princes aren't evil." Eddie had to shake her head at that clanger. Supernatural, powerful beings running around tossing shit like greed, envy, and gluttony about. Sounded like a real party.

"Your view of good and evil is narrow." Sophia had moved on to an eclectic mix of vases. "All these things that you deem as evil: lust, pride, wrath, avarice, envy, gluttony, sloth. They are merely facets of the journey of a soul to reach its wholeness. It is the same with the seals we archangels guard. The facets we guard were deemed by you humans as good, but even they can have a negative effect in excess." Sophia moved music and jewelry boxes out of the way of her duster, which was moving itself. No biggie. "Imagine someone who is excessively charitable for instance." *Wisp, wisp, wisp,* went that self-propelling duster. "They can cause as much damage to themselves as someone who has an excess of gluttony." She gave Eddie a minatory stare. "Humans need to start seeing things in a truer perspective."

Easy for Sophia to say. She was working with a much fuller dossier. "Back to the humans are gross thing." Eddie couldn't keep the edge out of her voice.

"Not gross." Sophia held up one finger like a governess. "Merely susceptible, particularly the younger souls. They are unable to help themselves, and having congress with them is like...er...a human adult preying on a child."

"Ugh." Eddie was running out of stretch now. Good news would be great at this point. "So, you're saying that my daddy is the hell prince version of a pedophile?"

Sophia grimaced. "That is oversimplifying the matter, but it is frowned upon to prey on a being with fewer defenses."

Potato-potahtoh. "Great."

SEVENTEEN

Eddie got back from the grocery store to find a black sedan parked outside the theatre's stage door. It wasn't a vehicle she recognized, and given how surprises were working out for her lately, she kept an eye on the sedan as she parked.

As she was hauling her groceries out of her trunk, a man in a dark suit and shades climbed out of the passenger side of the sedan. Tall, straight-backed, with dark hair graying at the temples, Eddie had never seen him before. The driver's door opened, and his younger twin emerged. They stood by their vehicle surveying the back of the Edwardian building which housed the theatre.

"Ms. Ward?" The older man removed his shades and tucked them in the breast pocket of his suit jacket.

Call her paranoid or merely suffering from an overactive imagination, but Eddie was getting *Men In Black* vibes with these two. The hair on her nape prickled, and she took a step closer to the door. "Can I help you?"

"I think it best if we talk inside," the older one said.

His buddy stood with his hands folded in front of him and his head turned in her direction. Although she couldn't see his eyes, Eddie would bet her groceries he was staring right at her.

Having faced down a rakshasa demon, whatever the hell —*arf, arf*—that toad thingy was, an imp, two hellhounds, a hell prince, an archangel, and a pissed off diva, Eddie wasn't about to roll over for two suits. "That would really depend on what you're doing here and why you want to see me."

"Ms. Ward." He straightened the cuffs on his jacket. "I'm afraid I'm going to insist we have this conversation inside. Preferably somewhere private."

"Yeah." Still not going to let these suits into her theatre. "And I'm going to have to insist you state your business before that happens."

The younger man took a determined step in her direction. His companion put out his arm to stop him. "No need for that, Oliver." He gave Eddie a thin smile. "Not at this point. Actually, Ms. Ward, we are here to speak with Deandra Ward. She will know who we are."

With spidey senses tweaking, Eddie played dumb. "Dee?"

"That is correct." Tall, dark, and intimidating nodded.

"She's not here right now." And she stopped there. "If you leave a name, or your card, I can make sure she gets back to you."

"Inside." The younger shifted his jacket aside and revealed a handgun holstered to his side. "Now."

Eddie had seen prop guns aplenty, but this might be the first time she was actually looking at a real gun, as in one that could make her dead or very, very sore. Rock meet hard place. Putting aside, for a very brief instance, these two were giving her a squicky feeling, inside that theatre she had a handful of other problems—see the list of what made her so brave in the parking lot.

Not-gun guy stepped forward. "Edme, we know." He leveled her with a heavy look. "We know what this theatre masks. We are guardians."

"What now?" *Shit, shit, shit, shit, double shit.* Maybe if she pretended she didn't know what that meant, they would go away. And how had that been working for her lately? Refer again to the list of what made her brave, currently infesting her theatre. How was it taking so long for Dee to get back from Alaska?

The bogeyman was now at the door, and Eddie was out of room to tap dance.

"Edme." He shook his head at her. "You live here with Rosabella and Deandra. You were born here and have been raised here. While I commend your diplomacy, I also have to ask you to stop trying to bullshit us." He nodded to the stage door. "I suggest we take this inside."

"Inside?" The place Dee had impressed on her they absolutely did not want the guardians to be.

He stared her down. "Inside." Turning to the younger man, he motioned Eddie's grocery bags. "Make yourself useful, Oliver."

Oliver's faced tightened as if he'd rather be shooting people than being useful, but he snatched her bags from her hands and marched to the door.

Staring at him standing there with her toilet paper and peanut butter, Eddie weighed her options. Dee had told her never to contact the guardians, but they'd pretty much rendered that moot by arriving here anyway. Hand to her heart, she'd never called them, yet here they were. The other part of that warning had been that she never tell them she was the one guarding the hell gate now while Dee lived out her fantasy of younger men and cruises. They still didn't know that part.

Eddie had grown up keeping the secret of the hell gate, and as they were guardians, there was no point in trying to keep it secret from these two. They already knew it was here and what it did. In fact, they probably knew more about it than she did.

A faint glimmer of hope shone through her clouds. These were the guys with the answers. They were human right? Just like her—maybe. They were also the guys who could possibly clear her little problems out for her.

Palming her keys, Eddie approached the stage door and opened it.

They followed close on her heels.

"Edsie!" Lillian fluttered down the corridor toward her. "Edsie, I have a huge problem." She stopped when she caught sight of the two men with her. "Oh, hello." She held out one elegant, pale hand. "Lillian Hampstead." She giggled. "Aka Lady Macbeth."

"*Macbeth*?" Oliver growled. "You're doing *Macbeth*?"

"We are." Lillian flashed her gleaming white smile and fluttered her lashes. "Such a masterful piece of theatre, and we shall do our best to do it justice."

Oliver glowered at her. "Deandra knew to never—"

"I must say when Bianca first suggested it, we had our doubts." Lillian laid her hand against the cleavage threatening to make a break for it over the bodice of her fire-engine red top.

"Chris Fellows." The older guardian shook Lillian's outstretched hand. "And you look familiar to me."

"Oh, well." Lillian fluttered and giggled. "I did start out as a professional actress before I found my higher calling of wife and mother." She wrinkled her nose at him. "Of course, that was years ago."

"It can't have been that many years." Chris turned on the charm with a full wattage matinee-idol smile.

"Stop." Lillian playfully batted his arm. She eyed the two men with interest. "Are you friends of our Edsie's?"

"Long time acquaintances." Chris maneuvered himself between Eddie and Lillian. "And if you'll excuse us, we need to catch up."

Before Eddie could register how he'd done it, she was marching down the stairs to the basement, with Oliver on her heels.

When they reached the basement, both men dug out a phone and opened an app Eddie shouldn't have had access to.

Oliver nodded at Chris. "The hell gate has been active recently."

"Are we surprised, given the play being performed?" Chris turned to Eddie. "Have either you, your grandmother, or your mother had a recent encounter with a witch?"

"A witch?" Eddie was ashamed of the squeak that came out of her mouth. "You mean, other than the witches in Ma—the Scottish play?"

Oliver sneered. "Don't play dumb, Ms. Ward. Our records also indicate that you have never been to training camp. Got an explanation for that?"

She really didn't, and Eddie shook her head.

"Could you call your grandmother?" Chris glowered at her. "She does need to be here to explain the recent activity and why it hasn't been reported through official channels." He sighed. "To be truthful, Edme, there are so many irregularities around his facility, I'm surprised we haven't sent a team out to check on it before."

She had no idea where Dee was, but then, neither did they. Eddie dug out her phone. "I can try."

She kept the screen hidden from view as she pressed Dee's number.

"Voicemail," she reported as Dee's message played. "I can send her a text."

"And warn her that we're here?" Oliver took a threatening step closer.

Eddie didn't like the way he was looking at her, and she especially didn't like the large crystal dagger he'd produced from his inner jacket pocket.

"Do I need to warn her?" Eddie kept her eyes on that sparkly, deadly looking knife.

"We have an issue here, Edme." Chris gave her an apologetic look. "You appear to have access to information you shouldn't. And as Oliver said, you have never received any guardian training." He spread his hands palms up. "It really is nothing personal, but I'm sure you can appreciate the problem if some of this information escaped to the general public at large."

"Umm." Eddie stepped back. She wasn't at all comforted by the fact that it wasn't personal. With Oliver heading her way with that goddamn knife, it felt intensely personal. "I really don't know that much."

"You know too much." Chris motioned the door to the hell gate. "You are clearly aware of what that door hides."

She shook her head. "No, I don't. Dee always told me never to come down here."

"And yet you have shown no surprise at the mention of levels of activity around the hell gate." Chris looked almost apologetic. In a homicidal kind of way.

Dammit. She knew she should have taken acting lessons. "That doesn't prove anything?"

"Edme." Chris shook his head. "Our understanding is that you have been unofficially operating this hell gate without certification."

Operating the hell gate. How the hell did one operate a hell gate? "No, I haven't."

"You should listen to her," Shade drawled from the basement door. "She's fairly clueless if you want to know the truth."

"Asmodeus," Oliver hissed and rounded on Shade with the knife.

Shade kept his eyes on the knife. "A heaven forged weapon? Is that necessary?"

The conversation was mostly gibberish to Eddie, but she was relieved that Shade was there. That, more than anything, was a mark of how crappy this situation had become.

"And I prefer to go by Shade." Shade straightened and sauntered closer to Eddie.

She resisted the urge to hide behind him. Shade was not a safe place for her to run.

"You know the rules, Shade." Chris folded his arms. "You cannot be here."

"I do know the rules." Shade shifted his shoulder in front of Eddie. "And doesn't that make you a little curious as to why I am here?"

"Irrelevant," Chris snapped.

Oliver moved so quickly Eddie had barely registered it before the crystal dagger was sunk in Shade's chest and he dropped to the floor.

"What have you done?" Eddie dropped to her knees beside him.

Shade's eyes locked on hers, his hand twitched convulsively around the dagger's hilt. "Don't trust them," he whispered. "Don't trust them just because they're human."

"Hell princes are not allowed on this plane." Chris stood over Shade with a dispassionate expression. "Neither are archangels." He glanced at Oliver. "If Shade is here, Uriel can't be far behind."

Shade's gaze locked with hers. Blood bubbled on his lips, but he seemed to be beseeching her. He tried to speak, choked, and coughed up blood.

"Is Uriel here?" Chris crouched down to her eye level. "Edme, do you know where Uriel is?"

"No." She shook her head. Shade had gone gray and was looking worse by the second. He gave her an approving nod. "What have you done to him?"

"Heaven wrought weapons are poisonous to hell princes." Chris stared at Shade. "You must understand, Edme. They have so much more power than us. They're not like us. They don't think like us, and they do not value us as equals. We have a few tricks to equalize things between us."

"What things?" Eddie wanted to yank the dagger from Shade's gut. "You're killing him."

Chris laughed and stood. "Oh, Edme, you know nothing. Only another hell prince or an archangel can kill a hell prince." He toed Shade with his tasseled loafer. "Us wielding heaven wrought weapons merely hurts them enough to make them easier to handle." He chuckled. "We have a theory on how our weapons would impact Nephilim, but they're so rare and not enough information has been gathered."

Eddie froze.

Shade's gaze met hers. Pain registered in the gray depths of his eyes, but also that plea again. He was asking her to keep silent about what she was.

Chris turned to Oliver. "Toss him back."

"No!" Eddie threw her torso over Shade. "You can't do that. We don't know what will happen to him if you do."

"Not really my problem, Edme." Chris shook his head. "I see you have fallen under his spell, which is unfortunate." He gave her a disparaging look. "You do realize that he is the embodiment of lust. Like most women, you are incapable of thinking past your unruly hormones."

Eddie was torn between her desire to rip his fucking throat out and protecting Shade. Now she was definitely not telling them where Uriel was.

Chris moved behind her. "Apologies, Edme, but I have no choice."

An shock sizzled through her neck followed by a hard *click*.

Shade's eyes widened on the collar around her neck.

"What are you doing?" Eddie grabbed at the collar. It made her hands tingle and she dropped it.

Chris gathered her hands and yanked them behind her back.

Only then did it occur to her to fight, but it was too late. Cuffs clicked shut on her wrists.

"Those are also heaven wrought," Chris said. "You won't escape them."

Through a haze of panic, Eddie watched him grab Shade's leg and drag him through the door to the hell gate.

The hell gate flared, and Chris shoved him through.

"That's it." He stood and dusted his palms. "Now we wait for Deandra to explain." He glanced at Oliver. "Find that fucking archangel. She can't be far."

EIGHTEEN

Oliver and Chris left the basement, shutting the door behind them, and taking any available light other than the slight glow of the hell gate.

Eddie couldn't drag her eyes away from the hell gate. Shade was an asshole, and she shouldn't care that he was now in hell, gravely injured and vulnerable to Wrath. And yet, she did care. She tried moving, and shocks lanced through her neck and arms from the cuffs and the collar. She experimented and managed to butt shuffle to the nearest wall.

Soft padding sounded from above to her right. Four glowing red eyes materialized out of the dark above the propane tanks, and then came the two hounds they belonged to. Graceful, despite their size, they dropped to the floor beside her. Eddie wanted to cry with relief at the sight of them.

The hound who reached her first sniffed at her collar and recoiled. With a doggy groan, he lay down beside her, his huge body pressed against her leg. The second hound dropped into place on her other side and put his big head on her lap. "We're in trouble here, guys."

Hound one twitched an ear. "I'm glad you guys are here." She pressed her head against the wall. She could barely move, and she couldn't stand. It felt like the strength was being leached from her muscles. The warm press of the hounds was comforting. She needed something to distract herself. "I really should give you guys names."

The head on her lap raised and red eyes locked on her. "How about Spike?"

He lifted a lip and flashed a fang.

Not Spike then. "Fluffy?"

The other hound growled and pawed her leg.

"Not Fluffy either." She strained her ears for any sound from the theatre, but the silence was broken only by the low hum of machinery. Where were those guardian shitheads now, and what were they doing to her theatre? God, she hoped Uriel had found a good place to hide. "I don't suppose you guys could warn Uriel?"

Not Spike gave her a pitying glare. With nothing else to do, she studied his broad face. "I think something strong and noble. Definitely dangerous."

He nodded and his eyes gleamed.

It hit her suddenly. "Cronus?"

The hound cocked his head and then grunted and lay his head back down on her lap.

She turned her attention to the second hound. "Now we need something similar for you. I'm assuming here that you're as opposed to Fluffy or Spike?"

It gave her a pitying look. "Mars?"

He growled.

"Atlas?" The hound might have rolled his eyes.

"Zeus?"

Cronus growled this time. Maybe they knew their mythology.

Anything could be happening while she was stuck down here. They could be laying a trap for Dee, but Eddie couldn't reach her phone. It lay on the floor about three feet away from her feet, the screen lighting up every now and again with incoming notifications. Had rehearsal started yet today? Had anyone noticed she was missing? Lillian had seen her with the guardians. Surely, she would start to ask where Eddie had gone. Pardon her—Edsie.

Jesus, she despised that nickname. She was starting to understand why the hounds were getting fussy over the naming game. "Xerxes," she said.

Xerxes winked at her and stuck his tongue out the side of his mouth like a particularly vicious and edgy looking golden retriever. "Xerxes it is then."

Cronus and Xerxes. She liked it.

"Pssst."

It came from the same place the hounds had, and Eddie craned her head back as far as the collar would allow.

Yesterday's eyes widened. "What are you doing?"

Really? *Really!* She let the sarcasm load up her voice. "Hanging out with the lads."

"Well." Yesterday leapt down from the propane tank. He eyed her collar. "That does not look well."

"Can you take it off?"

Yesterday snatched his hands behind his back. "Oh, no, no, no, no, no." He wrinkled his nose. "Heaven wrought. Can't touch that." He tilted his head. "In fact, I am not sure why they are not burning you to a crisp."

"They do that?" Eddie had definitely felt a sparking sensation when Chris the cocksucker had put the collar on.

Xerxes snarled at Yesterday.

Yesterday leapt back. "I'm from hell." He shrugged. "What do I know of heaven wrought objects?"

Dammit! She changed tack. "Can you warn Uriel?"

"Oh, Uriel knows." Yesterday waved an airy hand. "She knew the guardians were here before you did. She is not stupid enough to be caught by the guardians."

Which said what exactly about her? It was too depressing to contemplate. She needed to get these bloody heaven things off her and get out of this basement. The how escaped her. Time dragged by, her ass cheeks grew numb, and she may have dozed off.

Footsteps sounded outside the door. "Hide," Eddie whispered to the hounds. She was not letting the guardians get their hands on her lads. The hounds leapt atop the propane tank and disappeared into the darkness.

Yesterday followed.

Knowing they were there gave her a smidge of hope that the situation wasn't one hundred percent dire.

A crack of light opened around the door. Eddie blinked at the suddenly bright light surrounding a tall, male figure. Chris snapped on the overhead light and momentarily blinded her.

"There you are." He chuckled as if he'd made the most hilarious joke ever. "I hope your time alone has given you a chance to reflect." He snort laughed. "Reflect? Get it? No light?"

Eddie had no idea how long she'd been down there. It would have to be way longer for that joke to even raise a titter from her.

Chris strolled closer. "I have a few questions for you."

"I don't know anything." Eddie shifted closer to the wall. If she was in real danger would Xerxes and Cronus protect her? That would put them in danger. She tried to check out the darkness surreptitiously. "You even said so yourself."

"Don't be obtuse, Edme." Chris's tasseled loafer nudged her thigh. "I will get the answers to my questions."

Oh, that was a good one. Straight outta the mouth of a

Bond-level villain. "Don't tell me, this will hurt you more than me?"

"No, Edme." He chuckled, and the hairs on her nape sprung to attention. "This will most definitely hurt you more, but don't think I will hesitate to do what needs doing."

Well, that was reassuring. Fucking. Not. "I honestly don't know anything," she whined.

"Interesting." He crouched beside her. "And most interesting of all is that rakshasa bite on your arm. Not only do you have one and are living to tell the story, but it's healing." He flashed his teeth in a parody of a grin. "Why don't we start with that?"

"A what now?" She pulled her best clueless face. "A grasshopper bit me the other day."

"Edme." He clicked his tongue and shook his head. "Let us assume you are speaking the truth, which I highly doubt. When was the last time you were bitten by a grasshopper?"

Creasing up her face, she pretended to think it over. "I was bitten by a spider last autumn, but a grasshopper now..." She looked him dead in the eye as she asked, "What did you call it?"

Chris sighed and stood. "Very well." He took a sparkly knife out of his pocket. "Let's start with something simpler. Where is Deandra?"

"Right here, motherfucker," Dee said.

Chris's eyes widened, he half turned toward Dee's voice. There was a loud *thwack* and he dropped to the floor like a stone.

Eddie got her legs out of the way just in time. She felt not one jot of sympathy for his head pounding into the concrete floor. Shithead had been about to carve into her with his unicorn-sparkly dagger.

"Hi, Eddie-girl." Dee stood where Chris had been with a crowbar in her hand. "It looks like I got here just in time."

"Well done." Uriel sauntered up behind Dee and stared down at Chris dispassionately. "What a thoroughly unpleasant man." She grimaced. "The other one is not much better, but we have him contained."

Contained? What did that mean? Questions for another time. Eddie dropped her chin toward the collar. "They put this thing and cuffs on me. They said they were heaven wrought."

Tutting, Uriel knelt beside her. "I told Gabriel that we should never have given the guardians heaven wrought weapons." She pulled a face. "But Gabriel never listens." She clicked her tongue and shook her head. "Gabriel always knows better than anyone else. It's very infuriating."

She reached behind Eddie's neck, and the collar clicked open. She freed Eddie's wrists next. "I'll just hold on to these." She wrinkled her nose at the collar and cuffs. "No need to tell Gabriel."

Eddie was so fucking happy to see Dee. She scrabbled toward her and flung her arms around her grandmother. "Thank Christ, you're here." She didn't know if you should say Christ in front of an angel but couldn't find a fuck inside her to give right now.

"Oh, Eddie." Dee's wiry arms fastened around her. "Don't cry, darling. I'm here now."

Eddie was shocked to find she was crying. Sobs gummed up her throat and all she could do was nod. She had so many questions, but right now relief was uppermost in her mind.

Uriel cleared her throat. "I hate to be insensitive, but this piece of crap will wake up soon."

"Right." Dee pulled back and cupped Eddie's face. She took a shuddering breath. "Right."

"Let me buy us a moment more." Uriel grabbed Dee's

crowbar and gave Chris another head whack. That put Eddie's potential blasphemy in perspective. She crouched next to Dee. "First things first, where is Shade?"

"They stabbed him with one of those sparkly knives and threw him back." Eddie glanced at the gently swirling hell gate.

"Bugger!" Uriel stared at the hell gate. "I was worried about that."

Eddie had worries of her own. "Dee?" She looked into her grandmother's eyes, searching for the truth. "They said I'm…" She couldn't say that word.

Dee swallowed, her eyes softening behind her pink leopard print glasses and nodded. "Nephilim."

"It's true?" The foundation of Eddie's world quaked. Dee would never lie to her. Except, hadn't she lied by omission all this time? All this time, like her entire life, and Dee had never mentioned a word.

Dee slumped and the corners of her mouth turned down. "I'm sorry Eddie-girl, and I never wanted you to find out."

"But, Dee." Eddie tried to put the right words together. "You told me nobody knew who my father was. That he was one of the men Rosabella dated."

"I couldn't tell you, darling." Dee cupped her face. "Knowing what you are puts you in danger."

"Especially from this lot." Uriel flicked her fingers at Chris. "If you think our lot are intolerant of Nephilim, we're a welcome party in comparison to these fuckers."

Eddie's head reeled. "Rosabella got freaky with a hell prince."

"Well." Dee pulled a face. "You know your mother."

"Hmm." Uriel pursed her lips and sniffed. "Not discriminating I take it."

"Hey!" Dee rounded on Uriel before Eddie could respond. "That's my daughter you're talking about."

Uriel held her hands up. "Sorry, Deandra." She wrinkled her nose. "But a hell prince."

For some crap alone knew why reason, Eddie felt the need to defend Rosabella. "They're hot. At least, Shade is…was." For all they knew he could be in a thousand pieces by now. And that really bothered her. "We need to get him back." She gave Uriel her best no-bullshit look. "You're an all-powerful archangel. You get in there and get him back."

"I can't." Uriel grimaced. "I mean, technically I could, but if I go through that portal"—she blew a breath—"pardon the pun, but all hell will break lose."

"I don't care." Eddie needed Uriel to get some perspective here. "Shade could be dead."

"He's not dead." Uriel tapped her chest. "I would know if he was."

"How comforting," Dee drawled. "Would you know if he was in trouble?"

Uriel shook her head. "No. I would only feel the catastrophic shift in the balance if he ceased to be."

Catastrophic shift in the balance seemed a good enough reason for Uriel to get her shiny ass through the hell gate. "You need to save him."

"It doesn't work like that." Dee gave Eddie's hand a comforting pat. "If Uriel arrives in hell, it will be seen as an attack, and war between heaven and hell will ensue." She cleared her throat. "And earth would get caught in the middle of the battle."

Eddie was tired of information being parceled out. "Maybe heaven and hell should work together, if everything I've been told is true."

"There's a lot you don't understand, Eddie-girl." Dee

glanced at Uriel. "There is a sacred compact in place between heaven, hell, and earth. Any break in that compact would be terrible."

Uriel nodded. "Like apocalyptic terrible." She waved her hands—elegantly, of course. "Like end of existence as we know it terrible." She patted Eddie's shoulder. "Besides, even if I did get permission to journey to hell, I have work to do here. Those guardians will need managing if any of us are going to make it out of this in one piece."

Eddie looked from Dee to Uriel. There was a lot of existence ending threats hanging around. "Well, if you put it that way." And yet Shade was stuck in hell, not at full strength, with Wrath trying to end his ass. "But if Wrath gets to Shade, won't it be the same kind of terrible?"

"It will be." Uriel nodded. "And that's why we need you."

NINETEEN

Xerxes and Cronus flanked Eddie as she stood on the edge of the hell gate.

"You'll be fine, Eddie." Dee gave her an encouraging nod. "You're of hell and earth, and can therefore cross the boundaries without a problem."

At Eddie's feet, the hell gate swirled muddy green and orange. "I thought Nephilim were rare."

"Extremely," Uriel confirmed.

"Then you don't know for sure what will happen if I step through there?" They needed to decide what truth they were going with, especially if they were asking her to step through a portal to hell.

Cronus pressed closer to her side.

"The hounds will protect you," Uriel said. "They will also help you find Shade. They can track him better than anyone."

"But it's hell." Eddie didn't really know why she had to explain this.

"Um, Eddie." Dee stepped forward and jerked her head to a still unconscious Chris propped up against the propane tank.

"I'm fairly sure the guardians are only one step away from putting together what you are." She cleared her throat and winced. "And when they do that, hell might be the safest place for you."

Uriel hummed. "That is certainly true." She plastered a bright smile on her face. "And you know hell is nothing like you think it is."

No, Eddie didn't know that, and neither did Uriel. "How would you know? You've never been there."

"Not true." Uriel held up her forefinger. "I can go to hell by invitation, and I have been there before." Her smile brightened. "It's really a fascinating place. Very interesting."

"You're telling me hell has a great personality?" Eddie edged away from the portal.

Uriel looked confused. "I don't think a place can have a personality."

"Right." Sarcasm was clearly wasted on supernatural beings. Other than Shade. He got that sexy smirk on his face and called her bullshit. He was also a dickhead, and she didn't know why that kept slipping her mind. "Tell me again why I need to go through there."

Dee stepped closer and took her hand. "Eddie-girl, I know this is tough for you to accept, and I'm to blame for that. Maybe I should have told you what you were, but I was trying to protect you." She jabbed a thumb at Chris. "From them." She glanced at Uriel. "And from them."

Giving the hell gate a meaningful glance, Eddie asked, "What about them?"

"Well, one of them is your sire," Uriel said. "We know it's not Shade." She counted on her fingers. "It couldn't be Belphegor, Mammon, or Leviathon because they incarnated as female this time around." She shrugged. "So that leaves Lucifer, Wrath, and Beelzebub."

"See, Eddie." Dee grabbed her shoulders and squeezed. "You only have to worry about three of the seven."

Eddie rolled her eyes. "Great."

"I'd wager on Lucifer. Wrath doesn't do relationships," Uriel said. "And Zeb has been in love with Levi for centuries."

"Who?" She was having trouble keeping all the hell princes straight, and now Uriel was introducing new beings to the mix."

"Oh, sorry." Uriel flapped her hand. "I'm not the only one who hates my name." She gave Dee a significant look. "Elderly, middle eastern men did not do the best job of naming us." She shook her head. "I mean...Uriel. Is it any surprise I prefer to go by Sophia?"

"Look at me, Eddie-girl." Dee clasped her face and turned Eddie to face her. "Don't worry about any of that. This is the crux of the matter as I understand it. Wrath is out to end Shade. Shade is not capable of stopping him right now. If Wrath succeeds, it will create a catastrophic imbalance that could implode the whole fucking lot of us." Dee looked into her eyes. "You following me so far?"

Yep, she was getting the message loud and clear. Eddie nodded.

"I'm a guardian, and Uriel is an archangel. If either of us go through that portal without an invitation, it would be seen as an act of war." Dee clicked her fingers. "War between heaven, hell, and earth...catastrophic imbalance. You still with me?"

"Uh-huh." Eddie swallowed past the lump in her throat.

"You're Nephilim, so you could be more powerful than the lot of us."

"Um...Dee." Uriel held up her hand. "That remains supposition at this point."

"Get over it," Dee snapped at Uriel. "You're not the biggest dog in the fight."

Xerxes gave a doggy chuff and lolled his tongue out at Uriel.

Dee turned her attention back to Eddie. "Darling, I would never send you through that portal if I thought it wasn't safe for you. Is there danger?" Dee nodded. "Absolutely. Do I think you're strong enough to survive it?" Dee nodded again. "I would not even be thinking about sending you through there if I didn't."

"And take this." Uriel handed her the crystal knife. "It will help even the odds if you need it."

Eddie eyed the weapon with misgiving. The cuffs and collar had sent electric type shocks through her. "That's made from the same stuff as the cuffs and collar, right?"

"Yes." Uriel nodded. "But if you keep your grip on the handle, it'll be fine. If you were a demon or hell prince, however..." She grimaced.

That handle didn't seem thick enough to block the nasty tingles. "You sure about that?"

"Just keep the blade from contacting your skin directly." Uriel tore a strip from Chris's shirt and wrapped the blade. Then she tucked it into the waistband of Eddie's leggings. "None of the nasties down there can touch it. It'll scare the crap out of them."

Eddie did not like the sound of nasties but she couldn't feel anything from the dagger. "What—"

"She'll be fine." Yesterday dropped from the top of the propane tank and used Chris's head as a steppingstone. "Because I will be her guide."

Dee and Uriel stared at him.

Undeterred, Yesterday swaggered over to Eddie's side. "Yes, I am an imp. Yes, I have been here all this time. And yes"—he jabbed a stubby thumb at his chest—"I know all Eddie needs to know to survive hell." He took a deep breath and grabbed

Eddie's hand. "You're going to want to take a deep breath. Now!"

Sooo...this was hell. Who knew?

Not a flaming lake or a fiery pit in sight. Just a lot of gray dusty emptiness. She'd been expecting...more. The ground was gray, the sky was gray, and the silence was absolute. She swore she could even hear the pounding of her heart. "So this is what hell looks like."

"This is not hell." Yesterday rolled his eyes. "This is the portal."

"I thought the hell gate—never mind." She should quit asking questions. Shit didn't get any clearer even when she got answers.

Xerxes and Cronus shook themselves and pricked their ears.

"Eddie." Yesterday dragged out the syllables of her name. "The hell gate is the door, as it were. This," he motioned the barren landscape, "is the passageway."

"Oh-kay." Then there was a doorway around here somewhere. She turned in a circle and took the nothing in. "So where's the door out of the passageway?"

Cronus took off at a slow lope.

Xerxes nudged her thigh, and Eddie followed Cronus. At least somebody knew where to go. She hoped.

Up ahead, Cronus stopped and turned and looked at her.

And then Eddie saw it, a swirling gray vortex that blended with the landscape.

"That's the door?" she asked Yesterday.

Yesterday stared at her askance. "Do you see another doorway anywhere?"

Nope. She saw sweet fuck all, but a mouthy imp giving her 'tude.

Before she could think about it, Yesterday grabbed her hand and stepped into the swirling mist.

Sooo...this was hell. Just to confirm, she turned to Yesterday. "Is this hell?"

"This is hell." Yesterday spread his arms like he was selling real estate.

"It's...hot." Humidity clung to her skin. Lush, verdant growth surrounded them. From the dense foliage, creatures buzzed and chittered. The air smelled fragrant of blossoms and spice. A thousand shades of glossy green, blue, and purple rioted through the jungle around them. Eddie had never been to the amazon, but she had a feeling it might look something like this. "And so jungly."

"This is Shade's demesne." Yesterday still had his hand in hers, and it felt hot and sticky, but she wasn't letting go.

Hazy sunlight filtered through the tree canopy, catching here and there on sprays of virulently colored blossoms. It was verdant and sensual and fertile, and the perfect setting for lust.

She wanted to lie down in the lush vegetation and feel the warmth on her skin. She wanted to watch insects move through the blossoms and feel the ambient warmth wrap around her.

Xerxes snarled and looked at her. He stared pointedly at the ground at his feet.

Enough of the frolicking Eve fantasy, she had a mission to complete.

The feathery plants at Xerxes's feet had been flattened into a roughly humanoid shape. Bright spots of red blood looked garish against the glossy green vegetation. Eddie crouched for a closer look. "Was Shade here?"

Xerxes huffed. Eddie was beginning to recognize the ways they spoke to her. "You can track him, right."

"*Yes.*"

Eddie stared at Xerxes. Had he spoken in her mind?

"*Yes. We are in hell now and can access our full power.*"

"Shit." Eddie jerked back and plopped to her ass in the plants.

Xerxes's tongue lolled out the side of his mouth. "*Was that a command, mistress?*"

He had jokes. Xerxes had jokes.

"What are you doing?" Yesterday stared down at her with a bemused expression on his face.

Eddie had to laugh. And yes, her laughter did have an edge of hysteria to it. "I'm talking to Xerxes."

"Xerxes speaks?" Yesterday eyed the hound with misgiving.

"He said—" Eddie cleared her throat and forced the next words out her mouth. "He said that he has access to his full powers here in hell."

"*He said we.*" Cronus had a deeper, slighter huskier mental voice than Xerxes. "*Meaning you as well. Here, you have access to your full powers as well.*"

"I have powers?" Eddie looked from one hound to the other, and then at Yesterday.

"*He knows not,*" Xerxes said. "*That one likes to pretend he knows all about hell, but he knows little more than you.*"

All things considered, Eddie would take the hounds' word over the imp's.

Cronus nudged her shoulder. "*Ask him when he was born?*"

"*Yes.*" Xerxes chuckled. "*Ask him that?*"

Yesterday did have some inconsistencies to explain. She turned and pinned him with a stare. "When were you born?"

"Really?" Yesterday coughed and scuffed his feet through

the lush greenery. "I think we have more important things to worry about."

Oh, and Eddie recognized an evasion when she heard it. "When were you born?"

He muttered something she didn't quite catch, and Eddie leaned closer. "Say that again."

"Well." Yesterday heaved a massive sigh. "You know I am called Yesterday?"

Oh, no. She better not be putting the right two and two together. "When were you born?"

"The day before I came through the hell gate." Yesterday took a preemptive hop back from her.

"Truth," Cronus rumbled. *"Finally."*

Vegetation bled damp through the seat of her yoga pants, but Eddie didn't move. She let the repercussions of what she'd heard roll through her mind. "If you were born the day before you arrived on earth, how can you know so much about hell?"

"Excellent question, mistress," Cronus said.

Maybe she should object to being called mistress, but Eddie was into it, so sue her.

Yesterday puffed up his chest, reminding Eddie of a plucked chick. "I know everything about hell."

"Lie," Cronus said.

Turning to Cronus, Eddie voiced her fear. "But he's my guide through hell. He told Uriel and Dee that he could guide me through hell."

"Mistress." Cronus pressed his large body against her. *"You have us."*

TWENTY

Eddie lost all sense of time as they followed a fat, lazy green river. Cronus led the way, and Xerxes kept on her heels. Yesterday trotted behind. He'd given up pleading his encyclopedic knowledge of hell a while ago. It could have been hours, it could have been minutes, Eddie had no idea.

She felt good. Strong. And like she could walk forever. Strength surged through her muscles; the air felt wonderful on her skin. The place seemed to beat to a rhythm in time with that of her heart.

"Can we rest?" Yesterday whined from behind her. "I'm hungry."

Eddie didn't feel tired, or hungry. Was this part of her full powers or something?

"*Hide.*" Cronus trotted back to her. "*We will shield your presence.*"

Whatever that meant, but Eddie wasn't going to stand here asking questions when Cronus wanted her to hide, while they were tromping through hell. She dived behind the tangled trunk system of a large tree and pulled the fronds of a fern-like plant over her head. The undergrowth rustled, and Yesterday ducked behind her. "Wrath's demons," he hissed. "Stay very quiet."

He had Eddie at demon.

The hounds crouched on either side of them, Xerxes pointing his rump at Yesterday in a way Eddie was willing to swear was no accident.

The bass murmur reached her first. Their voices were harsh and guttural, but Eddie didn't dare take a peek.

"*Lower demons,*" Cronus said. "*As stupid as they are ugly.*"

Now she desperately wanted to see what they looked like. She remembered the creatures from her dream of them beating up Shade.

"I smell that imp," one of the demons said.

Xerxes glared at Yesterday accusingly.

It could be any imp. One glance at Yesterday's face, and Eddie came down on the side of nope. They were definitely talking about him. He'd told her he'd had some trouble in hell. Just what kind of trouble had the little shit stirred up down here?

"*We need to leave the imp,*" Cronus said.

Tempting, but she couldn't do it. She tried thinking a thought at him. "*We can't do that.*"

"*We?*" Cronus stared at her. "*I can assure you that Xerxes and I could leave him happily.*"

"He is near," a second demon said. "The scent is still strong."

"*You are sure you cannot leave him?*" Cronus asked.

Getting more tempting. Tempting-er. No, definitely more tempting.

Loud sniffing interrupted her mental babbling. How big

was that demon's nose that she could hear the air whistling through his nasal passages? "There is something else."

Grunting and growling followed. "What is that?"

"I'm not sure."

A low, rumbling growl made the hair on Eddie's nape stand on end. "Hell hound," a demon snarled. "Asmodeus's vermin are near."

Vermin? How dare they. I mean, the hell hounds wouldn't win a beauty competition against a golden retriever, say, but she would hardly call them vermin. She gave Cronus a reassuring pat to let him know she didn't consider him vermin at all.

"The opinion of a lower demon is nothing to me." Warmth tingled in her mind, almost like he was trying to comfort her. *"They are to me as what you would call a cockroach is to you."*

The need to peek burned in her. From the sounds of their voices and footsteps, those demons were big.

"Stay down." Cronus stared at her. *"They cannot know what you are."*

"We must tell him the hounds are here," a demon said.

"Who's he?" Eddie thought at Cronus.

"I am guessing Wrath."

"If the hounds are near, then Shade must be," another demon said.

A raspy-voiced demon said, "There is the scent of another. A scent I do not know. Could it be what the master seeks?"

Which meant they didn't have Shade. And that, at least, was good news. Bad news was that last bit from the one who sounded like he smoked four packs a day.

"Could it be me they're talking about Wrath looking for?" That time she'd dreamed of Wrath, he'd looked right at her, like Shade had.

Cronus pressed closer to her. *"We cannot know for sure."*

"We also cannot afford to assume it is not," Xerxes said.

Feet stomped, vegetation rustled, and the demons' voices grew more distant.

Eddie risked a quick look. Naked, muscular backs were moving away from her. And that's where the vaguely human thing ended. The demons' bottom halves were a mix of hooves, claws, and flippers. Their skin colors ranged from dark gray to burgundy, with a disturbing mixture of scales, spikes, and feathers in some cases.

"They know we are here," Xerxes said. *"We will need to be more careful."*

"They know about him." She jerked her thumb at Yesterday. The two of them were due for a little heart-to-heart. "And they know about you. And they could have picked up on me."

Yesterday snorted. "Let's not let them get any clearer on you."

The inside of Xerxes and Cronus's minds remained carefully blank.

Yeah, that was not good.

"There is another thing that is not good." Cronus padded forward, his large muzzle swinging side to side. *"This is Shade's demesne, and Wrath's demons should not be here."*

"We need to find Shade and get out of here." Eddie dropped into step with Cronus.

"Agreed," he said and nudged her to get her moving.

Turns out Cronus had all sorts of opinions, and now that she could hear his thoughts, was not shy to share them. Over the course of who knew how many hours, she learned that Wrath was an asshole, and he and Shade did not get on. If you could call routinely attempting to disembowel and or flay each other not getting on—and Eddie rather thought you could. However, Wrath's latest attempt to win the never-ending war between the two demesnes had been particularly brutal, and

Wrath appeared to be going for the no more Shade option, which was problematic for reasons Uriel had mentioned, and Cronus chose to repeat at length.

With Shade's disappearance—cue him coming through the hell gate into her theatre—the violence had escalated, and Wrath's demons were making a new home for themselves. Shade's demons, including the hounds, were not at all happy about their new tenants and were looking to make them leave as soon and as violently as possible. Violence seemed to be a big thing here, and given that here was hell, it shouldn't be at all surprising.

What did surprise her was the lack of brimstone, sulfur, and flaming tar pits.

"Each demesne is an outward manifestation of its prince," Cronus told her, after a look scornful enough to make Eddie want to check she wasn't wearing her undies over her leggings. As they tromped along beside the languid green river with living thingies chittering, chattering, and clucking around them, Eddie had a foray into fantasy that maybe gluttony's demesne looked a bit like Willy Wonka's chocolate factory. She could totally go for a chocolate river.

Xerxes had been scouting around them for most of the journey, and he reappeared to their left. *"Village ahead,"* he said. *"She is hungry and should rest."*

She was hungry, but not tired, which was odd considering the big pink ball in the sky that passed for the sun here had made its way all the way across the sky, and now long purple and blue shadows were creeping across the land.

"I can keep going," she said to Xerxes.

"You have power here." Cronus said, *"Your hell prince side is active in this realm, and it lends you greater strength and powers."*

"What powers?"

Cronus gave a canine shrug. *"We will know only when they manifest. Nephilim are an unknown quantity."*

"Like shooting fireballs out my eyes and stuff? Or being able to pick up buildings and toss them at Wrath? Or maybe I can fly?" Eddie would like to be able to fly.

Xerxes snorted, and Cronus gave her another of his scathing looks and said, *"You don't have wings."*

Just to be clear, Eddie stayed on topic. "But the eye fireballs could happen?"

"We will need to get you something to eat," Cronus said and stopped. He looked at her hopefully. *"Unless you hunt."*

"Nope." She gave Xerxes her own hopeful look. "Maybe you could hunt for me?"

"What we hunt, you could not eat, mistress," Cronus said.

Which was probably a good thing, considering she had no way of cooking anything and certainly didn't fancy the idea of disemboweling and skinning, descaling, or plucking whatever they found for her. "It's fine. I can go a bit longer."

"We know not how long it will take us to find the master." Cronus stared at Yesterday.

Yesterday blinked at him. "What?"

"We need a cloak or something to disguise the mistress."

"Disguise?" That sounded ominous. The only reason she would need a disguise was if she was planning to wander around amidst demons, and she definitely didn't have that in mind.

"The village up ahead is quiet," Xerxes said. *"We can purchase something for you to eat and move along."*

"Yesterday can go and get me something." Quiet or not, Eddie didn't want to hang out with demons.

Xerxes nudged Yesterday with his muzzle. *"This one stinks of Wrath."*

"Hey." Yesterday threw his stubby arms up to stop himself from face planting. "Why don't one of you two go?"

Excellent question, and Eddie waited for the answer.

Both hounds blinked at her, and then Cronus said, *"We are hell hounds."*

"And?" She was going to need a bit more than that.

"The master deploys us to harvest demon souls. If we enter that village, there will be widespread panic," Cronus said.

"Night is falling," Xerxes said, and then trotted back into the heavy growth as if that explained everything.

"Demons are more powerful at night," Cronus said. *"Wrath will be hunting for us, and by extension, you. We need to get you some food and find somewhere safe for the night."*

Eddie ignored her growling belly. "If Wrath's demons are everywhere, then that means they could be in that village. And the closer I am to other demons, the more chance there is I can be discovered."

"She has a point," Yesterday said.

Cronus growled and snapped his massive fangs at Yesterday.

On a yelp, Yesterday disappeared into the bushes. "I'm just saying."

"You are Nephilim; your scent is not recognizable here, and your human half needs to eat," Cronus said. *"Your hounds are not content for you to be hungry."*

Her hounds. She did like the sound of that.

"And we have nothing for you to eat," Cronus said.

"I'm not that hung—" Her belly growled and made a liar out of her before she could finish that sentence. "It won't be the first time I've missed a meal." She looked around her at the verdant growth. "There must be something here I can eat. Find us somewhere safe for the night, and I'll forage as we go."

"The master will not be happy about you going hungry either," Xerxes grumbled.

"Shade will have to suck it up." Eddie put on her big girl stage manager voice. "It's getting darker as we stand here and debate. Let's find a place to rest for the night."

"I can show you what to eat." Yesterday swaggered forward.

Cronus snorted and rolled his eyes. *"That one is incompetent. You should allow me to ingest him."*

"Nope." Eddie was reasonably sure on this point. "No ingesting."

"Who's ingesting what?" Yesterday popped out of the undergrowth with a handful of berries. "These are perfectly safe for you to eat."

Cronus gently pushed her aside and sniffed the berries. *"He speaks the truth."*

"There we go then." Eddie accepted the berries and made a great show of eating them. "See, I'm not even hungry anymore."

Pretty true, considering her stomach felt like her throat had been cut.

THE HOUNDS LED her to a small grotto beneath a waterfall as the last of the day's light was waning. Eddie sank to the soft sand with a sigh of relief. Thank goodness she'd worn comfortable shoes because she must have walked about a thousand kilometers. Maybe not that many, but a lot in any case.

"We should be safe here for the night." Cronus settled down beside her.

A gentle spray from the falls covering the grotto entrance had dampened the sand behind it, but didn't extend far enough to reach her. She was dry, she had the hounds, and she had a safe place to sleep. It wasn't really all that bad. With night falling, though, Eddie's nerves started to tweak and jitter at her. Cronus had said hunting demons were more active at night. She'd never slept out in the open, never even been camping, and she felt exposed and vulnerable.

Cronus curled his big head around her hip. *"We will not allow anything to happen to you."*

She didn't want to think about all the things that might happen to her, so she pointed to the falls. "Is the water safe to drink?"

"Oh, yes." Yesterday swaggered over to the falls and stuck his hands into the middle of it. He made a big business of slurping water out of his hands. "See, perfectly safe."

Eddie wasn't about to trust her life to him, so she kept her attention on Cronus.

"The water is safe," Cronus rumbled. *"And the imp can go out and forage for more fruit for you."*

Yesterday trotted to the back of the grotto, dropped to the ground and curled into a small ball.

"He's tired." Eddie didn't have the heart to send him out into hell's night. "And I can wait until morning."

"You are too soft," Xerxes settled himself at the grotto's entrance. *"He would be treated more roughly in Wrath's court."*

Eddie settled herself as comfortably as she could and rested her head on her hands. "Blame it on my human side."

BETWEEN HER HUNGER and sleeping rough, Eddie didn't expect to sleep well, but the next moment Cronus was snuffling in her ear. *"Wake, mistress. We should resume our journey."*

Eddie freshened up as best she could with the falling water

and followed the hounds out of the grotto into a soft, balmy morning.

Soft pink light bathed the jungle and glinted off the heavy dew that had fallen on the plants. It was kind of magical and brightened her outlook on the day.

"Xerxes found the master's scent in the night." Cronus padded along beside her. *"We draw closer."*

That was good news, and Eddie's step felt lighter as she forged forward. "Where's Yesterday?"

"Foraging for you," Xerxes said. *"I am not as kind to the infernal pest."*

"You can do the mind speak thing with him?" Eddie hadn't seen any evidence of that the day before.

"No." Xerxes peeled his lips off his massive fangs. *"But these work as well as words."*

Well, yes they would. Eddie's belly chose then to remind her it hadn't eaten since yesterday morning. Yesterday should be all right. He came from hell.

It was cooler in the early morning, and the humidity felt gentle against her skin.

As they walked, she found a few more of the berries Yesterday had given her and they helped appease her hunger. A distraction would help. "Tell me about the other hell princes," she asked Cronus.

And Cronus did like to share knowledge. *"The master's demesne is bordered by Wrath on the east and Lucifer toward the west. Mammon's demesne resides to the north and Bellephegor's to the south. Mammon and the master do not interact much, and Bellephegor keeps to herself."* He paused to take a great sniff of the air before resuming both their walk and his lecture. *"Lucifer and Wrath are even greater enemies than the master and Wrath, and keeping them separate is vital for the balance of hell."*

Eddie wanted to ask why, but Xerxes reappeared with Yesterday dangling from his jaws.

"Put me down." Yesterday wriggled in Xerxes's grip. He waved a small sack at her. "I brought food."

That was reason enough for Eddie. "It's okay, put him down."

Xerxes dropped Yesterday face first into a large lime green bush.

"You did that on purpose." Yesterday struggled out of the thick, twisty branches and sniffed indignantly. "There was no need for that. I found something for her to eat." He waved the sack at Eddie.

"Eat." Xerxes's red eyes glinted at her. *"All is quiet for now, and we can rest."*

He didn't need to tell her twice, and plopping to the ground, Eddie reached for the sack. She withdrew an oblong object that looked like bread and gave it a sniff.

"It is bread," Cronus confirmed. *"And safe for you to consume."*

She took a tentative bite and was pleasantly surprised by a flavor that rested somewhere between pumpernickel and sunflower seeds.

The sack also contained some links of sausage. Not trusting any potential meat products, she offered the links to Yesterday, who gobbled them up in a blink.

A large wheel of a cheese-like substance looked safe enough.

Taking Cronus's nod of approval as the go ahead, Eddie bit into the cheese. A rich, smoky flavor had her taking a second bite before she could second guess herself. She put any thoughts of what had provided the milk to make the cheese firmly out of her mind. Using the dagger Uriel had given her, she carved off a wedge and jammed it between two hand torn hunks of bread. Turns out, Uriel hadn't lied, if she held the knife by the handle, it didn't cause shitty tingles.

Cronus eyed her knife warily, and his hackles rose as he took a few steps away from her.

A couple more bread loaves in the sack gave her hope for dinner that night. She dearly hoped she'd be sharing them with Shade.

Beneath the additional loaves, she found a large, golden-crusted pie. It smelled like the berries she had been eating, and Eddie's mouth watered.

"I am also hungry." Yesterday fixed his beady eyes on the pie. "I have traveled far to find the food for you."

Eddie took out the dagger to cut him a piece.

"Thief!" A demon burst from the undergrowth.

Yesterday yelped and ducked behind Eddie.

Both hounds lunged for the demon and pinned it to the trunk of a tree. Large, droopy white flowers plopped down around the demon's head as it gaped at the hounds.

Xerxes growled and tensed.

"Stop." Eddie sprang to her feet, sure the hounds were about to do their soul harvesting thing.

"It cannot live," Cronus said. *"It has seen you."*

"Don't end me," the demon blubbered, eyes huge and terrified in its green face. "I didn't know the imp took my food for you."

"It was just lying there." Yesterday peered out from behind Eddie.

"You stole the food?" Eddie couldn't believe it was only occurring to her now to ask where Yesterday had gotten the sack.

Yesterday took a step away from her. "I didn't think it belonged to anyone."

"He took it right from me," the demon said. "I only put it

down for a minute to gather my offspring for their meal."

And then Eddie saw them, two smaller versions of the large green, vaguely reptilian demon hiding in the bushes and staring at the hounds with terror. Looking closer, the demon did have a vaguely feminine quality to her.

"You're their mother?" She motioned to the smaller demons.

The demon blinked at her. "Mother?"

"She birthed them," Cronus clarified, and with that, sealed their fate. Eddie would not be responsible for killing a demon and her children, however odd they looked. "Let her go," she said to the hounds. She put the pie back in the sack with the remainder of the cheese. "I'm sorry. I've already eaten one of the loaves of bread and some of the cheese. And the imp ate the sausage."

"Mistress." Xerxes kept the demon pinned to the tree. *"She could tell others about seeing you and us."*

Eddie pushed past him and held the sack out to the demon. "I'm sorry but I don't have any money to pay you."

"Money?" The demon glanced at the sack and then back at Eddie. "What is money?"

"We have no currency in hell," Cronus said. *"We barter or provide a blood oath as repayment. And you cannot give her blood, or she might guess what you are."*

"I'm afraid I have nothing to trade for what I took," Eddie said.

"You're welcome to what we have." The demon eyed the hounds nervously. She waved her hand at the sack. "Keep it."

Eddie glanced at the children, and she couldn't do it. They could be hungry, and this could be all the food they had. "No, it's fine. Take your food."

The demon snatched the sack from Eddie's hands.

"Let her go." Eddie's tone was more forceful than she

intended, but the hounds backed away far enough for the demon to slide away from the tree.

She edged backward toward the two little ones. "You look human." She clutched the sack to her chest as she stared at Eddie. "But you smell...different."

Xerxes snarled and stalked her.

The demon stumbled back and away from him. "Never mind. You travel with the master's hounds." She kept retreating until she drew level with the children. "I saw nothing. I know when to mind my business."

"It is dangerous for you to let her go," Cronus said. *"We were hoping to avoid notice, and now, word will spread that we are here, and we travel with a being that is part human."*

She thought of her reply to him as the demon gathered her children and ran into the depths of the forest. "Not everything needs to end in violence."

Cronus eyed her with compassion. *"This is hell, mistress. Everything is violent, and nothing about that is unnecessary."*

TWENTY-ONE

The rest of the day passed uneventfully, and Eddie chose to focus on the scenery.

She wouldn't say the hell hounds were angry with her, but they were definitely keeping the communication on a need-to-know basis. Even Cronus couldn't be cajoled into one of his long-winded soliloquies.

Around dusk, Eddie broke. "We couldn't kill a mother with two children."

"Eh?" Yesterday peered at her.

Xerxes rolled his eyes and disappeared on another scouting mission.

Cronus it was then, and Eddie tapped his mammoth shoulder. "It wouldn't be right. If we killed the mother, then who would look after the children?"

"Mistress Edme." Cronus heaved a canine sigh. *"This is hell, and things do not proceed here in the same way as they do on earth."*

At least he was talking to her. "Enlighten me."

"That demoness will have a litter of four to five pups every year. Some will live, most will not. She was a saurian, and they reproduce

at an alarming rate." He glowered at Yesterday. "*And like imps, they are not to be trusted.*"

Still, Eddie couldn't be responsible for the death of someone who happened to have their lunch stolen by the wrong imp. "It wouldn't be right."

"*There is right, and there is necessary,*" Cronus said. "*And here in hell, those distinctions could cost you your life.*"

She couldn't say she was sorry, so she settled for, "I understand, but I'm not made that way."

"*If you want to survive here, you may have to become that way.*" Cronus looked around them and sniffed. "*We will need to find shelter for the night.*"

He didn't bring up feeding her, and given how earlier had gone, she certainly wasn't going to risk raising the issue. "Any sign of Shade?"

"*Xerxes informs me he passed through here very recently.*" Cronus veered off to the right and pushed his way through the dense vegetation. "*There were signs that he was followed, and signs of a fight.*" He turned and looked at her. "*You must prepare yourself, mistress. The master is still gravely injured.*"

"Shouldn't we push on then?" Finding Shade had become more critical than ever.

"*The danger of night is too great.*" Cronus nudged aside some low hanging branches with his head. "*Xerxes is within, and all is safe.*"

Again, hell surprised her with the cave Cronus led Eddie to. Entrance hidden by unruly vegetation, a downward sloping tunnel opened into a wide, humid space. Phosphorescence on the walls and roof lit the space in a gentle blue light. It felt safer than where they'd sheltered the night before.

"*The master was here,*" Xerxes said and found a small nook in the rock and curled himself into a ball.

Cronus was only slightly more cooperative and suggested

she get some rest before he found his own nook and closed his eyes.

Still too keyed up to sleep, Eddie watched them for a long moment before turning away and exploring the cave a bit. A few meters of careful exploration with the hounds still in sight led her to a smaller cave with an electric blue pool in the center puffing out moist warm air.

When in Rome—or a cave in hell—and all that. Eddie tested the water temperature with her hand before giving in to temptation and stripping down and climbing in. Water lapped playfully against her skin as she edged forward. Deciding not to take a chance on the depth, and ignoring the possibility of aquatic beasties, she perched on a submerged rocky ledge and put her head back against the pool lip. Blue light playing across the cave's roof in hypnotic patterns, along with the warm water, lulled away her lingering tension.

With no soap, she did her best to wash off the worst of the grit and sweat and dunked her head beneath the water. Time slowed to the soft trickle of water and the warm touch of the thick air.

The saurian demon had said she smelled of Wrath. Her trip to hell was turning out to be one surprise after another. Not that she had anything to compare it to. The odd trip to Ottawa or Toronto hardly counted as comparable.

As soon as the hounds woke from their naps, they would be off again, and she may as well take their example.

She climbed from the pool and dried herself on her clothes before fighting her way back into them. Leggings versus damp skin—the struggle was a constant. Back in the main cave, she picked a spot between the two hounds and propped her back against the wall.

Cronus belly crawled closer to her and pressed against her side. After some deep grumbling, Xerxes flanked her on the other side. The hounds gave off a lot of heat, and their fur was silky and soft. Eddie's eyelids drooped as her muscles relaxed. As she drifted off to sleep, her bite tickled, and she rubbed it. Was it smaller? She'd thought it might be when she was bathing, but she'd think about that after a quick rest.

"Nephilim." A persistent prodding at her forehead woke Eddie.

Crouched beside her, huge eyes gleaming iridescent in the dark, was Yesterday.

Perhaps it was a comment on the development of their relationship that Eddie no longer demanded he stop that. Yesterday wouldn't listen anyway.

"What?" She swatted his poking finger away.

She was curled into a little spoon with Cronus, her head resting against his belly. Completing the furry circle around her, Xerxes was awake and glowering at Yesterday. The hounds had made a nest for her of their bodies, and she felt rested and strong.

"Wrath's demons are everywhere." Yesterday put a sensible distance between himself and Xerxes. "If you don't get moving, they'll have you surrounded."

Cronus snuffled and yawned. Eddie got an up close and center of rows of serrated, long teeth that reminded her she was using a monster as a bed.

He opened one eye and looked at her. *"You are rested?"*

And hungry, but Eddie kept that to herself. She wasn't up for another hard lesson in hell this morning. "Yesterday says we should get moving."

"He is annoying but not wrong." Cronus shifted to stand, and Eddie clambered out of the hound circle and stood.

Despite a night sleeping rough, her muscles felt fluid and

powerful. This morning, the bite had disappeared into a faded red mark. She rubbed the spot. "My bite's gone."

"You have power here." Cronus got up and did a downward dog stretch that was flat out adorable. *"It will be interesting to see how it manifests further."*

Eddie wasn't sure she and Cronus shared the same definition of interesting.

Xerxes stood, shook himself and stretched, and then padded out of the cave.

As she scrambled into the new day, a breathtaking dawn of lavender and rose greeted Eddie. It struck dew droplets on the vegetation around them and filled the air with tiny rainbows.

"Here." Yesterday tugged at her shirt. He held up a handful of scarlet berries. "You can eat these."

Not prepared to take his word for that, Eddie hesitated. They looked like an enticing cross between a blueberry and raspberry, but given her location, she wasn't taking the chance.

"They are safe," Cronus said. *"For once, the imp has proven useful."*

Xerxes disappeared through the thicket ahead of them and Eddie fell into step with Cronus. The berries were eye-wateringly tart with a slight spicy sweetness that wouldn't make them her first breakfast choice, but they certainly stopped the low complaint growling from her stomach.

She had no idea of time here, and plants blurred into a confusing jumble as they trudged on through the jungle. Occasional bursts of gloriously bright flowers broke the greens, blues, and purples all around her. The hounds had told her the demesne reflected the hell prince, and the jungle did make her think of Shade. If she was the sort to stage the odd orgy, the jungle surrounding her would be a great choice.

She spared a thought for her theatre and what was going on back there. Dee would have it all well in hand, but she did worry. She had no hope of Rodders actually wielding a plunger himself, or Lillian finding a sympathetic ear in Dee. Chris Fellows must have recovered consciousness by now, and she wondered what Dee had done with him.

"Hide." Xerxes dropped out of a tree beside her and nearly scared her to death.

Eddie dived behind an indigo bush that resembled a rubber plant.

She heard them before she saw them and held her breath as a small procession of hooves, claws, and feet passed her hiding spot and disappeared into the jungle.

"Wrath's." Yesterday confirmed for her as they got moving again. "They're everywhere. They even attacked a settlement yesterday and are now occupying it."

Eddie wasn't about to take Yesterday's word on that, so she looked at Cronus.

He nodded. *"Xerxes confirms what the imp says. We will need to avoid settlements until we find the master. He will deal with the interlopers."*

If Shade was in any condition to deal with anyone, and that was a big if in Eddie's mind.

As the sun rose like a giant opal in a crystalline sky, the heat and humidity of the day increased. Eddie's usual choice of black leggings and a black T-shirt felt like they were boiling her like a lobster in a pot. Her hair had turned into a thick, frizzy mass and clung to her sweaty face and neck. Despite sweating like a cheese at a picnic table, Eddie wasn't overly thirsty. They stopped occasionally at streams or water pools to drink, but other than being hot and grumpy, she didn't seem to need much.

Cronus told her which fruits she could eat, and she ate those as they trod on through the forest. It might have been a nice hike, if not for the constant ducking and hiding to avoid roving bands of demons. It seemed like the longer they walked, the more regular the groups of demons became. Some were Wrath's, but others, Cronus and Xerxes were confused by. Demons, she learned, stayed loyal to one hell prince but some of the groups they encountered were a mix of hordes. Neither the hounds nor Yesterday knew what to make of that.

It was another thing to add to Eddie's growing list of stuff she didn't like. She didn't like the heat, she didn't like the hiding, and she didn't like them making her life difficult. Her mission was to find Shade, sort out whatever was wrong with him and get back to her theatre. Her lovely, air-conditioned theatre.

Xerxes's disappearing act was getting annoying as well. She wanted to hang a bell around his neck so he'd quit scaring the shit out of her every time he reappeared. And Cronus never stopped talking. *Yakkity, yak, yak* in her head all the time. Like she cared which part of Shade's demesne they were in, or how far from Wrath's border his demons had traveled. As for the mixed hordes, she didn't know why he insisted on remarking how odd it was, and then going on an endless warbling of speculation. She also didn't need the fucking botany lesson he had going on.

And where was Yesterday? She didn't know why the little turd had bothered showing up in her life at all, if all he did was disappear for large portions of the day. Well, if he got himself in trouble, he could damn well get himself out of it. The hounds were her hounds, for her protection, not taking care of some annoying yellow squirt with a flexible relationship with the truth.

Xerxes was scouting around them, looking for danger,

between sessions of reappearing suddenly and scaring years off her life.

She huffed a tendril of hair out of her eyes. Damn thing drifted back and tried to Velcro itself to her skin. Giving it a yank hard enough to threaten its roots, she tucked the tendril into her ponytail.

"You are well?" Cronus side eyed her with his creepy red eyes.

What was with that? If Shade had created the hounds, couldn't he have done it without the vampire peepers. Those eyes creeped her the fuck out. "I'm hot," she snapped.

"We will stop to drink," Cronus said.

"I don't want to stop for a goddamn drink." Cronus and his stupid suggestions were making everything worse. "I want to find Shade and get out of here." She glared around her, willing the other furry asshole to appear. "I thought Xerxes said we were getting near."

Cronus blinked at her. *"We do draw near."*

"No, we don't," Eddie yelled, and then lowered her voice before one of Wrath's shit for brains demons heard her. "If we were getting close, then we would have found him already. But we haven't, have we? All we do is walk and walk and fucking walk." Her voice had risen again, and she had to breathe deep to get a handle on her temper. She wanted to hit shit, and kick it, and yell at it. Well, she was already doing the latter.

Cronus stopped and stared at her. *"You become incensed."*

"Bullshit." She bit down on her molars to stop from bellowing at him. "I'm hot and sick of walking, and my fucking hair won't stay out of my face." She ripped out her hair tie, taking a handful of strands with it, dragged her hair back until her eyes watered and tied it up again. That would teach it to keep getting in her face.

Xerxes materialized right in front of her.

"Shit!" Eddie leapt eight feet back. "Stop doing that." She glowered at him. "Warn me before you appear, or next time I might hit you. I know krav maga." She jammed her hands on her hips. "I've been to...three lessons, and I can take you out."

Xerxes looked at Cronus.

Cronus stared at her.

"What?" They could stop side eyeing each other about her as well.

Yesterday crawled out from beneath a stupidly pink ferny thing. Why did all the plants here look like the inside of a vagina? Nobody wanted to see that everywhere. He sidled closer to Cronus. "Why is Eddie shouting?"

"I'm right here." Eddie poked his huge, round forehead. "And I'm yelling because you're all pissing me off. This place is pissing me off. Shade is pissing me off, and this whole situation pissed me way the fuck off days ago."

All three of them gaped at her.

"I think you should calm down," Cronus said.

"Oh my god!" Eddie yelled. Her anger ripped free in a glorious, blinding rage. "You did not just tell me to calm down. You did not just say that."

"Mistr—"

"When in the history of assholes telling women to calm down has that ever worked?" She crossed her arms and glared. "Give me one time. Just one. I'm waiting." She tapped her foot for emphasis. Then got tired of waiting because she had a shit ton more to say. "I dare you to ask me if it's my time of the month. Do it!"

"Mistress?" Cronus and Xerxes took a step back.

"The only reason I'm here is because of that overgrown fucking horndog you call master. Here in this pissing oven with these stupid plants." She gave a tree trunk a solid kick and it didn't hurt...much. "This is nothing to do with me. Nothing.

There I was minding my own business, looking after that shitty hell gate because Dee had to go off and get her oil changed by a man young enough to be dating me." She jabbed her chest for emphasis. "And my mother is too fucking flaky to be trusted with a pencil, and suddenly it's Eddie must take care of the hell gate." The unfairness of the situation dripped acid into her system. "Well, Eddie is sick of taking care of shit for other people. Sick of plunging their fucking toilets, lighting their stupid shows, cleaning up after their untalented asses, and listening to their constant fucking whining. Eddie has had enough. Enough!"

Xerxes froze and his head snapped to the right.

Cronus's hackles rose.

And the biggest rhinoceros-like motherfucker Eddie had ever seen crashed out of the forest with his sights set on her.

Cronus bellowed in her head. *"Run!"*

Taking all her bottled-up fury, Eddie shot after Yesterday and the hounds.

TWENTY-TWO

Eddie ran as if she was being chased by an eight-foot behemoth with a head like a rhino and a horn the size of her arm—because she was. Weaving through the forest, leaping over fallen logs, sliding under low hanging branches with a grunting, snorting beast on her tail, it took her a while to notice that the hounds were keeping up with her and not the other way around.

Yesterday had shot up a tree, and she was dimly aware of him crashing through the branches above their heads. At least, she hoped that was Yesterday and not some hideous buddy of Rhino man. For someone who was routinely, and willingly, picked last in gym class, she was doing great. Her muscles responded like eager puppies to her need for speed, breath whooshed smoothly out and into her lungs, and she fell into a hypnotic rhythm. She'd heard about runners experiencing this kind of trance but had put it down to exercise freaks suffering a lack of oxygen to the brain. Hell had turned her into a fitness fanatic, and if that wasn't a metaphor in the making, she didn't know one when she saw one.

She leapt a sparkling stream like a gazelle and kept going. She ducked, weaved, twisted, and turned like a gymnast going for a perfect ten. She was a super-human, running machine, fleet of feet, nimble and—

"You can stop now." Cronus cut into her mental celebration. *"We've lost him."*

Eddie couldn't resist a fist pump to self as her breathing was barely even elevated. She did a couple of hamstring stretches because it seemed like the sort of thing cardio crushers should do.

Cronus eyed her walking lunges with his head cocked. *"You are feeling better?"*

She was feeling better. The heat didn't bother her quite so much, and she didn't feel the need to rip the world a new one.

With a doggy huff, Xerxes pulled another disappearing act.

Eddie fell into step with Cronus, who also looked like he had another three months of running left in him. Guess she'd had the hell equivalent of a mental health walk. Which brought her round to the uncomfortable topic of her earlier grouchiness. "Um...about earlier."

"Your emotions are being affected by hell," Cronus said. *"You are not to blame for your anger."*

Easiest apology she'd ever given, but not an apology at all, so she said, "Still, I'm sorry for being so irritable. Does hell make everyone grumpy?"

"You are Nephilim." Cronus stopped and sniffed the air.

Eddie gave it a go but all she got was heavy, sultry jasmine with an earthy undertone. "Which means?"

"Your reactions could be anything." Cronus shrugged. *"Although it is worth noting that your emotions skewed to anger, which I would have expected in Wrath's demesne. Here."* He swung his head to the forest around them. *"I would have expected an emotional response more closely aligned to lust."*

Eddie shoved that in her brimming box of unanswered questions and kept on walking.

Cronus swung his head to her left. *"Xerxes comes."*

A heartbeat later, Xerxes appeared. *"I have found the master."*

And Eddie's good mood took another leap forward.

EDDIE'S MOOD plummeted as she got her first look at Shade.

They followed Xerxes into a similar cave to the last one, only to find Shade lying in his congealing blood, broken and bloody, beside a small pool.

"It is bad," Xerxes said.

No shit, it was bad. Eddie crouched beside Shade, bile churning in her belly. She wanted to help him but was terrified to touch him.

Cronus threw back his head and gave a long, mournful howl.

"Stop." That certainly wouldn't help and could bring down more of Wrath's demons on their heads.

Stopping mid-yowl, Cronus blinked at her. *"He is in agony."*

But still with them, and some days you had to take your wins as you found them.

"Keep him warm." She motioned the hounds closer. Eddie only knew the bare basics of first aid, and keeping someone warm seemed a good starting point. "Now." She could call and fire multiple lighting, sound, and special effects cues without breaking a sweat, and she needed that Eddie to show up now. After ripping off her T-shirt, she dipped it in the water. "First, let's assess the extent of the damage."

Some distant part of her was panicking, but she kept it on lockdown and wiped away the crusted blood.

"His pain is our pain." Xerxes stared at her mournfully and tipped his head back.

"Nope." Eddie grabbed his snout and pushed it down again. "There will be no mourning howls." Yet. Hopefully never, but she continued to clean Shade's face and torso. Long, deep gashes dissected his ribs and oozed bright, red blood. A jagged tear down to the bone went from his hip to his knee. His breath rattled through the smashed bones of his nose. Fuck, when they went for blood down here, they didn't mess around. The gaping wound from Chris stabbing him with the heaven blade had grown nasty around the edges.

Shade's skin was gray and hot to the touch.

The cons of her situation were clear. The pros: her, two hounds, and a heaven-forged blade, which was useless in this situation.

"Lust." Cronus stared at her over Shade's bruised and blood-smeared chest. *"He heals with lust."*

That may be, but Eddie kept her tone even as she said, "I hardly think he's in any condition for that."

"Your lust," Cronus said with a penetrating gaze. *"Your lust could help."*

"What do you expect me to do?" Eddie had tried to be nice about her explanation. "He's near death, and you want me to get freaky with him?"

Xerxes raised his chin again and inhaled.

"You do that, and I'll stab you," she snapped at him.

She wouldn't—well, she might—because panic was starting to take hold.

"Lust is an emotion." Cronus glowered at her as if she was the one making ridiculous suggestions. *"Feel it."*

"Lustful thoughts?" Eddie surveyed the broken and bleeding form between them. Getting a good fantasy rolling was going to be a problem and felt all kinds of wrong. But given her lack of better options...Eddie took a deep breath and closed her eyes.

"Skin contact is best," Cronus said.

Placing her hands gingerly on a marginally less battered part of his forearm, Eddie screwed her eyes shut. She pictured Shade as she had first seen him, lying beside the hell gate. Nope! He'd been pretty battered that time too. For a near-enough immortal being, Shade seemed to be walking close to the mortal line a lot.

She tried harder. Shade leaning against her bedroom door-jamb, all long, lean, and muscular, exuding CFM vibes.

"More," Cronus whispered.

Shade pinning her against the wall, every hard inch of him pressed against her. His deep, raspy voice in her ear. *"I can do anything I want with you."* His breath warm against her neck. *"Your body is mine to play with."*

And he'd been right. Her body would have obeyed him without question.

Xerxes made a noise like a deep-throated purr.

Her memory leapt to Shade in her bedroom, lying over her and waking her up. The silver glow of his eyes, the taste of him when she'd kissed him—honey and musk—the silk of his hair between her fingers. His hard, hot body rubbing against her, driving her need into a frenzy. She ached for him, more of him, all of him.

Him sitting in her bed, sculpted chest bare, sheets pooling around his trim waist. His hand rubbing his chest, disap-pearing beneath the sheets.

That time he'd stopped, but in her imagination, Eddie let his hand slide beneath that sheet. His hand gripped his shaft, his slate eyes went slumberous, and a flush rode the high jut of his cheekbones as he stroked. He murmured her name as he watched her. She couldn't see beneath the sheets, but she saw the up and down stroke of his hand, watched the tendons flex in his wrist and forearms.

Her imagination stripped the sheets away, and now she could see his hand on that perfect cock as he pleasured himself. She wanted that and more.

She wanted him spread naked on a bed, sweat gleaming off the defined planes of body, his cock erect and straining. Except now, he was spread eagled like a delicious offering in front of her. Red silk ties bound him to the bed posts. The hand stroking him was hers. In her palm, he was hard and velvety. His gaze bored into hers, demanding she touch him, take him, use him. Eddie had no idea where this fantasy had come from, but now that it had bloomed, she went with it. She added a blindfold to those slumberous gray eyes. He licked his lips, arching his back as he fought the restraints. She had the power. She could taunt him, and tease him, promise him what he wanted and then withdraw that offer with a soft laugh.

He was hers to do with as she pleased. Hers to command.

"Eddie?" Shade's voice popped her fantasy like a soap bubble, and she opened her eyes.

He was staring at her with a quizzical expression, almost as if he could... Dear God, let him not have seen what she'd been conjuring up. "Can you read minds?"

"Read minds?" Shade flinched and eased himself into sitting. He was still pale, but much better. "No, but I sensed your lust."

"Your wounds." She leaned closer. Where gaping, jagged wounds had oozed blood, now thick pink scars had replaced them. "They're healing."

"Yes." Shade cricked his neck. "Your lust gave me what I needed to heal." His smirk held only a shadow of his former arrogant expression, but there nonetheless, and she took hope from that. "Told you before, you're like a nuclear reactor."

Feeling vulnerable and exposed on the lust front, Eddie went with a sidestep. "It was all imaginary."

"Imagination is often the best aphrodisiac." And he had to be feeling much better because he followed up with his signature Shade smolder.

"Right." Eddie stepped back and put some space between her and the Shade slow burn. "He's looking better. What now?" She looked to Cronus for an answer.

"The master will tell us." Cronus lay down and lowered his massive head to his dinner-plate paws. *"We are his to command."*

"I'm not," Eddie said, not even in her imagination did she give him control. She stamped down on the erotic images trying to make space in her brain. The dominance fantasy was a whole new playground.

Shade stood, slowly and gingerly, testing out his muscles as he did. "What are you doing here?"

"Well." Eddie kept it short and sweet. "After stabbing you and tossing you through the hell gate, the guardians weren't happy with what was going down and locked me up."

Shade's head shot up and his gaze skewered her. His voice was a low, menacing whisper, "Locked you up."

"But Dee came and freed me." Eddie skipped a few details. "And Uriel and Dee said the best thing to do was send me through the hell gate. One, so I could find you, and secondly, for my own safety." She remembered the dagger. "Oh, and Uriel gave me a special knife."

She searched her waistband for the weapon. Strange. It wasn't tucked into the small of her back where she'd left it. She'd gotten so used to carrying the thing, she hadn't been aware of it, or now, its absence.

"Uriel gave you a heaven forged weapon?" Shade eased a

crick in his lower back. "Forgive my lack of excitement at encountering another one."

He was looking stronger by the minute. It was hard to believe he'd been lying in a puddle of his own blood, barely breathing. If she hadn't been standing there, she might have believed she'd dreamt the entire thing. Maybe she was dreaming. And all of this—the rakshasa demon, the frog thing, Shade, Uriel, her being Nephilim—was all part of some detailed dream.

Except she knew it wasn't, and she turned away from Shade to find the knife. It hadn't slipped out of her pants. She couldn't see it anywhere on the cave floor.

She turned to the hounds. "Do you guys have it?"

"*No,*" Cronus said.

Xerxes narrowed his eyes at her and shook his head.

"Where is it?" The sharpness in Shade's tone brought her hackles up.

"It's here somewhere." Eddie retraced her steps since she'd entered the cave. There was no sign of the shiny dagger. Just because she didn't remember taking the knife out, didn't mean she hadn't done that. She searched the nooks and crannies of the cave, but that didn't take nearly long enough. A nasty feeling wriggled through her. "It's not here."

She remembered distinctly picking it up after her bath in the other cave and tucking it back in her waistband. Now her mind played tricks on her, and half convinced her that she had left a heaven forged blade in a random cave.

"*You had it when we were chased,*" Cronus said. "*You were holding it.*"

"I did have it." Thank God, Cronus had remembered that, because she hadn't. Reaching for the knife had been instinctual.

Shade's chin shot out, and he glowered at her. "But it's not here now? Do you mean you don't have it?"

"It's hardly a cryptic fucking statement," Eddie snapped, done with him and his judgy. Shit, shit, shit. It must have dropped out of her pants. It could be anywhere right now. "It's not here."

"You had it when we entered the cave," Cronus joined the search with his snout to the ground. *"I recall you took it out when we first entered."*

"Yes!" She had done that because traipsing into a cave unarmed had seemed like a spectacularly stupid move. "Then it must be here."

Xerxes shook his head. *"The weapon is not here."*

"It must be." She'd had it in her hand, then she'd seen Shade and crouched beside him. She must have put it down to touch him. The floor beside where Shade had lain was as empty as it had been ten seconds ago. Dread pooled in the pit of Eddie's gut. She'd lost the heaven forged blade. Uriel would have her head for this. Plus, she now had no way to defend herself, and despite Uriel's assurances that demons wouldn't touch the thing, somewhere in this hellscape, some other being could be carrying it around right this minute.

"The imp is also missing," Xerxes said.

Knowing that nothing had changed in the last few minutes, Eddie still looked around the cave. "He was here when we found Shade, and he can't have gone because you would have seen him leave."

Cronus shook his head. *"We were not paying attention to him. We had entered a trance state to amplify your emotion."*

"You mean he walked out of here, and none of us saw him go?" Eddie had seen Yesterday almost disappear into thin air at the theatre, but why would he go now? "He wouldn't leave me.

He promised Dee that he would be my guide, take care of me." She couldn't believe Yesterday would steal from her.

Except...

"He's part of Wrath's court." Shade's jaw set in a grim line. "And imps lie. So, we can be reasonably certain if Yesterday did take the blade, he's heading to Wrath with it."

TWENTY-THREE

They were arguing about what to do next—Eddie made a compelling case for back to the theatre—when Shade stood up, announced their destination as his palace, and headed for the cave entrance.

Eddie glared at Shade's back. The man refused to listen to reason. "What do you mean we're going to your palace?"

"Because that's where we'll find Wrath." Shade peered around him before stepping into the thick, warm night.

Eddie traipsed after him. "You don't know that for sure."

"The master knows all," Xerxes said and padded after Shade.

Shade turned and waited for her to catch up. "I do know that because the demons that were pursuing me said as much."

"Exactly." Eddie lowered her voice as the night stillness wrapped her like a blanket. "The same Wrath who left you bleeding and dying on the cave floor. Seems like finding him is the very last thing you should do."

"His demons did this to me." Shade stared at Xerxes by his side.

Xerxes stilled and took a tremendous sniff of the air before he nodded to Shade.

Shade strode into the forest.

Not fancying the option of being left behind, Eddie trotted after them.

"If Wrath is at your palace, then so are his demons." Eddie caught up with him, and Cronus flanked her. "It makes no sense for you to go strolling in there to get the shit beat out of you again."

"None of this makes any sense." Shade frowned as if mentally cogitating the situation. "Wrath and I fight often." He shrugged. "It's a way of relieving the boredom. But he has never tried to end me before."

"We should go back to the theatre." Eddie gave reason and logic another whirl. "We can talk to Uriel about it and see what she says."

"Uriel has no say in hell," Shade bit out. "And she will have problems of her own shortly."

"Problems?" Eddie had a plate full of problems right now and no desire to add another dollop. "What kind of problems? Why would she have problems?"

Shade stopped suddenly and turned to her. Taking her by the shoulders, he gave her a gentle shake and said, "Breathe, Eddie."

"I am breathing." She pulled air into her starved lungs. Problems for Uriel meant problems for Dee and her theatre. "Explain."

"Uriel should not be on earth either." Shade started walking again. "The guardians will not like it that she or I have strayed into their realm. And if what you told me is true, the guardians will be furious that she sent you through the portal with a heaven forged weapon. It's not done." He flinched. "Not without consequences in any case."

"Does that mean Dee is in trouble?" Eddie's gut tightened. She didn't want to think of her grandmother having to deal with those asshat guardians who had locked her in the basement. When Dee had virtually shoved her through the hell gate, she hadn't thought to ask about the consequences for Dee. And given the way the guardians had treated her, she absolutely should have. What if they had hurt Dee? "Shade, we have to go back. My grandmother could be in danger."

"Your grandmother can take care of herself," Shade said. "And she will be under Uriel's protection."

Oh, that was comforting. Not! "You just said Uriel will have problems of her own."

"Eddie." Shade threw her a fulminating stare. "Uriel is an archangel. An all-powerful being, and she can take care of herself and Deandra."

"An all-powerful being like you." Eddie didn't want to rub salt in his recently healed wounds, but someone had to provide the reality check. "So all powerful that you were lying half dead on a cave floor less than an hour ago."

"Exactly." Shade growled and shook his head. "That should not have happened. None of this should be happening."

Eddie stopped walking and stared at him. "None of this makes any sense to me."

"No, it doesn't." Shade took her arm and tugged her forward. "Which is why we need to get to Wrath."

She was losing her ever loving mind. That was the only explanation. Talking to Shade was verbal circumlocution. She gave up trying to follow the conversational thread and wailed, "I don't understand."

"None of us do." Shade wrapped his long fingers around hers. "Wrath should not be trying to kill me, because if he kills me the entire construct collapses, so in essence, killing me is tantamount to killing himself at the same time." He held up his other hand. "And Wrath is many things, but a suicidal fool is not one of them. So"—he nodded as if satisfied with the world around him—"we need to find him and ask him what the fuck he thinks he's doing."

Rolling up on a hell prince and demanding he tell them what the fuck he was doing didn't strike Eddie as a great idea, but she trudged on beside Shade. What were her alternatives? She would need someone to show her back to the portal. The hounds, Shade, and Yesterday were her only options, and Yesterday was MIA.

So, yes, she was walking into a showdown with an omnipotent, immortal being with a pissy attitude. Awesome.

"So, Eddie." Shade glanced at her out of the corner of his eye. "I want to speak with you about something you said."

She'd said a great many things to him, so she waited for specifics.

"About my ability." Shade developed a keen interest in the foliage around them.

Eddie cast her mind back. "Which one?"

Shade laughed, and it was an unfairly attractive sound. It made her want to make him do it more often. Rather than looking at his stupidly beautiful face, she indulged in a botanical study. The plants vaguely resembled earth plants but with disorienting subtle differences, like the green was too intense or the glossy leaves gleamed too brightly.

"I only have the one clear ability." Shade sounded sincere, but the humility left her floundering.

"I don't know about that." Eddie could think of a few nifty tricks he could pull. "There's the super strength." She counted them off on her fingers. "Super speed, the flying." And honesty compelled her to admit, "That's very cool. I'd love to be able to fly." As there didn't seem to be a plethora of advantages to being Nephilim, wings should come with the gig.

Shade waved a dismissive hand. "All immortals have the speed and the strength. No." He cleared his throat. "I was talking about my...er...unique ability."

"Your—" And then she got it. And she was suddenly not so sure she wanted to have this conversation. "You mean the lust thing?"

"You had a strong reaction to it," Shade said.

Heat seared Eddie's cheeks. She'd been all over him, just about dry humping him in an effort to get relief. "Not by choice."

"What..." He stopped and gaped at her and then smirked. "Not that." His smirk widened into a grin. "I was speaking of your objection on moral and ethical grounds to me incurring lust in people who are unaware."

"Right." Her face might explode if she got any more embarrassed. "Of course you were." Eddie kept right on walking.

Shade didn't move. "You are ashamed of your reaction to me?"

"Is there a point to this?" Eddie slapped a hanging vine out of her face.

"Eddie?"

Just when she started to think of him as less of a prick, he managed to set her straight.

"Eddie?"

"What?" She refused to look at him.

"You're going to wrong way." Shade chuckled. "And I don't wish to embarrass you. I wanted to say you were right."

That and the wrong way thing stopped her dead, so she turned and stared at him. "Are you apologizing?"

Shade flinched. "I wouldn't call it apologizing per se." He scuffed the ground. "More of an acknowledgement that you were right."

Eddie wasn't about to let him slide by that easily, and she

folded her arms and stared him down. "Tell me how I was right."

"Well." He shoved his hands in his pockets. "First you must understand that beings, such as myself, have very little contact with humans. We are much more...accustomed...comfortable, you might say, to dealing with other immortals." He made a vague hand gesture. "Demons and such."

"Uh-huh." Eddie added some foot tapping to let him know she was running out of patience with him.

"The rules of hell are not the same as the rules in the human realm." He studied the toe of his boot. "There is more flexibility when dealing with demons." He held up a hand to stop her from speaking. "Demons are not like humans. If given an opportunity to act in one way or another, a demon will nearly always take the violent path."

She wasn't going to argue with him about demons. Mainly because she was on shaky ground there. But the other thing—his lust thing—she was clear on that. "It sounds like you're making excuses for your crappy behavior to me and Lillian." And whoever else he'd done that thing to.

"I wasn't thinking about how it would affect you." He grimaced. "That's not strictly true. I knew how it would affect you, and I chose to continue because I needed healing. I didn't think beyond my needs in the situation."

"What's changed?" Not that she didn't appreciate the apology—sorry, the acknowledgement that she was right.

"I have already vowed it will not happen again." Shade took a left turn and got walking again. "And I mean that. But I also wanted you to know that I understand why it shouldn't happen again, and I agree with your reasoning." That last bit was said so fast Eddie had to trot to hear it.

She drew even with him, but he kept his fast pace going.

"There is another thing," he said.

She couldn't wait to hear it. He was full of surprises today. "Oh, yes."

"Your reaction to me." He flicked his fingers between them. "That is extraordinary."

"In what way?"

Xerxes and Cronus both growled.

The bushes around them rustled, and demons emerged.

Shade stilled, his face hard.

Eddie was getting a bad feeling. "They aren't yours?"

"No," he snarled.

"Asmodeus." A demon with an oversize bald head stepped forward. "We have been looking for you."

Eddie didn't know how Cronus and Xerxes hadn't picked up their presence.

"They were masked," Cronus said, his gaze moving from one demon to the other. *"These are higher level demons. You should run and hide. We will find you."*

More rustling undergrowth and more demons surrounded them. And because the fuckery wasn't done with them yet, another bunch added to the first. There must be close to forty bodies surrounding them, and all those bodies were armed. As much as running and hiding sounded like the best option, it was now off the table.

Shade swelled, and a strange glow turned his skin to molten gold. His low rasp made the hair on her nape stand on end. "Stand aside."

"Now, Asmodeus." The demon spread his hands like he was ready to give them a sweet deal on the rust bucket parked in the back of the lot. "We have been instructed to find you and bring you to our master. We can't leave here without you."

"And who is this master?" Shade sneered. "Because you are of Mammon's horde." He pointed to another. "And you reek of Belphegor."

Another mixed horde. Eddie reached for the dagger that was no longer there. Adrenalin dumped into her system, swelling through her muscles and speeding up her heart rate.

"You miss the point," the first demon said. "But we grow weary of all the chatting."

Shade nodded. "So be it."

His wings whooshed out of his back in a gleaming black and gold sweep. Blue light danced off the filaments like a crow's wing as Shade launched into the air.

"Dammit." The bald demon shook his head. "I thought he might do that." He turned silver eyes on Eddie. "And now he has forced my hand."

Cronus leapt in front of her, and Xerxes went for the demon, but faster than she could blink, the demon was behind her. Something icy pressed against her neck.

"Don't," the demon said. "Or I'll slit her throat."

Shade paused, midair, his eyes frigid.

"And that goes for you fuckers, too." A massive demon with a canine snout dropped to all fours and sunk arm-length fangs in Xerxes's shoulder.

His yelp of pain resounded through Eddie's mind.

Red dropped over Eddie's vision and flash-fire rage coursed through her.

Everything slowed around her as her body responded to the fury inside her. The knife at her neck disappeared as she lunged back and cracked her head into whoever was behind her. With strength she didn't know she possessed, she grabbed its arm and flung it ten feet across the clearing into its buddies.

Demons yelled and scattered. Fangs flashed, claws swiped, fur, skin, and blood flew.

Eddie was rage, she was vengeance, she was unadulterated might.

Dimly, she was aware of strikes against her flesh, but Eddie shrugged them off like insect bites.

Shade and the hounds joined the fray.

A switch had flipped in her brain, and Eddie knew only the need to defend and protect, the sharp desire to inflict pain on those that would threaten her and hers. She plowed through bodies. Claws sprang from her fingertips, and she slashed and gouged, ripped, and mangled. And all the time, anger roared through her like an out-of-control freight train.

"Eddie." Strong hands wrapped around her and held her against a chest.

She lashed to free herself, sinking her claws into the being that held her.

"Fuck!" Her attacker yelled. "It's me, Eddie. It's Shade. You can stop now."

"Edme." Cronus whined in her head. *"Please, mistress. Return to us."*

And then Xerxes's voice, pragmatic and stoic. *"She is crazed. Caught in a rage thrall."*

"Thanks," Shade panted in her ear. His arms tightened around her. "Got that much."

Crazed? Eddie's breathing slowed, and the red haze drained from her vision. She barely ever lost her temper. She didn't get crazed. And she certainly didn't get caught in a rage thrall.

As the rage receded, her other senses kicked in. The stench of demon almost gagged her. And then she looked around her and she did retch. Black and red demon blood had drenched the plants around her. Dismembered parts of God alone knew what lay twitching and mangled around her. Gore dripped off leaves and splatted on the ground.

"It's over." Shade's voice was deep and calm in her ear. "They're gone. It's over."

A dismembered head lay at her feet.

Slowly, carefully, Shade took his arms away from her and stepped around to face her. His gray eyes peered deeply into her. "Are you with us?"

Eddie nodded, her horrified gaze moving past him to the carnage around her. Blood dripped from her hands and plastered her clothes to her body. Bits of bone and tissue clung to her hair.

An eyeball was stuck on her index finger, and she shook it off.

Horror replaced the rage, and she leaned over and emptied her stomach.

"It's okay, Eddie." Shade rubbed her back.

It was so not okay, but Eddie didn't trust herself to speak. She shook her head and heaved. She'd done this. How could she have done this? Yet, she knew soul deep that she had.

"You were defending yourself," Shade murmured and kept soothing her spine. "It would have been far worse for us if you hadn't."

"Defending myself?" Eddie squeezed her eyes shut, but the grisly images were imprinted on the inside of her eyelids. What had happened in this clearing was so beyond self-defense it was nearly funny. "I can't..." She turned in a slow circle to view the full extent of her destructive rampage. "I don't..." What had done this was so beyond human that it made her head want to explode. But that thing had been inside her. She had done this.

"*We helped,*" Xerxes said and pressed his big head against her shoulder. "*You did not do it all alone.*"

"Is that supposed to make me feel better?" Eddie wanted to scrub the gore off herself, but everywhere she looked there was more blood and viscera. Her clothes were saturated. Her skin was covered. She looked at Shade, willing him to help her, to make it all go away. "I have to get it off me."

Shade nodded. "Let's clean you up."

Eddie tried to walk, but her legs buckled.

Catching her, Shade swung her into his arms. He glanced at Cronus. "The river."

Cronus swung his head and pushed through the thick vegetation. *"It is near."*

Eddie could barely force air into her lungs. She didn't deserve to breathe after that awful thing she'd done.

Shade followed Cronus through the forest until they reached the bank of a slow, lazy river, and then he walked right in.

Warm water lapped at her legs and then submerged them as Shade strode shoulder high into the river. A thought formed deep inside her and rose to the top of her mind. It popped and she looked at Shade as she said, "I'm not human. I'm a thing."

"I know, Eddie." Shade's gray eyes gleamed with empathy, and his expression softened as he studied her.

Tears pricked her eyes. "I'm a monster."

"You're not a monster; you're Nephilim." Shade clasped her to his chest with one arm as his other hand cleaned the ghastly remains of her actions from her. "And I have a fairly good idea who sired you now."

TWENTY-FOUR

Shade had tenderly washed all the awful shit off her in the river and then carried her to another cave, this one as lovely as the others, but Eddie barely noticed. She was exhausted in the aftermath of her rage episode, and a hundred parts of her ached and twinged from where her victims had fought back.

As he laid her tenderly on the cave floor, she made a token protest. "Shouldn't we keep moving?"

"That can wait," he said as he scooped together some blueish stones. With a nifty click of his fingers, he set the stones alight. "Let's get you dried off and warmed up."

If she'd been feeling anything close to her usual self, Eddie would have been impressed as fuck by the fire lighting finger thing. As it was, she was grateful for the gentle heat and the cheerful flicker of the flames.

Xerxes and Cronus lay across the cave entrance.

Nephilim. The word reverberated through her brain. Some women hated their asses, or their thighs. Others wanted to be prettier or have thicker hair. Her? She hated the very essence of what she was. A thing she'd lived in blissful ignorance of until today. Even when Uriel and Shade, and then Dee, had confirmed that she was Nephilim, it had felt like being told you had freckles or a genetic predisposition to a certain disease, a distant and vague truth about her that may or may not impact her daily life.

Sweet Jesus, being Nephilim was not that at all. For her, it meant rages that would literally shred beings into thousands of pieces. She closed her eyes and pressed her palms into them. The Eddie she knew scooped beetles into jars and carried them outside rather than kill them. She felt like a murderer when she stepped on ants. And now she was a murderer, a destroyer.

Shade settled beside her, his body warmth a welcome comfort. He took her hands from her eyes and held them between his palms. "Stop, Eddie."

Unable to look at him, she stared into the fire. There were no good words to respond to him. How could she stop hating herself for what she'd done? She deserved every moment of self-loathing.

"This may surprise you, but we hell princes are not great with emotional stuff," he said.

It dragged a reluctant bark of laughter out of her.

"We're not raised that way." He threaded her fingers with his. "We're pretty much raised to smash and destroy. We guard seals to all the worst qualities that humanity can indulge in. We are the physical embodiment of what the Christians like to call deadly sins."

Wondering where he was going with his admission, Eddie turned and looked at him.

"Being here in our demesne is where we're at our strongest." He winked at her. "I'm at my most irresistible here, you know?"

"Really?"

He grimaced. "Yes, really. And apparently not nearly as irresistible as I've come to believe."

Eddie wouldn't say that much, and she wasn't going to open her mouth and admit that thought either. Shade was beautiful, and part of her craved being near him, but no good would come from her declaring as much, so she waited.

"Half your DNA is hell prince." He rested their clasped hands between his upraised knees. Her forearms lay against the bunched muscle of his thighs. "You can't change that, any more than if you had a human sire who had given you blue eyes or diabetes."

"I'm not sure those two things belong in the same sentence."

"I told you." He smiled and raised his chin. "Hell prince. Incredible cosmic powers, low emotional intelligence."

"I'm surprised you've even heard of emotional intelligence."

"I pick shit up fast." He kept her hand in one of his and put an arm around her shoulders. "Part of the incredible cosmic powers. It doesn't mean I always understand what I learn."

His arm around her shoulders felt way too nice, and she considered shrugging him off, but the thought didn't make it into action. "Are you going to make some kind of meaningful point here?"

"I wouldn't get your expectations that high," he said and tucked her close into him. "My point is simply this. Your sire was a hell prince. His seal power is inside you, and while you're in hell, you cannot stop it from rising to the fore."

"Great." Shade should stink of blood and sweat, but the undertone of musk and honey clung to him. "You're saying I should get used to ripping demons in half?"

"You didn't kill them, Eddie." His gray eyes met hers. "Only a hell prince can end a demon. They'll reform in another shape and come after you again."

"But I'm half hell prince, so I might have killed them." Eddie would love to believe him, but the carnage she'd wrought wouldn't allow her that comfort.

He frowned in thought. "That's a good point. I didn't think of it like that. But"—he squeezed her hand—"the fact remains that here in hell, the rule is vanquish your foe or they will vanquish you. It's that simple."

It wasn't for Eddie. "I'm not made like that. I wasn't raised like that."

"I know, Eddie." His face softened as he studied her features. "And I'm sorrier than I can say that you got dragged into this and are now confronting stuff that you shouldn't have to. If none of this had happened, if the seals had remained stable, and the hell gate closed, you might have gone on being the same Eddie you were, going about your same life, and none of this would be your reality."

"Might have been?" Eddie was regretting there had ever been a time when she'd wished for a different life.

He grimaced. "At some point, your Nephilim side would have manifested."

"I hate it," she whispered. It made her doubt everything she'd always believed about herself.

"Don't say that." He kissed the top of her head. "You're a special soul, Eddie, and we're all better off that you are amongst us."

Bitterness leaked into her voice as she said, "Because I'm a half-hell prince, half-human freak?"

"No, Eddie, because you're you." Shade tightened his grip until Eddie could legitimately call what he was doing cuddling. "But this is now your reality, and you're going to have to adapt. It's not fair." His voice softened. "And it's not right, but it is."

"Are you telling me to get over it?"

"Maybe." Shade rested his cheek on her head. "But only in the nicest possible way."

Get over it. Simple as that.

"Today was not your fault, Eddie," he murmured. "You didn't do anything wrong. You did what you had to do. And I'm not going to lie, you probably saved the lads and me from a fairly shitty hour or two."

Weirdly enough, he was making her feel a bit better. If not better, then certainly more resigned. She was Nephilim, and that meant things she was only beginning to discover. "I hope I never have to do that again."

"Me too," Shade whispered. "I hope that for you too. Now try and sleep. The lads and I will keep watch."

Shade shifted until Eddie was lying with her head in his lap. Her features were soft and gentle as she slept. Her dark hair lay in a silky cloud over his thighs.

Belly-crawling, Cronus sniffed her. *"She is well?"*

"She's okay." As okay as she could be.

His newly healed wounds ached like a motherfucker. Today's fight had them bitching at him all over again.

What she'd done today still left him reeling. He'd seen fights aplenty, but the smooth viciousness that had flowed from Eddie had shaken him to his core. Nephilim.

Her delicate bone structure seemed too fragile to contain the power he'd witnessed today. In the heat of battle, her glorious blue-green eyes had flashed bright blue and shone with rage. He'd only ever seen one being exhibit that, and the conclusion that led him to was barely palatable.

Eddie sighed in her sleep and burrowed closer to him, more

vulnerable in sleep than she would allow herself to be when awake.

Fierce protectiveness pounded through his blood. She had the spirit of a warrior, yet he wanted to shield her from all harm. He chuckled to himself as he pictured her reaction if he ever told her that. Eddie was savagely independent. Growing up as she had, he understood how she'd become that way. Dee had provided the only stability Eddie had known. Her mother and father had abandoned her, and those assholes in the theatre used her for her flawless competence.

She had so many questions, and he had pathetically few answers for her. Recent events had shaken him from his complacency. For thousands of years, he and his fellow hell princes had drifted along in the same manner. They fought, they struggled for power, every now and again, they joined forces against the archangels, but they stayed constant.

The rules had changed, and Eddie had been caught up in that. He wished he could have spared her, but fate didn't work like that. It tangled all of them in its webbed skeins and twisted their existences together.

Still, fate would not stop him from doing all in his power to keep Eddie safe. Maybe at the end of this, he could return her to her life.

The idea left him feeling oddly adrift.

Eddie would not have believed it possible, but the next thing she knew, she was blinking awake.

Shade must have moved, because she was lying curled up on her side, facing the fire.

"Psst!" A familiar yellow head popped into her line of sight. "Wake up before he eats me."

Yesterday cowered in front of her, a very angry Cronus towering above him and dripping long, sticky streamers of saliva on him.

"Yesterday." Her eyes were gritty, and her body felt like she'd been asleep for a while.

"Of course it's me." Yesterday sidled away from Cronus.

Cronus slammed one big front paw down on him and flattened him face first to the cave floor.

"Eddie," Yesterday yelped. "He's going to eat me."

A distinct possibility, but Eddie had experienced all the bloodshed she could. "He won't eat you."

"*I might,*" Cronus said.

"Why don't we find out where he's been first?" Eddie levered herself into a sitting position. Her muscles felt strong and sure, and the grogginess faded quickly. Any residual pains from her fight had also disappeared.

"Mvebeensryingferya," Yesterday mumbled into the dust.

Eddie motioned Cronus to lift his dinner plate paw.

With a grumble, Cronus complied but stayed within snapping distance.

"You disappeared." Eddie stretched and yawned. "And so did my heaven blade."

Cronus growled.

"I didn't take it." Ears twitching, Yesterday kept his gaze on Cronus's jaw. "I swear I didn't."

"*His word means nothing.*"

Eddie didn't need Cronus telling her what she was already thinking. "I think you did, and so does Cronus. And we both want it back."

"I don't have it." Sweat trickled down Yesterday's cheek. Or it could have been Cronus slobber. Either way, it wasn't a good look.

Eddie didn't need to look intimidating. Cronus pretty

much had that covered. So, she stuck to the questions. "Where is it?"

"I don't know." Yesterday swallowed and licked his thin lips. "I don't have it. I promise. I don't have it."

"I want to believe you." And she did. "But you did take it."

"Look." Yesterday tried to shift away from Cronus. Cronus growled, and he froze. "I came here. At great risk to myself." He splayed his hand over his chest. "Great risk. To let you know that Wrath knows where you are, and he's coming for you."

"He could be lying."

"But he might not be." Eddie checked around the cave for the two she didn't see. "Where are Shade and Xerxes?"

"They have gone." Cronus averted his gaze.

"I can see that." Eddie stood and stopped right in front of him. Her heart missed a beat, and the pit of her stomach dropped. "But where have they gone?"

"To ensure your safety," Cronus said. *"We are to remain here until they return."*

"Hello?" Yesterday waved his arms. "Are you listening to me? I told you Wrath is on his way here now." His voice went shriller. "Not his demons. Wrath himself is on his way here, and you have to leave."

Cronus stuck his head in Yesterday's face and snarled. *"We are to remain here."*

"I know you think I took your blade thingy." Yesterday's eyes rounded like small moons. "But I'm telling you the truth. Wrath knows where you are, and he's coming for you."

With a grumble, Cronus shifted and padded to the cave entrance. *"If he lies, I eat him."*

Seemed fair enough to Eddie. "How do you know he's on his way?"

"Because I was with him." Yesterday rolled his eyes. "I am from his court, and I went to see what was going on. I can slip in and out without anybody knowing." He batted his eyes at her. "I did it for you, Eddie. I risked myself to spy on Wrath for you."

"He's a feral runt," Cronus said. *"But he is not lying about Wrath. I can smell him coming."*

"Shit!" Eddie ran to the cave opening and peered into the undergrowth. Although what she hoped to accomplish mystified her, it seemed like the right sort of thing to do. "What do we do?"

If Shade were here, she could ask him. And then she wanted to slap herself for having that thought. She didn't need Shade. She was a strong, indepen—nope, not working. She still wished Shade was here.

"I'm glad you asked." Yesterday scuttled up beside her. "Because I've given this a lot of thought."

Cronus snapped at him.

Yelping, Yesterday leapt behind her. "You're Nephilim, right, and from what I heard in Wrath's court, you can repair the hell seals."

"Is that true?" Eddie looked at Cronus.

He tilted his head. *"It's not completely impossible."* Glaring at Yesterday, he said, *"Nephilim wield the power of two realms, and that gives them greater powers over the seals than even the hell princes."*

"Does Shade know this?"

"Of course Shade knows that." Yesterday rolled his eyes, recovering his courage now that he was hiding behind her. "And Uriel knew it too. That's why she was so keen for you to come down here." His expression grew cunning. "It also explains why Shade is letting you stay and why Wrath wants to get his hands on you so bad."

He'd lost her on that part. And why was she feeling oddly let down that Shade had known this. It's not like she wanted him to keep her around for the pleasure of her company. A subtle vibration rumbled through the earth and into the soles of Eddie's feet. "Is that Wrath?"

Cronus nodded.

"How come I don't feel that when Shade is around?"

"*Wrath is—*"

"Does it matter." Yesterday grabbed her hand and tugged. "You need to get out of here."

"*Master commanded us to stay.*" Cronus looked troubled.

"You can't." Yesterday hissed. "The best thing you can do is get to Shade's seal and repair it. Then Shade can fight Wrath. It'll end in their usual stalemate, and you go home."

She looked at Cronus. "Would that work? Could I do that?"

"*I do not trust the imp.*" Cronus's shoulder muscles tensed as if he was getting ready to fight. "*But he is right about Wrath, and we have minutes to decide.*"

"Well." The vibration under Eddie's feet was getting stronger. "I'm not saying yes to the seal, but I am saying yes to getting the hell out of Dodge."

TWENTY-FIVE

Cronus led the way into Shade's palace via a bewildering series of caves and underground tunnels. It had taken a day to reach the palace, and they'd slunk into the tunnels as night was falling. Eddie had no idea how far they'd traveled, but with the ever-present vibration through her soles, she'd been motivated to cover the distance fast.

As they journeyed through the tunnels, the harbinger of Wrath receded. "Does this mean we've lost him?"

Yesterday snorted. "Wrath is a hell prince. You don't just lose them."

"*Perhaps.*" Cronus padded along in front of her. "*It is also probable that Shade's aura is so strong within the palace that it masks him.*"

Yesterday looked smug. "No way Wrath is giving up on you, Eddie."

Her vision seemed to be near perfect in the dark. Accurate enough to make her want to wipe the smirk off Yesterday's face. There went her temper again, sparking and spitting like a hot ember. Eddie breathed deep and counted to ten. Then another ten, and for good luck, she made it an even thirty.

The dim tunnel walls grew smoother and more honed as they walked. And now Eddie felt the pulse of Shade's magic in her middle. It was like a slow seduction by her own body. The air smelled of musk and jasmine and caressed her skin like a soft touch.

The corridor ended in a gleaming onyx set of stairs leading up.

"Let me check first." Cronus ascended the stairs slowly, his nose working the air, his hackles slightly raised.

He reached a large polished wooden door at the top and turned and nodded.

Eddie hurried after him.

The door was carved with images of demons and people. Very naked demons and people, doing very explicit things. Eddie's cheeks heated, and she hurried through the door after Cronus.

"Oh." She gasped as she stepped into the palace. Towering marble columns held a domed glass roof suspended above a lush atrium. Silken curtains fluttered languidly in the perfumed breeze and writhed around the columns like exotic dancers. A large rectangular pool filled the center of the atrium, colorful fish darting through its lapis lazuli depths. It was a space dedicated to beauty and pleasure. Big surprise. Not so much.

"We dare not linger." Cronus nudged her with his nose. *"The seal is this way."*

Despite the danger, Eddie wanted to linger. She wanted to sprawl in one of the shadowy alcoves filled with cushions that lined the atrium. She wanted to slip off her shoes and dip her feet into the water.

"Not bad." Yesterday jammed his hands on his hips and looked around him. "But I was expecting more cavorting."

"The master embodies lust." Cronus gave Yesterday a decidedly ungentle nose shove that sent him sprawling. *"That does not mean he indulges in lust all the time."*

Now Eddie had questions. Yes, more damn questions. She hurried to catch up with Cronus. "What does that mean?"

"Mistress." Cronus stopped and stared at her with his red eyes. *"There is a time for discussions, and I would suggest this is not it."*

"Okay." He was totally right, but she still wanted to know. "Is Shade here?"

"Close," Cronus said and nudged open a soaring wooden door.

Eddie caught another glimpse of anatomically impressive acts as she hurried after him. This room was even larger than the first. Three rows of pillars held up the ceiling, which was lavishly painted with busy figures. She wanted to stop and stare. The figures depicted above her were so beautifully painted they seemed to writhe and pulse with life. Or maybe that was just inside her. Need washed over her, peaking her nipples and pooling in her core.

A giant onyx throne covered in red silk took pride of place at one end of the hall on a raised dais. Eddie could picture Shade lounging amongst the scarlet silk. The image ramped up her rioting hormones another embarrassing notch.

Cronus padded to the throne and slipped behind it.

A set of double doors opened without him touching them, and a tsunami of lust almost dropped Eddie to her knees. She wanted and craved so many things. Her body was afire with need.

And there, in the middle of small a chamber, was what looked like a ten-foot round metal drum with sigils etched into its brassy surface. As she drew closer, Eddie saw slivers of light break through the sigils.

It became difficult to walk with the full-on lust override going on in her body. Sweat trickled down her face and snaked down her sides. Her shirt clung to her clammy skin. The friction of her leggings against her flesh was almost painful in its intensity.

"It is the seal." Cronus looked at her sympathetically. *"It is leaking lust."*

"What do I do now?" Eddie panted. Her skin felt too sensitive to touch. The closer she drew to the seal, the stronger the sensations coursing through her grew.

"Wow." Yesterday trotted up to the seal. "Even I'm getting tingles, so you must be ready to—"

"What do I do?" She snapped. She did not want to talk about Yesterday's tingles or her current discomfort.

Yesterday looked at her scornfully. "You fix the seal."

"How?" She gritted her teeth to keep from groaning her need.

"Dunno." Yesterday sniffed. "You're Nephilim." He jabbed his thumb at the seal. "Fix it." His face twisted into a grimace. "Major tingles."

Eddie's muscles shook, and her insides felt liquified as she stood in front of the seal. She wanted to rub herself against it and bring herself relief. Jesus, she hoped Shade didn't walk around feeling this every day. Or maybe she wanted that more than her next breath.

"Eddie!" Shade's voice snapped through her reverie.

She was half convinced she'd conjured him up through sheer desire as she turned toward the door. "You're here." Her voice came out raspy and breathy. An invitation to play with her. A plea to put her out of her misery.

"I told you to wait in the cave." Shade stalked closer, Xerxes on his heels.

"I couldn't." Eddie moaned as a fresh wave of need washed over her. "Wrath."

"Master." Cronus lowered himself to his belly and cowered. *"Wrath came. We were no longer safe."*

"I felt him." Eddie gasped as another onslaught hit her. "He was coming for me."

"And here he is." A tall, muscular form stood in the doorway. Wings streaked with red and burnished gold filaments framed a being that could only be Wrath.

Shade whirled, unfurling his wings as he did.

Wrath's gaze flicked to Eddie. Clear blue eyes in a chiseled, angular face. The face of a fighter, all harsh lines and implacable purpose.

"You dare," Shade roared, and a gleaming gold sword materialized in his hand.

"You were true to form, Yesterday." Wrath glance at the imp. "I may let you keep your head."

Eddie wanted to delve into that last comment, but a horde of demons crowded in the doorway behind Wrath. Huge, misshapen bodies carrying weapons and leering at Eddie and Shade.

And suddenly Eddie was angry. The red haze dropped over her vision, and she stalked Wrath. "You." She bared her teeth at him. "I have had enough of you."

Wrath blinked at her. An expression flickered across his face, too fast for her to catch. In her current temper, Eddie didn't give a fuck. "You will fight me," she bellowed.

"Eddie." Shade stepped in front of her. "No!"

Cronus threw back his head and howled.

Power crackled and crashed in the air around Eddie.

"Magnificent," Wrath whispered.

"This ends here." Shade shifted her back and closed with Wrath. "No more."

Wrath dragged his gaze away from Eddie and to Shade. Fury tightened his features as he drew his own weapon, a massive double axe. "So be it."

"Stop them." Xerxes flung himself between the two hell princes. The power barrage between them flattened his fur to his back and dragged his jowls away from his teeth. He implored Eddie with a look. *"You must stop them before they destroy us all."*

Fury pounded through Eddie where there had been lust moments ago. She craved the feel of flesh and bones sundering beneath her fingers. With a battle cry, she leapt between Wrath and Lust. She threw up her hands, and the doors to the room slammed shut on Wrath's demons. "You fight me." This was her war. There stood her foe. "And your demons stay out of it."

"Fight you?" Wrath's eyebrow rose. "You are not my match, Nephilim."

"Am I not?" Eddie felt like she could rip the columns from their bases and beat the shit out of him with them. She could crush the stone beneath her feet. "Try me."

"Get her out of here," Shade snapped to Cronus and Xerxes.

"Master." Xerxes looked between her and Shade.

"You protect her first." Shade scowled at him.

"Fuck. That." Eddie lunged for Wrath.

Wrath moved faster than she could track. He fastened his fist into the front of her shirt and tossed her across the room, as if she weighed nothing. "My fight is with Shade. Not you."

Steel clashed, booming through the room as sword met axe. Sparks showered the hell princes as their weapons locked in the bind. Muscles straining, they glared at each other with pure hatred.

Shade shifted his weight and kicked Wrath's knee. Bone cracked, and Eddie wanted more. She wanted to break bones herself.

Barely stumbling, Wrath righted himself and swung his axe on a low arc for Shade's middle. The blade whistled through the air where moments ago Shade's midriff had been.

The fight started in earnest. It was like a silent signal had gone off in both their heads and released the beast inside them.

Every blow of steel, every strike against flesh echoed through Eddie, feeding her blood lust. They moved so quickly, strike, parry, thrust, deflect, that she had trouble following them. Blood trickled from a gash on Shade's shoulder. A deep wound to Wrath's thigh pumped blood down his leg, yet neither hell prince seemed to notice.

Shade ducked and sent Wrath careening into a pillar.

Plaster dust and pebbles rained down.

The building shook around them. The force of their blows reverberated through stones and mortar and shook the floor beneath her feet.

"They will end us all." Cronus whimpered. *"The seal is driving their blood lust."*

Large cracks opened in the floor. Chunks of marble crashed to the ground around the fighting hell princes.

"Get it together, Eddie," she whispered. Someone had to get control of this situation or Cronus was right, they'd all end up destroyed. She didn't know what that meant in the cosmic or universal sense of hell princes, archangels, and people sandwiched between them, but the way they were tearing the palace apart didn't auger well.

The fight had increased in ferocity, and there was no way to get between them. Not if she wanted to keep her limbs attached, and she rather did.

Eddie circled the fighters, looking for a way through.

The ceiling groaned and cracked. Ash and stone chips rained down around them, thudding to the ground.

Xerxes and Cronus flanked her, silently urging her to get on with it.

Wrath lurched closer to her, his back to her.

Swooping down, Eddie hauled a massive piece of fallen mortar off the floor. Raising it as high as she could, she crashed it down on the back of Wrath's head. A massive *boom* of power shuddered through the room.

Everything went still.

Even Shade gaped at her, chest heaving.

Wrath half turned, stumbled, and dropped to his knees. "Edme," he rasped before crashing face first on the floor.

Eddie wasn't going to wait around for him to recover. Given the fight she'd witnessed, she didn't give him longer than a few seconds.

"Let's go." She grabbed Shade's arm.

Shade pulled away from her. "The seal," he gasped. "You must repair the seal."

"Not today," Eddie yelled. And not with Shade leaking blood all over the floor.

As if on cue, the doors to the chamber flew open and demons boiled through the gap.

"Here." Yesterday darted forward and tossed something at her.

Her hand snapped out on reflex and caught the heaven wrought blade. The demons stopped short and hissed at her.

The heaven wrought blade gleamed in Eddie's fist.

"Eddie." Shade held his hands out. "Be very fucking careful with that."

From the floor, Wrath groaned and struggled to his feet.

"What do I do with it?" Eddie didn't want this much power. It was too terrifying.

"You buy us time." Shade darted forward and wrapped his fist around hers. "I cannot touch it. But you can." Yanking her closer, he thrust their joined hands down and stabbed Wrath in the shoulder with the blade.

Eddie screamed.

Wrath threw back his head and bellowed.

"Get up." Shade hissed into Wrath's ear. "Or I'll angle this straight into your heart.

"You wouldn't dare," Wrath panted through gritted teeth. Agony contorted his face into a grimace.

"But she might." Shade jerked his head toward her. "And it's going to fucking hurt."

Eddie wanted to yank her hand away from Shade's grip keeping it on the hilt, but the hovering demons kept her right where she was.

"Want to bet your life on how much we know about Nephilim powers?" Shade growled. "Who can know what a heaven blade wielded by a Nephilim can do."

Wrath went still. "Now what?"

"Now we get the fuck out of here?" Eddie wasn't going to stay and face the odds. "And you're our ticket out."

TWENTY-SIX

"Y ou made me stab him," Eddie hissed as Shade draped an unconscious Wrath over Cronus's back. Blood dribbled down Wrath's side and on Cronus's fur. She tried to wipe it away with her sleeve. "Isn't he heavy?"

"I am well, mistress." Cronus snuffled her neck. *"I am stronger than I look."*

Cronus looked like he could shoulder a truck, but still he was her hound, and she didn't like the idea of him being used like a pack mule.

"When I'm stronger, I'll carry the fucker," Shade said and winced. "Aren't you worried about my wounds?"

"Maybe." She was, but she didn't want to show it.

Shade looked pale in the dim light of the corridor they'd come through to reach the palace.

"Rough, Eddie." Shade grinned at her. "You're a tough woman to impress."

She noticed for the first time since they'd fled the room with the seal that Xerxes was sticking to Shade's side. Almost like the hound was providing physical support. "You're not trying to impress me." Eddie peeked at him out of the corner of her eye. "Are you?"

"Maybe." He grinned. "So what's your plan?"

"My plan?" Eddie stopped in her tracks and gaped at him. This was his demesne, his stomping ground.

"Your plan." Shade pointed to her. "You wanted us out of the palace. You knocked out Wrath. You stabbed him with the heaven wrought blade."

That was too much. "I did not stab him. You made me do it."

"Semantics." Shade tried to suppress a wince, but she caught it anyway.

"Do you need a shoulder to lean on?"

Shade jerked his head at Xerxes. "I have one." A smolder sparked into life in his storm-cloud eyes. "What I need from you, Eddie, is entirely different."

She couldn't believe this guy. "Are you flirting with me? Now?"

"Lust." He raised an eyebrow at her. "It's how I heal."

"Right. Well." Eddie had had her fill of lust for one day. Given the way her body had taken over near the seal, she'd probably incinerated her way through an entire lifetime of lust. "You'll have to make do with Xerxes." She studied Xerxes for any sign of strain. "Only don't hurt him."

Shade huffed and shook his head. "Rejected for my hound."

"I thought you said they were my hounds."

"Our hounds." Shade kept on giving her bedroom eyes. "Look at us. We're co-parenting already."

Eddie snorted to let him know what she thought about that.

"Sooo." Yesterday scuttled along beside her. "What is your plan?"

Given he'd stolen the blade in the first place, Eddie didn't trust him. Not to mention what Wrath had said about him. Then again, he'd given her the blade when she needed it most. The jury was out on Yesterday, and she didn't have a plan. When she'd hit Wrath over the head, she'd only been thinking about stopping him from tearing the world apart, and Shade with it. Also, the fate of life as she knew it had played into her actions, but not on a conscious level. Truthfully, she hadn't been thinking at all.

"I assume Wrath's demons will come after him?"

Shade chuckled. "You can bet your sweet ass they will."

"Stop flirting." He seemed to have a thing about her ass, and truthfully, she wasn't mad at that. "Okay." She forced her stage manager brain into action. "This is the situation as I see it. One, the lust seal is breaking and that's really, really bad."

"Correct." Shade pursed his lips. "And I've been thinking that Wrath's behavior might indicate he is having trouble with his seal as well."

"Really?" Eddie tucked that information into her calculations. "Isn't he always...well...wrathful?"

"Yeah." Shade stopped and grimaced before shambling forward again. "He's a temperamental son of a whore, but it's out of control lately." He gave her a slow and thorough eye sweep. "Rather like my lust."

This guy took objectification to the next level. He didn't even like her. She was just a convenient supply of lust for him. Rather like an all he could consume red light district. "I'm not going to warn you about the flirting again." She could face down divas in full tantrum with the stare she gave him. "I have a heaven blade and I'm not afraid to use it."

Shade grinned.

"So." Eddie went back into planning mode. "We know we have one seal in trouble, and a strong possibility of a second." A thought occurred to her. "Could the possible weakening of the wrath seal have anything to do with my loss of control?"

Shade thought that over and then nodded. "Possibly. But, like I said before, you're Nephilim, so it's all guesswork."

"Right." She tucked that in her mental Unknowns column. "Let's stick with the verified facts. The lust seal is breaking. Wrath wants to end you." Wrath's arms and feet dragged on the ground on either side of Cronus. He didn't look like he could swat a fly, but Eddie wouldn't forget seeing him in action in a hurry. "We have Wrath, and as long as we do, his demons will have to be careful." She motioned the heaven blade sticking out of Wrath's back. "In case I end him."

"Partially." Shade stopped again and caught his breath before taking what looked like a painful step. "Like if you end me, you end our hounds. If you end Wrath, you end his demon horde." Shade took another careful step. "But also because they are created to protect their hell prince. It's their reason for being."

"Oh. That's a neat system. Protect yourself by protecting your hell prince?"

Shade nodded, sweat trickling down his face.

He shouldn't be moving if he was injured. "Shouldn't we find somewhere for you to rest and recover?"

"No time." Shade shook his head. "And I'll slit my own throat with that blade if you even suggest I ride Xerxes."

Kind of made Eddie wonder what pride was like if lust had a chip this big on his shoulder. She hoped she never found out what pride was like. But then curiosity got the better of her. "Who is pride?"

Shade blinked at her subject change and shrugged as if it were obvious. "Lucifer."

"The Lucifer?" At last, a hell prince she'd heard of. But hang on. "Isn't Lucifer the king of hell?"

"Huh!" Shade glowered at her. "Only if you hear him tell it. Fucking king of fucking hell." He spat. "That prick."

Eddie was going out on a limb here as she asked, "So, not the king of hell?"

"No," Shade snapped. "Just a hell prince like the rest of us with no shame about pushing himself forward and an out-of-control ego."

Out-of-control egos were a theme around here. Back to the original topic. "According to Yesterday, I can repair the seal." And she couldn't stop herself from adding. "A detail you did not share with me."

"In theory." Shade studied her through narrowed eyes. "It's only a theory because, as I've said a number of times, we don't know what Nephilim are capable of, because there aren't many of you."

Not being the only one sounded comforting to Eddie. "When you say not many, how many?"

"I only know of two in my lifetime, and they're both dead." Shade shrugged. "Guardians killed one, and the archangels got the second."

"Ouch." Eddie was beginning to feel like a hunted woman. Uriel and Dee had said she was safest in hell, but with an unconscious hell prince who wanted her dead, and his demons who wanted her dead even more, she wasn't feeling that. Then again, on earth the guardians had it out for her. Uriel had tried to help her. "Even if I can repair the seal, I don't know how. And hanging around it until we find out isn't an option."

"Agreed." Shade nodded and flinched. "Fuck, that shithead hits hard."

The futility of walking hit her, and she stopped. "Where are we going?"

"I thought you knew that." Yesterday rolled his eyes at her.

"We can't stay here." Eddie waved a hand around to indicate hell. "We can hide, but it's only a matter of time before his demons find us, or he wakes up."

"You could cut his throat," Shade suggested.

Eddie couldn't believe he'd said that. "Firstly, I thought you said I couldn't kill him, and secondly, and I probably should have made this the first point, I am not slitting anyone's throat."

Shade shrugged. "It won't kill him, as long as you don't sever his head from his neck entirely." He grinned. "But it will hurt like a motherfucker and take him a while to heal from."

"Still not slitting anyone's throat." She couldn't believe she was having this conversation. She couldn't believe any of this. Except it was undeniably happening. "And why am I the one who needs to do the stabbing and the slitting?"

"Demons can't touch that blade," Yesterday said.

"You did." Eddie glared at him. "When you stole it."

"I wrapped it in leaves and moss, and I'm a lower order demon." Yesterday didn't look one iota apologetic for his theft. "It doesn't affect me like it affects the more powerful demons."

She was so tired of running around in the dark—literally and figuratively. "Huh?"

"It's a weapon of enormous power," Shade answered her. "The more powerful the hell being who handles it, the greater the power the blade has. For Wrath and me"—he shrugged— "it's near fatal."

That stopped Eddie in her tracks. "Near fatal?" She stared at the weapon hilt sticking out of Wrath's back. "Then that is killing him right now."

"Eddie." Shade sighed. "Technically, you stabbed him and not me. Only a hell prince can end another hell prince." He nudged Wrath's head. "And he's still with us."

"But when I stabbed him with it, I weakened him?"

Shade nodded. "It does enough damage to seriously slow us down."

At this stage, Eddie wasn't sure they weren't all making the rules up as they went along. "Right." Back to her original point. "That still leaves us with no options on where to go."

"Back through the hell gate," Shade said.

Eddie shook her head at his obtuseness. "Did you miss the part about the guardians being there?"

"Uriel can handle them," Shade said. "And the situation here is going to need a full gathering."

"Gathering?"

"A meeting." Shade glanced at Wrath. "If his seal is in trouble too, then the situation is worse than we imagined. We need a full gathering of archangels and hell princes, and earth is the most neutral place to do that."

The idea of such a gathering terrified Eddie. "In my theatre?"

"Your theatre is a hell gate." Shade smiled placatingly at her. "It will be fine."

Eddie wasn't so sure she wanted to take that chance. "As members of this so-called alliance or treaty or whatever, don't the guardians attend such a gathering?"

Shade's grin was wolfish as he said, "Yes, but we can handle them."

"You told me it was a three-way alliance." The way Shade said handle made her fear for the guardians. Then she remembered Chris Fellows and didn't give so much of a crap.

"I said we had struck a deal," Shade said. "It doesn't mean that all parties are aligned. Just that we agreed to certain terms for the well-being of the whole."

As much as she'd like to protest on behalf of humanity, Eddie wasn't a big fan of the guardians she had met. They didn't appear to be the listening types. "So we go back to the theatre and call this gathering?"

"Yes." Shade looked grim. "I'm not looking forward to the prospect. None of us will. And it's only in the direst of circumstances we risk being together like that."

"Because you all fight?"

Ahead of them, light appeared at the end of the tunnel.

"We'll have to move fast when we get to the end of the tunnel." Shade indicated Wrath. "And we can't risk him waking up."

Eddie knew she wasn't going to like what was coming next. "And?"

"That knife needs to stay where it is. It keeps him weakened." Shade looked entirely too happy about the prospect.

"I told you—"

"Eddie." Shade's voice went colder than a February wind. "We can't risk him waking."

Without waiting for her agreement, he grabbed her hand and twisted the dagger in Wrath's back.

Flesh parted beneath her fingers and Eddie screamed.

Wrath's body jerked and Cronus grunted.

"I can't believe you did that." Eddie snatched her hand away. He'd made her stab someone. Again.

"How distressing," a man drawled.

Eddie whirled.

A tall, dark-haired being strode down the tunnel toward them. His broad shoulders almost blocked the light from the outside jungle.

Eddie had the nasty feeling she was about to meet another hell prince.

"Fuck off," Shade snarled.

The stranger drew close enough for Eddie to discern his features.

His long hair hung to his shoulders in a silky sweep. Dark, soulful eyes stared at her from a classically handsome face. Humor clung to the sensual sweep of his mouth. "Hello."

"Hi," she croaked. If Shade was gorgeous, this being was the pinnacle of male perfection. It almost hurt to look at him.

"What are you doing here?" Shade straightened and glared at the newcomer.

"Shade." He tutted as he tilted his head and studied Eddie. "Aren't you a tasty little morsel."

"Back the fuck off." Shade stepped between Eddie and the stranger. "She's mine."

"Yours?" He raised a perfectly sculpted dark brow. "If you want to get technical about it, then she's—"

Shade grabbed him by the neck. "What do you want?"

"Don't be a dick." The stranger shrugged him off and straightened his dark, button-down shirt. "And I came to offer you my help." He waved a languid hand to the jungle. "You're not going to get far without me."

"And why would you do that?" Shade growled.

"Why?" He laughed, an attractive deep sound that created shivers up Eddie's spine. "Because anything that pisses off my brother, works for me." He peered past Shade's shoulder at Wrath. "And as you've done way more than piss him off, I am at your service."

Eddie couldn't contain her question any longer. "Who are you?"

"Me." He turned a beautiful smile of flashing white teeth and deep dimples her way. "Why, sweetheart, I am Lucifer, but you can think of me as your savior."

TWENTY-SEVEN

Outside the passage, Lucifer had gathered Shade's demons. They all looked delighted to see him, and equally delighted to see Wrath's condition.

Shade looked at the horde surrounding them and frowned.

"What is it?" Eddie wasn't up for another nasty surprise.

"There are too few of them." Shade's frown deepened.

Lucifer straightened his cuffs and led them to a flashy chariot thing drawn by six glossy dark creatures that closely resembled horses. Except for the glowing red eyes and the vicious, sharp teeth. "Noticed that too, did you?"

"Has Wrath destroyed them?"

A towering, ruddy-skinned demon with sharp horns bowed to Shade. "Go, master. We will make sure you are not followed."

"My thanks." Shade nodded. "Where are the others?"

The demon growled. "Gone. Their disloyalty has been noted."

"As much as I'd like to blame Wrath for this, my horde is suffering a similar thinning." Lucifer swung himself gracefully into the chariot and held a long, elegant hand out to Eddie. "Allow me, sweetness."

Eddie considered rejecting the hand, but not wanting to appear petulant, she allowed him to help her into the chariot. Strictly speaking, Lucifer was more beautiful than Shade. His features were more finely drawn and clean, his dark eyes pools of mystery, and his mouth a perfectly sculpted sweep, but he was almost too beautiful. It was like trying to look directly into the sun.

Shade dropped Wrath's inert form into the bottom of the chariot, leapt up beside Eddie, and put himself between her and Lucifer.

"Protective, are we?' Lucifer drawled. "No need, Asmodeus, after all she is my—"

"Not yet," Shade growled. "We haven't covered that yet?"

More secrets. What a surprise! GAH!

Lucifer studied her with his fathomless onyx eyes, and Eddie resisted the urge to fidget. She felt like a specimen on a slide. Then he gave her a dazzling smile and took up the reins of his chariot. "Hah!"

The demonic horses shot away at such a speed that Eddie's head snapped back on her neck. Stumbling, she nearly stood on Wrath. His eyes were open, studying her through a haze of pain.

Catching her by the hips, Shade steadied her. His voice was rough and deep as he murmured, "Hang on to me."

As much as Eddie wanted to decline his offer—being close to Shade, touching Shade, gave her ideas she had no business having—the chariot was gathering speed by the second. Her hair streamed out behind her. Shade's demon horde dropped far behind as they went so fast the ground blurred beneath the wheels.

Lucifer handled the reins nonchalantly as if they weren't

defying physics with their forward momentum. He turned and spoke to Shade. "It started about the same time as the trouble with the seals."

Eddie resisted the urge to tell him to watch where they were driving as bushes and trees flashed past. She dug her fingers into Shade's arms and held on tight.

"At first it was only one or two missing from the horde." Lucifer shrugged and changed the reins from his left to right hands. Reaching inside his pocket, he pulled out a silver hip flask and took a healthy sip. "But it's been steadily getting worse. By my last count, I'd lost well over two hundred thousand from my horde."

It begged the question of how large each hell prince's horde was, but Eddie was too busy hanging on for dear life and trying to not scream.

If anything, the horses were moving faster now. Colors blurred as they streaked past and the wind in her face robbed the breath from her.

Shade turned her head into his chest.

It helped with the wind but gave her lungs full of Shade's unique honey and musk smell.

His voice rumbled through her as he spoke, "I thought it was Wrath destroying my demons."

"As much as I'd like to plant the blame on him." Lucifer toed his brother's inert form. "I believe there is something else afoot."

Wrath groaned.

"Speaking of afoot." Lucifer raised a booted foot and drove the knife hilt deeper into his brother.

"Shit!" Eddie didn't like Wrath, but that seemed needlessly cruel. "What are you doing?"

"You don't want him to gain his strength back, my sweet."

Lucifer grinned at her. "He's a grumpy bastard at the best of times."

"So if Wrath isn't destroying my horde, who is?" Shade didn't appear to have any problems with Lucifer's actions.

"That, Asmodeus"—Lucifer offered him the hip flask—"is the pressing issue we need an answer to."

"Here's a better question." Shade sipped from the hip flask, and then offered it to Eddie. "Why are you helping us?"

Eddie eyed the flask dubiously. Then again... *What the hell? Get it! Arf arf.* Now she had jokes. Smooth single malt met her tongue in a burst of peat and smoke.

"My reasons are my own," Lucifer said, and flicked the reins over the horses' backs.

Shade snorted. "Aren't they always."

The scenery blurred into streaks of color with no distinguishing details. Eddie had no idea how fast they were going. She was also certain that for her peace of mind, she didn't want to know.

At the speed they'd been traveling, it shouldn't have surprised Eddie that they arrived at the hell gate within about thirty minutes. A journey that had taken her days had ended in a flash. A terrifying and stomach-churning flash, but over nonetheless.

She looked about for Xerxes and Cronus. There was no way they would have been able—

The hounds emerged from the forest with their tongues lolling and their eyes gleaming brightly.

"They enjoy a good run." Shade grinned at her.

At lightning-fast speeds apparently. "Is Yesterday with you?"

Cronus's massive flanks heaved as he panted. *"That plague will never be fully banished."*

Yesterday did have a way of popping up when least expected.

"And now, sweet Edme, I must say goodbye." Lucifer gave her a knee trembler of a smile. "For now, that is. I am sure we'll be seeing a lot more of each other."

Shade growled and got his shoulder in front of Eddie. "You're not coming through the hell gate?"

"Not as yet." Lucifer leapt into his chariot. "I have a couple of leads I want to follow up down here. See if I can get any answers to the disappearing demon debacle."

A flick of his wrist set the chariot in motion, and away he shot.

Eddie turned to Shade. "What now?"

"Now." Shade bent and tossed Wrath over his shoulder. "Now we go back through the hell gate with this fucker, and he can tell me why the fuck he is so intent on ending me."

She hated to be the one to point out the obvious. Not really because it gave her a tenuous feeling of superiority over all the immortals around her. "Um, Shade. You can't go back through the hell gate." There was something satisfying about being right. "One, because you're not supposed to be on earth. And two, because there are guardians up there waiting for you." She jabbed a finger at Wrath. "I'm assuming they won't take too kindly to him either."

"Eddie." Shade raised his eyebrow at her. "I am a hell prince. Nobody tells me where I can and cannot go."

EDDIE STEPPED through the hell gate and into her basement ahead of Shade and Wrath. And nearly ran smack into Chris Fellows.

"Edme." He looked disappointed in her. "You and I really need to talk further."

Xerxes pushed past her and got between Eddie and Chris. His low, menacing growl reverberated around the empty room.

Taking a cautious step back, Chris eyed Xerxes. "And I'm afraid that really is not allowed."

"He's not a that. He's a hound." Eddie laid a hand on Xerxes shoulder. Taking a leaf out of Shade's book, she raised her chin. "And he goes where I go."

Cronus came up on her other side, hackles raised, red eyes glinting at Chris.

What girl wouldn't feel safe with these two by her side? And to think, she'd wanted an ordinary dog. She might still want an ordinary dog, as long as it got along with her hounds.

"That's a problem." Chris shoved his hands into the pockets of his pressed gray pants. "Hell hounds are forbidden on this plane." He cocked his head and studied her with cold, gray eyes. "So are Nephilim. As I'm sure Asmodeus has already informed you."

Speaking of Shade, where the hell was he?

The hell gate swirled, and he stepped through, Wrath balanced on his shoulder.

Shade dropped Wrath to the floor. "Guardian, I assume?"

"Indeed." Chris gave him a mocking head bow. "You knew my predecessor."

"Yes." Shade leaned over Wrath and studied him. "Considering he did not stab me with a heaven wrought blade and throw me through the hell gate," he drawled. "Forgive me for not congratulating you on replacing him."

Chris shrugged. "You know the rules."

"Indeed." Shade pointed to the dagger. "Would you, Eddie?"

"What?" Eddie wasn't sure what he was asking.

"Remove the blade." Shade straightened.

Chris took a step toward Wrath.

Cronus snarled, and he backed off.

"I don't think so." Shade grinned, all teeth and no friendliness. "The blade was given to Eddie, and she is the one who must handle it."

A muscle ticked in Chris's jaw as his frigid gaze slid over Eddie. "She has no right to that weapon. Only guardians may handle heaven wrought blades."

Six men stepped out of the gloom behind Chris, all dressed like *Men in Black* lite.

Chris looked smug. "And we must insist on the rules being followed."

"And archangels. Don't forget about them, Guardian." Shade toed Wrath. "You gonna just lie there, motherfucker?"

"I was thinking about it." Wrath groaned and flopped to his side.

Chris tensed, and his posse all palmed similar weapons to the heaven wrought blade. Swords, daggers, and rapiers, and all made of the unmistakable crystalline substance.

Eddie glanced at Wrath to find him watching her. A strange little smile played around the surprisingly pillowy sensuality of his mouth. In a face as roughhewn as Wrath's, the softness of his mouth drew your attention to it. "Hello, Edme," he murmured. He jerked his head at the blade. "Be a good girl and get that out of me."

Sword in one hand, Chris brandished it at Xerxes and stepped closer to Eddie. "I don't want to hurt you, Edme. We can resolve this without violence." One of his men aimed a crystalline crossbow at Cronus. "But if you remove that blade, then we will be forced to see it as an act of aggression."

Said the man with weapons pointing at them. Eddie didn't know what to do. She glanced at Shade.

He nodded. "Do it."

"But—"

"Eddie." Wrath's pale blue eyes met hers. "Remove the blade, and do it now."

Not a fan of being given orders, Eddie still went with the devil she knew. She lunged for Wrath and ripped the dagger from his shoulder.

Everyone moved at once.

Xerxes threw himself at Chris.

Cronus leapt and stood over her.

With a whoosh of air, Shade's wings appeared on his back.

Blades flashed like diamonds as the guardians attacked.

Wrath threw himself into action, taking on the guardian closest to him. He looked pale and was moving slower than Shade, but she couldn't fault his fighting style. Sheer poetic brutality as he downed his first opponent and turned for the next.

In the churn of feet and legs, Eddie cowered under Cronus's belly, as weapons clanged, men grunted and shouted, flesh smacked into flesh.

For two beings who had been trying to end each other hours earlier, Wrath and Shade made a tight unit. Shade had disappeared his wings, and they stood back-to-back and fought the guardians.

The guardians retaliated like no normal human could, their movements faster than Eddie could track.

Xerxes yelped as he took a bolt to the shoulder.

"No." Eddie had to get to him.

The enormous hound stumbled and then righted himself.

Black blood gushed from the wound, and he backed away on unsteady legs, snarling and shaking his big head.

"We need to get to him." Fury thrummed with Eddie's

pulse. Nobody hurt her hound. Eddie tried to move one of Cronus's caging legs.

Cronus growled at her. *"You are to stay safe."*

"I will help him." Her voice had dropped to a low, menacing growl.

The guardian with the crossbow took aim at Xerxes.

"Go." Cronus moved aside. *"I will shield you."*

Eddie leapt for Xerxes, her jump taking her all the way across the room. Her eyesight had sharpened, her hearing identified each of the sounds happening around her, and she smelled blood and power in the air. She hit the floor with her hip and slid up beside her hound.

The guardian with the crossbow blinked at her.

"Don't," she snarled.

Her gaze sharpened on his finger on the trigger. He fired.

The bolt headed through the air toward her as if in slow motion. Eddie snatched it out of the air and crushed it in her fist. She wanted to rip his limbs from his body and beat him with them.

"Yes," Wrath shouted. "Give me that rage, Edme."

Cronus's voice reached her through her angry haze. *"Mistress, you must control it."*

Cronus's furry body moved between her and the guardian.

Yes, she must control the rage. Memories of what had happened last time she let the haze go crowded her mind. She couldn't do that again, wouldn't do that again.

The guardian gaped at her, his crossbow trembling in his hand.

"Lower your weapon," Eddie said. "Or face my wrath."

The man blinked and pointed his weapon to the floor. He'd gone an unhealthy shade of pale, his eyes huge and staring.

"Breathe," Cronus said. *"You cannot release your wrath here."*

Fury still pounding in her blood, Eddie breathed deep and turned to Xerxes.

Grabbing the shaft, she gritted her teeth and yanked the bolt out of Xerxes.

He snarled in pain but staggered back to his feet.

Brushing her ponytail, a bolt *thunked* into the wall near Eddie's head.

Motherfucker! Eddie spun on the crossbow firing piece of crap.

"Stop her," Shade bellowed.

Both hounds got between Eddie and the remaining guardians.

Four guardians lay downed as Wrath and Shade moved on Chris together.

In one giant bound, Xerxes had the crossbow guardian pinned beneath a paw.

Still wanting to rend the bastard, Eddie ducked out from behind Cronus and snatched the crossbow out of his hand. Loading another bolt, she turned the crossbow on Chris. "Put it down." She motioned the sword he was about to swing at Wrath. "Put that fucking sword down, or I'll gut you like a trout."

"The power she holds." Wrath breathed deep. "It is…"

Shade glanced at him. "It certainly is."

Chris froze, gaze locked on her weapon. "You're not a violent person, Edme. You don't even know how to use that."

"Wanna bet?" She wanted nothing more than to see the bolt sink into his throat. "You twitch, and I will end you."

Chris glared at her. "Nephilim," he spat.

"That's right." Eddie grinned at him. "And I'd be very careful about the next words that leave your mouth."

"Look at her," Wrath murmured. "Strong and fierce."

"Eddie!" Dee came running into the room. Her eyes widened as she took in the scene. "What have you done?"

Eddie was not sure if the question was addressed to her or the two hell princes.

"Hello, Deandra." Wrath gave her a tight smile. "Do us a favor and gather up those heaven wrought weapons."

Deandra studied the room for a second before she started gathering up weapons. "This is not good, Wrath. So not good."

"Unavoidable, I'm afraid," Wrath drawled. He was watching Eddie again, and it made her want to fidget. It wasn't the way Shade looked at her; there didn't seem to be any sexual intent in Wrath's eyes. But it was still an uncomfortably intent look.

She jabbed Chris in the chest. "On your knees."

"You're making a mistake, Eddie." Chris dropped his sword with a clang and sank gracefully to his knees. "You're on the wrong side."

"Says the man who attacked me." Eddie scoffed.

"Not you." Chris jerked his head at Wrath and Shade. "We attacked them. They're not supposed to be here. Bad shit happens when hell princes gather on this plane."

There was only one person in the room Eddie could be sure of, and she looked at her grandmother. "Dee?"

"He's not wrong." Dee had an arsenal clutched to her chest. "But he's also not right. There's something more going on here, and right now, we need to put aside our differences and find out what it is."

"We have a treaty." Chris snarled and glared at Dee. "And you are one of our order. You are betraying your order."

"And that's my granddaughter," Dee snapped. "And you bet your ass I'll betray the order to keep her safe."

A waft of roses preceded Sophia into the room. Her wings were out, and her hair shone golden in the dim basement. She looked at Chris and then the other guardians lying around. "Oh dear." She shook her head, her blue eyes troubled. "This is not good. This is definitely not covered by the treaty."

"Fuck the treaty." Wrath growled. "My daughter comes first."

"Oh, fuck." Dee dropped her armload to the floor with a clatter. "I really wish you hadn't said that."

Chris's gaze grew calculating as it landed on Eddie. "Wrath's daughter?"

Eddie was following the conversation fine, but she didn't know why everyone was looking at her.

"That much became fairly obvious when we were in hell." Shade took a careful step toward her. "Eddie?"

"What?" Eddie kept her crossbow against Chris's jugular. "Why is everyone staring at me?"

"Tell her." Wrath glowered at Dee. "Or I will."

"We had a deal." Dee glared right back.

"She was not part of the deal," Wrath said. "I was not even told about her. so regard our deal as null and void."

Dee nodded. "Fair enough."

It felt like a swarm of wasps had taken up residence between Eddie's ears and were interfering with her hearing information and processing it.

"Eddie?" Shade stopped beside her. Sweat shone on the defined planes of his chest. "I was going to tell you when we came back. But this lot were waiting for us." He jerked his head at Chris.

Eddie shook her head to clear her muddled thoughts. "Tell me what?"

"Uriel." Wrath sighed and motioned the angel. "Could you immobilize our human friends?"

"I'm not sure." Sophia chewed her raspberry pouty bottom lip. "The archangels are not going to be happy about this."

"None of us are happy about this," Shade said, his eyes tender on Eddie. "But Eddie is my first concern right now."

"Oh, for fuck's sake." A blond man mountain stalked through the basement toward them.

The signature glow of an archangel clung to the bronzed perfection of his bare arms and shoulders. The almost preternatural perfection of his features made Eddie stare. Eyes greener than grass swept the basement and took it all in. "What the fuck have you done now, Wrath?"

"Me." Wrath's wings sprang up behind him. He drew back his lips in a growl. "I have protected my get."

The newcomer stopped and stared at Eddie. He grimaced. "Nephilim."

Eddie's slow brain chewed out a conclusion it didn't like and immediately rejected it. She turned to Dee. "Dee? What's going on, Dee?"

"Oh bugger!" Dee's shoulders slumped. "Eddie, this is Ramiel. Archangel counterpart to Wrath, and here because Wrath is here."

"None of you should be here." Chris scowled at all of them. "This is a direct contravention of the terms of the treaty."

Ramiel turned to Chris with a look of distaste. "Be quiet, human. You will speak when you are spoken to." He heaved a massive sigh and pulled a set of handcuffs from his belt. Crouching beside Chris, he cuffed his hands behind his back. "And those will keep you civil until I tell you that you can speak."

"You dare." Chris struggled against the cuffs.

Ramiel held his massive hands out in front of Chris. "Be quiet before I smash your head like a fig. My patience is stretched thin as it is."

Eddie was insanely relieved when Chris took the threat

seriously and snapped his mouth shut. She did not want to see head crushing. Nope. That would really suck.

Standing again, Ramiel turned to Wrath. "Explain yourself."

"Shade has been trying to end me." Wrath disappeared his wings. "I have had to resort to extreme measures to protect myself. And now he has come to earth to use my daughter in his war against me."

"What?" Sophia recovered first and spun on Wrath. "You attacked Shade. He had to hide on this plane to get away from you while he was grievously injured."

"I never touched him." Wrath threw up his hands. "My horde and I have been hunting him after he and his attacked us and nearly wiped out half of my horde."

Ramiel glared at Shade. "You tried to end Wrath?"

"No," Shade bellowed. "He's the one who is trying to end me."

Wrath yelled something back, and then Sophia shouted at him. Ramiel bellowed at Sophia. And they were all yelling at each other.

Eddie had heard enough and not nearly enough. With her fingers in her mouth, she let out a piercing whistle.

All four beings turned to stare at her.

"Right." Eddie's hands shook as she smoothed her hair back. "I'd like us to circle back to the daughter thing."

TWENTY-EIGHT

"Dee?" Eddie stood and stared blindly at the view of the town of Paradise outside her bedroom window. With it being summer, the small park across the way from the theatre was filled with people. A woman was power walking the paved path around the perimeter. The woman was nodding along to whatever was playing through her AirPods. Eddie had been that woman, not even three weeks ago. She'd been going about her normal life, thinking she was a normal woman, in a normal world. Now she had archangels and hell princes arguing in her greenroom, and apparently, she was the child of one of them. She glanced at Dee sitting cross-legged on her bed in a bright pair of lime green leggings and an off the shoulder cerise shirt. "Is it true?

"Oh, Eddie-girl." Dee pushed her turquoise tortoise shelled glasses up her nose and sighed. "I really hoped we would never have this conversation." She rested her palms on her knees like a spry Buddha. "Your mother was...lively. She had a mind of her own."

Eddie snorted at that one. Rosabella had been born on a

tear and continued to live her life that way. "But a hell prince?" She pictured Wrath's mammoth shoulders and resting asshole face. "And that one?"

"She always did like a bad boy." Dee grimaced. "And you may not feel like this now, but judging by who else she had swarming around her back then, you got the best option."

Wow! The women in this family had horrible taste in men. Dee with her cradle robbing, Rosabella with…well, whoever, and her with this ridiculous thing she had for Shade. When she thought about it like that, she didn't judge her mother too harshly. They had a way about them, these hell princes, and it was more than their ridiculous good looks. Not to say the looks didn't nudge a woman's hormones on a bit, because they definitely did.

"By now you know how they all feel about Nephilim." Dee waved her hand in the direction of the raised voices drifting up the stairwell. "I wasn't going to let anyone harm you."

Eddie didn't bother to hide her hurt. "But you never told me the truth."

"Eddie, the truth was a hard one to tell." Dee's kingfisher blue eyes filled with tears. "And as you grew older and none of your powers manifested, I began to think…hope…that you would never have to discover who you truly were. I wanted you to have the most normal life you could."

"Other than living on top of a hell gate?" In the park, a family were having a picnic under the shade of a towering maple. As a child, she'd dreamed of being part of a normal family—mom, dad, siblings. Instead, she'd been the home-schooled granddaughter of the outrageous woman who ran the local theatre. Not forgetting being the daughter of the woman everyone hid their husbands from.

"Other than that," Dee said. "And we were born into that. Guardians are always from the same families. It's how the council controls the information from getting out." Dee shrugged one shoulder. "It's the sort of thing that could create widespread panic if people found out about it."

As Eddie had been experiencing a low-level panic since this entire thing had begun, she could get that, and she nodded. "Now what?"

"Now, we need to deal with that situation downstairs." Dee uncurled from the bed and stood. She launched into a sun salutation.

"Where's Jean-Claude?"

"I left him on the cruise." Dee popped her hips up into a downward dog. "He's a lovely boy, but not the brightest, and all this would be too much for him."

It was all too much for her, Eddie wanted to wail. "I don't suppose we could kick them all out and tell them to sort it out somewhere else?"

"No." Dee unrolled into mountain pose. "We want to keep them where we know you're going to be safe. And between Wrath and Asmodeus, here seems the best place." Dee clapped her palms together in prayer. "What is the situation with you and Asmodeus?"

"Nothing." Eddie didn't even want to go there. She felt things for Shade, for sure, but then he was the hell prince of lust, so anyone with a pulse would feel things for him. "He came through the hell gate injured, and I helped him. That's it."

Dee cocked her head and stared at Eddie. "Hmm?" She started a second sun salutation. "We should go down there and see what's happening."

"Do we have to?"

"Yup." As limber as an eighteen-year-old, Dee folded forward. "The guardians are in there, and we need to keep an eye on them."

"But you're a guardian." Eddie was sure she'd pull a muscle if she tried yoga.

"I'm a different kind of guardian," Dee said as she table-topped her back. "I don't believe the hell princes are evil or that the archangels are on a power trip." She popped into a lunge. "And I definitely do not believe all Nephilim should be destroyed."

"Thanks for that." There was one silver lining.

"Eddie-girl." Dee approached her and cupped her face in her hands. "You're my granddaughter, and I love and adore you. I am not going to let anything happen to you." She tapped Eddie's nose with a forefinger. "But we can't hide up here and pretend none of this is happening. There's obviously a big problem in hell, and our hell gate is getting all the action. We need to make sure that we're part of whatever next steps are taking place."

Eddie closed her eyes and inhaled the familiar mint and vanilla scent of Dee. "Are you sure we can't hide."

"Eddie." Dee chuckled. "The hiding thing didn't work out as well as I'd hoped with you. And besides"—she gave Eddie's head a little shake—"you should make an effort to get to know your father. You might like him."

Eddie didn't see that happening, and she pulled a face. "Let's go and see what they're all talking about."

Eddie and Dee shouldered their way into the packed greenroom.

With so many impossibly beautiful beings in one place, Eddie found it impossible not to stare.

A red-haired angel dressed in a beautiful tailored gray skirt suit stood in the middle of the greenroom with a tablet in her hands. Her fiery hair was neatly contained in a gleaming chignon. She was trying to make herself heard above the noise of so many raised voices. Everyone seemed to be talking at once.

Shade sauntered over and took Eddie's hand. "That's Gabriel," he murmured. "Try not to shove that tablet up her ass. It's what we're all doing."

"This is most irregular," Gabriel shouted, her eyes on the tablet screen. "It completely contravenes all the terms of the treaty."

Chris was on his feet, thrusting his forefinger at Gabriel. "Wrath and Asmodeus broke the terms of the treaty by assaulting me and my men." His men stood behind him, hands uniformly folded in front of them. Including the one who had fired that bolt into Xerxes.

Eddie gave him a look to let him know all was not forgotten or forgiven.

Ramiel spotted Eddie and stood. "The Nephilim is here."

He didn't raise his voice, but his words brought instant silence to the greenroom. All eyes swung Eddie's way and stuck.

"Nephilim." A huge archangel dressed like a gladiator glared at her. "Abomination."

Growling, Wrath leapt to his feet. "You touch one hair on her head, and I will end you, Michael."

"Don't make me laugh." Michael sneered. Like all the archangels, he was beautiful, but his was a harsh, brutal sort of beauty that made Eddie take a step back.

"You won't be laughing when I shove your head up your ass," Wrath roared.

Michael's wings sprang from his back, pure white with gleaming silver filaments. His shoulder-length hair blew back as if he had his own fan operating. The term avenging angel sprang immediately to mind. He put a broad hand on the hilt of a gleaming, opalescent sword hanging from his waist. "I will end you, hell scum."

"Stop it." Gabriel and her tablet leapt between the two of them. "There will be no weapon drawing. In fact, it's article twelve subsection A of the treaty." She tapped on her screen. "The drawing of weapons—provoked or otherwise—will be regarded as an act of war and responded to accordingly."

Chris smirked at Wrath. "What about willfully hiding a Nephilim?"

Gabriel's porcelain brow creased in a delicate frown. "There is no mention in the treaty of Nephilim."

"Because they're not supposed to exist." Michael sneered.

Yep, hot as fuck but a total asshole. One out of five stars for Archangel Michael, Eddie would not recommend. She spread her arms and tried to mimic his sneer. "And yet, here I stand."

"There you stand." Gabriel sighed and massaged the spot between her eyes. "There really is no precedent for this."

Lucifer sprawled, legs stretched out in front of him on one of the couches. He winked at Eddie. "Hello, sweetness. We meet again."

"You knew about the Nephilim?" Gabriel swung her arctic blue eyes on him. "And you did not report her to Rafael." She tapped at her screen. "You are well aware of the necessity of princes and angels sharing pertinent information."

Lucifer grinned at Gabriel. "Did I mention how fabulous your ass looks in that skirt."

Her ass did look amazing, but Eddie still glared at him on behalf of objectified women everywhere.

"My ass always looks fabulous," Gabriel said without missing a beat. "Which does not address your negligence."

"Would we call it negligence?" Lucifer pursed his bow-shaped lips. "I only discovered I had a niece this morning."

Wrath stomped over and kicked his legs. "She's nothing to you."

"Beg to differ." Lucifer yawned. "As much as I would rather change it, you are my brother, and that would make sweetness my niece."

Eddie was not a fan of the sweetness thing, and as much as she wanted to deny it, if Lucifer was Wrath's brother, then that did make him her uncle. Ugh! How was this her life now?

"Go near her, and I will—"

"End me." Lucifer crossed one ankle over the other. "You seem to be trying to end a lot of us at the moment."

"Indeed." Ramiel stood with his shoulders propped on the wall. "You will need to answer for your attack on Asmodeus, Satan."

"Satan?" Eddie turned to stare first at Wrath and then Lucifer.

"Common misconception." Shade's warm breath stroked the side of her neck. "Two different princes, twins. Lucifer rather likes it that everyone thinks they're one and the same." He pulled a face. "Wrath, not so much." He put his hand on her waist and drew her closer to him. "Best to stand out of the firing line."

His hard body pressed against her back and Eddie resisted the urge to lean into his strength. The smell of him surrounded her and made her want to melt into him. His advice, however, made sense, and she stayed where she was.

A pretty brunette with honey-toned skin and huge green eyes emerged from behind Ramiel. "I'm sure Satan has a good explanation."

Wrath looked at her and smiled. "Hi, Haziel. It's been a while."

"Hi, Wrath." She twinkled at him. "Too long." She turned

her lovely smile on Eddie. "I like your daughter. She's very pretty, and she seems nice."

"She's magnificent." Wrath's chest expanded. "And she fights like a berserker."

"She fights?" Michael's gray eyes grew a tad less hostile. "Is she any good?"

"What do you think?" If anything, Wrath's chest got even broader. "She is of my bloodline."

"She needs to die," Chris said.

Shade moved so fast, Eddie didn't even see him until he had Fellows pinned against the wall by the throat. "You will not touch her."

The other guardians drew their weapons. Wings flared, eating up what little space there was. Weapons appeared like measles around the room.

"No weapons." Gabriel brandished her tablet. "And the Nephilim lives."

"Nephilim are an abomination," Chris choked out.

"Bullshit," Ramiel snapped, then blithely ignored that he'd expressed pretty much the same opinion earlier when he said, "They are rare and unknown, but that does not make them dangerous."

"I saw her during the altercation downstairs. She's strong, and she's fast." Chris glared at Wrath. "Wrath confirms it. He says she goes into a fighting rage. That makes her dangerous."

"Only to you." Shade's low voice was loaded with menace. "And only if you so much as blink in her direction."

"Let's all remain civil," Gabriel murmured, not looking up from her tablet.

"And you." Chris rounded on Dee. "You can consider yourself struck from the council."

Dee snorted and folded her arms. "You can't do that. I was born into guardianship, and I will stay right where I please."

She closed on him with a vicious expression. "Why don't we talk about how you hounded my daughter and forced me to place my granddaughter in hiding."

"Rosabella was hounded?" Wrath's wings whooshed out again, and death beamed from his eyes. "By this worm."

"Put those away." Ramiel spat black and red feathers as he struggled around Wrath's wingspan.

"Gabriel?" Another gorgeous male angel sauntered into the greenroom. "I have the reports you requested on activity to this hell gate."

Did anyone in heaven or hell have so much as a minor skin blemish?

Tall, broad, and muscular—ho hum, weren't they all—with copper skin and piercing light gray eyes, his bone structure seemed to be carved out of glass. Sensual, pillowy lips stretched into a polite smile as he nodded to her. "Good afternoon. I am called Raguel."

"Raguel!" Shade smiled and clapped the newcomer on the back. "Gabriel keeping you locked in that mausoleum of hers?"

Raguel blushed, adorably it might be added. "I am happy to serve my archangel. Always." The glance he sent Gabriel's way should have set the archangel's panties aflame, and Eddie got the impression Raguel would like to serve Gabriel in all sorts of ways.

Holding out her hand for his report, Gabriel behaved as if he wasn't standing there. "And have we any more information on the demon incursion on earth?"

"What demon incursion?" Chris shot to his feet.

Dee stepped up and cold cocked him.

Guardians surged for her.

Wrath, Shade, and Raguel closed ranks in front of her.

"I think you owe her that one," Shade drawled. "For all you've put her through."

"I can't believe you condoned what Dee just did." Gabriel finally looked up to scowl at Shade. "You are putting this entire operation in jeopardy with your impulsive actions." She sneered. "Although I can hardly expect more from a hell prince."

"What's that supposed to mean?" A hell prince with shoulder length, raven dark hair and amber eyes loomed over Gabriel.

It occurred to Eddie that she should be paying attention to the other occupants of the greenroom, but it was all too overwhelming.

"Calm down, Zeb." A dark-haired beauty with onyx eyes and a swagger to match her leather breastplate put her hand on his arm. "You know what they're like." She rolled her eyes. "Judgy."

"We are not—"

"Sanctimonious pricks," someone else shouted.

And it was on.

Wings flared, feathers flew, weapons appeared in hands, and there was shouting, lots and lots of shouting. Voices bounced off the walls and made Eddie's head ache. They were going to bust the entire theatre apart if this carried on. And Eddie had had enough. She channeled her best Wrath energy and bellowed. "Enough!"

The mirror behind the sofa shattered, and glass rained down on stunned archangels and hell princes.

"Enough." Eddie wound her neck back in and modulated her tone. "One. Two. Three." She snapped her fingers. "All eyes on me."

"Spectacular," Wrath murmured.

And that was kinda nice and made her feel a little fuzzy inside toward him. With all angels and princes staring at her, she didn't have time to enjoy the situation. "Now," she said, in the voice she saved for refereeing Lillian and Peter, "this is not helping. And I think we can agree, we have bigger problems to focus on."

Gabriel recovered first. "I have a list."

Everyone groaned.

Undeterred, she surged forward. "Item one: the war between Wrath and Shade."

"He started it," Wrath and Shade yelled.

"Item two." Gabriel raised her voice. "We have demons missing from hell."

Ramiel turned to Wrath. "You're missing demons? Why didn't you tell me?"

"Judgy," the dark-haired, black-eyed beauty murmured.

"We're all missing demons," Lucifer drawled, and stretched his arms over the back of the sofa. "We're shedding them like fucking semiplumes."

Eddie made a mental note to look up what semiplumes were, but everyone else seemed to get the reference so she kept her question inside.

"Leviathon?" Gabriel turned to the dark beauty.

She crossed her arms and nodded.

"Belphegor?"

A diminutive silvery blonde stood quietly against the microwave. "I thought it was just me."

"Are you going to go through each one of us?" Lucifer yawned and stretched his arms above his head.

"Gabriel." Raguel cleared his throat. "According to my reports, each demonarchy is missing members. There has also been a sharp increase in demon activity on the earth plane. Our angels are monitoring it, but it seems extensive."

"Well, fuck." Michael grunted. "That can't be good."

"You think?" Zeb, who Eddie rather thought must be Beelzebub, gave him a flat stare.

"Do you have actual numbers?" Gabriel glared at Raguel.

He shook his head. "Not as yet, but I'm working on it."

"I don't see what you expect me to do without accurate data." Gabriel scowled at Raguel before jabbing her forefinger at her tablet. "I need accurate data."

Shade smirked. "What you need is a good fu—"

"Is there anything else on your list?" Eddie was not having another explosion in her theatre.

"Right." Gabriel straightened her lapels. "Item three."

Lucifer groaned. "How long is this list?"

"Item three." Gabriel pinned him with an admonitory stare. "The hell seals are breaking. All of them."

Absolute silence descended.

Wrath stared at Gabriel. "Shouldn't that have been item one?"

TWENTY-NINE

And on that, thank fuck, everyone seemed to agree. Shade despised gatherings but the breaking of the seals demanded nothing less. And the damage was not limited to Wrath's and his demesnes. All the hell princes were reporting missing demons and damaged seals.

The meeting broke up shortly thereafter, with the hell princes going back to check the status of their seals and to see if they could discover where the demons were disappearing to. The angels went off to do whatever Gabriel had on her list for them to do.

Shade made sure to shoulder check Michael as he passed. Fucking war archangel, always blade happy and quick on the draw. And hell princes got the bad rap?

Michael glared back at him. "Watch yourself."

"Or what?" If Michael had been his counterpart, they would have ended each other millennia ago. "You going to take out your little sword and wave it about?"

Ava grabbed Michael by the front of his breastplate. "Come on, big guy. Let's go terrify a few guardians."

Shade winked at Ava. Avarice amused him, and with a real name like Mammon, he respected her right to call herself Ava. He wouldn't turn his back on the tricky prince, but she was quick and funny.

The guardians slouched off, grumbling and shooting dagger looks at everyone, but they also subsided in the face of a much greater danger.

The look Chris shot Eddie as he left got Shade's fighting blood pumping. That man did not like Eddie and was looking for a way to show her how much. Well, the shithead would have to get through Shade first. And judging by the glower Wrath was wearing, Shade had backup.

Finally, it was only Uriel and Ramiel with a smiling Haziel pouring wine for everyone on one side of the greenroom, and Wrath and him on the other.

Eddie stood in the middle and drained her first glass of wine. She was pale but composed, and Shade wanted to hold her and also cheer for her. She had a spine of steel and had rolled with the huge shitfest that had been dumped on her with incredible resilience.

Popping up behind Eddie, Haziel refilled her glass with a smile. "It helps."

Haziel was a true sweetheart and Shade's favorite kind of angel. As a seraph, she was one order below an archangel and served Ramiel with a lot more loyalty than the arrogant prick deserved. For that, Shade truly pitied her.

Uriel was the only archangel he could tolerate.

"Right." Eddie took another slug of wine and pointed to him and Wrath. "You two need to talk. Both of you are convinced the other one is trying to end you. You don't have to be Lassie to work this out."

Who the fuck was Lassie? Shade gave her a blank stare.

"Dog from a human movie," Haziel whispered to him. "Super smart and saves her humans."

Well, it beat Eddie's other descriptors for him, and he was taking it as a sign she was warming to him.

"Is it possible that there is a third party creating the conflict between you?" Eddie frowned, her aqua gaze shifting from him to Wrath.

Wrath surged to his feet. "Who?"

Typical Wrath! Act first and think later. Shade rolled his eyes.

"I don't know that," Eddie snapped at Wrath, not in the least intimidated by the fucker's bad temper. Damn, she had pluck. "We are just now exploring the possibility there could be a third party."

"It makes sense." Shade got on board with the conversation. Both he and Wrath were convinced the other was the aggressor. A third party would explain that. He glanced at Wrath. "I vow I never attacked you first."

Bristling, Wrath said, "Are you suggesting I attacked your first?"

Eddie sighed and held up her hand. "Shade is not suggesting anything of the kind. He merely said he hadn't attacked you first."

"Yes, daughter." Wrath sank down into the sofa. "And I vow on your life that I was not the aggressor either."

"See. Now we're getting somewhere." Eddie spread her hands, and smiled at them as if they'd made her proud.

As a supernatural being who had spent most of his existence pleasing himself, Shade wasn't sure what to do with his overwhelming need to please another being.

"So you were both convinced the other attacked first?" Ramiel snapped his fingers and held up his glass for a refill from Haziel.

Eddie stiffened, and Shade wanted to pound his face into the dust.

Uriel glared at him. "Keep up, Ramiel. And thank your angel. She serves you; she's not a serf or a minion,"

See, that's why he liked—okay maybe not liked totally, more tolerated—Uriel.

Coloring brick red, Ramiel turned to Haziel. "Thank you."

"You are most welcome." Haziel beamed at Ramiel.

The gossip mill had it that Haziel had warmer feelings for Ramiel. Shade opened his senses to the energy coming from Haziel.

Huh! Interesting. Lots of admiration and devotion, but low on the lust meter. In fact, Ramiel barely moved the needle on lust for Haziel. Of course, knowing how these things worked, Haziel might not be aware that her feelings for Ramiel were less carnal and a lot more cerebral. Being the sweetheart she was, Haziel was probably confusing *agape* for *eros*. Eyeing Ramiel's rigid posture and buttoned up demeanor, he toyed with the idea of giving matters a nudge. But Eddie would have his balls for that, and he'd made a promise to her.

"Why did you attack?" Changing tack and focus to Wrath, Shade leaned his elbows on his knees. "I mean, what made you think I was attacking?"

"Your horde," Wrath said. "I found your horde on my land. I captured one of them, and he confessed that you had a plan to end me and take over my demesne. He said you had a way to end me and keep the balance." He shrugged. "Obviously, I could not allow that to happen. It is my sole purpose to keep the wrath seal safe. Even from the other hell princes." He glowered at Shade. "A short time later, I was hunting you, and more of your horde attacked and almost wiped mine out."

"Hmm." Shade let that sink in. If he were not with the horde hunting Wrath, could either of them be certain the horde had been acting on his instruction. "But I was not with them?" His own information source had been very suspect. "And Yesterday came to me and told me you were hunting me."

"Yesterday, again." Sighing, Eddie nibbled her bottom lip. A bottom lip he wouldn't mind nibbling, maybe sucking it into his mouth, but she didn't trust him and, worse, she didn't trust her feelings for him. He'd only used his lust influence on her twice. The other times she'd accused him of influencing her emotions, she'd been wrong. Her desire for him came from her, but again, her mistrust prevented him from taking things further. And they also had the current epic fuck up happening around them to deal with first.

"Stop looking at my daughter like that." Wrath growled. "I do not accept it."

"Hey." Eddie blushed and glared at Wrath. "I get to decide what and who I accept. Not you."

With a grumble, Wrath crossed his arm over his mammoth chest. "We will discuss."

"No, we will—"

"Eddie." Shade interrupted them before Wrath could screw things up further. Not that he cared about shielding Wrath, but Eddie deserved to get to know her sire. "Let's focus on the more important issue for now."

"Okay." Eddie took a deep breath. "When you say the seals are cracking, what does that mean?"

Her question surprised him. "You saw what it meant. You were there at my seal."

"Yes." She waved a hand and looked adorably flustered. "I know what the actual cracking looks like. I was referring more to the effects and the results of those effects. Did either of you notice any discrepancies before you noticed the seals cracking. Maybe you two should compare notes, there might be similarities or differences."

"She must get her intelligence from her mother." Shade gave her a warm smile. She'd zeroed in on their greatest weakness as hell princes; the inability to cooperate.

Wrath snorted, and then shot Eddie a guilty glance.

With a head shake, Eddie got them on track again. "Back to the seals."

Shade gave it some thought. The seal had existed for so long that he didn't really pay close attention to it. It was just there. A constant in his existence. But Eddie was right, something must have made him check it and discover the problem.

Wrath sat up straighter and opened his mouth. With a humph, he subsided again.

As per usual, no help from that quarter.

"There must be something." Uriel sat forward.

"Power fluctuations." It came to Shade in a rush. "Before we noticed the cracks, there were a series of surges in power through the seals. That's what made me check it."

"Again!" Ramiel threw up his hand. "This was not reported to me. What is the point of having a system of counterbalances if there is no communication between us?"

Uriel shook her head at him. "So not the point."

Yeah, he more than tolerated Uriel. She was decent, for an archangel.

Cocking his head, Wrath considered Shade's statement. "Now that you mention it, I did notice one or two shifts in the aggression of my horde. Like they'd been charged up."

"So we have demons disappearing from hordes. We have demon hordes attacking without either of you present, and we have power surges through the seals. As well as the cracking." Eddie summed it all up for them. It made him feel dumb as a stump that he hadn't bothered to step back and put the obvious together.

"Also, we have increased demon activity on this plane. And

from what Lucifer and Raguel said earlier, it appears the problem is widespread," Uriel said.

"You can never trust a word my shitstain brother says." Wrath sat back and folded his arms. "But Zeb, Ava, and Belle also mentioned missing demons. And Raguel is decent enough for a seraph."

"Hey." Haziel shot Wrath a wounded look. "What's wrong with seraphim."

"Nothing." Wrath flushed and avoided making eye contact with her. Instead he glared at Ramiel. "Other than the pissy archangels they serve."

Shade was momentarily distracted by the flare of energy around Haziel as she interacted with Wrath. An energy surge Wrath shared. Interesting indeed. "All the hell princes reporting their problems is noteworthy in itself." He forced his mind back to the more pressing issues. "Admitting such a weakness would be like handing the other hell princes an advantage."

"What sort of advantage?" Eddie perked up, her beautiful eyes keen and focused.

"In the war." He knew Wrath, Uriel, and Ramiel would get what he meant, but Eddie wasn't accustomed to their ways. "The seals are both ours to guard, and they provide our power. If one had a damaged seal, it weakens one. It was why Wrath's demons were able to injure me so gravely."

"Please." Wrath snorted. "They injured you because they were trained by me, and I am the superior fighter."

"Stop it, Satanus," Ramiel snapped before Shade could put Wrath back in his place. "Nobody is contesting your prowess."

Nope, Shade would question Wrath's so-called prowess all day long. The fucker confused a shitty personality with battle skills. "You are not the superior fighter; you merely have a horrible temper and the personality of an enraged bull." He couldn't resist tacking on the next part. "And we all know who the better lover is."

Haziel gaped at Wrath.

"I'll give you—"

"Stop it," Eddie snapped. She shot him a look laden with disappointment. "You're both hell princes, right?"

He didn't care that much. That jab had been worth it. And Haziel had definitely responded to the idea of Wrath and his bedroom prowess. If it weren't for Eddie, he could stir up so much shit right now.

"And you both guard a seal for a deadly sin?" Eddie continued.

Ramiel held up his forefinger. "The term deadly sin is a human construct, we prefer—"

"Right?" Eddie raised her voice.

Watching Eddie cut Ramiel off was almost as satisfying as doing it himself, and judging by the smug grin on Wrath's face, he felt the same.

They nodded in answer to Eddie's question.

"And you all exist in this delicate balance?"

Shade wasn't sure where she was going, but Eddie was smart and not tainted by their centuries of prejudice.

"And if one of you ends, the rest of you do too?"

Wrath tossed a glare at Shade. "Yup."

Dream on, fucker. Shade shot the glare right back.

"So why the hell are you constantly at war with each other?"

It took Shade a while before he replied, and he felt like an ass when he did. "Because we are hell princes, and it's what we do."

"That makes no sense."

"It really doesn't," Haziel murmured, earning herself a quelling look from Ramiel.

Wrath raised one eyebrow. "It makes perfect sense, daughter. It is our nature to make war."

Eddie kept them going down her thought path. "So if it's your nature to make war, could it be your nature to conquer some other prince's demesne?"

When you put it that way, it was a distinct possibility. Standing, Shade shoved his hands in his jeans pockets. "I mean...yes. That is the reason we go to war with each other." And now he got where Eddie was going. "Not that we expect to ever win another prince's demesne."

Uriel snorted. "War for the sake of war—how sensible."

Shade studied Eddie for a long moment, and then asked, "Are you suggesting one of the princes might be causing this issue in order to change the status quo? What was it that demon of mine said to you, Wrath?"

Wrath frowned. "He said you were trying to end me."

Hell fire give him patience. "The other thing. The thing about me having found a way to maintain the balance, end you and take over your demesne."

"Well, if you already knew, why the fuck did you ask?" Wrath huffed.

Ramiel scoffed. "No hell prince could find a way to end another and keep the balance."

"Why not?" Eddie held his disdainful gaze without flinching.

What Eddie was suggesting made a lot of potentially nasty sense. He glanced at Wrath to see if he was coming to the same conclusion. "I mean, it's possible. Not likely, but—"

"Lucifer," Wrath spat.

You never turned your back on Lucifer, particularly not when Eddie was in the room, and Shade whirled to face the door. "Where?"

"Lucifer." Wrath slapped his palms on his thighs. "If any

one of us had ideas above their station, it would be that turd weasel."

"Lucifer helped us." Eddie pointed out. "When we were escaping you."

Lucifer had helped them, but Shade knew better than to trust anything that—what had Wrath called him?—turd weasel did. Like Michael being all brawn and no brain, you could always depend on Lucifer having ulterior motives. Could Lucifer be behind all of this?

"On that, daughter"—Wrath stood—"you were never in any danger." He scowled at Shade. "This puny piss peddler however, I would have wrung his neck."

"You would have tried." Shade scoffed. Wrath was fucking delusional, and those insults needed serious work. "And really? Puny piss peddler?"

Wrath grunted. "I like alliteration."

Haziel stepped between them. "If this is possible, and if Lucifer is the guilty party, what motive would Lucifer have for helping you?"

"The oldest motive in the world," Shade said and caught another slight shimmer of energy as Haziel looked at Wrath. Oh now, that was just fascinating. "Divide and conquer. If he keeps Wrath and me at each other's throats, he can act on the others without our interference."

"It makes a valid point." Ramiel jerked his head at Shade. "Shade and Wrath are the most warlike of the hell princes. Belle is...well...indolent. Ava has more interest in acquiring whatever she can by whatever means necessary. Zeb will only act if Levi is threatened."

"Levi is a possibility." Shade considered Leviathon. If ever there was a hell prince who played their cards close to their chest, it was Levi.

Eddie huffed and gave him an impatient glare. "Levi?"

"Leviathon." Shade suppressed a chuckle. "Envy."

Frowning, Eddie thought that over. "She sounds like she might want what you have."

"It's not in her nature," Wrath said.

"She's envy!" Eddie snapped. "I would say it's very much in her nature."

Shade hated to add to her confusion. Eddie had so much to absorb and process, and he wanted to help her with that. "It's not that simple."

Eddie sighed. "It never fucking is."

"I am lust." He broke it down for her as plainly as he could. "I can inspire lust and control lust. If my seal is compromised, I embody lust."

"And if Levi's seal was compromised…" Wrath raised both eyebrows as he looked at Shade.

"Right." Shade took a deep breath. It was way too early to dismiss Levi entirely. "But I still think Lucifer more likely. Especially if his seal is breaking and giving him even more grandiose ideas."

"Either way." Wrath nodded as if he'd decided. "They both need further investigation. But first"—he looked at Eddie—"we should stabilize our seals."

Eddie grimaced and looked apologetic. "I went to Shade's demesne to do that, but I didn't know what to do."

"Wrath is your blood seal." Wrath beamed at her like… well…like a proud dad. "You are much closer bonded to it, and it would be a better seal to begin with."

"Ah, Eddie." A male human of middle to late years strutted into the greenroom. He stopped when he saw the occupants. He eyed Wrath and him like prime meat. "I wasn't aware you had company."

A professional mask descended over Eddie's features, and

Shade mourned her former openness. "What is it, Peter? Did you need something?"

"Umm." Peter circled Wrath, tapping his chin with a forefinger. "I don't suppose he acts."

Shade wanted to add that Wrath acted up all the time, but somehow he sensed that was not where this human was going.

"He can hear you and speak for himself." Eddie stepped in front of Peter. "Now what can I do for you?"

"Right." Peter gathered himself with a shake of his head and a shoulder straighten. "I don't suppose you've seen Bianca? She was supposed to be doing props for me, and she didn't appear for our meeting."

"You had a meeting?" Eddie looked guilty as hell.

Shade moved closer to her, aching to reassure her. With all that had happened, Eddie owed this human nothing. Indeed, her actions over the past few days had been to save humans like this one from the worst outcome of all.

"I sent you an email, Eddie." Peter tutted and gave her a disapproving look. "You really should check your email. I don't want to be this director." He spread his hand over his chest. "But you have also not been updating the Google drive."

Beating Shade to it, Wrath shifted closer to Peter and loomed over him.

"Are you sure you don't act?" Peter stared up at Wrath in wonder. "You'd make a marvelous MacDuff."

"He doesn't act," Eddie snapped.

Tilting his head, Wrath appeared to give this some thought. "I mean, I could—"

"No, you couldn't." Fixing Wrath with a loaded stare, she said, "The play is *Macbeth*."

"And?" Wrath frowned at her.

Eddie loaded more meaning in the name. "*Macbeth*?"

"Oh." And Shade got it. "You're thinking the witch's curse in *Macbeth* caused all this?"

"There's a wonderful old wives' tale about that in the the-ay-ter." Peter's eyes sparkled with interest as they locked on him. "And do you act? I can see you as Valmont. You'd be wonderful." His eyes brightened. "Lillian would be a superlative Merteuil. With Sophia as Madame de Tourvel." He sighed as if he'd stumbled on Nirvana. "Oh, Eddie. We simply must stage *Dangerous Liaisons*."

"He's right." Shade couldn't resist looking at Eddie. If ever a human character embodied him, it would be the Vicomte de Valmont. "I would make a perfect Valmont. You could even say I was made for the part."

Eddie clenched her jaw. "Let's talk about that later, Peter. And no, I haven't seen Bianca. It's not like her to miss a meeting."

This Bianca might merit further investigation. The curse of *Macbeth* was true only in as much as it needed a witch to activate it, and such a witch would then have the power to summon a hell prince through the hell gate. Many witches had given that one a go over the years, only to regret messing with what they didn't truly understand.

"That's what I thought." Peter stared at him, his gaze still holding their gleam of *Dangerous Liaisons* visions. "But she hasn't attended rehearsal for the last couple of nights either."

"I'll track her down." Eddie motioned Peter to the door. "In the meantime, isn't rehearsal starting now?"

"Yes." Peter threw one more longing glance at him and then Wrath. "If you do ever decide to audition—"

"They'll let you know." Eddie got him by the elbow and assisted him from the greenroom.

"This MacDuff?" Wrath looked after Peter. "Does he fight?"

"Yes." Eddie clapped her hands. "Back to the pressing issue, stabilizing the seals."

"Right." Shade couldn't resist touching her any longer and he flung an arm around her shoulders. He hated to be the one to break the bad news to her. "I'm afraid it's back to hell for you, my darling."

Wrath puffed up and scowled. "She is not your darling."

Shade smirked to piss Wrath off further. "She is if she wants to be." And he hoped with everything in him that Eddie did want to be his darling.

THIRTY

The trip through the nothing and then into hell felt much more comfortable this time. Dee—who had insisted there was no way she was not coming—handled it like a veteran. Xerxes and Cronus went through moments before Eddie, and the comfort of their presence made her feel braver. Also, the two hell princes standing at her back had a little something to do with that. But she might like the hounds better.

Maybe. If she could sort out her own emotions and trust them.

Carnage greeted them as they stepped into Shade's demesne. Demons were milling everywhere, weapons flashing, yelling war cries and generally trying to end each other.

"Oh, shit!" Dee grabbed her by the arm and yanked her back.

Eddie didn't know if it was a mark of how far she'd come or how low she'd sunk that she barely flinched.

All activity stopped as the princes appeared. Their power

emanated from them in palpable waves that made the hair on Eddie's arms stand on end.

Demons froze mid battle. A sword clanged against the ground.

"Cease!" Wrath yelled. His voice echoed through the forest surrounding them.

Shade sauntered closer to Eddie and jerked his head in Wrath's direction. "What he said."

"My prince?" A massive blue demon whose head had a central horn like a rhino stepped up to Wrath. "You wish for us to cease?"

"I not only wish it." Wrath looked at him like he'd scraped him off his shoes. "I demand it immediately. The war is over."

Low mutters sprang up amongst the demons. A few weapons were tucked away, but for the most part, they remained frozen in their fighting tableaus. Over to her left, one demon had a knife halfway in another's chest.

Rhino demon sniffed and locked on Eddie with pale yellow eyes. He dropped to his knees and lowered his gigantic head. "Seed of our sire. Hail!"

It was like someone had jerked the rug out from beneath half of the demons as they hit their knees as well. She was going to go ahead and guess those belonged to Wrath.

"Umm..." Eddie glanced at Shade and then Wrath.

"They recognize your position as my daughter," Wrath said with more than a touch of smugness. "As such, they grant you authority over them."

Eddie had enough trouble controlling her theatre people. She did not need a demon horde looking to her for instruction. "That's okay." She kept her tone light and airy. "They don't need to do that."

"Yes, they do," Shade said. He lowered his head and whispered in her ear. "They are demons, Eddie. They fight, they fuck shit up, and they kill. They need to know you're off that list."

His proximity warmed her skin and made her nerves skitter. She took a self-preserving step away and nodded. She would talk to Wrath about the demon thing later, when she got her brain out her pants again. Shade had called it right at the theatre. He was Valmont, and she would do best to remember that. The women who had tangled with Valmont hadn't ended up in a good place.

"This is the Nephilim Edme," Shade shouted. "And she is under my protection."

There was more kneeling, slower and less enthusiastic this time.

"She is under *my* protection," Wrath bellowed.

This wouldn't end well. "She's standing right here," Eddie snapped. "And she has hell hounds to do the protecting."

Xerxes and Cronus threw back their heads and howled. The genuflection Eddie could do without, but a girl with hounds could go anywhere and pretty much do anything.

Cronus looked at her, his tongue hanging out of his mouth as if he were laughing. Damn straight, she and the hounds understood each other perfectly.

"And I'm her grandmother," Dee yelled with a raised fist. "Mess with one of us, and you mess with both."

Eyes sparkling, cheeks flushed, Dee seemed to be having a whale of a time.

With a grin, Shade looked at Dee.

"What?" Dee straightened her utility belt. "Been a guardian my entire life. Never got to do anything interesting until now."

Dee was dressed the part, as well, in combats and a camo long-sleeve T-shirt. Biker boots laced halfway up her calves, and all manner of tools and weapons dangled from her belt.

When Dee had reached for the bandana to tie around her forehead, Eddie had stepped in and stopped her. There was a limit to GI Granny.

Wrath turned back to Rhino demon. "I want a list of every missing demon in the horde."

"Every one?" Rhino demon blinked, and his lids shut vertically.

Raising an eyebrow, Wrath's tone grew silky. "Problem?"

"No!" Rhino demon's spine snapped straight. "As you command, so shall it be done."

"And find me that little shit Yesterday," Wrath snarled.

"Yesterday?" Eddie perked up at his name. She hadn't seen him since he'd tossed her the heaven wrought blade in Shade's seal room.

"Yes." Wrath motioned her and Dee to proceed through the two hordes. "He's one of mine, and I've been connecting some dots."

The hordes stayed on either side of them, but dropped into orderly lines.

It didn't exactly blow Eddie away that Yesterday was in the middle of the trouble. He had a knack for placing himself in harm's way.

"Meaning?" Shade folded his large hand around Eddie's.

"Meaning it was Yesterday who brought me the news that your demons had aggressed on mine." Wrath glared at their joined hands but kept moving. "And it might interest you to know that he bargained for his continued existence by giving me your whereabouts once you entered hell."

Cronus growled. *"I shall rip its throat out. I shall eviscerate it and eat its guts."*

There was more in that vein, but for the sake of her stomach, Eddie tuned him out.

Yesterday had betrayed her. It had worked out fine in the

end, but the little turd had not known that when he'd sold them down the river. Anger stirred inside her and rose like slow tendrils of steam through her bloodstream.

"Um...Eddie." Shade looked down at their hands. "That's a strong grip you've got there."

Her fingers had tightened around Shade's and were squeezing. "Sorry." She released her grip. "The news about Yesterday pissed me off."

Shade chuckled. "Fair enough, but you might want to keep an eye on your temper while you're in hell, and particularly when we get to Wrath's demesne. You're at your most powerful here."

Eddie would never forget what had happened when she'd lost her temper with those demons who'd attacked. She never wanted a repeat of that.

As if reading her thoughts, Shade's expression gentled, his gray eyes like liquid silver. "They will have reanimated by now," he said. "You did not end them."

Which, given that she'd pretty much ripped them into pieces, begged the question, "What does it take to kill a demon?"

"A lot." Shade shrugged one shoulder. "And a stronger demon or a hell prince can end a demon. Although you might be able to, given who sired you. But you need to either crush their hearts or rip their heads off. Anything else, and they simply recover."

"Tough bastards." Dee sniffed and jammed her hands in her pockets. She eyed the two hordes following them. "I wouldn't want to take on this many, but we were trained how to fight them at the guardian institute."

That was news to Eddie. Dee had been typically light on what went on at guardian training camp. "You were trained to fight demons?"

"And angels." Dee nodded. "Guardians are aware of being the weaker party, and it makes them nervous."

"They weren't in any danger." Wrath huffed. "Until they attacked my daughter."

A grumble of assent rose from Wrath's horde.

He was getting very comfortable with the D word. It wasn't bothering Eddie as much as it had when she'd first heard it. And Wrath wasn't technically wrong about the daughter thing. She looked at him striding beside her like a conqueror across Shade's demesne. "I have questions."

"And I have answers." Wrath nodded. "Not all the answers, but some."

It didn't seem like a conversation they should have with everyone listening, so she nodded and kept walking. She also should be removing her hand from Shade's, but if felt oddly comforting, so she left hers in his.

The border between the two demesnes was surprisingly close, and they reached it after only half a day of walking. She stepped over the border and into an entirely different place. The two hordes crossed the border in the dull tramp of heavy feet and the clank of weapons.

Shade's demons looked a bit uncomfortable, but they kept moving.

Power prickled over her skin and settled into her muscles.

Wrath's demesne was different from Shade's and reflected his different temperament. The landscape here was rocky and mountainous. Soaring forests of hardy trees crowned the cliffs around them. Heat from a red sun in a cloudless purple sky beat down on the earth, and dust rose in ochre puffs as they walked. A raging torrent tore through the ravine to their right, foaming and hissing and sending a fine spray of mist into the air. It was the sort of place that almost demanded she strap on a backpack and some hiking boots and conquer it.

Their route led them up an incline and between treed, towering cliff faces before disgorging them onto a wide, craggy plain. A fortress guarded the plain from its position atop a hill.

Wrath pointed. "My home."

It made perfect sense. The place looked impenetrable with towering ochre walls standing sentinel. If you had a temper and a habit of making war on your neighbors, you'd need strong walls.

As they approached the fortress, arrow slits opened and crossbows appeared, which seemed to be unfortunately aimed at their heads.

"No need to worry," Wrath said and stepped in front of their party.

A pause followed, and then a portcullis creaked up. Behind it, heavy towering doors opened. More demons stood inside the fortress and bowed their heads as Wrath entered.

He ignored them and kept walking across a cobbled courtyard toward a stone staircase. Another large set of wooden doors opened as they ascended.

A large second, smaller courtyard with twin fountains lay on the other side. Lush plants softened the space and made it less utilitarian. Intricate and beautiful mosaics broke up the floor and ringed the top of the pillars. It was simple and beautiful at the same time, and Eddie approved. Whereas Shade's castle had felt like a shrine to pleasure, this one was a balance between pragmatism and beauty. It suggested a gentler side to Wrath.

A demoness in a medieval gown appeared through an arched doorway. Clasping her hands in front of her, she bowed her head. "Master, we have made preparations for your guests and for the honored daughter."

"Good." Wrath stopped beside her. "May I introduce you to Vexia? She is my steward and house manager." He turned to Vexia. "You are familiar with Asmodeus. This is the guardian Deandra, who is also the grandmother of my daughter." His beaming smile was warmer than the sun overhead as he looked at Eddie. "And this is the Nephilim, Edme.

Vexia clasped her hands and bowed her head again. Her long red hair was neatly braided down her back, and other than her pale skin and tawny cat eyes, she looked almost human. "This home is honored by your presence. Your wants are my wants, your needs are my needs. You have but to ask, and it shall be done."

Wrath unbuckled his sword and handed it to Vexia. "I think a cool bath and some refreshments in their rooms would be a good start."

She bowed again and vanished into thin air.

"So cool," Dee breathed, and Eddie couldn't have said it better.

"She's a higher order demon," Shade said. "They have some nifty tricks and look closer to human."

Wrath motioned them deeper into the home. "This way."

"Huh." Shade looked around him. "I always liked this place."

With a snort, Wrath glanced at him. "And you know how much your approval means to me."

"Absolutely fuck all?" Shade chuckled.

Wrath nodded and led them through a large arched opening, but not before Eddie caught his smirk. Not exactly chums, but it was a step in the right direction.

A soaring winged staircase in ochre and cream marble led upwards to the cool, shaded depths above. Tapestries adorned the walls, providing splashes of color in the restful interior.

"This is incredible," Dee whispered as they started up the stairs. "I've looked after that stupid hell gate for my entire life, and now I'm in hell." She widened her sparkling eyes at Eddie. "I'm actually in hell."

Eddie had to smile at Dee's enthusiasm. "I was expecting a lot more fire."

"Right??" Dee giggled. "Makes me wonder what heaven looks like."

"Probably a lot fewer clouds than we're expecting."

"Heaven is similar to this." Shade leaned in closer to them. "Each demesne tends to reflect the personality of the archangel." He grinned. "So, Gabriel for instance, lives in a fucking filing cabinet."

THIRTY-ONE

After lolling long enough to go pruney in a tub that resembled an ancient Roman bath, Eddie pulled on a white linen lounging set that Vexia had brought her. Double doors opened on one side of the bathing chamber—because no way she could dub this room something as mundane as bathroom—and Eddie wandered through gauzy white curtains onto a wide, deep balcony. She was high enough up to see beyond the fortress walls to the savannah stretching out for miles in all directions. A harsh line of jagged mountains pushed up through the grasslands to her right.

The fortress couldn't be approached other than by traveling uphill across a plane with no concealment. Was Wrath similarly unapproachable? Did she care?

Well, yes, she kind of did. For a girl who'd grown up dreaming of a father to rescue her from her awkwardness, she very much did care. And Wrath had seemed more than amenable to establishing a connection with her.

Dee had only stayed in their large, airy bedroom for long

enough to summon Vexia and then she'd gone on a tour of the fortress.

"Eddie," she'd said as she strapped on yet more knives. "This may be the one and only time I see this, and I want to see all of it."

A black speck flew low to the ground over the savannah, growing larger at a rapid pace until she caught the red flecks in Wrath's wings. He soared over the fortress walls, and then veered straight for her balcony.

Eddie had been half expecting a chitchat with daddy dearest since the theatre, and she braced.

Hovering in front of her balcony, Wrath bowed his head. "Daughter."

"Um...Wrath." She tried for similar insouciance, but the word stumbling ruined the effect. She didn't know what to call him, and dad seemed wrong on so many levels.

He motioned the balcony. "May I?"

"It's your balcony." Eddie braced her hips against the stone balustrade that guarded the edge as Wrath lowered himself about ten feet away from her. The draft from his wings sent her damp hair flying.

Landing, he furled his wings, and they disappeared into his back. "Stretching my wings," he said.

If Eddie had wings, you could bet your ass she'd be out there stretching them.

A demon appeared through another set of doors that led to a sitting room she and Dee had as part of their suite. Distressingly rodent-like, the demon bowed to Wrath and then her and set up a large jug and two glasses on a table before scuttling away again. He must have been a lower order demon. Look at her getting all up on her demonology.

"I thought we could...have words." Wrath cleared his throat and motioned the jug. "Wine?"

Wine sounded like a perfect accompaniment to words. "Yes, please."

While he poured, Eddie studied him covertly. She tried to find some trace of her features in his. Perhaps her darker hair when Rosabella's hair was lighter brown? Maybe in the square line of their jaws, or the fullness of their bottom lips? She definitely got her blue green eyes from Rosabella, but she was taller than her mother and less curvy.

Wrath held a glass out to her filled with a pale, straw-colored wine. "I hope this will please you." He joined her at the railing. "We make it here, but we do not have your human mastery of the perfect grape."

"I guess you have bigger things to worry about." Eddie accepted her glass. Cool to the touch, the wine caught the roseate light of a sinking sun.

Wrath chuckled, and it was a warm, comforting sound. "Perhaps just other things to worry about. Our insistence on making war doesn't leave time for more refined hobbies."

Eddie sipped her wine and was pleasantly surprised by its crisp, floral taste. "It's good."

"It is based on a Sancerre." Wrath motioned with his glass. "That was your mother's favorite white wine."

As most white wine found a place in Rosabella's heart, Eddie was surprised he remembered that detail. Ouch! The judgy thing appeared to be contagious, and clearly, she had some suppressed anger and mommy issues to work through.

The purple sky was darkening to indigo as the red sun blazed gold on the horizon.

"I shall begin with answering what would be my first question were I you. Why you have never seen me before now." Wrath took a seat on one of the oversize lounge chairs near the table. "The answer is simply that I was unaware that I had a child until Yesterday told me as much."

"Wait. What?" Eddie needed to unpack that piece by piece, beginning with, "Yesterday knew I was your daughter?"

"He guessed you were Nephilim." He studied her with those cool blue eyes. "It was only once you were in hell and your true nature revealed itself that he identified your sire."

You would think she was getting immune to all the ways Yesterday had played her. "He could have told me."

"Imps are…" Wrath pulled a face. "Dishonest by nature. They lie. It's what they do."

"Like you make war?" Frankly, the *we are this way because we were made that way* argument was getting stale.

Wrath flinched. "Touché. Would you like me to punish him?"

"No." She sighed. Not because she didn't want to smack the little shit in his stupidly big mouth, but more because *she'd* like to do the smacking. "But trusting him in any way seems to be risky."

Wrath grunted and sipped his wine.

Guttural shouts sounded from the courtyard and then receded. As Wrath didn't seem concerned, Eddie decided not to be. "So, you didn't know I was your daughter until recently?"

"Yes." He nodded, his expression somber and pensive. "Had I known, Eddie, I would have come sooner. I would have made sure you were protected. When I left the earth plane, Deandra made me promise not to return. But had I known I had a daughter, I would have broken that promise."

That must have been the deal Dee had spoken about when she'd first seen Wrath. Dee must have known Rosabella was pregnant when she'd extracted that promise from Wrath. Even knowing Dee had done what she'd done to protect her, it still smarted. Then again, Dee had given her a relatively normal life up until now. If Wrath had come for her, she might not have had that. She might have grown up here, and perhaps without Dee in her life. A tangle of emotions tightened in her chest. Everywhere she turned she found more questions. She couldn't deal with them right now.

Mouthwatering smells drifted in with the evening breeze. If she'd been attempting to have a conversation with anyone else about anything else, the evening might have been companionable. But as it was, she wanted to fidget. She caught Wrath side eyeing her and guessed he was no more comfortable with the situation than she was. "How did you meet my mother?"

"Rosabella?" He started and looked guilty as hell. "I met your mother when I came through the hell gate. About…" He cleared his throat. "Twenty years ago?"

"Twenty-six," she said. He didn't even know how old she was.

"Yes." He nodded. "Well, twenty-five, because you…and Rosabella was expecting…and…er…human biology being what it is."

"Right, twenty-five." His awkwardness put her more at ease and Eddie took the seat opposite him.

"We…that is to say, hell princes." He stopped a moment. "Archangels too I believe, have a weakness for humans." He took a huge slug of wine. "We find humans somewhat irresistible. It is…er…mainly for this reason that…congress between us and humans is forbidden."

"You find us irresistible?" Eddie found that hard to believe. Near perfect beings who, judging by what she'd seen thus far, were all ridiculously beautiful, found humans irresistible.

"You are not human, daughter." Wrath grimaced. "Not entirely human, but I am sure you are also irresistible." He went bright red, and his eyes widened in horror. "I mean, not to me. I am not…I do not. I speak merely of the way I have seen

Shade look at you. And the other demons. And a couple of the archangels."

According to her father, she was crack for supernaturals. Seemed like a missed opportunity. "Why? What is irresistible about us? You're the physically perfect beings."

"When you exist with physical perfection, it ceases to be perfection and becomes the norm," Wrath said. "We are also immortal beings. Whereas humans are so immediate and raw. They know their time is short, and that changes the way they embrace existence. We find it entrancing."

"Huh." Eddie let that percolate through her brain. "And me? If you're immortal and my mother was mortal, what does that make me?"

"Long-lived enough to be close to immortal." Wrath refilled both their glasses. "Now that your powers have been activated, so has your longevity."

"And if I hadn't come through the hell gate?"

Wrath tilted his head and considered her question. "That I cannot answer. Nephilim are so rare." He raised his glass to her. "And thus special."

For someone who'd been told she was going to live a helluva lot longer than she had originally supposed, Eddie was remarkably calm about the information. She would have thought she'd be happier about the news. "And Dee?"

"Is mortal." Wrath looked saddened. "That is another reason why we limit our exposure to humans. Once we grow attached to them, we spend a long time mourning them once they are no longer with us." He stared out at the view. "The temptation for us is always to find a way to keep them with us indefinitely. It can lead to some disturbing consequences. Even hell princes and archangels do not have power over life and death."

And there was the giant downside. Eddie needed to think

more about that, but not right now. "So, you came through the hell gate and what happened? Where did you meet my mother?"

"At the theatre." The sinking sun softened the harsh lines of Wrath's face. "She was on the stage dancing. I didn't mean to stop, but she was so graceful and so lovely. She had this passion for life that drew me to linger."

Expression tender, Wrath lost himself in his memory.

"You liked her?" It seemed Rosabella's allure ran the gamut of the male species.

"I loved her," he murmured. "Perhaps I still do." He turned to look at her. "I see in you all the best of your mother."

A lump clogged in Eddie's throat, and she blinked rapidly. There must be allergens down here making her tear up. She didn't want to like Wrath, but his openness appealed to her.

"She had fire and energy," he said. "She had this determination to embrace what life she had and bend it to her will."

That didn't sound like Eddie. "I'm not like that. Rosabella and I are very different."

"Maybe." He shrugged and sipped his wine. "But I see what I see, and you are only beginning to discover your true self."

The incident with the demons put in a memory appearance. "And apparently, I have a temper. A really fucking bad one."

"That would be from me." He smiled, and it made her want to tell him all her secrets. "I believe Shade has already told you that all those demons would recover." Elbows to his knees, he leaned forward. "And if it makes you feel any better, what you did to them would have been nothing compared to what I would have done to them if they had harmed you."

"Did you send them?"

"No." All softness fled Wrath's face, and his eyes glittered. "There were definitely of me, but I suspect they were a group of the demons who have escaped my horde." His hard gaze met hers. "But I will find them, Eddie, and I will make them sorry they so much as scratched you."

Fuck. Eddie's mind reeled. It was like the ultimate missing parent fantasy come to life, yet she felt wrong footed and awkward. She didn't know what to say to hearing all the things her heart had craved for so long. "Okay."

"Know this, Eddie." His stare held her captive. "You are precious to me."

The lump grew, and she stopped pretending that she didn't want to bawl her heart out. "Okay."

"I do not care that Nephilim are hunted and killed. You will not be harmed in any way. I will end the world before I allow that."

"You really need to stop saying shit like that." Her heart felt like it would burst out of her chest.

"Okay." Wrath smiled and sat back. "For now."

She needed to change the subject. But first, more wine, so she finished her glass.

Wrath leaned closer and refilled it.

"If you loved my mother, why did you not stay with her?"

Wrath hung his head and stared between his hands. "Rosabella did not love me." He sat back and sipped his wine. "Not as I loved her."

Rosabella had a hit 'em and leave 'em policy with men, but even she couldn't have been happy passing on this one. "She didn't love you? Are you sure?"

"Quite sure." Wrath's smile was tinged with sadness. "I asked, you see, and she was nothing if not honest."

Eddie leaned forward to catch all of what he said next. "What did she say?"

"She said she wanted to be free to live her life on her terms." He motioned around them. "I made this palace over in a way I thought would please her, but she did not want to stay here. She sought your earthly diversions and pleasures over what I could offer."

Sadly, that did sound a lot like her mother. She had chosen that same freedom over being Eddie's mother. "She left me too," she said.

"I know." His expression hardened. "And when I find her, I will make my opinion on that clear."

Alarm spiked through Eddie. "You won't hurt her."

"Of course not." He gaped at her. "I would not hurt the woman who holds my heart, but she has harmed our child, and that is not acceptable."

Oh, boy. And there he went again with the saying the right thing. She blurted out the first thing that came to mind. "Why don't I have wings?"

"Wings?" Wrath laughed. "You want wings?"

"Only because I don't have them," she babbled. "I mean, I never really thought about it until I saw you and Shade." That was not strictly true. "I mean, of course I've thought about it. You know, what kid didn't want to fly, but not since then. Much."

Wrath shifted in his seat. "Nephilim do not get wings. Some demons do. All angels, of course. And the hell princes and the archangels also all have wings." He cleared his throat. "But wings are not really all that great."

"How?"

"Well." He chugged his wine and refilled. "They can be cumbersome. It takes a long time to learn how to use them. And"—he held up his forefinger—"they hurt like nothing else when they get injured."

Eddie smelled the earthy waft of bullshit. "You're lying."

"You're right." He threw back his head and laughed. "Wings are the best."

THIRTY-TWO

A knock on her door interrupted the comfortable silence that had fallen between Eddie and Wrath.

"Shade," Wrath said and jerked his head toward the door. "He is here."

"Are you always aware of each other?" Eddie had so much to learn about the new landscape she found herself in. Fortunately, she now had a father to teach her. Not that Wrath with his built like a brick shit house badassery would ever fit comfortably in the dad category. But you worked with what you had.

Wrath stalked to the door. "Each of us has a power signature." His grin was pure evil. "It makes sneaking up on each other a challenge." Wrenching open, the door he barked, "What?"

"And good evening to you, Satanus." Shade's husky warm drawl floated over to Eddie. The man even sounded like sex, which given who and what he was—not a total surprise. "I came for Eddie."

Gah! He made that sound like an invitation she desperately wanted to RSVP *Hell, Fucking Yes.*

"I'm here." She edged around the barn that was Wrath. Satan. Her father. Damn, but that was going to take some getting used to. It would make an interesting Bumble profile. *One HELL of a good time.*

Actually, that might work...never mind.

"Hey, Eddie." Shade's smile was molten sunshine and sweaty nights. "You okay?"

Wrath puffed up like a barnyard rooster. "Of course she is okay. She is with me."

"Seeing you like this." Shade slid a languid, challenging gaze over Wrath. "Overprotective father. It's not a look I thought I'd see you wear."

"Fuck you," Wrath snarled.

Shade winked. "I'm flattered by the sentiment, big guy, but I'm more interested in other members of your bloodline."

"Did you need something?" Eddie got in there before feathers flew.

The look Shade gave her nearly set her lounge pants on fire. "So many things, Eddie," he said. "But for now, I thought we should concentrate on the seals."

Wrath nodded and then scowled at Shade. "The way you look at my daughter makes me want to rip your guts through your asshole."

"Colorful." Shade grinned. "And I cannot change the way I look at her. It is beyond my control."

Eddie stared at Shade. What did that even mean? Beyond the rather obvious Valmont dialogue. "You want to look at the seals?"

"Yes." Shade's gray eyes swung her way and softened. "There's going to be a lot of emotion for you to carry as you get closer to the wrath seal. And because it's your birth seal, it's going to be worse than my seal."

It would take a while before Eddie forgot the way unadulterated lust had consumed her, and she'd been standing across the room from it.

"I can help with that because of our shared blood." Wrath put a hand on her shoulder. "I can bear the wrath for you if you agree to allow me to link with you and carry the burden."

"What does linking mean?" She looked to Shade for her answer. Wrath may be her biological father, but Shade had been the closest thing she'd had to an ally since the entire mind fuck had gotten rolling.

Shade glanced at Wrath before turning back to her. "It means allowing him inside your inner being. He will be able to feel what you feel, think what you think, experience what you experience. He means to take the wrath from you and channel it through himself." He shrugged. "It will help, but I understand how you feel about hell princes having access to your inner being."

"What did you do?" Wrath shoved Shade's shoulder.

Shade barely moved. "I did some...inadvisable things when I first met Eddie."

"Did you hurt her?" Wrath crowded Shade.

"He didn't hurt me." Eddie was now officially cast in the role of peacekeeper. "But he did...never mind." She turned back to Wrath. "You can help me when I get closer to the seal?"

"Yes." He nodded but kept his glower on Shade. "It will make the emotion more manageable for you. I am wrath. The emotion is part of me and easier for me to manage. And as you came from me..." He shrugged.

Shade snorted. "Although, once you're done, he may start a major war to mitigate the effects."

"No wars." Eddie was clear on that point. Her entire purpose here was to avoid war. "Or we don't do a damn thing."

Wrath nodded. "No war, daughter. This I vow to you."

"Okay then." Eddie didn't relish going up against a seal again, but the end of life as she knew it provided enough incentive to get her nodding again. "Now?"

Shade grimaced. "The sooner the better, Eddie. With the seals unstable, they will be affecting other areas of creation."

"You mean like earth?" The way the lust seal had affected her taking place on a global scale was terrifying to contemplate.

He nodded. "Damaged seals will leak what they contain through to earth."

And she was meant to stop that. Sheer, unadulterated panic swept through her. She wasn't the heroic type. She was pretty sure she was the find somewhere good to hide type. For fuck's sake, she managed a community theatre in rural Ontario. Now the fate of the world rested on her inadequate shoulders.

Stepping forward, Shade cupped her face. His beautiful face filled her vision. The tender expression in his eyes robbed her of breath. "Breathe, Eddie," he whispered. "You've got this. You are more than you believe yourself to be."

Wrath grunted. "He's not wrong."

But it packed so much more punch when Shade said it to her.

"Eddie-girl!" Dee came barreling down the corridor toward her, Vexia following quietly behind. Dee glanced at Wrath and then Shade and wrinkled her nose. "Anyway, darling, this place is amazing. I found a ballroom." She chuckled. "I mean, a real ballroom with chandeliers and everything."

"I need to host on occasion," Wrath murmured with a flush.

"I mean." Dee planted her hands on her hips. "Who has a ballroom?"

"Not that often." Wrath cleared his throat. "I mean, the hosting, but it does happen."

"Archangels do like to waltz." Shade winked at her. "All except Gabriel, who likes to mark the music's rhythm and criticize every missed note."

Dee paid them no mind. "And I also found this massive banqueting hall, with these long tables." She slashed her hand through the air. "Like Hogwarts."

Eddie hated to spoil Dee's fun. "We were talking about repairing the seal," she said. "That it should happen now."

"Oh." Dee looked at Wrath and then Shade. "Okay, but is it dangerous?"

"Anything dealing with this amount of power can be dangerous," Wrath said. "But Shade and I will do all that we can to mitigate against that danger."

Deflating, Dee glanced at Vexia. "What do you think? Is it safe for my granddaughter to repair the seals?"

Folding her hands in front of her, Vexia bowed her head. "I serve Lord Wrath. I do not think."

"Dammit, Vexia!" Dee glowered at her. "Didn't we talk about this when we were going through that art gallery thingy?"

"Yes, Dee." Vexia kept her gaze on the ground.

Eddie decided to exercise the power Wrath had given her. "I want to hear your opinion."

Vexia glanced at her and blanched. "Mistress?"

"I want to hear what you have to say." It was her ass on the line after all and another opinion could help.

"I think there is little choice, mistress," Vexia said. "If you do not repair the seal, we will all cease to exist. And Lord Wrath will do all that he can to keep you safe."

"Eddie?" Shade took her hand in his and interwove their fingers. "I know my seal scared you, but we need you."

Fucking hell! She hated that he put it that way, because now she really didn't have a choice. "Let's heal this son of a bitch."

WRATH'S THRONE room looked like a medieval great hall with a huge wooden throne on one end shrouded in furs, a large firepit in the center, and heavy wooden beams crisscrossing the ceiling. Eddie shivered as she remembered it from when she'd dream walked here. A few of his demon horde slunk through the shadows, watching them pass with wary expressions.

Eddie could feel the pull of the seal. Already she wanted to smash things and rip one of the weapons off the wall and start bathing in the blood of her enemies. Like at Shade's palace, the seal was kept in a small room behind the throne. The ceiling was so low it almost brushed Wrath and Shade's heads, and smoking braziers did little to dispel the gloomy, dungeon-like feel of the chamber.

The seal was polished pewter with a faint red glow around it, and it tugged on Eddie. Rage suffused every part of her being as her lips curled back from her teeth in snarl.

"Wrath!" Shade gave her a worried glance. "She's feeling it already. You need to do something."

With a nod, Wrath closed his eyes.

Eddie felt a tap on her awareness and the warm, steady presence of Wrath.

"Open your mind to him," Shade said close to her ear. "Let him take the emotion from you."

She wanted to punch his beautiful face for the next to useless advice. "How the fuck do I do that?"

"Think of it like opening a door or drawing back a curtain." Shade's palm provided a steady pressure in the small of her back, anchoring her to the room, preventing her from grabbing Wrath's sword and hacking off heads.

She tried to do what Shade had suggested, but she didn't want to open her mind. She wanted to slam her defenses shut and fight.

"Breathe, Eddie," Shade murmured. "You are stronger than you think."

She was stronger. She was mighty. She was fury. She was vengeance and rage.

Her mind opened a tiny chink, and Wrath surged through. He coaxed the barriers of her mind further apart.

"Open your heart now to him," Shade said.

No. Every part of Eddie rebelled. Her heart was hers to protect and guard.

"Here hold this." Shade pressed the pommel of his sword into her hands. Probably not a good idea considering how she wanted to rip the world apart, and now had the means to carve it apart. But the sword felt familiar and comforting, and she drew courage from it and opened her heart.

Wrath flooded through her chest, warm and comforting, but still invasive.

Her anger receded a bit.

Wrath took up more space in her being, and the fury abated enough for Eddie to feel like she could breathe again.

"We're going closer to the seal now," Shade said, his palm pressing against her back. "It's going to get worse the closer you get. You can sense Wrath within you. Give him the emotion."

Shade at her back, Eddie stepped closer.

A red haze blanketed her vision, just as it had in the forest. Fury lashed through her blood. Her muscles swelled and blood pounded through her veins.

And Wrath funneled it from her.

He stood to her left. Sweat poured down his face, his eyes bulged, a vein beat in his temple, and the eyes locked on her were blood red.

He was doing this for her, and Eddie closed the distance to the seal.

Rage lashed at her. Even with Wrath's help, she felt the need to wreak destruction boiling inside her, calling to her to rip and rend.

"Put your hands on the seal," Shade murmured. "Feel it. Feel what needs to be done."

Through the haze of punishing anger, she sensed the seal. It rang through her being like a gong was struck. The dissonance hit her like a body blow and pushed her back.

"Hold him!" Shade yelled.

Three demons attempted to contain Wrath as he writhed and fought against them. His wings were out, and his power buffeted the room. Rocks cracked and debris rained down around them. More demons piled on the thrashing hell prince.

Eddie stepped back to the seal. If she didn't do this fast, the entire castle might come down around them. When she connected with the seal again, she homed in on the dissonance.

"What do I do?" Panic morphed into fury inside her.

"Concentrate, Eddie." Shade bracketed her from behind, his body shielding her from Wrath's wildly fluctuating power and the falling debris. "You are Nephilim. You have the power within you to do this. Let that power speak through you."

Wrath roared, and demons went flying.

More demons threw themselves at him.

Wrath ripped into them like a bezerker. Still they kept coming, trying to contain him.

"Concentrate, Eddie," Shade whispered. "He's got this."

The dismembered corpse of a demon crashed into the wall beside her.

"Eddie!" Shade raised his voice. "Stay focused."

Focus. She tried to shut out the war happening around her.

"Find the part of you that is your mother," Shade said. "Your hell prince side is already active; find your humanity."

Find her fucking humanity? How the hell was she supposed to do that?

A memory popped into her mind. She was about eight, in the park with Dee. Dee was laughing while she fed the squirrels.

"They're rats with tails, Eddie-girl." Dee smiled at her.

"That's it, Eddie," Shade whispered. "Give it more."

She was twelve now, and she and Dee were watching a scary movie. Dee's arms around her made her feel safe and secure. Eddie felt again the delicious sensation of being scared, but knowing she was safe.

Wrath bellowed a sound of pure rage. An answering yell built in Eddie. A two-foot crack opened up across the ceiling.

"More, Eddie," Shade shouted.

And Eddie closed her eyes and remembered. The times she'd laughed, the times she'd cried. She relived her sixteen-year-old heartbreak. The delight of running through the sprinklers on a hot summer day. The elicit thrill of hiding under the covers with a book and a pint of ice-cream. She kept the memories coming. All the delights and the tribulations. Every absurd and wonderful part of being human. She lived the contradictions and the struggles, the triumphs, and the thrills.

Until with a final note, the seal rung true. Or almost true.

She tried harder, but she could not feel that final piece of dissonance. It was like trying to fill in a missing piece of pie.

Shade tightened his hold on her hips. "What is it?"

"It's better." Eddie panted like she'd been running a marathon. "But it's not all fixed."

"Wrath?" Shade called. "Can you feel what she feels?"

"Heaven." Wrath grunted. He was on his knees beneath a pile of moaning, bleeding demons. "She has healed earth and hell in the seal, but she doesn't have heaven within her to complete the healing." He dropped face first on the ground. "It's better, but it's not entirely fixed."

Shade wrapped his arms around her. "You can let go now, Eddie."

She took her hands off the seal. The quiet after the storm almost hurt her ears.

Peeling off demons, Wrath rose to his feet. His wings dragged on the floor behind him, and his head hung down. "Let's agree not to do that again in a hurry."

Eddie opened her mouth to whole-heartedly agree when the world went black. She was dimly aware of Shade catching her before everything went dark.

THIRTY-THREE

Eddie woke in the bed in the room Wrath had given her. Warm arms encircled her, and a hard body cradled her. She'd never felt safer or more cherished in her entire life.

She knew it was Shade, and she lay still, relishing the moment.

"You're awake." His voice was husky in her ear. "You've been asleep for a long time."

She didn't want to move and lose the lovely feeling. "How long?"

"Most of what passes for a day and a night here." He nuzzled her nape. "Dee has almost explored the entire castle by now. She's beginning to look like she wants to take her adventure on the road."

For a moment, Eddie allowed herself to wonder what it would be like to have this all the time. To wake up beside a being who made you feel like the world was a better place. Except, it wasn't real. Nothing with Shade was real; it was all a byproduct of who he was. Or was it? There were times it felt so real, but maybe she just wanted it to be so much, that she made it so. It was way too early and she was way too short on caffeine for mental torture.

Edging away from him, she hung her legs over the side of the bed. She ignored the sense of loss moving away from him opened in her chest. "It's not done." She really didn't want to go through another session with a seal, but she had to be honest. "It's better, but it won't hold."

"Yeah." Shade rolled to his back and tucked his hands behind his head.

Eddie ignored the wonderful ripply muscle crap happening over his torso. Dammit, but when they'd chosen a form for the embodiment of lust, they hadn't been messing around. Or had he chosen his form? Perhaps he had a super-hot mother and father out there somewhere? All valid questions, but perhaps better deferred to another day.

"Eddie?" Shade was watching her with that lambent, sultry look he had down pat.

Perhaps over time she would become immune to it. "What?"

"I don't think you should fix my seal."

Eddie gaped at him. Wasn't the mending of the seals the entire reason any of this was happening. And then she got it. He didn't believe she could do it and was trying to let her down kindly. It shouldn't hurt as much as it did. After all, she hadn't been able to complete the job on her blood seal, why would he trust her with one she wasn't even bound to. Grabbing the sheet, she tucked it around her and stood. "I see."

"Eddie." Shade's voice compelled her to look at him, but she couldn't let him see her vulnerability.

She stomped for the bathroom. "I have to get dressed."

"Eddie." The bed creaked and his feet padded closer. "I don't think you do see."

"It's fine." She snatched open the bathroom door.

A big hand came over her shoulder and shut the door. Shade's naked body crowded her against the door. "I don't believe you do see."

"I couldn't complete the repair." Eddie tugged at the handle but with Shade holding the door closed, she had little chance of opening it. She could always use her hell strength, but she didn't like what happened to her when she did.

"The repair drained you, Eddie." Shade's breath caressed the shell of her ear and created goosebumps all down her neck and arms. "And I am not able to link with you like Wrath did. I can't help you, Eddie, and I can't risk you draining yourself."

If that's even what he meant. "It's not your decision. As you are all so quick to point out, I'm Nephilim. I'm the only one who can do this."

"But that doesn't mean you're expendable, Eddie." His hands dropped to her hips. "Not to me anyway."

It was tough to remember he was lust personified, and she couldn't trust what she felt for him when he said things like that. "I have to at least try."

Shade sighed and pressed his head against hers. "You're so stubborn, Eddie."

"Blame my father." She needed to get away from him and get her rampaging emotions under control again.

His grip on her hips tightened. "I'm not talking about the seal now, Eddie. Well, not just the seal."

"What then?" Her heart started an uneven pound against her breastbone.

"Us." He brushed his lips against her temple. "The way you don't trust me."

Her response was automatic and Canadian politeness at its dumbest. "I trust you."

"No, you don't." His raspy chuckle vibrated against her

shoulder blades. "You have decided because of who and what I am, that this is only about sex for me."

"It's not that." And honesty compelled her to be more specific. "Not only that."

He pressed his nose into her neck and drew in a deep breath. "Tell me."

She'd do anything he asked when he used that tender, hoarse note in his voice, and that was part of the problem. "It's me when I'm with you. How do I know if anything I feel is real and not just lust?"

Shade stilled and then sighed. "It comes down to trust, I guess, and I haven't exactly done much to earn that from you."

Or had he? Certainly, Shade had done some highly questionable fucking shit when he'd first arrived, but after that, she wasn't so sure. It was all too confusing. "Can we just focus on the seals?"

He sighed and let her go. "Okay, Eddie. Let's get that out of the way, and then we can talk."

"Okay." She yanked open the bathroom door and scuttled inside. Once safely on the other side, she shut the door behind her and leaned against it. It took several deep breaths before she felt calm enough to carry on getting dressed. That conversation she'd promised to have with Shade, she was nowhere near ready to have. Maybe he'd forget about it. Yeah, probably not, but you had to have dreams.

SHADE STARED at the closed bathroom door and quelled his desire to kick it off its hinges. The shower went on, and he pictured Eddie slowly peeling her clothes off and getting beneath the warm water.

"Fuck." He pressed his forehead against the door and

breathed deep. His own seal strength was biting him in the ass. For certain, he could go in there and draw lust, send it out in ever strengthening tendrils until Eddie was powerless to resist him.

But Eddie was right about that, and he had never taken a being against their will. He'd used his lust to draw healing strength from beings, like he had with Lillian in the theatre. He'd even used it to manipulate an outcome, and definitely used it to cause trouble amongst his fellow supernaturals. But he'd always stopped short of taking advantage of the lust he engendered and using it to take a being whose sexual will was not their own.

And because he had never known without doubt that it was him and not his lust ability that beings craved, he had lived a lonely existence. While his fellow hell princes slaked their lust with each other, high order demons, an angel or two, and apparently humans, he lived more chaste than them all. Not a soul would believe him if he told them, so he didn't, and allowed their perceptions to color him as the conscienceless debaucher of innocents, the great seducer.

And now he was paying the price, both for this seal and for his apathy in correcting assumptions.

BATHED AND DRESSED, Eddie met Shade and Dee in Wrath's throne room. Only to find Shade already there with a full horde, all of them armed and looking ready to travel.

In the center of the room, legs akimbo, arms folded, Shade and Wrath stood glaring at each other.

"They're arguing." Dee rolled her eyes. "Just for a change."

Eyeing the bellicose pair, Eddie chose discretion. "Want to give me the Cliff Notes?"

"Shade wants to take you back to the theatre." She waved her arm to indicate a horde to the left. "And those are his goon squad." Her arm circled over to the right. "And on this side, we have Wrath's goon squad. Both are vehement that they alone should be allowed to protect you."

And this for a woman who'd made a life out of doing things for herself. "Oh, boy."

"Yup." Dee tucked her thumbs in her utility belt. "Shade was under the impression we would be going back to the theatre without Wrath. Wrath is of the opinion that you will leave his home over his dead body."

"All right then." There really was only one thing to do. Eddie clapped her hands for attention. "Dee and I are leaving. Whoever wants to come with us needs to move out."

"Very good, Eddie-girl. I taught you well." Dee chuckled, leaned closer and whispered, "Where are we going?"

"Shade's demesne." Eddie had another seal to do battle with, and after that...she really didn't know. Nowhere felt like home right now, not with the guardians running rampant through her theatre.

Weapons and armor clattered behind them as the hordes got ready to follow, and then Shade appeared beside her. A frown creased his beautiful face. "I forbid you to go to my demesne."

It irked her that he'd guessed her intention so easily, but the forbidding thing annoyed her a whole lot more. "Then you and your army can keep me out." She couldn't resist a smirk. "Or you could try."

"And she'll have my army at her back," Wrath said, blissfully ignoring his former position of not letting her out of his demesne. Honestly, these two needed to go back to kindergarten and learn how to play nicely with others.

"Eddie, you're not being reasonable." Shade's face softened

in a way that made her want to give him whatever he asked. "The seal could be dangerous for you, and I can't help you. I cannot expose you to that kind of potential danger."

"Then we'll find that out when we get there." As much as his words made the pit of her stomach drop, she had a job to do, and the sooner she did it, the sooner life could return to normal. Whatever that would look like. Probably without Shade, or Wrath. It didn't matter; she'd been quite happy with her life before they'd appeared in it. She would be happy again. Somehow.

"Think about what you're proposing." Shade dropped into step beside her as she strode toward the throne room door. "Wrath won't let you go without him and his horde. And we cannot allow Wrath and his demons into my demesne. There will be repercussions."

"He allowed you and your lot into his." It's like they made war on each other even when there was no reason to. In this case, there was every reason not to. "And the extra man...er... demon power will come in handy. You'll keep your lot under control, and Wrath will do the same with his." A lifetime of diva wrangling came to her aid as she said, "Or are you not certain you can keep your horde under control? In which case—"

"Eddie," Shade growled and stepped into her personal space.

"I'm sure this managing part of your personality is inherited from your mother's side." Wrath joined them.

Dee thumped him on the bicep. "You keep thinking that, big guy."

"Okay then." Shade drew his shoulders back, and it was a distractingly good look on him. "I refuse to let Wrath into my demesne."

"Hah!" Wrath squared up to him. "I refuse to enter your

demesne, and your welcome in mine is now revoked. Any demon—"

Eddie gave a piercing whistle. She was done with the two of them. "One, two, three." She clapped out the numbers. "All eyes on me."

Every pair of eyes in the throne room locked on her.

Eddie swallowed the nerves that much demonic attention created. "I'm here to see if I can repair the seals. Wrath's will hold. Shade's is still a mess. I'm not leaving until I look at it. I'm going to Shade's palace to see what I can do. Everybody else can make their own decisions."

"I'm with you." Dee moved closer to her.

Xerxes and Cronus dropped into place on her other side.

Shade threw her a frustrated glance and then glared at Wrath. "She really is your daughter, isn't she?"

As they took the long walk to Shade's demesne, going slowly enough to accommodate Dee, Eddie had plenty of time to wish she had one of those handy chariot things Lucifer whipped around in. Wrath was suspicious of Lucifer, but if it was him causing all the trouble, why had he helped her and Shade get away from Wrath's demons? Then again, given that they hadn't actually—or she hadn't—been in any danger, maybe he'd done it to cause more strife. Not that it appeared much ingenuity was required to cause dissent around here. An ill-timed sneeze was enough to set off a spot of bloodletting.

Case in point, a couple hours in, Shade left her side to go and sort out two of his demons who were getting nasty with each other. Being here was so divergent from where she'd always thought her life would take her and who she'd thought she was.

"Daughter." Wrath appeared beside her. He cast an approving look at her. "You are strong."

Stronger than Dee, for certain. Dee had been forced into a litter carried between two of those rhino demons. She was currently fast asleep, and all the demons around her whispered and quietened their footsteps, on pain of death from Wrath if they woke her.

"I suppose I have you to thank for that," she said.

Cronus came up on her other side and threw Wrath the stink eye. He didn't like any other hell prince being too close to her.

Wrath chuckled. "They protect you."

"Yes." She patted Cronus's shoulder. "I always wanted a dog, and now, two hell hounds have adopted me."

Nudging her other hand, Xerxes inserted himself between her and Wrath.

Wrath growled at him.

Xerxes growled right back.

"I wanted to speak with you." Wrath cleared his throat. He threw a scowl at Xerxes. "Privately."

"There is nothing you can say to her that we cannot hear." Cronus turned his blood-red eyes on Wrath.

Eddie chuckled. Having these two with her gave her a strange sense of normal. Her new normal apparently. "They're discreet."

"Right." Wrath shoulder checked Xerxes. "When we were linked." He studied the landscape around them with a thousand-yard stare. Eddie was getting the sense that any personal discussions made Wrath uncomfortable. "I did not go digging through your mind and feelings," he said. "But it was impossible not to…"

Eddie believed him, but it was still rather unsettling to

think of your father having access to your most private thoughts. "Okay."

"The thing is, Eddie." He took a deep breath. "I realize that I am late to this fathering thing, and I have no right to interfere in your life."

Why did that make her sure he was about to do some interfering?

"But I need to speak to you about Asmodeus."

Was she psychic now? "What about him?"

"Asmodeus is lust." Wrath rubbed his nape and sighed. "He makes people feel lust. He makes them feel lust for him as well."

The incident with Lillian rose fresh in her mind. The things he made her feel as well had her tied up in emotional knots. "Yup, seen that."

"And humans are…" He cleared his throat and studied the horizon. "Even Nephilim, because of your human part, are subject to confusing lust for something…er…deeper. More profound."

Wrath had seen into parts of her she didn't even want to visit. She couldn't afford to admit the possibility that her feelings for Shade were more than just physical. If her cynical side was right, and none of it was real, she had the nasty sense she'd be in for a whole universe of hurt. "You mean love."

"Yes." He looked relieved. "Humans are such emotional creatures. It is why we guard the sins and the virtues and keep them in balance. Imagine a world in which, say my demesne, wrath, was allowed free reign."

Eddie was pretty sure she'd seen horror movies that did that.

"And your feelings for Shade, whilst pure and wonderful, are perhaps…not real."

Wrath was so uncomfortable having this conversation, it helped her over her own awkwardness.

"I'm not sure I have any feelings for Shade. And I have in no way put a name to those feelings." She held up her hand to stop the denial she could see building on Wrath's face. Had he seen more in her heart than she was willing to face? "I know that I have felt lust for him, and he does affect me in a certain way." Her face heated, and she joined Wrath in studying the land around them. "But I also don't know how much of that is coming from him and how much is coming from me. And until I do, there will be no acting on any of those...er...urges."

"Good." Wrath heaved a massive sigh. "I would hate for you to be hurt by this, Eddie. The relationship between myself and your mother did not end well. Even were Shade's feelings for you genuine, there is still the matter of you live in one realm and he lives in another. He cannot leave hell, and this is not the place for you. The human part of your soul would wither and die here. You would have none of your friends, your theatre, Dee, no—"

"I get it." She ended the recitation before it got more depressing. She knew what Wrath was saying, and honestly, he wasn't saying anything she hadn't thought, but it hurt to hear, nonetheless. Some ridiculous part of her wanted to believe the way Shade was with her meant more. That same part wanted to believe in fairy tales and happily ever afters. It also wanted to bellow fuck the consequences and throw her headlong at the tempting possibility of more with Shade. "Nothing will happen between Shade and me. When this is over, I will go back to stage managing, and he will go back to his demesne."

Her heart twisted sharply, and her belly dropped with a sickening lurch. Sucking in a deep breath, she tried to convince herself that she would be fine with that future. *Liar*, whispered her heart. *Nothing will ever be the same without Shade.*

"Good." Wrath gave a curt nod. "That is good."

The needy little girl in her took the reins and she asked, "What about you? When this over, will I see you?"

"Daughter." Wrath's face softened, and he smiled sweetly. "Not the combined forces of hell princes, archangels, and guardians could stop me from seeing you."

Tears pricked her eyelids, and she felt warm and squishy inside. "Good."

"Yes, good." Wrath cleared his throat.

They trudged on in an uncomfortable silence for another minute or so before Wrath waved a hand toward his horde. "I'll just go...er...control...something."

"Good idea."

He trotted away with an alacrity that demonstrated again how uncomfortable emotional conversations made him.

"Eddie." Cronus pressed his massive body closer to her. *"Your sire means well."*

Xerxes grumbled.

"He would like to protect you and do for you what he was unable to do before," Cronus said.

She'd gone all these years without a father. Having one now would take some getting used to. "I know."

"His motives are pure, but he does not know all." Cronus's hot breath warmed her nape. *"He speaks from his experience, and that colors his view of matters."*

"Trust the master," Xerxes said.

And right there was the problem, she didn't trust Shade, and she for damn sure didn't trust her feelings for him.

THIRTY-FOUR

A couple of what felt like hours later—Eddie had no way of telling time here—a green smudge appeared on the horizon. After her conversation with Wrath, she'd stuck close to Dee.

Shade appeared. "My demesne." He turned those beautiful eyes on her. "The lads tell me your conversation with Wrath has upset you."

"You did?"

Cronus and Xerxes refused to meet her eyes and kept their gazes stuck on the horizon.

Shade took her elbow and gently moved her away from Dee's litter. "Want to tell me about that conversation?"

"No." He already knew too much, and she felt vulnerable and exposed. "What I discuss with my father is between us."

His lips quirked, but his gaze remained intent. "Not when I am the subject of that conversation."

Eddie glared at the hounds. "What exactly did they tell you?"

"They told me that Wrath warned you against me."

Shade's jaw tightened. "That Wrath has told you not to trust that your feelings for me are real."

That was quite some chinwag the hounds had had with Shade. Heat strained her cheeks, and she couldn't look at him. Her confusion and conflicted feelings would only be too clear for him to read. She'd never been any good at poker. "If you already know everything, why did you ask?"

"I don't know how you feel." Shade's hand on her arm drew her to a stop. "I only know how I feel, and Wrath does not speak for me."

Her mouth dried, and she dared a peek at him. "How you feel?"

"Eddie." Shade cupped her face and turned her to look at him. A sweet, tender expression warmed his eyes. His voice grew deeper and infinitely gentle. "I would love to declare myself to you right here and now. But this is not the time or place, and I sense that you are not ready to hear what I have to say."

Say it anyway, she wanted to yell past the blood rushing through her ears.

"I also understand you have fears because of who I am and what I am. So that leaves me with only one option." He smiled.

"And what's that?" All the breath felt like it was being sucked out of her lungs.

"A courtship." Shade nodded. "I shall woo you with all the purpose and conviction of a being who has lost his heart to another. I shall give you time to get to know me, and to learn to trust me. And Eddie"—he leaned closer and dropped his voice to a raspy whisper—"I am both very persuasive and indefatigable."

Her heart beat an irregular rhythm and felt like it was flinging itself against her ribs like a caged bird. "Why would you do that?"

"Because I quite simply adore you, Eddie. And I cannot contemplate the centuries ahead without you."

"Wha—"

A shout came up from Wrath's horde, and Shade spun in that direction. "Later." He pressed a quick kiss to her mouth before turning and striding away. "What is it?"

Eddie nearly threw herself at him and dragged him back to finish their conversation.

"I'm not certain." Wrath strode toward the demon who'd shouted. He spoke in the harsh guttural dialect for a moment before trotting over to Shade. "Someone's coming." He pointed to the horizon on the left. "And judging by the size of that dust cloud, it's a big someone."

"Arm!" Shade yelled to his horde, and both Wrath and Shade ran to the front of their hordes.

Xerxes and Cronus crowded closer to her.

"Who is it?" Eddie squinted in the direction they were all staring at, but she couldn't see—

"Demons. A large horde," Cronus said. *"Much larger than ours."*

A faint cloud of red earth smeared the harsh line of the horizon. It doubled, and then tripled in size, moving closer at an unbelievable speed.

"Dee." Eddie spun back to her grandmother. The urge to protect her grandmother thrummed through her blood. If there was going to be some kind of battle, Dee was horribly vulnerable.

Dee was awake and sitting up on her litter. Her head swung this way and that as she tried to work out what was happening around her.

Demons were slapping on bits of armor and unsheathing weapons all around them.

"Eddie." Dee looked more excited than scared. "What's going on?"

"I'm not sure." The cloud had resolved into demon forms in its depths. "But that doesn't look good."

"A war," Dee breathed. "I'm about to see a hell prince war."

Eddie gaped at Dee. How did she not understand how vulnerable she was? Eddie had seen demons fight, even had the unpleasant distinction of having fought them. "This is bad, Dee, very, very bad."

"It doesn't have to be." A demon materialized behind Dee. "It all depends on what you do next, Edme."

Cronus and Xerxes snarled and closed around Eddie.

Three impressions hit Eddie in a tsunami. The demon who had spoken was carved, chiseled, and beautiful, with a face that would make a model weep. Secondly, he now had his perfectly muscular arms around Dee and had dragged her against his shredded chest. And thirdly, and possibly most importantly, he held a jet-black knife against Dee's throat.

It took her brain a moment to sort the order, and then rage pounded through her. The voice that came out of her mouth sounded nothing like hers as she said in a low, deadly snarl, "Release her."

"I don't want to harm her, Edme." The demon smiled. Sparkling, straight white teeth flashed in a knee trembler of a smile.

Fury kept Eddie's knees locked and ready to leap.

"Ashe," Cronos growled.

Eddie didn't give a fuck what his name was, she wanted the son of a bitch away from Dee. She palmed a sword.

"Don't," Cronos snapped. *"He carries an obsidian blade. One nick, and your grandmother will be cut from the fabric of existence."*

Forcing the battle rage coursing through her to calm down, Eddie took a deep breath. "What do you want?"

Around them, the hordes were all locked in battle with the arriving horde. The armies crashed together in a primal roar.

"I want you." Ashe spoke as casually as if beings were not being hacked to pieces all around them. An arm flew past his face, and he didn't even flinch. He flashed his charming smile, which Eddie would like to make him eat with his perfect teeth. "Not in that way, Edme, but I want you to come with me."

The arid planes were filled with demons, and more were flooding in by the second. It was difficult to spot who was on which side, but the circle surrounding them grew bigger and bigger. Demons yelled, weapons flashed, blood spattered in a gory vortex of dust and destruction.

Fury washed over her in a tide, and Wrath came up behind her. "Eddie."

"Hello, Wrath." Ashe cocked his head. His curved horns began above his ears and curled neatly to his neck.

"Ashe," Wrath growled. "You end today."

They all seemed to know the fucker with an obsidian blade at Dee's neck. "He has an obsidian blade," Eddie whispered to Wrath.

"I see that." Wrath tensed. "What are you doing here, Ashe?"

"At this moment?" Ashe grinned. "I would say that is fairly obvious."

Wrath's snarl made the hairs on Eddie's nape rise. "Does Lucifer know what you are doing?"

"What do you think?" Ashe raised a dark eyebrow. Other than his grayish skin and the horns, he looked exactly like a human male. The intense blue of his eyes flashed. "You cannot win, Wrath. Surrender."

"Over my dead body," Wrath growled.

"Or hers." Ashe pressed the knife closer to Dee's neck. Skin dented beneath its gleaming black blade.

One breath, and Dee would be over. Eddie couldn't let that happen. "If I come with you, you'll let Dee go?"

"Of course." Ashe looked calm and reasonable. They could have been discussing the weather, other than the nasty knife at Dee's throat. "And you have my assurance that I will recall my horde."

A demon head *thunked* to the ground between them.

"Do it now," Eddie whispered. "Recall your horde."

"Now that would be stupid," Ashe said. His blue eyes gleamed. "With two hell princes running wild." He winked at her. "My position is somewhat precarious, Edme. And your grandmother is the only guarantee I have of leaving this place with my existence continuing."

"Take me instead." Wrath got his shoulder in front of Eddie. "Take me in Eddie's place. If you and your horde leave here without harming my daughter, I vow I will come with you quietly."

Ashe gave that some thought. "An interesting proposition," he murmured. "Calix!"

A second demon, this one looking like a centaur, joined him. "Aye."

"Give our lovely hell prince the amulet."

Calix dug in a pouch around his belt and pulled out an amulet. He tossed it at Wrath, and it landed at his feet.

A large red gem glowed in the center. Eddie didn't know what it was, but it made her stomach roil, and she knew Wrath shouldn't go anywhere near the damn thing.

"I will take you instead," Ashe said. "But only once you bind your powers."

"Never." Wrath's wings flexed behind him. "We will fight you first."

Ashe laughed. "Look around you, Wrath. Your horde is disappearing as we speak."

Eddie never took her eyes off Dee.

Dee's gaze met hers and fierce determination blazed across the distance at them. Dee looked like she was about to do something courageous and fucking stupid. "Don't," Eddie yelled at her. "Wrath, please. She's everything to me."

"Fine." Wrath snatched up the amulet.

It flared to life in his hand.

With a roar, red light surrounded him and drove him to his knees. His face contorted in a rictus of agony.

Eddie felt her wrath pop like a soap bubble inside her.

"Don't be fucking stupid, Ashe." Shade spoke from behind Eddie. "You know you can't win against me."

"Do I?" Ashe grinned. "And yet I already have one hell prince rendered as helpless as a baby."

Wrath groaned and collapsed into a heap.

"That leaves me to contend with." Shade stepped closer.

"I will cut her." Ashe looked pointedly at the blade at Dee's neck. "But I made a deal with Wrath. I don't need him, just his power. Hand me that amulet, and we'll all leave you to go on your way again."

Eddie put her hand out to stop him. "Shade, he has that obsidian knife."

"I see it, Eddie." His calm tone reassured her. "How do you want to play this?"

There was no thinking about it. "I need Dee safe."

Ashe grinned at her. "Good choice, Edme. She has no value to me." He motioned to the amulet. "That, however, I can really use." He jerked his head to the pouch. "Bring that to me, Edme, and I'll release your grandmother."

"Eddie." Shade grabbed her arm. "Don't go near him." He glared at Ashe. "Get your lackey to fetch it."

"I'm not a patient demon." Ashe pressed the knife even further into Dee's skin.

Dee held her breath.

Darting forward, Eddie snatched up the pouch and held it out to Ashe.

"There's a good Nephilim." Ashe grinned. He grabbed the pouch, then shoved Dee toward Shade.

Shade lunged to catch Dee.

Wrath lurched to his feet.

And the obsidian blade dug into Eddie's throat.

"You should know better than to trust a demon, Edme. We lie." His arm clamped around her waist, stronger than iron. The obsidian blade at her neck was enough to keep Eddie dead still. "Didn't the imp teach you that?"

"Eddie!" Shade jerked for her and stopped. "Don't fucking move."

Eddie was way ahead of him.

"What's he doing?" Dee looked from Shade to Ashe.

"Let her go." Wrath stumbled like a newborn calf and shook his head. "We made a deal. You were to take me."

"That's not going to happen," Ashe said. "But my ruse did allow me to disable your power." He held up the amulet pouch. "And now it's mine, and the only part of you I need."

The world lurched around Eddie, and darkness descended.

SHADE STARED at the empty room that was Eddie's bedroom. He didn't remember much about the trip back from the battleground where Ashe had abducted Eddie. Vague flickers of Dee screaming, the hounds howling, and Wrath bellowing all merged together.

Inside, he was hollow, empty. Eddie was gone, and none of them had any idea where. They knew she was still alive because Wrath could sense her out there somewhere. If she was dead, her sire would feel it.

"Shade." Uriel appeared in the doorway, her beautiful face somber and subdued. "They're all here."

"All of them?"

She sighed. "All except Lucifer."

Of course Lucifer was missing. He hadn't the courage to face him and Wrath after what he'd done. He would be skulking somewhere between the three realms, and he had Eddie with him.

Ashe was Lucifer's second in command. After the shock of Eddie's abduction had worn off, he and Wrath had spoken. There was so much about what had happened that was wrong. Ashe and his horde of misfits from all seven demesnes had been so much more powerful than they should have been. They'd managed to overpower both his and Wrath's hordes in the battle in which Eddie was lost. Somehow Lucifer had found a way not only to gain the loyalty of demons from rival hell princes but also to transfer power to his horde.

Eddie was gone. His vision darkened around the edges. Fury and loss filled the aching emptiness inside him.

"Shade?" Uriel touched his arm. "We need to start the gathering."

In the greenroom below, the hell princes and archangels had gathered at his request. The others could concern them-selves with the seals and the state of the world. Shade wanted only one thing; he wanted Eddie back, and she had best be safe and unharmed, or he would end the world. And Wrath would help him do it.

~

THE LAST THING Eddie remembered was that demon, Ashe, shoving Dee at Shade and then grabbing her. There had been a flash of light, and then blackout.

Until she came to somewhere about as unidentifiable as the inside of a refrigerator, and not much warmer. She was lying on a narrow metal bed bolted to the wall. A thin mattress and an even thinner blanket were the only concessions to comfort.

To her left in the roughly three by three meter room was a stainless-steel sink and a toilet. Both also bolted to the wall. A large, studded door—also metal—faced her cot with a dark window in the top third.

Committing to the metallic decorating theme, the walls and ceilings were also made of seamless sheets of stainless steel. She was trapped in a metal box.

A plastic bottle of water stood on the floor beside her cot.

Raging thirst encouraged her to crack the seal and give it an experimental sniff. It smelled like water. She dipped her finger into the bottle and tested a drop with the tip of her tongue. It tasted like standard bottled water. Not the fancy kind, but the grocery store kind.

Still, Eddie had seen enough spy movies to know about things like tasteless and odorless drugs, so she kept her sip small.

As far as a quick examination of her body could tell her, she hadn't been harmed in any other way. But someone had removed her clothes, and she now wore a shapeless gray track-suit and thick socks. She pushed that thought into a box in her mind. If she thought about someone stripping her while she was unconscious, she would lose it.

A more thorough examination of her cell revealed a depressing lack of any possible way out, other than through the door.

She added how long she'd been here to her growing tally of shit she didn't know.

It was light in the cell, but she couldn't see any source for that light.

Fear, her new companion, tightened her throat. She couldn't sit here and wait for whatever was coming, because she was willing to bet it wouldn't be good. After getting up from her cot, she hunted around the space again for clues.

The only sound came from the soft pad of her feet against the floor. She turned the tap on, and then flushed the toilet to break the oppressive silence.

"Okay, Eddie." The sound of her voice grounded her. "You need to think."

She'd been in hell, almost at Shade's demesne, when Ashe and his demon horde had attacked.

"The attack must have been a diversion," she said. Had she been the target all along?

The air stirred, and she became aware of a chemical smell. Her head grew light, and she had to sit down before she fell. Her knees gave out, and she dropped on her cot. She'd been drugged. Eddie wanted to fight the effect, but her brain felt slow and her eyes heavy.

The door hissed open, and a large figure materialized from the dark corridor into the light of her room. "Hello, Edme."

It took her sluggish brain a while to put a name to the figure. "Ashe." Her voice sounded slurred and raspy.

He held up the tray in his hand. "I brought you something to eat." Strolling closer, he laid the tray beside her on her cot.

Eddie blinked at it and tried to bring it into focus. "You drugged me."

"Not me personally," Ashe said. His voice sounded like it was speaking to her from down a long tunnel. "But, yes. If you were human, that would have knocked you out, but as it is..." He shrugged.

"Where am I?"

Ashe chuckled. "Why do people always ask that first?"

Now Eddie was not on the top of her game, but it seemed like a perfectly reasonable question to her. "Wanna know."

"Of course you do." Ashe patted her shoulder.

Eddie tried to jerk away from him and nearly threw herself off the cot.

"You should eat," he said. Then he smirked as if he'd made a joke. "Obviously, you don't feel like it now, but when the drug has left your system." Up close, his blue eyes radiated a gross parody of sincerity. "The food and water is not drugged. The air, however, we will have to give you a little something every now and again to keep you under control." He straightened. "It makes working with Nephilim so much easier."

Working? If she were in one of those damned spy movies now, she would demand to know what they planned to do with her. But as her tongue felt ten times larger and glued to the top of her mouth, she didn't bother. "Fuck off."

"Yes." Ashe folded his arms across his broad chest. "That seems to be the most common next response as well."

"Fuck off," she muttered. The water bottle seemed a long way away, and it was taking a huge effort to try to persuade her arm to reach for it.

Ashe snatched the bottle off the floor and opened the cap. Handing it to her, he said, "It isn't drugged." Then he took a sip as if to prove it to her.

Eddie eyed the distance to the open door and the dark corridor beyond. Given that she hadn't been able to locate the water bottle, she didn't rate her chances.

"Here." Ashe held the bottle to her mouth. "Your mouth must feel like you've been licking a desert."

Given her situation, Eddie judged this as not a hill she wanted to die on and obediently took a sip.

"You'll want to pay attention to this next bit," Ashe said. "I'm about to do my evil genius monologue."

Only half of those words made sense to her, and Eddie blinked at him. Evil genius aside, he was stupidly good looking. Even with those horns curling around the sides of his head. "You're a demon."

"Yes." Ashe cocked his head at her. "And you're Nephilim."

Not too long ago, she'd been plain Edme Ward, stage managing the Paradise Theatre for the community theatre company in Clayton, Ontario, and very definitely human. Or so she'd thought.

"Which is why you're here." Ashe gave her another sip of water. "You have power, Edme, and we need that power."

She took another sip and waited for the promised monologue. Her brain and mouth weren't connecting enough for her to frame a question in any case.

"It's why I was able to defeat Shade and Wrath." He put the cap on the water bottle and put it back beside her cot. "Nephilim power is an amazing thing. It's like a shot of supercharged adrenalin to our demon powers."

Leaning close to her ear, Ashe lowered his voice. "It's why everyone is so frightened of you," he whispered. "They're scared they won't be able to control you. And Edme"—his gaze met hers again—"they're right to be frightened. You can do what we can't. As the daughter of a hell prince and a human, you can draw your power from both the earth and the hell realms."

None of this made sense to her, and she focused on the tray. A sandwich and an apple sat side by side, both of them wrapped. They'd even given her a cookie, and that struck her as so absurd that she wanted to laugh.

"Ashe." Another voice dragged her attention to the door.

Another demon entered her cell. Her fuzzy brain recognized him. Long, equine features made his face more animal than human, and he had four horse-like legs.

She couldn't remember his name. Ashe had called him something.

"Calix." Ashe drew himself up.

His chest swelled, and he grew larger. Or was that her drugged up brain making shit up?

The apple was bright green and shiny.

"They say to get on with it." The horse demon held out a shiny object to Ashe. A large, bulbous crystal dangled at the end of a heavy chain.

Ashe clicked his tongue and looked at her. "Calix has horrible manners. He's a lower order demon, and they're not known for their small talk."

"Do it." Calix grunted and slapped the shiny thing against Ashe's chest.

Eddie winced at the sound of a fist thumping into flesh, but Ashe didn't even flinch.

"I really am sorry, Edme." Ashe even looked like he might mean it. "But this is going to hurt like fuck."

After dropping the chain around her neck, he stepped back.

Eddie blinked down at the stone against her breastbone.

The stoned flared to life, and agony smashed into her.

EPILOGUE

*s the seals weaken...*

THE MAN STARED at the rear of the dark-red, broken-down sedan currently occupying his designated parking spot. He paid $300 a year to have that parking spot, and now somebody else was in it. His name and unit number were quite clearly displayed on the plaque on the wall in front of the parking spot. It's not like he could even excuse the offending car owner of being ignorant.

Options flashed through his mind. He could call the super, but at this time of night, the man was already one six pack down in front of the television. He could find another spot in the visitor's section, but the measly four spots given to visitors were already full for the night. He could leave a note on the windshield and find a parking space several blocks away.

Anger surged through him, and his foot tapped the accelerator. Tempting, so very fucking tempting. He was tired. He'd had a living shit of a day, tidying up after his boss and making sure the world only saw the carefully curated public image the politician wanted them to see.

"Fuck my life," he whispered as he caught the reflection of his own eyes in the rearview mirror. Plain, brown eyes. Dull brown, not even an interesting shape or color in an immediately forgettable face. Just another mediocre human churning their way through a predictable life until death finally came.

His car engine surged and reminded him he still had his foot on the gas.

Always taking a back seat, never making waves, being useful in the dark while people stupider and less worthy took the limelight. Always a bridesmaid and never a bride in the giant shit show of life. A little gray man scuttling around in the dark whilst others got to dance in the sun. A nothing who couldn't even have the parking he'd rightly paid for.

You don't have to be that man, the voice whispered in his mind. *You used to be somebody. You had dreams. You had ambitions.*

Rage hit him in a flash blast.

Enough! Enough eating shit for other people. And he slammed his foot down on the gas pedal.

~

Somewhere in Africa

. . .

THE VIEW from outside his window was spectacular. The entire city spread before him in twinkling lights. You couldn't pay for a view like this one. And the reason you couldn't was because you had to claw your way up through the grimy underbelly of politics to be able to look out this window and see the world beneath your feet. You had to be prepared to turn off your conscience and ignore your scruples. And once you had abandoned all decency, you got to stand where he was, and be who he was. One of the most powerful men in the world.

But only one *of the most powerful.* That nagging truth had been pressing on him lately.

He should have felt on top of the world. Beyond the large wooden doors that sealed his office, hundreds of people scurried and toiled to make his whims a reality.

Those twinkling lights in front of him represented the lives of millions of people whose destiny he controlled. One decision from him dictated how much money they took home, their safety, their existence. He closed his eyes and waited for the familiar power rush. Instead, he felt empty. It had all become so meaningless.

The thing about ascending to the heights was that there was always another mountain to be scaled. There was always more to be had.

You could have that more. The thought popped into his mind and blossomed. *You could have anything you wanted. Everything you wanted.*

∾

A BAR in London

. . .

"CAN I BUY YOU A DRINK?" With a nonthreatening smile, he eased onto the stool beside the brunette.

She turned, and the smile died on her scarlet painted lips. "No, thank you."

He'd been watching her for the last hour. She was here alone and didn't appear to be waiting for anyone. The thing with women was that you had to be persistent. They loved to be pursued. A man—a real man—was a hunter, a predator. He motioned the barman and pointed to her glass and his. "You here alone?"

Frowning at him, she stood. "I don't want a drink, and I came here to be alone."

Women always said that when they wanted you to try harder, press harder. He leaned in, letting her smell his pheromones. "Now, we both know that's not true."

"Are you bloody serious?" She pursed her whore painted red lips and grabbed her purse.

The barman appeared with his drink and not the one he'd ordered for the slut. "You okay, miss?"

"Yes." She glared at him and snatched up her purse. "I was leaving anyway."

He watched her round ass twitching from side to side as she sashayed away. She walked like a woman who wanted it. She wore her enticing clothes because she was gagging for it. And now she thought to turn him down.

A low snarl echoed through his mind. *Take her,* the voice said. *A real man takes what he wants.*

∾

A PRIVATE ESTATE in France

. . .

"I apologize, madam." Not looking at all apologetic, her executive assistant bowed his head. "But your offer has been refused."

Fury drummed at her temples. She had made a fair offer. In fact, her offer had been more than fair. The useless little shit she had hired must have fucked up the negotiation. She'd hired him over the other applicants because he was pretty and would look good walking beside her.

She turned her iciest stare on him and was slightly mollified by his nervous swallow. "I beg your pardon?"

"Your offer." With shaking hands, he tapped on the tablet in front of him. "For the Degas, was rejected."

"Why?" She pinned him with a stare. Let the little shit sweat. She had been four years in tracking down a priceless Degas, one that the museums knew nothing about. A treasure hidden in the dark and passed from private collection to private collection for obscene amounts of money. And a treasure she wanted to add to her specially created art vault below her study where they stood.

He cleared his throat and smoothed back his perfectly styled hair. "They did not say why. They just sent a note saying it was refused."

The anger almost made her shake, and she forced herself to calm. When she reached for her champagne flute, she was proud to see her hand did not betray her emotion. "I want that Degas."

"I understand, madam." He had recovered his composure and spoke to her now as if she were a petulant child. "But the owner will not sell."

"Then make him." She sipped her champagne and touched her tongue tip to her lip to catch the drop of champagne left behind.

Her assistant frowned and tucked his tablet beneath his arm. "You want me to offer them more money?"

Money! She snorted in her mind, never one to be so crass as to make such a vulgar sound aloud. Everything always came down to money. "I don't care how you do it, but I want that painting."

"But—"

"Or you will be looking for another position."

He paled and snapped his mouth shut. A money-grubbing leech like the rest of them, her assistant was fond of his expensive apartment and his designer suits. She paid for every trivial luxury he, no doubt, lorded over his cronies, and all she demanded in return was loyalty and competence.

You deserve as much. You deserve everything; everything your heart desires.

Need more Hell Bound?

A hell prince bent on vengeance
An angel who cannot lie
A grumpy-sunshine supernatural adventure where the stakes couldn't be higher.

Haziel loves her archangel, Ramiel. She always has. So, when he sends her on a mission to monitor his opposing hell prince, Wrath, Haziel is happy to serve.

Once bitten twice shy, Wrath is hell-bent on finding his daughter, the Nephilim Edme. Certain Lucifer responsible for Edme's abduction and the growing demon rebellion in hell, Wrath is on the warpath.

He doesn't count on an unfailingly honest, vivacious seraph tagging along—an unwelcome and increasingly intriguing distraction.

Haziel is horrified when her feelings for boorish, frustrating Wrath start to complicate her mission. Not wanting to betray her first love, Ramiel, she fights her growing attraction.

Haziel and Wrath discover the demon revolution is a greater threat than the combined gathering of heaven, hell, and earth suspect. And the end of days countdown has begun as the first horseman of the apocalypse wakes.

While they battle a spiraling situation that heralds the end of all creation, Haziel is forced to choose between Wrath and Ramiel. And Wrath must overcome his bitterness and take a chance on a love that shouldn't exist.

Haziel stood at her assigned place behind Ramiel. As his second in command, she was always where he needed her to be. From this angle she couldn't see the emerald glitter of his beautiful green eyes, or the sharp perfection of his bone structure. She made do with admiring the broad sweep of his muscular shoulders and the gleaming bronze glow of his nape. Which made her officially the most ridiculous being in the room.

Although, not the most pitiable. That title was divided equally between Wrath and Asmodeus. They were both absolutely gutted by the missing Nephilim, Edme. Wrath as her sire paced the small confines of the room that everyone called a green room, but was mysteriously painted an unassuming beige. In fact, nothing in the room was green. Other than Ramiel's eyes.

**Buy your books directly from me at
Sarah Hegger Books**

For first dibs on news, deals, and giveaways, and so much more, join the @Home Collective

Or if Facebook is more your thing, join the Sarah Hegger Collective

Anything and everything you need to know on my website http://sarahhegger.com

About the Author

Born British and raised in South Africa, Sarah Hegger suffers from an incurable case of wanderlust. Her match? A hot Canadian engineer, whose marriage proposal she accepted six short weeks after they first met. Together they've made homes in seven different cities across three different continents (and back again once or twice). If only it made her multilingual, but the best she can manage is idiosyncratic English, fluent Afrikaans, conversant Russian, pigeon Portuguese, even worse Zulu and enough French to get herself into trouble. Mimicking her globe trotting adventures, Sarah's career path began as a gainfully employed actress, drifted into public relations, settled a moment in advertising, and eventually took root in the fertile soil of her first love, writing. She also moonlights as a wife and mother. She currently lives in Ottawa, Canada, filling her empty nest with fur babies. Part footloose buccaneer, part quixotic observer of life, Sarah's restless heart is most content when reading or writing books.

Also by Sarah Hegger

Sarah Hegger also writes as Sarah Edwards

Paranormal Romance

The Hell Bound Series

Lust

Wrath

Pride

Avarice

Envy

Sloth

Urban Fantasy

The Cré-Witch Chronicles

Prequel: Cast In Stone

Vol l: Born In Water

Vol ll: Purged In Fire

Vol III: Raised In Air

Vol IV: Cradled In Earth

Vol IV ½: Forged In Fate

Vol V: Joined In Spirit

Sports Romance

Ottawa Titans Series

Roughing

Contemporary Romance

Passing Through Series

Drove All Night

Ticket To Ride

Walk On By

Ghost Falls Series

Positively Pippa

Becoming Bella

Blatantly Blythe

Loving Laura

Willow Park Romances

Nobody's Angel

Nobody's Fool

Nobody's Princess

Medieval Romance

Sir Arthur's Legacy Series

Sweet Bea

My Lady Faye

Conquering William

Defying Roger

Henry's Honor

Love & War Series

The Marriage Parley

The Betrothal Melee

Western Historical Romance

The Soiled Dove Series

Sugar Ellie

Standalone

The Bride Gift

Bad Wolfe On The Rise

Wild Honey

PRAISE FOR SARAH HEGGER

Drove All Night
"The classic romance plot is elevated to a modern-day, wholly accessible real-life fairy tale with an excellent mix of romantic elements and spicy sensuality."
Booklife Prize, Critic's Report

Positively Pippa
"This is the type of romance that makes readers fall in love not just with characters, but with authors as well."
Kirkus Review (Starred Review)

"What begins as a simple second-chance romance quickly transforms into a beautiful, frank examination of love, family dynamics, and following one's dreams. Hegger's unflinching, candid portrayal of interpersonal and generational communication elevates the story to the sublime. Shunning clichés and contrived circumstances, she uses realistic, relatable situations to create a world that readers will want to visit time and again."

Publisher's Weekly, Starred Review

Hegger's utterly delightful first Ghost Falls contemporary is what other romance novels want to grow up to be." – Publisher's Weekly, Best Books of 2017

"The very talented Hegger kicks off an enjoyable new series set in the small Utah town of Ghost Falls. This charming and fun-filled book has everything from passion and humor to betrayal and revenge." –
Jill M Smith, RT Books Reviews 2017 – Contemporary Love and Laughter Nominee

Becoming Bella
"Hegger excels at depicting familial relationships and friendships of all kinds, including purely platonic friendships between women and men. Tears, laughter, and a dollop of suspense make a memorable story that readers will want to revisit time and again."
Publisher's Weekly, Starred Review

"...you have a terrific new romance that Hegger fans are going to love. Don't miss out!"
Jill M. Smith – RT Book Reviews

Blatantly Blythe
"Ms. Hegger has delivered another captivating read for this series in this book that was packed with emotion..." Bec, Bookmagic Review, Harlequin Junkie, HJ Recommends.

Nobody's Fool
"Hegger offers a breath of fresh air in the romance genre." –
Terri Dukes, RT Book Reviews

Nobody's Princess
"Hegger continues to live up to her rapidly growing reputation for breathing fresh air into the romance genre." – Terri Dukes, RT Book Reviews

"I have read the entire Willow Park Series. I have loved each of the books ... Nobody's Princess is my favorite of all time." Harlequin Junkie, Top Pick

www.ingramcontent.com/pod-product-compliance
Lightning Source LLC
Chambersburg PA
CBHW051135300726
48978CB00011B/286

9 781990 731259